HERE LIES ARTHUR

PHILIP REEVE

■ SCHOLASTIC

For Geraldine McCaughrean

First published in 2007 by Scholastic Children's Books
This edition published in 2008 by Scholastic Children's Books

An imprint of Scholastic Ltd
Euston House, 24 Eversholt Street
London, NW1 1DB, UK
Registered office: Westfield Road, Southam,
Warwickshire, CV47 0RA
SCHOLASTIC and associated logos are trademarks and
or registered trademarks of Scholastic Inc.

10 digit ISBN 1 407 10358 X
13 digit ISBN 978 1407 10358 7

A CIP catalogue record for this book is available from the British Library.

Printed by CPI Bookmarque, Croydon, CR0 4TD

Papers used by Scholastic Children's Books are made from
wood grown in sustainable forests.

1 3 5 7 9 10 8 6 4 2

www.scholastic.co.uk/zone

NOTE ON PRONUNCIATION

Before English existed, people in Britain spoke a language similar to Welsh. At the back of the book, there is a guide to how some of the names and place names in *Here Lies Arthur* might have been pronounced.

HIC IACET ARTHURUS, REX QUONDAM REXQUE FUTURUS
Here lies Arthur – King that was, King that will be again.

Sir Thomas Malory, *Le Morte d'Arthur*

SOUTH-WEST BRITAIN

AROUND AD 500

Even the woods are burning. I plunge past the torched byre and hard into the shoulder-deep growth of brambles between the trees, but there's fire ahead of me as well as behind. The hall on the hill's top where I thought I'd find shelter is already blazing. I can hear men's voices baying like hounds on a scent, the hooves of horses on the winter earth like drums. I see their shadows long before the riders themselves come in sight. Fingers of darkness stretch from their raggedy banners, reaching through the smoke which hangs beneath the trees. I duck sideways into a brambled hollow and wriggle deep. Thorns tug at my dress and snag my hair. The ground's frosty. Hard and cold under my knees and fingers. Fear drags little noises out of me. I squeak and whimper like a hunted cub.

But it's not me these horsemen are hunting. I'm nothing to them. Just a lost girl-child scurrying across the corners of their war. They thunder past without seeing me, the firelight bright on spears and swords, on mail and burnished helmets, on shield bosses and harness buckles and fierce faces lit up like lanterns. Their leader's out in front on a white horse. Big, he is. Shiny as a fish in his coat of silver scales. The cheek-guards of his helmet ripple with fire-gleam and his teeth between them are gleaming too, bared in a hard shout.

You've heard of him. Everyone's heard of Arthur. Artorius Magnus; the Bear; the *Dux Bellorum*; the King that Was and Will Be. But you haven't heard the truth. Not till now. I knew him, see. Saw him, smelled him, heard him talk. When I was a boy I rode with Arthur's band all up and down the world, and I was there at the roots and beginnings of all the stories.

That was later, of course. For now I'm still a snot-nosed girl, crouched in the brambles, giddy with the thump and stink of horses and so still that you'd think I'd been turned to a stone by my first glimpse of the Bear.

I didn't know then who he was, nor why he'd led his fierce, shiny riders to burn my home. All I knew was it was unnatural. Wrong as snow in summer or the sun at midnight. War's a thing for autumn, when the harvest's in and the rains not yet come to turn the roads to mud. When men can be spared to go harrying into other lands and carrying off other men's grain and cattle. So what do these horsemen mean by coming here in winter's dark, with the trees bare and the hay-stores half empty and cat ice starring and smashing on the puddles they ride their horses over? Are they even men at all? They look to me like Dewer's Hunt. They look like the Four Riders of the world's end I've heard the monks talk about up at

4

Lord Ban's hall. Though there's more than four of them. Five, seven, ten, more than I can count, heaving uphill on a steep sea of horse-muscle.

Uphill, and past me, and gone. Their wild voices blur into the crackle of burning brush and the steady bellowing of scared cattle from the byres. I sneeze on the smoke as I make myself move, slithering across the flank of the hill, over the knuckles of tree-roots, over the granite boulders furry with moss, through sinks of dead leaves in the hollows. Don't ask me where I'm going. Away from the burning. Away from those angry riders. Just away is good enough for now.

But then I reach the road, down at the bridge where it crosses the river, and there's another of the raiders there. His horse has come down in trampled mud at the bridge's end and the battle has left him behind. He's on foot, furious, flailing at the horse with the flat of his sword. A young man, his white face framed by wings of red-gold hair, a thin beard clinging to his jaw like fluff the wind has blown there. His eyes are full of angry tears and a desperate hunger for blood. Even the blood of a girl-child, I realize, as I somersault out of the scratchy undergrowth and land thump on the path before him. He forgets the horse and comes at me. With his blade in front of me, the steeps and fire behind, I turn, looking for a way out.

Ways out are all I have been looking for this evening, ever since I woke in my master's house to find the thatch ablaze, the women screeching, the men scrambling sleepily for staves and spears and sickles. I remember how the shadows of horsemen flicked past

5

the open doorway. How my master had run out shouting and how a sword came down on his head and made the women screech louder. How I scrambled between the horses' legs and over a fence the pigs had trampled down in panic. Gwyna the Mouse they call me, and like a mouse I always have the sense to scurry out of trouble.

Except that now all my quickness and cunning have brought me to this: a dead end, cut off short by a shouting boy.

And for once I'm more angry than afraid. Angry at myself for running into his way, and angry at him and his friends for their stupid, unseasonal war. Why couldn't they stay at home, wherever their home is? I dart at the boy, and he flinches back, as if he thinks I mean to fight him. But mice don't fight. I duck by him quick, feeling the wind of his sword past my face, hearing the hiss of sliced air. I run towards the bridge, where his terrified horse is heaving up, mud and white eyes and a smoke of dragon-breath. I go sideways to avoid it, and lose my footing on the ice, and fall, and keep on falling.

And I leave the fire and the noise behind me, leave everything, and dive down alone through darkness into the dark river.

The first shock of that cold water jarred my teeth and made my lungs go tight. I surfaced in the shadows under the bridge, and heard the boy above me, screaming curses at his horse. I turned circles, paddling with my hands. This mouse could swim. Raised near the river, I'd been in and out of it as long as I could remember. In summer me and the other children of the place came down at evening when the day's work ended to splash and shout until the light died. In autumn, master had me dive in to set his fish-traps. Open-eyed in the hubble and swirl below the rapids, I'd wedge the long wicker creels in place, then lift them out later full of plump, speckled fish.

So I took a deep breath and dived, kicking out hard, letting the river drag me away from sword-boy. Gritty water pressed against my eyes. I could only darkness, with here and there an orange fire-gleam slanting down. It was easier to find my way by touch. I pawed over slimy boulders to the first bend below the bridge and came up for air, yelping and gasping in the clatter of the rapids. The current tugged at me, reminding me of all the things that haunt rivers, ready to drag unwary children under with their long, green hands. I was scared of them, but the raiders scared me more.

I slid down into a calmer pool and trod water there, listening for the sounds of battle. There was nothing, only the voices of the river and the woods. Far off, the farm where I'd grown up was burning like a dropped torch. I wondered if all master's household were dead. There had been no love between me and them – I was just a hanger-on, the whelp of some dead slave-woman. But still that farmstead was the only home I'd known. Out of pity for myself I cried and cried, adding my tears to the river till the cold clutched and shook me and set all my teeth a-rattle.

At last, just to keep warm, I started swimming again. Downstream, letting the river do the work. I kept my head above the surface this time. If you'd been watching from the bank you'd think you'd seen an otter, scared from its hole by the fighting upriver and heading for quieter fishing grounds. I swam until the trees parted above me to let the sky show and the river widened into a deep pool. Another river joined it there, coming down off the moors and tipping into the pool in a long fall, pale in the moonshine like an old man's beard.

There, cold as a ghost, wet as a drowned dog, I came ashore, heaving myself out by the tangle of tree-roots that reached out of the bank. I flopped into the litter of beechmast and dead leaves between the trees and made a little ball of myself, trying to hug some warmth back into my juddering, shuddering limbs. The noise of the water filled my head. Where would I go now? What would I eat? Who would I serve? I didn't know. Didn't care either. There was no more feeling left in me than in a hearthful of cold ashes. When feet came scuffing through the fallen leaves and stopped beside me I didn't even look up, just knelt there, shivering.

It was dark under those trees. I couldn't see the man who lifted me and carried me away from the pool. I couldn't see his waiting horse, though I felt it snort and stamp when he hung me over its saddle like a blanket-roll. I didn't see him till we reached shelter. It was an old building from the Roman times, big and pale in the owl-light, half sunk in furze and trees. He led the horse right inside, and small, loose tiles slid and scraped beneath its hooves as if the place was floored with teeth, or knucklebones. He lifted me down from the horse's back and laid me in a corner. I was too scared to look at him. He moved about quietly, kindling a fire. Big shadows shifted across the walls. Traces of paint clung to the plaster. Ivy hung down thick through the rotted cage of rafters overhead, rustly and whispering. I squinched my eyes shut. I thought if I was small enough, and still enough, and quiet enough, he might forget me.

"Hungry?" he asked.

I opened one eye. He was crouching by me. He wore

a shabby black travelling cloak fastened with a flashy, complicated brooch. A jangle of charms and amulets hung round his neck. Horse charms, moon charms, paw of a hare. Magic things. In the shadow of his hood his face gave away no secrets. Sallow, sharp-nosed, beardless. Was he a priest? He wasn't dressed like one, but I'd never seen a man clean-shaved who wasn't a priest or a high-born warrior, and this was no warrior. Fine-boned like a hawk, he looked. Quick and birdy in his movements too. And his eyes were hawk's eyes, patient and clever.

What did he want with me?

"Hungry?" he asked again. He stretched out the palm of his hand towards me and suddenly a hunk of bread was between his fingers. I shuffled backwards, pressing my spine against the wall. I was afraid of him and his magic bread.

He laughed. "It's only a trick, girl. Look close." He folded his hand over the bread and when he opened it again the bread was gone. He waggled his fingers and the bread was back. It perched on his palm like a baby bird. He held it towards me again but I closed my mouth tight and turned my face away. I didn't know much but I knew to fear magic.

Another laugh. A ripply sound, like water running in the first thaw of spring. "Scared it'll make you sleep a thousand years? Or witch you away to my kingdom under the hill?" He pushed the bread back inside his clothes and went about his business. He took a saddlebag from his horse and opened it, pulling out a cooking pot, a sack of food, a stained old blanket that he

11

wrapped around me. All the time he talked to me softly, the way a farrier whispers to a scared horse.

"I'm as mortal as you, girl. I am Myrddin. The bard Myrddin. You know what a bard is, don't you, girl? A traveller and spinner of tales. There's my harp, bundled in oilcloth, see? It was *I* who thought *you* came from the otherworld. Creeping out of the lake like that. You must swim like a fish. I thought you were the lake-woman herself, come up from her home under the waters to steal my heart away. But you're a little young yet, aren't you, to be stealing anything but apples and barley cakes? How many summers have you seen? Nine? Ten?"

I managed a shivery shrug. Nobody had ever told me how old I was. Nobody had ever asked before.

"And have you a name?" He crouched down again on the far side of the fire and watched me. He threw back his hood, baring cropped, greying hair. The flame light stroked his face and gleamed in his eyes. He wore a look you could have taken for kindness.

"Gwyna," I said.

"So you can speak! And where have you come from, Gwyna?"

"From my master's farm. Up that way." I pointed with my head. My voice sounded very small and dull compared with his, as though the river-water had washed all the colour out of it. But it made the lights in his eyes flare up like embers when a breeze catches them.

"You've come from Ban's place?"

I nodded numbly. Ban was my master's master: lord of the fort on the hill above my burned home, and all the lands you could see from that hill.

"But it must be miles from here. . ."

"Not so far by river," I said. "I swam all the way."

"Like a fish." He was looking at me different now. I started to feel pleased. Nobody had ever cared much what I was or did before.

"I swum under water half of it," I said. (I didn't know it then, but I was sealing my fate with that silly boast.) "It's my job to set the fish-traps at fall-of-leaf. The cold don't worry me. I can open my eyes down under water and I can hold my breath. . ."

"How long? Show me?"

I gulped in a great breath and sealed my lips tight behind it. I watched him, and he watched me. Blood thumped in my neck, and the back of my head. I felt proud of myself. It was easy. I couldn't see why people bothered breathing, it was so easy to get by without. And still this Myrddin watched me. After a while the breath I'd taken started to grow stale inside. A bit of it seeped out my nose. The dam of my lips cracked, letting out more. I gasped, and the game was over, and still he was watching me.

"Better and better," he said. "Perhaps the spirits of the lake did send you to me, after all."

"Oh no, sir! It was the burning, and the riders. . ."

I stopped. Here by the warmth of his fire the battle seemed far off and strange, like a dream I'd had. But I hadn't dreamed it. Outside, the sky was turning pale above the bare branches. Birds were stirring. Day was brewing. "Oh sir!" I said, "They came with fire and swords and horses! They came killing and burning and hollering!"

13

Myrddin wasn't worried. "That is the way of the world, Gwyna. It has been so ever since the legions sailed away."

"But they'll come here! We must hide! We must run!"

"Peace, child!" he said, and he laughed. He caught me by both shoulders as I tried to scramble to the door. His horse sensed my fear and whinnied softly, stirring its tail, wafting a smell of dung towards us. Myrddin said, "You've nothing to fear. Not now. Not if you're with me." He sat me down again, shushing and crooning to calm me. "You know who those riders are, Gwyna? They are the war-band of Arthur. You've heard of Arthur, haven't you?"

Well of course I had. I never thought to meet him in my own woods, though. Arthur was someone out of stories. He fought giants and rescued maidens and out-foxed the Devil. He didn't ride about burning people's shippens down.

I said, "It can't be. What would he want here?"

Myrddin laughed and scratched his chin, as if he was trying to work out the easiest answer to that one. At last he said, "Arthur offered your Lord Ban his protection, in exchange for gold and other tributes. But Ban thought the price too high, and refused. That was foolish of him. Now Arthur has come to take Ban's holdings for himself. And he looks to me to help him do it. I ride with Arthur's band, see. I spin tales for him, and about him. I parted from him a few days since and came here by a different way, scouting out the land. If you know how the land lies a battle can be half won before it's started. Sometimes there's no need for a battle at all."

I took a moment to understand what he'd said. When I did, I was scared of him all over anew. What had I done, to make God deliver me up to a friend of the raiders?

"You've turned paler than porridge," he said. "But you've nothing to fear from me, and nothing from the Bear either. It'll make no odds to you who your lord is. Except that if I can make Arthur strong enough there might be peace again, like our grandfathers' fathers knew back in the days when Rome held this island. Strength like Arthur's could be used for good, see, just as the strength of old Rome was. That's why I help him, Gwyna. And I have a sense that you can help him too."

IV

He talked and talked while I sat drying out beside his fire, and the grey day brightened grudgingly above the woods. He was in love with words. He found his own conversation so interesting he didn't notice that he was the only one talking. I just sat watching, listening, while he spoke of places I'd never heard of: Elmet and Rheged, Ireland across the sea, Din Tagyll where the ships from Syria put in. Oh, I snatched a few familiar names out of the word-storm. I'd heard of bad King Gworthigern, who let the heathen Saxons settle in the east, and how they rose up and tried to steal the rest of Britain too. And I knew a song about Ambrosius Aurelianus, who led the armies of the Britons through battle after battle until he smashed those Saxons flat at Badon Hill. But mostly Myrddin's words flowed past my ears like water.

"When Ambrosius died," he said, "there was no man strong enough to take his place. The army he built to fight the Saxons came apart into a hundred different war-bands. Now they fight each other, and leave the

Saxons sitting tight upon the lands they stole in the eastern half of Britain. Some of those war-bands serve the small kings of the hill-country. Some serve the big kings of Dumnonia and Powys and Calchvynydd. Some are landless men, loyal only to their captain, grabbing loot and territory where they may. Arthur's band is like that. But Arthur's is the best, and one day, with my help, Arthur will be leader over all the rest as well. Then he can finish what Ambrosius started: push east and drive the Saxons into the sea."

I was only half listening. I was more interested in the stew Myrddin cooked up while he talked. I'd never thought I'd see a nobleman cook his own food. It was watery stuff, flavoured with onions, and dry meat a-bob in it. I ate all I could and then fell asleep, propped up in a corner with my head on my scabbed knees. In my dreams the woods were still on fire.

Woken by voices, I jumped up. I'd slept the day away. Afternoon sunlight bled down through the mat of weeds and wormy rafters overhead and made patches on the floor. The horse was half asleep, head down. Out among the trees two men were talking. One was my new friend, or master, or whatever he was. The other I did not know.

I crept past the horse and peeked. In the shade of the trees that grew around the old house's door stood another horse, a white one with a mane the colour of old snow. A man sat on it, looking down at Myrddin. The newcomer was a warrior, with a leather breastplate, and a sword at his side. His thick, red cloak had run in the rain, dribbling pink stains down his horse's rump. His helmet was off, and his sandy hair stirred in the breeze.

I went closer. I didn't think I'd be noticed. Noblemen don't notice people like me, any more than they notice the stray dogs and cats that flit around their halls. I heard the newcomer say, "The Irishman is on his way. He'll bring all the men he can muster, and ours are tired after the fight. If it comes to a battle. . ."

"It will not come to that," Myrddin promised. "Don't you trust me, Cei?"

"Not an inch," said the rider, laughing. Something made him glance my way, and he started as he caught sight of my face watching him from the shadows. Then he kicked his horse's flanks and turned it away. It looked strong and fast, that horse. It had been well looked after, and well fed on other people's hay.

"We meet at the river, then?" I heard the rider shout.

"The pool above the ford," called Myrddin, one hand up, waving, as the rider went away between the trees. "Where the waterfall is."

As the hoof beats faded he turned and saw me watching. He came towards me smiling, and I was still so little used to being smiled at that I just stood there basking in it till he reached me. He took me by one arm and pushed me back inside. "There is work to be done, Gwyna."

I looked at the dark loaves of dung his horse had dropped on the floor. I wondered if he wanted it cleaned up.

"Didn't I say you'd help me help the Bear?" he said. "Arthur needs a sign. There's an Irishman who rules those wet moors that rise up south of here. He's Ban's man, and if he chooses to avenge his overlord it will be a hard strife, and a waste of good men. Better for everyone if he can just welcome Arthur as his lord in Ban's place. Arthur could use an ally here in the west.

I've spoken with the Irishman, and he's agreeable. But his people won't trust a man who carries the sign of Christ on his shield. The ways of the new God lie thin in those hills of his, like first snow. Just a pretty coverlet. Dig a little and you soon find old ways and old gods underneath."

I shivered. It must be bad luck, I thought, to talk so carelessly about gods. I crossed myself, and made the sign against evil. I didn't want to anger any gods, not new nor old.

"So the old gods are going to make Arthur a present," Myrddin went on, fumbling among the furs and cloths behind his saddle. "A sign to show they are on Arthur's side."

"What sort of sign?" I asked, afraid.

"I'll show you."

His quick hands undid the fastenings on a long bundle of oilcloth. Something golden caught the light. A sword hilt. I'd not seen many swords, but I knew enough to know this one was special. The pommel and the crosspiece were red gold, inlaid with swirls and curls of paler metal. The hilt was twisted round with silver wire. The blade shone like water in the folds of the cloth.

"Swords are important to the Bear," said Myrddin. "And not just for fighting with. They mean something. A sword thrust through a stone was the badge of Artorius Castus, who saved us from the Picts and Scots in olden times, and from whom our Arthur claims descent. The gods will send this sword to Arthur from the otherworld, to show that they love him as they loved the old Artorius."

He was holding out the sword to me as if inviting me to touch it. I drew back.

"It has a name. Caliburn."

"Is it really from the otherworld?"

"Of course not, child. I bought it from a trader down at Din Tagyll. But we can make men *think* it is from the gods."

If I'd been a man, or even a boy, I might have said, "What do you mean, 'we'? I want no part in enchantments." But I was only Gwyna the Mouse. It was my lot to do as my elders told me, even if I didn't understand.

Myrddin tousled my matted hair. "And maybe some god *is* watching over us," he said. "Something sent you to me, that's for sure. I had planned to have the Bear row out and find the sword on a ledge beneath that little waterfall, hid among the rushes there like Moses in his basket. Spin a story afterwards to explain it. But now I have a better notion. And now I have you, my little fish. . ."

He left the horse tethered there, and hustled me away through the woods. All he took with him was the sword, bundled in its roll of cloth. The air was growing cold. Myrddin nodded and said, "There will be a mist upon the water."

How could he know such a thing? What demons told him so?

"You'll be wondering how I came into Arthur's service, I suppose?" he asked, striding ahead of me through the thickets.

I'd been wondering no such thing. It was no place of mine to wonder about his life. But I knew that he was going to tell me all the same. I sensed he was nervous, and that talking for him was a way of keeping fear at bay.

"It's a good story," he promised, talking at me over his shoulder as he went stalking through the wood. His breath fumed in the cold air, wreathing him in smoke. "You should hear how the men tell it round their campfires. They say I worked for Arthur's father, that old villain Uthr, who was captain of Ambrosius's cavalry. It seems this Uthr had an eye for the girls, and one spring it lighted on one called Ygerna, that was wife to some small lord down in Kernyw. Lust lit up his brain like a gorse-fire. You could see the smoke pouring out of his ears. But what to do? Ygerna's husband was jealous. Kept her penned in his fort and let no man come near her.

"So Uthr called on me, and on my powers. One night, when his rival was off raiding some neighbours' cattle-runs, I transformed Uthr by magic into his image, and he slipped into the fort and into Ygerna's bed without anyone guessing. And the child conceived that night was Arthur, and his victories outshine old Uthr's as the sun outshines the moon."

Shoving my way through dead bracken at the magician's heels, listening to all of this, I wished I could just make a run for it, and take my chances with whatever wild beasts and wicked spirits lived in this maze of trees. Running had always served me well before. But running from Myrddin would be different, wouldn't it? If he had the power to transform one man into the likeness of another, then he could surely catch me and transform me into anything he chose. A frog. A toad. A stone.

"Of course, it's all nonsense," Myrddin said. "You'll have to learn that, Gwyna. Just because someone tells a story doesn't mean it's true. I have no magic powers. I'm just a traveller who has picked up a few handy conjuring tricks along the road."

"Then how did you change Uthr into another man?"
I asked.

"That's what I'm telling you, girl. It never happened.
Old Uthr took that fort by force, and carried off Ygerna
along with all his other trophies. Probably tired of her
within a week. There's no difference between Arthur and
any other of Uthr's landless bastards, except that Arthur
has me to spin stories like that one about him. You see,
Gwyna, men do love a story. That's what we're going to
give them this morning, you and I. A story they'll
remember all their lives, and tell to their children and
their children's children until the whole world knows
how Arthur came by the sword of the otherworld. And
here we are!"

We had reached the pool. Late afternoon sun lit the
oak-tops on the far shore, but the water lay in shadow,
and a faint silver breath of mist hung above it, just as
Myrddin had promised.

How had he known? He had just said he could not
work magic, but how else could he have seen into the
future?

A horn sounded, away downriver. Myrddin hurried
me along the shore. We pushed through undergrowth.
The armoured leaves of a holly-tree scratched my face. A
narrow ledge of rock led to the waterfall. Ferns grew
thickly here. The spray rattled on their leaves. Fleshy
and pointed they were, like green tongues. Among
them, almost hidden, I saw a faint path snaking in
behind the water's white curtain.

Myrddin turned and put the swaddled weight of the
sword into my hands. Then he took me by both

shoulders and stooped to stare into my face. Dark as good rich earth, his eyes were, and a quick to-and-fro flicker in them like the dancing of candle-flames as he watched me, searching, expectant.

"They are coming. I'll tell you what you must do, little fish, and you must listen well."

The sun crept west, and the tree-shadows shifted on the far shore. I crouched alone on the damp, narrow shelf behind the waterfall. The shout of falling water filled my head, but the spray barely touched me. It was a magic place. From a few paces away I must be invisible, yet I could look out through the water-curtain and see Myrddin quite clearly as he paced about in the sunlight on the eastern shore.

His face turned suddenly in my direction. He was too far off for me to make out his features, but I guessed it was a warning look. I looked at the trees behind him, and after a moment I saw light on metal, and the shapes of men on horses. They came out of the woods in a line, wary. Round white shields with the symbol of Christ on them, ☧, in red. Arthur's men. I looked for the sandy-haired one called Cei who had come to Myrddin earlier, but I could not tell which was him. The riders had their helmets on, and most rode white horses, and all wore red cloaks.

I knew Arthur when I saw him though. A red horse-tail fluttered from his helmet, and between the cheek-guards his teeth flashed in a white grin as he urged his horse down the shingle into the shallows. He was talking to Myrddin, but I could not hear their voices.

Then someone pointed across the pool towards the western side. More riders were coming down through the trees on the steep hillside there, and men on foot ran lightly between them. Spears and hunting bows. A big man with a black beard riding ahead of the rest. He stopped, and his men with him. They looked at Arthur's band. Some waved their weapons and shouted. Insults, I suppose, now I think back. Men stand taunting each other for hours sometimes before a fight begins.

But there was to be no fight. Myrddin was holding up his arms, shouting something back over the water. He swept his hand across the pool, reminding the Irishman's men that this was a magic place, a gateway to the otherworld. Telling them that that was why Arthur had come here, to pay his respects to their gods.

Now Arthur was dismounting, handing the reins of his horse to a boy who came running forward to take them. I could see men on both shores looking at each other in surprise as Arthur walked into the pool.

I said little prayers under my breath as I slipped off my old wool dress and wadded it into a crack of the rock behind me. I gripped the sword Caliburn in its oilcloth wrapper and took deep breaths. I didn't think I had the courage to do what Myrddin had ordered, but I hadn't the courage to disobey him, either. The air was cold. The water would be colder. I shuffled on my bottom to the edge of the rock shelf and let myself drop into the whirl of foam under the waterfall.

"They'll all be watching the Bear," Myrddin had said.

"Not every day you see a great warlord take a bath in all his gear. Or out of it, for that matter. No one will see you."

I hoped he was as right about that as he had been about the mist.

I surfaced cautiously under the fall. Water drilled down white all round me. For a moment, confused by the swirling and the noise, I didn't know which way I was facing. Then I saw Arthur pushing across the pool towards me. He was up to his chest; up to his shoulders. In the middle of the lake he had to half swim, which he did awkwardly, weighed down by his armour, his red cloak spread on the water behind him. Then, as he entered the tongue of rippled, roiling water that spread from the foot of the fall, the pool shallowed again and he rose up standing, waves lapping at his chest. Just as Myrddin had promised me he would.

I ducked under water, as I'd been told to. It was easy to stay down with the weight of the sword in my hands and no clothes to float me up. My bare feet sank into the thick dough of leaf mould on the bottom. I blundered forward with my eyes open, scrambling through the crown of an old drowned tree, slithering in its slimy, rotted bark, stirring up such a tumble of peaty flakes that for a moment I could see nothing at all. And then, close ahead of me, I saw the square gleam of Arthur's belt-buckle, the tower of his armoured torso. I blinked the grit from my eyes and looked up and saw his head and shoulders high above me, out in the air. For a moment our eyes met. His were wide under the iron eyebrows of his helmet. Wide and filled with wonder and something that I did not recognize, because never in my life had anyone been afraid of me before. Then my own long hair swirled up over my head and hid him. My lungs were drum skins, and my heart was pounding on them.

"Do it slowly, gracefully," Myrddin had told me. But when I tore the oilcloth wrapping from the sword it almost floated free, so I had to snatch it down and stuff it between my knees and poke the sword up with my spare hand. I felt it break the surface. My hand, out in the air, felt even colder than the rest of me. The sword was too heavy. I could feel it wobbling. My fingers were so numb that I knew I couldn't keep a grip much longer on the wet hilt. Why didn't he take it from me? Bubbles seeped from the corners of my mouth. Why didn't he take it?

He took it. I snatched my empty hand back into the world of fishes and used it to clinch my nose shut, holding the air inside me until I had swum back under the plunge of the fall, where I could surface again. I gulped down a mix of air and water and scrambled to the rock shelf, not a bit like a fish or an otter or any other water-thing, but frantic and graceless. I was too cold to care if anyone saw me or not as I climbed up into my hiding place. But when I looked back through the falling water, they were all watching Arthur slosh ashore, holding Caliburn high over his head so that it burned with sun-fire. Some waved their arms; some ran about. Their mouths wide open in their beardy faces, shouting things I couldn't hear.

I found my clothes and crawled into them, and felt no warmer. I lay down on the damp stone behind the waterfall and hugged myself and shuddered, and my teeth rattled, rattled, rattled.

VII

I must have fallen into a shivering sort of a sleep. When I woke, the light beyond the waterfall was almost gone, and someone was pushing towards me along the hidden track among the ferns.

A voice called softly, "Girl?"

I'd not thought to see Myrddin again. Why would he even remember me, now I'd served my purpose? Yet here he was. He must have thought of further uses for me.

"I'm sorry to leave you cold here, and such a time! You played your part well. You should hear the stories they're already telling, our men and the Irishman's. How the lady beneath the lake gave Arthur a magic sword. . . That hand rising out of the water. . . If I'd not known better, even I might have thought. . . For a moment there, with that sword shining against the shadow of the rocks. . . Even Arthur believes it! He's used to my tricks, but he really thinks I conjured up the lady of the waters for him. . ."

I wondered sleepily how anyone could have been fooled by my dirty, trembling hand, holding up a sword too heavy for it. I did not know then that men see whatever you tell them to see.

He wrapped me up in his cloak and carried me gently back along that precarious path to the shore, where his horse was waiting. Unused to gentleness, I let myself relax. By the time he heaved up me up on to the horse's back I was half asleep again. He rode with me along the forest track, holding me in front of him like baggage. By the time I woke we were passing the burned timbers of my home and starting uphill towards the fort Arthur had captured the night before. The huts that had ringed it were gone. Only their black bones remained, dribbling ghosts of smoke into the twilight. The gate was smashed open. Strangers stood on the walls. The church and the house where the monks had lived were burned and broken too, and the stones were cracked and crumbly from the fire. Dead men lay about. Outside Ban's hall the dragon banner blew, dark against the bat-flicked sky. Shouting came from the open door, and laughter. Myrddin dismounted and boys ran to take his horse. They didn't notice me as he lifted me down. Bundled up as I was, I suppose they thought I was a bag or a blanket.

He carried me in his arms along the side of the hall. It was a long building, with stone walls that tapered at each end and a steep thatch towering above. I could hear sounds like the roaring of wild animals from inside, where Arthur and his men were celebrating their victory and sharing out Ban's treasure and his women.

31

At the end of the building a narrow doorway led into a honeycomb of small rooms. There in the half-dark Myrddin dumped me on soft bedding and left me, tugging a curtain closed across the doorway as he went out. Through a high, tiny window the first stars showed. Firelight shone in around the edges of the curtain. I sat up and looked about me. Straw scrunched inside the plump mattress as I shifted. This must have been Ban's wife's room till last night, and some of her fine things were still in it, though they'd been tumbled and overturned as if a storm-wind had swept through the place.

A puddle of light showed on the floor near the doorway. I crept to it, and found a mirror of polished bronze. My own eyes blinked up at me, like a spirit looking out of a pool. I'd never looked in a mirror before. I saw a flat, round face, a stubby nose. My hair, which was normally the hopeless brown of winter bracken, hung in draggles, black with lake-water. I was a nothing sort of girl, no sooner glimpsed than forgotten. Why would Myrddin care what became of me? Maybe he planned to kill me, seeing as I was the only one who knew the secret of the sword from the water. . .

I started to think of escaping, but just then shadows moved across the spill of light beneath the curtain and I heard a man's voice quite clear outside, saying angrily, "You brought her *here*?"

I threw myself back on to the bed and pretended to be asleep. With eyes half shut I saw the curtain drawn open, then quickly closed again when the two men were inside. The newcomer was the man called Cei. He carried an oil lamp. He knelt beside me, but Myrddin stayed near the doorway.

"So this is the truth behind your trick," Cei said. I saw his ugly face in the lamplight turn to Myrddin.

"A good trick, too," said Myrddin. "Even you might have believed it if you'd not seen the sword and the girl before.

Cei still looked angry. He stared at me as if I was a wild cat that Myrddin had smuggled in. "Myrddin, Arthur himself believed what happened at the river! He is out there now, telling anyone who'll listen about how he saw the lake-woman. If he learns it was this child he'll kill you. If the Irishman finds out. . ."

"Then we must make sure that Arthur and the Irishman don't find out," said Myrddin. "But I must do something with her. I won't smother the girl like a kitten. She served us well."

Cei gave a shrug. I heard his armour creak. He said, "Then let her loose somewhere. She's nothing. Even if she does tell, no one will believe her."

"She deserves better than that," said Myrddin firmly. "After what she did for us? Our lady of the lake? You've seen the way the Irishman and his friends look at Arthur; as if he's half a god himself."

"So what do you mean to do with her?"

"I'll keep her by me. She'll be a useful servant."

"And men will say, 'The trickster Myrddin has taken a girl-child as apprentice,' and they will remember that white hand rising from the lake and the long swirl of hair and sooner or later the brighter of them will put one thing beside another and work out that today's spectacle was just another trick. And you will be finished, and Arthur too, maybe."

"Then what if she was not a girl?" asked Myrddin, and turned to look at me. I don't think he'd been fooled for an instant by my play of being asleep. "What do you say, child? How would you like the great Myrddin to transform you into a boy?"

I sat up and stared at him. I thought he was about to change me by magic, like he had the Bear's father. But that had been just a story, hadn't it?

He came closer and took the lamp from Cei and held it so the light shone on me. "Look. There's nothing girlish about that face. And no shortage of dead men's cast-offs to clothe her in. With her hair shorn and leggings and a tunic on she'd look like just another of the boys who hang round Arthur. She needn't even change her name, much. Gwyn will do."

"What do you say, child?" asked Cei.

Well, what would you say? Better a boy than a frog, or a stone-cold corpse. That's what I reckoned.

"Of course," said Cei, glancing up at Myrddin, "when a few more summers have passed there'll be no mistaking her for anything but a maiden."

Myrddin waved his words away like midges. He liked the thought of pulling this new trick. Outwitting everybody with his foxy cleverness. He said, "When a few more summers have passed, Cei, the story of the sword from the lake will be rooted so deep that nothing will blow it down, and then young Gwyn can become Gwyna again. Or maybe by then your brother will have outrun his luck and led us all into our graves, or your Christian god will have returned in glory and declared his paradise. So don't lurk there fretting like an old woman. Go and find clothes for my boy here."

Cei left, grumbling that he did not care for being ordered off on errands by a godless mountebank, but I guessed he did not mean it. The way he and Myrddin threw insults at each other told me they were old friends. When he was gone Myrddin said, "He's a good man, Cei. Arthur's half-brother. But he hasn't Arthur's ambition. Old Uthr's blood doesn't burn so fierce in his veins. A follower, not a leader."

I didn't say anything. It wasn't my place. I listened to the voice of my heart instead. It was busy asking me what it would be like to be a boy. Would I have to fight? Would I have to ride? Would I have to piss standing up? I was sure I couldn't do any of those things. No one would ever take me for a boy, would they?

VIII

But they did. Cei returned with a woollen tunic (oaten-coloured it was, with red borders) and scratchy homespun trousers which hung down to my ankles, bound round my shins with ribbons of soft leather. My shoon were leather, too, the first I'd worn. They made each foot feel like a fish in a trap. Then Myrddin took out a wicked-looking knife and cut my long hair so that it spiked up on end like hedge-pigs' prickles, and when he had brushed the trimmings from my shoulders I went out with him into the hall.

It was so full of noise and smoke and men that I could hardly see anything at first. Arthur's shield-companions were feasting with the Irishman's warriors, celebrating their new alliance in beer and meat. Wherever I looked some man's broad back was in my way, and all I could hear was their great bull voices bellowing. But the men drew aside when they saw Myrddin coming, and soon we got near the big fire where one of Ban's captured cows was roasting. There stood Arthur, with a knife in his hand and grease on his tunic, carving honour-portions for his favourites, slinging their meat to them along with jokes and laughter.

It was the first time I'd seen him without his helm and fish-scale armour on. He was less like a god than I'd expected. A solid, big-boned man with a thick neck and a fleshy face. His cropped, black hair was thinning at the front, and his scalp shone with sweat in the firelight. His eyes were small and dark, set deep, and they had a sleepy look, but they could become sly and thoughtful all of a sudden, or twinkle with merriment like a boy's. I guessed they might narrow easily with rage. A dangerous man, I thought. A bear of a man.

"Myrddin!" he shouted, seeing my master through the smoke and waving the meat-knife at him. "Where have you been? Get out your harp. Give us the story of our victory!"

Myrddin grinned at him, and said, "A good story is like good mead, or good beer. It needs to brew a while."

Men turned to look, and some shouted "Myrddin!" too, and gestured with cups, or hunks of meat, or upraised hands. I watched the way they looked at Myrddin, and I guessed that he was someone they joked about when his back was turned, but someone they feared too. After all, had he not called up the spirits of the waters that very afternoon?

"What's this?" asked Arthur, pointing at me with his knife. "You have a son, and never told us?" Laughter from the men about. Arthur laughed too, and shouted above the noise of the others, "Let's pray he doesn't take after his granddad!"

Myrddin claimed to be the son of a bard, but there was another story, too: that his mother was a nun and his father the Devil himself. I didn't know that then, mind. I thought all their rough laughter was at me. It battered me backwards like a storm of wind till I was pressed against my master's robes.

Myrddin laid a hand on my shoulder. "Gwyn's a kinsman of mine, come to be my servant. He travelled with me from Din Tagyll. Can't I have someone to fetch and carry for me just as you fighters do?"

Arthur's bright eyes were on me, spilling tears of laughter at his own joke. I thought he was sure to see the truth about me, and I felt myself shrink and blush, waiting for him to bellow, "That's no boy." But I was only a servant. Why would Arthur waste a thought on me? After a moment one of the Irishman's captains said in his moss-thick moorland accent, "This is Myrddin? The enchanter?"

Arthur turned to him, and I was forgotten. "The greatest enchanter of the island of Britain. Did I not see her face myself when she gave me this sword? The lake-woman. He called her up. Summoned her like I summon a servant-girl. What a face! Beautiful she was! And a swirl of golden hair, like. . ."

Words failed Arthur. He moved his hands around, sketching a swirl of white-gold hair in the smoke. His listeners were entranced. How could anyone doubt his story? Myrddin might lie to them, but Arthur was an open man; like him or not, you could see the truth shining out of his big face. "Naked she was, down under the water, and white as doves' down. . ."

A knot of men closed round him, and round Myrddin who stood beside him. They shut me out. A wall of backs. Thick belts and hanging swords. I turned away, and the talk of other men washed over me, full of unknown names, coarse laughter, talk of dead enemies and stolen women. I pushed among their tree-trunk legs, invisible to them as the dogs that truffled for scraps in the rushes on the floor. Then a hand touched mine, and I turned to find a face on a level with my own.

I started back, stepping on one of the dogs, which yelped and growled low. For a moment I'd thought the boy I was facing was the same one I'd met in the woods, the red-haired, angry one with the fallen horse. But when I looked closer I saw that this one was younger, closer to my own age, and grinning.

"I'm Bedwyr," he said. "My uncle Cei told me you're in need of a friend."

I nodded nervously, glad of Cei's kindness, yet fearful in case this lad could see through my disguise more easily than full-grown men.

"Come on," he said, "I'll take you to the horse-lines."

"Why?"

"So we can see that our masters' horses are safe for the night," he replied, still friendly, but looking surprised at how little I knew. "You are new to Myrddin's service, then? But you'll know how to groom a horse. . ."

I nodded again, but I didn't know. I knew that food went in at one end and dung came out the other, but that was all my knowledge of the tribe of horses. "I come from over the water," I told him. "From Armorica, that people call the Lesser Britain. My father was rich, and we had servants to do everything for us. But everyone was killed by Saxon pirates last spring, and now I am just a servant."

I don't know where the words came from. They seemed to have been waiting inside my head for a time when I would need them. I remember wondering if I would be struck dumb or dead or mad for telling such appalling lies. I remember thinking that Bedwyr was sure to know that I was lying. But I survived, and Bedwyr didn't question me. He felt sorry for me, and his eyes filled with tears. He hugged me in a brotherly, bearish way he'd copied from the fighting men and said, "How you must hate the Saxons. I hate them too. I'll kill hundreds and hundreds of them when I'm older, and a warrior like my brother."

He pulled me past a knot of men and pointed through the greasy smoke at where the lad who'd nearly killed me in the woods was stood, laughing too loud at some older man's joke. "That's my brother Medrawt," he said. "Our mother's Cei's sister, Arthur's half-sister. Medrawt will lead a war-band for Arthur one day. Me too, God willing. For now I'm Medrawt's man, in charge of his horse and his weapons. Medrawt fought in the battle last night, and killed a dozen of Ban's men."

I guessed I wasn't the only person who had been spinning tales about himself, but I looked astonished and impressed, which was what Bedwyr seemed to expect of me. Now that I could see them both I realized they weren't that alike, except they had the same red-gold hair and the same pale skin. Bedwyr was stocky and freckled and he had a friendly, laughing face, but

Medrawt had the look of someone who'd grown fast and lately, and still wasn't sure how to move inside his tall new body.

Bedwyr hugged me again. I tried not to shrink from his touch. I wasn't used to being touched, except by my old master's boot or the flat of his wife's hand. "We'll avenge them," Bedwyr said. He thought I was still moping about the poor murdered family I'd just invented. "Next summer," he said, "we'll ride side-by-side and wash our swords in Saxon blood! We'll be brothers, Gwyn."

"Brothers," I agreed, and wondered what he'd do when he found out I was more suited to be a sister. I trailed after him out the big door at the hall's end, trying not to walk too oddly in those odd, uncomfortable clothes. I didn't think I wanted to ride with a war-band, or wash my sword in anybody's blood, but I was glad of Bedwyr all the same.

Outside there was ice on the puddles and the sky was enormous with stars. The sentries talked softly on the walls. Frost made a fuzz of white fur on the helmets and shields piled up outside the hall. We passed a thicket of spears set butt-downward in the earth, where the heads of Lord Ban and his men had been spiked. I suppose it should have grieved me to see my own lord brought down like that, and the houses of his shield-companions roofless and his hall in the hands of Arthur's gang. But I didn't feel anything, except my leggings chafing and my new shoes nipping my toes. I followed my brother Bedwyr downhill in the dark to the horse-lines.

IX

On the whole, I preferred being a boy. The things boys do – even the chores – are better fun than women's work. Even the clothes are easier, once you grow used to them.

There's more to being a boy than wearing trews and cutting off your hair, of course, and don't let anyone tell you different. There's ways of moving and ways of standing still you have to learn. There's a way of looking at things as if you don't care about them, even when you care about them a lot. There are grunts that mean more than words. Boys have all sorts of rules among themselves, just like dogs. Rules about who leads and who follows. They don't talk about them, they just seem to be born knowing these things. I had to pick them up as best I could, by watching Bedwyr and the others.

There were about two score boys in Arthur's band, acting as servants and grooms, learning the ways of war from the older men. They sensed there was something different about me, right from the start, but I think they put it down to me being servant to Myrddin, who wasn't a soldier like their masters but a poet and maybe a magician. That made them too scared to bully me, which was good. And Bedwyr had decided to be my friend, which was better. Bedwyr wasn't the oldest or the strongest of the boys, but the rest looked up to him because he was Arthur's nephew and his brother was already one of Arthur's warriors. So they accepted me for Bedwyr's sake. They mocked me when I was too shy to piss beside them and burrowed off into the bushes on my own, but mockery is all part of how boys talk to each other. None of them ever guessed I was a girl. Myrddin was right. People see what they expect to see, and believe what you tell them to believe.

The war-band waited most of a month at Ban's fort, till the green spears of Easter lilies started jabbing up through the mud at the lane-sides. Then Arthur left the Irishman to hold Ban's lands in his name and rode away, taking with him a dozen hard warriors the Irishman had pledged to Arthur's war-band. As well as those men, the Irishman had promised to pay yearly tribute to Arthur: three ingots of tin from the mines in his hills, three loaves as broad as the distance from his elbow to his wrist, a tub of butter three hand's-breadths across and three deep, and a sow three fingers thick in her hams. It was less than he'd paid when Ban was his overlord. But he was a wily Irishman. As I helped my master mount his horse in the shadow of the gate I heard Arthur grumbling that he'd never see any of that tribute.

Myrddin said calmly, "It doesn't matter. At least the

Irishman won't move against you. That leaves you safe to turn your eyes east to the lowlands, where men will pay you taxes in gold, not butter, if they think you can keep trouble from their door."

Arthur looked sideways at him, thoughtful. He wasn't a clever man, Arthur, but he was clever enough to trust my master's judgement.

We rode downhill and turned east on the river-road, and the bare green branches of the woods soon hid the fort and the hill it stood upon. Two standard-bearers went in front, carrying Arthur's banners: the red dragon of Britain, like a long red sock with the foot cut out, and his own flag, a flat square stitched with the symbol of a sword thrust through a stone. Behind them rode Arthur, and his captains, and his sixty warriors, gorgeous in their red cloaks on their ghost-white horses. We boys followed, with pack-horses and spare mounts. By noon I was further from home than I had ever been, yet still we kept going. Britain was bigger than I'd thought.

Days went by. I got used to seeing the world from horseback. I rode a pony called Dewi that had been taken as plunder from Ban's pastures. Arthur had given him to Myrddin, and Myrddin gave him to me. The first time I got up on his back I fell straight off the other side into a dung-puddle and the delighted crowing laughter of the other boys. But I learned fast. Second time I stayed up, swaying, and Bedwyr showed me pityingly how to grip the reins, how to tug Dewi's head round to steer him, how to control him with the pressure of my knees and heels against his hairy flanks.

Strange, it seemed, to think I owned something so big

and beautiful and alive as Dewi. He was white with a hint of grey-blue dapple at his hind-end, strong in the leg and well muscled. I got to love the way his mane tufted, wood-smoke colour, and how he would put his big head down to nuzzle me when I was trying to bridle him. The squared ridge of his long nose, hard as a shield. His steady walk, the quiet power of him. Sat on Dewi's back, I felt like one of those creatures they have in Greece that Myrddin told us of one time; half man, half horse. I'd look down from his saddle at common people who could only stand and watch as Arthur's band went by. Now and then I'd catch sight of some little dirty girl-child with scabs on her knees and think, wondering-like, "That's what I was, till master changed me."

But though I knew it was true, it grew harder and harder to believe it. My new life was so different that the old felt like it had never been at all. Even I was coming to think of myself as a boy.

We rode through a land that was a patchwork of small powers. Strong men had hacked territories for themselves out of the carcass of old Britannia, and then they had had sons, and their sons had had sons, and each son had taken a portion of his father's holding till what remained were countless tiny kingdoms. Some were combined under the heel of a single overlord, Maelwas of Dumnonia in the south, or Cunomorus of Kernyw in the far west, or the kings of Gwent and Calchvynydd northward. But among the smaller kingdoms, and in the borderlands, a man might still forge territory of his own.

The country we travelled that spring wasn't exactly Arthur's, but the men it did belong to weren't strong enough to argue when he came riding up to their holdings with his band behind him and my master Myrddin at his side, shouting out words as fine as banners: "Make way for the *Imperator* Artorius! Make way for the *Dux Bellorum* of the island of Britain! Great Arthur will protect you from the Saxons!"

In truth, the Saxons had been beaten so soundly by old Ambrosius that they'd kept meekly to their lands in the east ever since, and the few small war-bands who came raiding over their border sometimes had never reached this far west. But if anyone dared voice that thought Myrddin would scowl like an owl and say, "Are your memories so short in this country? Don't you remember the terrors of the Saxons' war? The houses and churches on fire? Women and children snatched away as slaves? Bodies strewn in the streets, red with blood, as if they'd been crushed in a wine-press? It was men like Arthur who protected us then. And it's Arthur who will protect us again, when the Saxons return. Why, it's only the fear of Arthur that keeps them from swarming west and murdering you all! What do you think will happen to your homes and your children if you don't give Arthur the little he asks, to keep his brave fighters fed and clothed and mounted?"

I think Myrddin really believed what he said about those Saxons. You could see his fear for Britain's future in his eyes when he spoke of them. You could hear it in his voice. But I don't know what Arthur thought. Sometimes it seemed to me those Saxons were just a threat he used to make men part with their belongings. He would sit on his white horse while my master made his earnest speeches, and the people would look at him, and at his gang behind him, and go scurrying to bring him tribute and offer us shelter in their houses and food for ourselves and our hungry horses.

Once we ran up against a rival war-band, led by another man who also called himself *Dux Bellorum*, and there was a battle at a ford. I didn't see it, for I was back with the wagons. I heard the noise of it roaring and crashing like a far-off storm, and once the shrill screaming of a wounded horse. I couldn't understand what it was at first, but Bedwyr tensed like a hound that hears the hunt go by. When we crossed that ford later there were dead men in the water either side, leaking long ribbons of blood downstream.

Medrawt killed a man in that fight. It filled him with a shaky sort of laughter. He came and hugged Bedwyr and promised him a share of the stuff he'd taken from his dead enemy. I'd never seen him show kindness to his younger brother before. He was so conscious of being a man that he barely let himself look at us mere boys, except when he was barking at Bedwyr to clean his gear or tend to his horse or find him something more to eat. But Bedwyr loved him, and when I watched them laughing together I could see why.

"This is my friend Gwyn," said Bedwyr, tugging Medrawt towards me. "Gwyn's Myrddin's man. We're brothers in arms."

"Gwyn," said Medrawt vaguely, looking me up and down. Just for a moment I saw a little shadow of confusion pass across his face, as if he recognized me but could not remember why. Then it was gone. I was just a boy, and his brother's friend, and his blooding had put him in such a good temper that he threw me an iron bracelet he'd taken from the dead man's wrist.

Arthur hung the head of the rival *dux* from his saddle-girth till the stink and the flies grew too much. Then he lobbed it into a pool beside the road. I don't think he meant anything by it, except to be rid of the thing, but it pleased the war-band. They took it for a tribute to the old gods.

I'd learned, by then, the ways of all the different gods and spirits who watched over Arthur's band. Outwardly, most of the men were Christians, and their shields carried that red ☧ to show it. Crosses and tin medallions with Christ's alpha and omega sign jangled round their necks, in the hope that God would notice, and turn away the blades of enemies in battle. Some were earnest. Cei prayed every night, and looked sour and disapproving when Arthur threw that head into the water. But most were wary of the old gods too. You can't live in this land of mists and rivers and not know they're there: the lake-lady in her waters, the small gods of trees and stones. The new god has hushed and shrunk them, but he can't quite drive them away. And some of the band, like red-haired Gwri and his men from the wild uplands of Gwynedd, scoffed at Christ, who seemed weak and womanish compared to their own god, Nudd, the hunter.

And Myrddin? He had no gods. His head was full of

tales of magic and wonders, but in his heart he didn't believe any of them. He told me once, "There are no gods, Gwyn. No ghosts, no spirits. Nothing but our own fears and hopes. Gods are tales for children. They're tricks we play upon ourselves, to make it seem there's some sense in our lives."

"But you must believe in something," I told him, staring at all the charms and talismans that hung round his neck.

He laughed. "These? They're just for show. Simple people see them, and think I'm closer to the gods than other men. Men I meet on the road are afraid to rob me. But believe? I suppose some hand must have set this world moving. But I don't believe any god is watching over me, ready to help me if I make the right sacrifices and stamp me flat if I don't. It's a freedom, not believing. It gives me the power to look clear and hard at what other men believe, and use it to steer them."

Well, I'd seen the truth of that, hadn't I? But I didn't think it'd suit me, that sort of freedom. It seemed to me that going through the world without a god would be like going through midwinter snow without a cloak. I went on saying my prayers to Christ and his saints, and if they didn't answer them I'd sometimes try the old gods, too. I kept it to myself, though. It pleased my master to think he'd turned me to his own cold way of thinking.

"And Arthur?" I wondered once. "What does he believe?"

"Arthur's different. He believes in gods, both the old and the new. He welcomes their help when it comes. But

49

he won't grovel for it. He thinks he's their equal, and better than most of them."

The roads led us at last to the old legion fortress that was Arthur's base. A rampart high as the highest tree, and a wall upon the rampart, and a palisade upon the wall, and a tall gate with watchtowers. It held me spellbound as we rode up to it. How could men have built anything so *big*?

Inside the walls were scores of huts and some bigger, boat-shaped buildings hunched around a feast-hall. A smell of cooking fires, and animals wandering about the houses. Some of the men had women and families there. Cei's wife was a squat, cheerful, barrel-shaped woman, who had given him a daughter, Celemon. It was strange to see his hard face soften as he picked the girl up and swung her round him. Arthur had a wife, too: Cunaide, red-haired and beautiful as summer. I remember staring at all the gold she wore. She didn't look so very much older than me.

I expected my master would have a wife, or a woman, or at least a home, but he had nothing. While we stayed there we slept as we had slept on the road, bundled up in blankets at Arthur's fireside. Turned out Myrddin owned nothing but the things he carried bagged on the saddles of his horse and my pony. "I like to travel lightly through the world," he told me, when he saw my disappointment. "If you have nothing, no man can take it away from you."

There we left the war-band for a time and rode on alone, stopping at villages and hill-top halls. Without Arthur's army my master was able to travel easily into the territory of other lords, for a harper is welcome everywhere. It was that time of spring they call Blackthorn Winter, when blossom lies white on the hedge-banks like fresh snow. Sunlight dappled us. Over our heads the trees were putting on new leaves of fresh, shy green.

We travelled sometimes on old Roman roads which looked like God had made them, for what mortal could build roads that wide and straight? The going was easy there despite the weeds and bushes that had grown up between the slabs of stone. Now and then we went into some old town where men still tried to act like Roman citizens, despite the trees that were sprouting in their streets and the tiles that took flight from their roofs each time the wind blew. And each night Myrddin unwrapped his harp and told his tales of Arthur.

He wasn't much of a harper. It wasn't much of a harp, to be fair. I got to know it well, for a part of my duties was tightening its strings and carving new pegs for it, and oiling the wooden frame, and making sure it was tightly wrapped in lambskin and oiled linen when we went a-travelling. But however well I wrapped it, the damp of the road crept in somewhere, and it was a warped, battered, crack-voiced old thing. The sounds Myrddin plucked from it weren't beautiful, nor meant to be. They were just a stream of sound for him to set his words afloat on.

And what words! To people who had never left the valleys they were born in, Myrddin brought news of the wide world, and tales of the wonders of Britain. There was a lake in Brechiniog where Arthur had seen islands that floated on the water, and never rested twice in the same place. In the tin hills stood a stone which turned at dawn to warm each face in the rising sun, till Arthur hugged it in his arms so tight it couldn't move, and told him its secrets so he'd let it go. Arthur had stolen from the King of Ireland a magic cauldron which was never empty, and always full of what you wanted most to eat.

It was funny to see the way people bathed in his stories, believing every word. Funnier still when he told them of the lake, and the hand that had reached up out of it to offer Arthur his wonderful sword. And funniest of all was the feeling I had that even if I'd told them the truth, they would all have believed Myrddin's account over my own. "Everyone loves a story," he always said. And whatever Arthur did, Myrddin could turn it into a story so simple and clean that everyone would want to hear it, and hold it in their hearts, and take it out from time to time to polish it and see it shine, and pass it on to their friends and children.

"There's nothing a man can do that can't be turned into a tale," he used to tell me, as we rode from one hall to the next through the hills of summer. "Arthur can do nothing so bad that I can't spin it into gold, and use it to make him more famous and more feared. If the tales are good enough even the poor man who goes hungry from paying Arthur taxes will love him. I am the story-spinning physician who keeps his reputation in good health."

The stories kept changing, too, but that didn't seem to matter. Some people knew a different tale about a sword. They'd seen the symbol stitched upon the war-band's battle-flag, and a story had grown up about a sword wedged in a stone, and how Arthur had freed it to prove that he was Uthr's son, and heir to old Ambrosius. "Ah, that!" said Myrddin, when someone reminded him of it one night in a hall hard by the Usk. "That sword was broken, in Arthur's fight with the giant of Bannog, so the lake-woman gave him a new one, see? What, have you not heard about the fight at Bannog?" And he was away, spinning a tale of giants so rich and fierce that all his listeners forgot they'd never heard before about the sword-from-the-stone being broken, and Arthur needing a new one.

It started to seem that there were two Arthurs: the hard man who had burned my home, and another one who lived in Myrddin's stories and spent his time hunting magical stags and fighting giants and brigands.

I liked the Arthur of the stories better, but some of his bravery and mystery rubbed off on the real man, so that when we came back to Arthur's place in the harvest and I saw him again, I could not help but think of the time he had captured that glass castle in the Irish Sea, or sliced the Black Witch into two halves, like two tubs.

Myrddin said he was not an enchanter, but he worked magic all right. He turned me into a boy, and he turned Arthur into a hero.

XI

Here's a story Myrddin told that year, while we sat around the hall-fires, me and Bedwyr reunited, and the other boys and men of Arthur's band. He'd been talking to the Irishman's kin, and he'd got from them a tale their grandfathers had brought across the sea from Leinster. It was all about some old Irish god, but Myrddin took the god out and put Arthur in his place and when he told it by the harvest fire even the Irishmen listened rapt, as if they'd never heard of it before.

One Christmas, Myrddin said, Arthur gave a feast here in this very hall for his loyal companions. And as they feasted, the big door there blew open, and in roared the wild west wind, all filled with snow, and with the snow a giant dressed in green. Green cloak, green tunic, green boots, green leggings, and an armour-coat of long green scales like laurel leaves. A green sword at his side, green hair, green beard, teeth green as summer acorns in his green head. "Where's the governor of this gang?" says he, looking round (and I dare say his voice was as green as the rest of him). And when Arthur stands up he says, "I've heard of your bravery, Arthur. The courage of your shield-companions is known all across the world. Even the emperor in Rome has heard of them, and quakes at night with the fear that they might come and pluck his rotten empire like an apple." (Cheers, of course, at this bit.) "Well," says the green man (only the way that Myrddin has him say it makes his listeners stop cheering and laughing and lean towards him big-eyed, waiting). "Well, I'm here to test your famous courage."

And he takes out a great axe, its haft green with moss, its blade shining that silver-green of a spring lake reflecting new birch leaves. He lays it on the flagstones by the fire. *Chink*. He gazes round at the guests with his green eyes. "Any one of you," he says, "may strike my head off. Here, I'll make it easy for you. . ." And he goes down on one knee and bows his head, and pulls his green hair aside to bare his green neck.

Up jumps Medrawt, ever eager to show his strength and courage. "I'll meet that challenge!" he shouts. "I'll cut off your old green head with such a blow it will fly out of that door you've so rudely left open and all the way back across the sea to Ireland!" And he takes his stance beside the kneeling green man, and lifts up the axe, all sharp and shiny in the firelight.

"Just one condition," says our green friend, before the blade comes down. "If you cut off my head today, you'll have to let me cut off yours tomorrow. That's fair."

Medrawt hesitates. (The listeners chuckle, imagining the look on the young man's face.) He senses a trick. In tales like this there's always a trick, and nothing is ever what it seems. The gold you bring back from the otherworld turns overnight into dry leaves. The pretty lady is an old hag in disguise. Medrawt lowers his sword. His face is almost as green as the stranger's. (Listening to the tale, he laughs uncomfortably, and accepts the friendly blows and laughter of his comrades. He's pleased he has a part in the story, but he wishes it had been a braver one.)

Now up steps Arthur, and the listeners go quiet again. They know the real business of the story is beginning. "I won't let my men face dangers I won't meet myself," says the Arthur in the story. And he takes the axe from Medrawt and, quick as lightning, strikes off the green man's head. *Thump*. It rolls across the floor. A spatter of green blood comes out of the severed neck, sticky as sap.

Then the headless body stirs. It stretches, and rises to its feet. The guests gasp and stare in horror. (And Myrddin's listeners gasp and stare along with them.) The body walks to where the head lies and picks it up. The head's green eyes look about it. The green mouth grins. "I'll be back tomorrow night to take my turn," says the head. The body takes up the axe in its other hand, and the green man strides out of the hall and vanishes into the snowy, midwinter dark.

A long day of worry passes. Next night, the gates and doors are barred, and a guard is set all around the fort. But sharp at midnight the green man appears in Arthur's hall, as whole and sound as when we first saw him. Arthur's men rage and his women wail and weep, but Arthur stands up, brave to the end, and says, "I've made my bargain, and I'll keep it" (or something such – Myrddin put it better, and included a lot of stuff about how much Arthur cares for his men, and how he'll miss them). Then he kneels down, and bares his neck, and the green man raises his axe.

Crash! The blade smashes a flagstone in half. (That one there, between your feet, Sagranus.) Arthur is unharmed. He springs up, whole. The green man kneels to him. "Artorius Magnus," he says, "you're as brave as they say. I'll go back to my own country and tell them of your courage, champion of Britain."

In the silence as the story ends, I look about. I see their faces, and I feel the same look on my own. An enchanted look. It's not that we believe the story. We all know no green man really came here, or walked around with his head held in his hand. But we feel we've heard a kind of truth. Even Arthur feels it, lounging in his big chair with Cunaide at his side and his hound Cabal at his feet. For a moment, the real Arthur and the story Arthur are one and the same, and we know that we are all part of the story, all of us.

XII

A year has passed. It's my second summer as a boy. I've almost forgotten that I ever was a girl. The oak-tops in the cleaves below the fort are a green sea, stirring and shushing in the wind, and the hills beyond them reach away in hazy veils of green and blue to the real sea, which is a distant silvering along the joining place of world and sky. I've never seen that real sea close, but I'm about to. Arthur is taking a band of men south to gather taxes from fat farmers. And Myrddin is to go with him, and so am I.

I remember making the horses ready, the work of loading the pack-ponies, hanging their saddles with bags which we hoped would be full of gold when we came home again. I remember stopping nights at thick-walled halls where sulky headmen glowered at us as they grudgingly handed Arthur his tribute. The sky was blue, and the sun was golden, and the roadsides bloomed with meadowsweet and foxgloves. People in the farmsteads said Arthur had brought the summer with him, and that pleased him, though they'd have said the same to any great man who rode by with a gang of warriors behind him.

And I remember a villa in the hills, a Roman-ish place, with slaves to run it still, and plump red cattle grazing the pastureland. Gorse popping in the sunshine as we rode to it along a white track, dust clouding from our horses' hooves like smoke, and a hawk pinned on the sky high up. The owner of the place looked even sulkier than the rest when Myrddin told him that great Arthur was guarding this land against the Saxons. He said this was the territory of Maelwas, King of Dumnonia, and he had already paid his tribute.

"If this is Maelwas's land, where is he?" asked Arthur, smiling, looking puzzled. The men behind him laughed. Maelwas was a joke to them, the old king of a land too big for him. Arthur rode on their laugher, laughing himself as he went on, "I don't see Maelwas hereabout. We crossed into his country days since, and never a welcome have we had. I think Maelwas's lands are shrinking like the last patch of hair on an old man's head. I reckon you need someone else to guard you against those Saxons."

The landowner looked grim, and said he had already paid tribute.

"Then you'll pay it again," said Arthur, and he jumped down off his horse and walked past Myrddin and knocked the man down. He didn't draw his sword, just kept kicking and stamping until the man's face was one soft mask of blood and his teeth were scattered all about in the dry grass, yellow as gorse-flowers.

The man's servants and family looked on without

speaking or trying to help. Children snuggled into their mothers' skirts. When Arthur was finished some slaves came forward to drag their master away. "You see what can happen?" Arthur asked the rest, wiping blood-spatter off his face with a corner of his cloak. "You never know when a war-band might ride up here to burn your huts and take your cattle and your women and your gold. You need a strong friend to keep trouble at bay."

And Bedwyr and me going round with the bags while he spoke, and the servants running indoors to fetch gold coins and pewter dishes and a set of silver spoons with the symbols of Christ on the handles, and that hawk still circling high up.

After that Arthur pointed us east towards a rich church he planned to plunder. But at a ford along the road we met a band of men sent out by Maelwas, who had heard of our coming at last. Insults and arrows went to and fro across the water all through a sweltering day, but it was too hot to fight, and come the sundown we drew back into the woods on our side of the river, and the Dumnonii drew back into theirs. "Arthur doesn't need a fight with Maelwas," Myrddin said. "He has made the old man notice him. That's a start."

So we turned downriver to the sea, where there was a place that had been held by one of Arthur's old shield-companions once, a man called Peredur Long-Knife. He was ten years dead, this Long-Knife, and all his sons with him, but his widow was supposed to hold his lands still, and Myrddin reckoned she'd pay well for Arthur's protection.

We came at evening down a long combe, following aimless sheep-tracks through bracken and bilberries and the scratchy, purple ling, and there was the sea, all shiny pewter and as wide as the world. I'd thought it would be smooth and clear, like a great pond, but it was dark and rough and hummocked, heaving up in white-topped hills. I had to hide my surprise, for Bedwyr and the other boys thought I'd been across it in a boat when I came from Armorica to be my master's servant. I couldn't see how anybody could venture out on that restless greyness in a boat. I couldn't stop glancing at it, for fear it would rise up when I wasn't looking and drown the land. I didn't trust that sea one bit.

We rode down to the beach, and our horses snorted and jerked up their heads at the salt air. The sky was a wet slate, scratched all across by the hard voices of the gulls. There was a smell of rot from the tideline, and a village of round huts straggling up to a stronghold on a cliff-top. Door-curtains flapped in the damp air, and a few fishermen's children ran to hide among the drying nets as we rode by.

"Looks poor," said Arthur grumpily, as we came up the track to the stone-walled hall. "This was a wasted ride."

"Maybe they'll spare men, at least," Myrddin replied.

"Looking for more men from this place will be like groping for coins in an empty purse."

Around the rampart of the hall ran a gap-toothed palisade, with dead gulls strung up on it, perhaps in an effort to scare off their friends, who kept screaming overhead, daubing the place with white dazzles of shit. Inside the fence a rash of huts had sprouted. A chapel hunched low in the hall's lee with its back to the weather. A pack of men with half-shaved heads and flapping, crow-black robes spilled out of it to stare as our horses came through the unguarded gate, clip-clopping on the warped boards that made a roadway there. The tallest barred our way. Thistledown hair, he had, and fierce eyes. His robes stuttered round his skinny limbs, cloth so thin you could see his white flesh through the weave. His nose was red, though, and his words ran together, like a man who liked his wine. He held up his shaky hands in front of Arthur's horse.

"Turn back!" he shouted. "You are men of the sword, and the sword will devour you! Your hands are red with blood! I, Saint Porroc, command you in the name of the Lord of the Seven Heavens, turn back and leave this place!"

The sea-wind took his words and whisked them over the wall and away through the dry dunes and the shivering sea-cabbage. But not before we'd had time to hear them. All down the line of horsemen, riders reached for their swords. No man told Arthur to turn back. Not if he wanted to keep his head on his shoulders.

"But he's a saint!" I said, nervous.

"A self-appointed saint." Myrddin gave a soft, scornful laugh. "Britain teems with them."

Arthur, up at the head of the column, leaned on his horse's neck and grinned. "And does the lady of the place hire you and these other beggars to be her guards?"

(I looked at the hall. In the doorway, like a ghost, a woman stood watching us.)

"God guards this place!" the old man in the roadway bellowed. "And I am God's servant. You'll find no warriors here. No swords, no weapons. Nothing but the love of God."

I winced, expecting any moment to see Caliburn flash from its sheath and cut the thin, straining stalk of his neck. But Arthur's moods were always hard to guess. He just laughed.

"Out of my way, old man," he said.

A kind of mumbling howl went up from the black huddle of monks. Saint Porroc shouted shrilly, "If you kill me, God will whisk me up to Paradise, but you will whirl and scorch for ever in the fires of Hell!" But he didn't look happy at the prospect of martyrdom. He let slip a strangled shriek when Arthur urged his horse forward, and let it push him awkwardly aside. He stumbled and sat down hard in the gritty sand, where he held up his arms and started shouting Latin. His followers all copied him and their psalms and spittle blew past us on the salt gale as we went on our way up to the hall and dismounted outside.

Peredur Long-Knife's widow was a small woman with frightened eyes. A big driftwood cross hung round her neck on a rough cord which had made red weals in her flesh. Everything else about her was a shade of grey, as if the tears she'd shed for her lord and all his sons had washed the colour out of her. But she knelt before Arthur, and kissed the hem of his cloak, which I think pleased him after the welcome we'd had in the hills.

"I have no gold to offer you, and no warriors," she whispered. "This is a place of women. All the men went to the wars, and God did not see fit to send any of them home again. I have no sons now, only my daughter. Saint Porroc guards us. He has been kind enough to build his hermitage here upon my land. It is his prayers that protect us from sea-raiders and horse-thieves."

Arthur cast his eye over the daughter, who stood further back, staring at us from behind a fence of waiting-women. She was pretty enough, but only a child, no older than me. His gaze slid off her like water off metal and went roving among her older, prettier companions.

"We'll take no gold from you," he said, talking to the lady of the place, but with his eyes on one of the serving women. "A bed for the night, and straw for our horses, and a day's hunting. That's all we ask of Peredur Long-Knife's widow."

Peredur Long-Knife's widow looked past him to her saint, as if expecting help. None came. She seemed to gather herself, leaning for a moment against the doorpost while she struggled to recollect the right words and ways for greeting war-lords. With a watery effort at a smile she said, "You are welcome, my lord Arthur."

That night she served a feast for us. Killed and roasted a pig she probably couldn't spare (though I noticed that Saint Porroc's monks had pigs a-plenty in pens behind the little chapel). She was so frightened of Arthur that just looking at him seemed to hurt her. Arthur could have helped himself to her place without a thought, and everybody in the hall knew it; you could see it in the wary, watchful looks they gave him through the smoke. The monks outside knew too. When I slipped out to piss I saw a dozen of them standing outside their hump-backed huts, eyes on the hall. They knew they and their angry saint would be booted out if Arthur took the place.

But Arthur had no use for this drab, sandy holding, so far from his other lands. Anyway, he was in a giving mood. He ate the stringy pig and called it good, and drank Peredur Long-Knife's memory in gritty, vinegarish wine. He nodded approval when the widow's blushing daughter picked out a tentative, tuneless air upon her harp. He grabbed the serving girl who'd snagged his fancy and sat her on his lap and shouted to my master for a story.

So Myrddin, who'd seen the hunting-spears being sharpened ready for tomorrow's sport, told us the tale of another hunt that Arthur had ridden out on, and somehow the real hunt merged into a magical hunt where Arthur and his companions took the places of the old heroes, and the boar they were hunting became Twrch Trwyth, the great boar of the island of Britain, and they chased him deeper and deeper into dark old thickets of story until Arthur speared him and snatched from between his two ears the magic comb.

And we slept by the fire that night, wrapped in our cloaks, dreaming of riding through ancient woods, with the white tail of Twrch Trwyth flashing ahead of us and the spears in our right hands so sharp we heard the air sing as the blades sliced it.

I woke to a booming, sunlit morning. The doors of the hall were open, and a sea-wind was whisking up the ashes in the fireplace. The light kept dimming suddenly as a cloud masked the sun and bursting out again, golden, world-filling. Even the gulls sounded happier.

The men and boys of Arthur's band were waking up around me, scrambling to their feet and shaking the wine-fog from their heads. Bedwyr, all tousle-haired, tugged me away to ready our masters' horses for the hunt. He was itchy with excitement at the day ahead. "A hunt's not like war," he said earnestly. "In a hunt we're the equal of the grown men. Speed and wits may take the quarry, where weight and strength mean nothing. I hunted often in my father's lands when I was younger."

I nodded, trying not to show how I really felt about the idea of riding our wiry little ponies fast across those hummocky, tussocked cliff-tops. I tried to look as if I had hunted before, too; as if I'd spent my summers chasing the boar Twrch Trwyth instead of dipping for minnows in the withy-ponds. And when I thought about the tales Myrddin had spun for us in the firelight I found it wasn't so hard, after all, to imagine myself a great hunter. You could see the same thing in Bedwyr's face, and in the faces of the other men as they got ready, shouting for spears and calling dogs to heel. The spell of the story was still at work in us, and were we all eager to prove what heroes we were.

My master, stepping out blinking into the sunlight, tipped cold water on my imaginings. "You'll stay here with me, Gwyn."

"But your horse is ready, master," I said.

"Unready her, then," snapped Myrddin. "Do you really think I would risk my neck galloping through those tangle-woods? I leave hunting to the horsemen. Besides, they say that dragon's teeth and giant's bones may be found along this shore, and I mean to look for some. Fetch a bag, and come with me."

I blushed hotly, half relieved and half ashamed at being kept from the hunt. Other boys laughed as I tramped back to the hall. One of the men – Owain, maybe – called out, "Let the boy come, Myrddin," but of course my master would not relent. I knew what he was frightened of. Injuries are common on the hunting field. What if I fell, and someone tried to tend me, and discovered what I really was?

I could hear the horns sounding as I climbed the stairs to the chamber where Myrddin had been quartered (no blanket by the hearth for Arthur's enchanter). As I rummaged through his things for the old sack he wanted I could hear the clatter of the departing horses. I felt as if they were taking something of mine away with them as they rode along the cliff-road, through the gorse.

Coming back down I found no sign of my master. Started for the beach already, one of the women told me. I went round the hall's corner and saw Peredur Long-Knife's daughter stood alone in a little sad garden which someone had planted in the lee of the wall: half a dozen salt-wizened shrubs, ringed by a fence of white driftwood shards like the ribs of drowned sailors stuck upright in the sandy soil.

I could have gone by, but something drew me to her. I think I sensed that she was like me somehow. Set apart from other people. I wanted to know her, so I went towards her. She still didn't notice me. She was shading her face with one hand while she stared at the distant shapes of the huntsmen riding up the green cliff-side into the furze.

"Not seen their like?" I asked. I remembered how she'd stared and stared at them, the night before.

She looked round, startled to find me there, then smiling. "Never! They're so shiny! So beautiful! Is Arthur as brave as they say? He looks brave! When I saw you all coming up the hill yesterday I thought it was God's own angels come down to earth. . ."

"But weren't your father and brothers fighting men?"

"Were they? Were they? I never knew them, see. I never thought to ask. My mother doesn't talk of them. They died before I was born. There used to be a few old men with spears to guard us against sea-raiders, when I was little. But when Saint Porroc came he made my mother send them away, and burn the spears. He said God would guard us." Her eyes couldn't settle on me; they kept being dragged back to the cliff-top, and the far-off brightness of the riders' cloaks. "Saint Porroc says that men like Arthur are outcasts of God, and have no power over him. But Arthur just pushed him aside! I never saw anyone dare disobey the saint before."

I'd forgotten about Saint Porroc and his monks. They'd not seen fit to join us in the hall the night before, and by the time I woke they'd been hidden away in the chapel, which buzzed like a bee-skep with their angry-sounding prayers.

"Who is he, this Porroc?" I asked.

The girl looked shocked. "*Saint* Porroc!" she said

earnestly. "He is a great man of God. He came here two summers back, with his disciples. We are so blessed that he chose our hall! He is very close to God, you see. He punishes his body in all manner of ways to keep himself godly. He flays himself with brambles, and he never lies down on a bed to sleep but rests himself upon a heap of fresh-cut nettles."

"You've seen him do that?"

"No, no. But I heard him tell my mother."

I grinned. I'd already guessed, see, what kind of man this saint was. The Myrddin kind. Only difference was, he spun stories about himself, not Arthur.

"He has nothing," said the girl. "He urges my mother to be like him, so that she can come to God. He had her give away all our fine things, all her gold and silver that was left from Father's time, and all the best wine from our cellars."

"Who'd she give them to?"

She frowned, as if she'd never thought about that. "I don't know. Saint Porroc and his monks took them. He said they'd use them for the glory of God."

I squinted along the side of the hall. Now that the hunters were gone, Saint Porroc's monks were setting off to their work in the miserable straggle of fields below the rampart.

"Saint Porroc doesn't go with them?"

"He's too busy at his prayers."

"Ever been inside that church of his?"

"Oh no! Saint Porroc would not permit it! He talks to God and angels there!"

I thought about the wine-jars I'd seen in the ditch

behind the chapel. I could guess what manner of angels Porroc chatted to, while his hangers-on were weeding their bean-rows.

"Let's look," I said.

"What?" The girl took a step backwards, so as not to be caught by the thunderbolt that must surely strike me down. Looked up nervously at the sky, but it stayed blue. I could see the wickedness of what I'd suggested excited her. Living the way she did, all holy and prim in this hard-scrat place, the thought of wickedness was as sweet to her as honey. But she said, "Oh, you mustn't, no, no. . ."

I didn't listen. My year as a boy had primed me for mischief. My time with Myrddin had taught me enough that I wasn't scared of men like Porroc. If Myrddin won't let me go to the hunt, I thought, I'll have a hunt of my own, and flush out Porroc's secrets. I took my new friend by her hand. "What's your name?"

She hesitated a moment, and colour came to her cheeks, as if she was ashamed. "Peri," she said.

"Well, Peri," I promised, "we're going to give the Blessed Saint Porroc an angel to talk to."

XIII

Peri had to act the angel, I decided. Angels have long hair, don't they? And they're tall, like she was, and graceful. Anyway, I wasn't stripping off in front of her. Like Saint Porroc, I had secrets to keep.

"But he'll know me," she said, when I explained what we were going to do.

"He's half blind," I told her, remembering the way Porroc had screwed up his eyes to peer at us the day before. "Anyway, he'll not see your face. You'll have the sun at your back. The glory of God will shine about you."

"Don't talk about God that way! Oh, we shouldn't do this. . ."

She was as scared as I'd been the day Myrddin made me play the part of the lake-woman. Her fright made me feel braver. I snatched the dress she'd taken off and stuffed it into Myrddin's bag before she could change her mind. Slung the bag across my shoulders. Under her dress Peri wore a long, sleeveless, white shift. I untied her plait so her hair tumbled down. Dark, springy hair, gingery where the sunlight touched its edges. Hair I'd have envied, if I'd been still a girl. There was nothing else girlish about her. Her chest, under that white shift, was flat as a slate. Her jaw had a boyish squareness to it, too. But that fitted our purpose. Angels aren't girls.

They have wings, though. I fetched one of the gulls that hung along the rampart-fence and took its big white wings off with my knife. It didn't take me long to lash them to my belt and loop it round under Peri's arms, hiding it under her shift at the front. The wings were skewed, and at the back the belt and all the cordage showed, but from the front, with those white feathery points poking up over her shoulders, she looked. . . Well, angelic.

We went down to the church, me keeping watch for passers-by, Peri hugging herself against the chill of the wind. She was giggling nervously with the thrill of it. This was the most exciting thing that had ever happened to her, I suppose. I warned her to keep quiet. "Angels don't giggle," I said.

"How do you know?"

"The sort of angels Saint Porroc thinks about don't giggle, and that's the sort we've got to give him. Remember to keep quiet. He'll know your voice. He's never heard mine."

Saint Porroc had built his church without windows, but high on the wall above the door there was a hole to let smoke out and the light in. I scrambled up the roof and hung over the edge of the thatch to peer through it.

Upside-down, I saw the chapel's dim innards. An altar, with a swag of reddish cloth hung up behind it, and Porroc down on his knees in front of it.

That surprised me. I'd thought him a play-actor, pure and simple. Thought to find him sitting in a soft chair, sipping wine. But maybe there was some truth in his religion after all. Maybe he really did think he was God's servant. Maybe he'd been honest once, before he understood what a living he could make with his prayers and prostrations.

For a moment then I felt the huge peril of what we were doing. What if God was looking down on me, and didn't see the joke? But I couldn't go back now without looking a fool in front of Peri, and I didn't want that. I remembered what Myrddin had said. Porroc was a charlatan. God wouldn't care what tricks we played on him.

Down below me, my pretend angel stood outside the door, her long shadow stretching out from her bare feet. Her worried eyes upturned to mine. I nodded, and made faces at her till she gathered up her wits and nerve and shoved the door open, like we'd agreed.

Saint Porroc turned from his praying, and stuffed a cup of wine behind him somewhere. There was a scowl on his face as he swung round, but it dropped off him quick enough as the light from the open doorway hit his face.

What did he see? A dazzle of sunlight, and in the heart of it a white robe, and the light shining through two spurts of white feathers. His face went empty and amazed. He tried to shade his eyes. And I leaned close to my spy-hole and shouted through my cupped hands, "Porroc!"

There was a good echo in that high-roofed place. His name seemed to come at him from all around. He went down on his face, whimpering.

"God's lost his patience with you, Porroc!" I yelled. Not very angelic, but the best words I could find, and they seemed to work. Porroc writhed, a long black worm trying to burrow into the flagstone floor. "You love wine more than prayers," I told him, "and you rob the poor widow who gives you shelter!"

All that shouting was making me want to cough. I paused, swallowing, while Porroc wailed apologies at the floor.

"Go from here, Porroc!" I yelled. "Punish your body! Go to the cold sea and clean yourself!"

I looked down at Peri and hissed for her to move aside. She left the doorway and scrambled nimbly round the corner of the church. She'd barely made it when Saint Porroc shot out through the open door, like God's own boot had kicked him up the arse. Wailing, he ran through the rampart gate and away down the board-road towards the beach, and his monks in their fields left their work and hurried after him.

I slid down the thatch and flumped on the ground next to Peri. Coughing and laughing. Peri looked as if she still half expected God's finger to reach down and rub us into the dirt like two gnats.

"Come on," I said, when my cough had gone. "He's out of our way. Let's see what he hides in that hole of his."

Peri shook her head. Her bravery was all used up. She was fumbling with the belt, trying to drag off her heretical wings.

"Keep watch, then," I ordered, and ran into the dark of the church. Black as a pit, it was, after that sunlight outside. No wonder poor old Porroc had been dazzled when the door burst open. His wine-cup rolled across the floor, and the curtain behind the altar flapped in the breeze. I lifted a corner and looked behind it. And there, of course, among the cobwebs, I found all the things he had persuaded Peri's mother to part with in the interests of her immortal soul. Fine gold dishes, and bags that had a money-full look about them, and gold neck-rings and other jewellery in a well-made casket, and a whole crowd of those tall Gaulish wine jars in a corner, leaning together like drunks.

I laughed at my own cleverness, and went back outside. Peri had managed to get the gull-wings off, but she was looking at her shift in dismay, and wouldn't even listen to my story about Porroc's treasure. There'd been some blood left in the wings, and somehow in working herself free of them she'd smeared some across the breast of her white shift.

"The servants will see," she cried. "They'll tell my mother! Oh, what am I to do?"

"Take it off," I ordered.

She seemed fearful. "Look away."

I turned my back on her, and busied myself tugging her bundled-up dress out of the bag I carried. Behind me I heard her hiss at the cold as she pulled the stained shift over her head. "My mother said I must never let anyone see me unclothed," she said.

What was it made me look round? Just mischief, maybe. Just a desire to go against whatever Peri's godly mother said. Anyway, I glanced over my shoulder, and caught sight of her in her nakedness. Only a flash, like something glimpsed by lightning. But enough. It drove all thoughts of Saint Porroc and his plunder from my head and blew them away on the wind.

I'd known all along there was something strange about her. I'd not known what it was that kept pulling my eyes back to her face, to the line of her jaw and the set of her features. But I saw it now, and once I had, I couldn't imagine how I'd been so stupid not to see it sooner.

Peri wasn't a girl at all.

I looked away quick, before Peri caught me peeking, and held the dress out behind me with one hand. When I turned, she'd pulled it on. It looked all wrong on her, now I knew her secret. *His* secret.

"Why do you dress like that?" I asked.

"Like what?"

Could it be he didn't know? I saw nothing but honest confusion in those long-lashed eyes. No, this wasn't some quick disguise. His mother hadn't seen her guests coming and said, "Quickly, son, put on a gown, or they'll have you for their war-band." It takes time to grow your hair long enough to sit upon. It takes a better actor than Peri could ever be to mimic the movements of a well-born maiden; those downcast eyes and shy tilts of the head. This boy must have been treated as a girl his whole life long, and it had never occurred to him that he might be anything else.

I waved the bloodied shift at him, lost for what to say. "I'll wash this with my master's stuff. Bring it to you later."

"What about Saint Porroc?"

"My master Myrddin will know what to do with him."

We walked back towards the hall, side by side, a little apart. I said, "That name of yours. . ."

"It's Peredur," said Peri. "My real name's Peredur. "I know it's a man's name, but it was my father's, and as there are no men left to take it, my mother said it must be mine."

"It's a good name," I said, and mumbled something about looking for my master, and left him there. Hurried to the shore with my head full of questions. Why would Peredur's mother do such a thing? And how long did she mean for her son to live as a girl?

XIV

Down on the shore where the grey waves broke, Saint Porroc was tumbling like driftwood in the cold white surf. His monks stood on the sand, calling out prayers and praising God for this new sign of their master's holiness. I crunched past them along the top of a shingle bank towards a place beneath the cliffs where another black shape leant into the wind.

Myrddin looked round sharply as I drew close. "You took long enough," he said. "What mischief have you been making?"

I didn't want to tell him. I could imagine too well the storm that would break over me if he found out the trick I'd used to snare Saint Porroc. Anyway, I'd other things on my mind. "The widow's daughter is a boy," I said.

"And it has taken you all this time to notice?" said Myrddin. "Have I taught you nothing? I don't expect Arthur and his men to see more than the widow wants us to, but I didn't think you'd be fooled." He chuckled, kicking his way through the stinky hummocks of sea-weed. "The lady must be as great a magician as I am, to work such a transformation."

"But this is different!" I blurted. "I'm not like Peredur! I'm just *dressed* as a boy. He really thinks he is a girl. She's let him think it all his life!"

Myrddin didn't seem to be listening. He crouched beside a stone and traced a raised shape he found in it, a flinty whorl. "What is this?" he asked. "What *is* it?"

"I don't know, master. It looks like a ram's horn. Or a snail."

"A stone snail?" He shook his head. "The Creator is keeping secrets from us, Gwyn."

He looked up at me. He'd heard my question after all. "You can see the widow's reasons, surely? Imagine being her. All her life sons have been dropping out of her belly and into battles. One after the next cut down, and then their father. And while she's still stupid with the news of his death, she finds there's one more child in her. If you were her, wouldn't you do anything to stop this last lad from hurrying off to the same death as the others? Bring him up to know nothing of riding, weapons, hunting, any of the war-games young men play? Keep him safe at your side always?"

"But it won't work, will it?" I said. "Not for ever. He may fool people now, but once he grows a beard and his voice turns gruff, people will think it odd. Even he will notice that he's not like other girls! We should tell him the truth."

My master shook his head. "No, Gwyna." (He still called me Gwyna sometimes, when we were alone, as if to remind me of what I really was.) "The only way she'll keep that boy out of the wars is if we put an end to wars. Raise up one strong man who'll stop this petty squabbling. Bring peace back, and in that peace boys will be able to grow to manhood without learning how to butcher one another, and men of wisdom will turn their minds to greater matters, such as snails entombed in sea-stones."

He frowned, looking back at the hall, considering Peredur as if he was another freak of nature; another stone snail. "Yes. That boy has a strange road ahead of him, but he must find his way alone."

We walked back along the beach. Porroc was still in the sea. "Saint Porroc has all the fine things of this place heaped up behind a curtain in his chapel," I said.

I felt Myrddin's eyes on me. "And how do you come to know that?"

I shrugged. Myrddin looked at me, and then at the hermit, bobbing half drowned in the breakers. There was a laugh in his voice. "Perhaps you have learned something from me after all. . ."

When I got back to the hall that evening Peredur's mother watched me nervously, as if I frightened her as much as Arthur himself. Peredur was a good daughter, and must have told her about the strange questions Myrddin's boy had asked. Peredur did not join us that night to eat the venison that Arthur and his men brought back with them.

Next morning, while I was saddling our horses, Arthur and a few of his men went into Saint Porroc's chapel. The saint and his monks stood shouting curses at them, and warning them that Porroc had been sent a vision by the Lord only yesterday, and that the earth would open up and swallow Arthur shoulder deep if he defiled the hermit's holy place. Arthur paid them no heed. He came out with armfuls of gold, and his men behind him the same. He said, "These things we shall take as tribute. Henceforward, this place is under our protection."

As we rode away I looked up and saw Peredur watching from a window, gazing wide-eyed at the splendour of our cloaks and horses and our shiny swords. I waved, and he waved back, and I rode on, glad that I was not quite alone in the world.

XV

I thought often of Peredur on the long ride home, but once we reached Arthur's stronghold I soon forgot him. There was work for us boys in the fields below the ramparts, helping reap and stack the hay for winter silage, cutting and threshing the wheat. And harvest was barely in the barns before a messenger arrived. He was a nervous, chinless man, sent from a town called Aquae Sulis that prided itself for clinging on tight to the old Roman ways. He had come to ask for Arthur's help.

I wasn't there when he said his piece to Arthur and Myrddin, but word of what he'd come about soon spread. A Saxon raiding band was moving west, burning and looting. Aquae Sulis's hired soldiers had deserted, and now it lay defenceless. The council had demanded help from Maelwas, since the town lay on the fringes of his lands, but no help had come. So they begged Arthur to bring his war-band and save them.

It was the chance that Arthur had been waiting for. He needed a town under his protection if he was ever to be taken seriously as a power among the little kings of Britain. Aquae Sulis wasn't big, but it had been important once, and it was still rich.

I listened to the men talking about it as Bedwyr and I and the other boys got the horses and the weapons ready. The way they spoke made you wonder if the poor old citizens wouldn't be better off just letting the Saxons in.

North-east along the old roads, in autumn sunlight, with the dusty blue sky above and a line of white cloud on the horizon like the foam of a wave that never broke. Sleeping in the open, in the golden woods. Myrddin with his harp beside Arthur's fire, spinning us tales of victories gone by, and reminding us that it was near Aquae Sulis that Ambrosius had routed the Saxons in our fathers' time.

Aquae Sulis waited for us in a loop of silvery river, at the bottom of a green bowl of downland. A wall ringed the main part of the town, thrown up hastily during the Saxon wars, with fragments of old pagan tombs mixed in among the brick. There were gates in it, and people coming and going. Coming, mostly; packing into the town out of the rumour-haunted countryside. The guards were men in Roman gear. Big four-cornered shields with the sign of Christ on them. Rusty armour patched and mended. Their leader rode a bay horse, and walked it forward to meet Arthur in the shadow of the gate. "Valerius," he said. "I command the defences of this place."

"Artorius Magnus, *Dux Bellorum* of the Britons," said

Myrddin, riding out front as usual, to announce his lord.

Valerius looked at Arthur down his long nose. Arthur looked at the walls, the rubbish heaped up in the ditch below, the thistles on the rampart, the half dozen shabby spearmen guarding the gate. He grinned. "We're here to save you from the barbarians," he said.

Valerius just kept on looking at Arthur, and I reckon he was thinking the same I'd thought: that Aquae Sulis might be better off without Arthur's help. But then he gave a smile that seemed to hurt him, and his men stood aside, and Arthur went past him and into the town with the rest of us following.

Inside those walls wasn't much different from outside at first. The buildings near the edge of town were so overgrown they looked like up-croppings of mossy rock in a wood. In the gaps between them market gardens and small fields had been made. Cattle were nibbling at the grass that sprouted up between the stones of the road. In one place a crowd of beehive lime-kilns sent up their fug of smoke. Men with barrows and sledges brought down slabs of marble, pillars and pediments stripped from old Roman buildings, which they were turning into lime for their fields. They stopped and stared at Arthur's band, at the armour and the flags and the sheen of sunlight on the spear-points. Maybe they thought we were the ghosts of some old legion, marching in from victories in the west.

In those leafy, half-countrified parts of the town we stopped to make our camp and set up our horse-lines, and we boys ran about finding water and fodder for the beasts. But Arthur and my master and a half-dozen of the war-band went on with Valerius into the heart of the town.

And the further they go, the finer it gets. There's less ivy on the walls, and more tiles on the roofs, and someone has made an effort to scrape the dung off the pavements. But down near the river, morning mist hangs over what looks like a whole cluster of ruins. "What's happened there?" Arthur asks Valerius, imagining that raiders have already breached the walls.

"There was a temple there in olden times," Valerius replies. "The pagans used to wash themselves in the hot springs and make offerings to their idols. But the bishop of this place prayed a great prayer, and God caused the waters to rise and engulf it. No one goes there now."

The riders cross a place called the forum, which has no weeds at all, just a dried-up fountain and a prosperous-looking market. Hogs squeal and jostle in a pen of hurdles. Pewter-smiths are at work in an open-fronted shop. There's a smell of blood from a pillared building which has been turned into a butcher's shambles; gutted carcasses hanging up in the shade under the portico. Behind the stalls and the haze of blue cooking-smoke from the food-sellers, tall stone walls tower up like sea-cliffs. There are fine buildings here, and some are still in good repair. One is a big old church, but you don't have to look too hard at it to see that it was a temple once, dedicated to the Romans' emperor, who'd been their god too.

Arthur wouldn't be Arthur if he didn't start imagining his own statue perching in the empty alcove where that old emperor used to stand watch. He wants this place. Till now he's thought his little hard-won kingdom in the hills was an achievement. He's felt proud of himself whenever he thinks of all the farmsteads that pay him tribute. But now he sees it's nothing. Wet hills. Ruins. There'll be no happy homecoming for him to his fortress in the west. Not now he's seen Aquae Sulis. He wants it the way a man wants food and shelter after a month on the road. He wants a town. Maybe he'll change its name, like Alexander, once it's his. Arthuropolis.

On the steps of the church the town's council stand waiting. The *ordo*, they call themselves. They're trying to look like Roman gentlemen, but they're just a gaggle of silly old men, togged up in bed sheets. Their bare knees rattle in the autumn chill with a sound like someone knapping flints. The west wind flips their hair about like cobwebs.

"*Salve, Imperator!*" cries the chief magistrate, raising one arm as Arthur swings himself down out of the saddle. "*Salve, Artori, Dux Bellorum et Malleus Saxonici! Macte nova virtute, sic itur ad astra!*"

Arthur straightens his helmet and squints sideways at him. He likes to call himself the heir of Rome, but he's never learned much Roman talk. He grunts, and glances back at Myrddin to make sure the old man's not insulting him.

"We welcome you," the chief magistrate explains. He's eager to please, and this isn't the first time he's run up against blank looks when he's tried out his Latin. He comes flapping down the steps to where Arthur waits. "Christ our Saviour has heard our prayers, and sent you to protect us in our time of greatest need! The Saxons are only two days' march away. . ."

Arthur pushes him aside and stalks up the steps, peering into the church, into the faded glory of old Britannia. The *ordo* draw back and watch expectantly. A group of women hide shyly among the pillars outside the door. They are servants, mostly, clustering around their mistress, the wife of Valerius. Arthur's eyes meet hers for just a second before he turns to take in the view of his new town. He forgets her as soon as his back is turned. She's not his sort. Tall, bony, serious, with a long white neck. She looks like a heron.

Her name, he'll find out later, is Gwenhwyfar.

XVI

Big grey clouds marched in from westward. Cold handfuls of rain came down on Aquae Sulis like coins flung at a beggar. We found shelter in the town, ate what food the grudging citizens gave us, and took more when it wasn't enough. The people watched sullenly as we dragged the pigs out of their pens and the hens out of their runs and rummaged through their storerooms for bread and wine and apples, and cleared their granaries of corn.

That evening, when the rest were dozing round the fire in the house we'd taken for ourselves, Bedwyr and I went down to see the old healing springs that gave the town its name. I was curious because I'd heard Myrddin talk about the place, and I made Bedwyr come with me because I didn't care to go alone. The common people resented us, and while they were too scared of Arthur's men to stand up to him, I guessed they might feel braver if they could corner a boy alone in their labyrinth of old stone streets.

Bedwyr, of course, didn't see how much they hated us. Couldn't imagine that anyone could hate a lad as handsome and as brave as him, striding along with his sword at his side, in the hand-me-down red cloak he'd cadged from Medrawt. All that worried him were ghosts. And those towering houses did look like the homes of spirits in that damp grey light, and the drinking songs and shouts and laughter that splurged out of the buildings where Arthur's men were quartered sounded ghostly too, like the shades of Romans celebrating some forgotten victory.

Valerius had been lying when he said no one went to the springs. They'd been a place of power and magic since the hills were young, and however hard the bishop preached against them his flock kept going to the waters to cure their ills, as well as praying to his god. A dozen small paths wound shyly through the reeds and grass and alder-saplings, leading towards high stone buildings: bath houses, a half ruined temple. The doorways had been barred, and filled up with stones, but the walls themselves were crumbledown, and full of holes that a boy could easily slip through.

It wasn't long before Bedwyr and I were standing in a great hall, beside a muddy, misty mere that had once been the Romans' sacred bath. Square-cut pillars, tall as trees, rose from the water. Beneath the mud and moss the floor was paved with stone; you could feel the hardness of it when you walked, and see the paleness of it in places, showing through. Most of the roof had crashed down, making reefs of tiles and rubble in the water. The water was green as garlic soup, and it smelled like piss and vinegar. Stone steps went down into it, faint and yellowy under the surface.

"We shouldn't have come here," said Bedwyr, his voice tight-sounding, high with fear.

"Scared?" I asked, as if I wasn't.

"There are ghosts here," he said.

"Myrddin says there's no such thing," I told him. I was afraid as well, but I was too curious to run away. A strange warmth was in the air, and when I reached down and touched the water that was warm, too. How could there be warmth without a fire? I looked for one, but there were no flames anywhere, no smoke, only the steam rising from the water, hanging in veils between the crumbling pillars.

We crept along the pool-side, squelching through mud. Narrow doorways led off into rooms full of shadows and man-high nettles. We passed through one and crossed a narrow, mossy space, and looked through a sort of window into a place where the mist hung thick above another pool, and ferns and small trees grew from the walls, and evening sunlight came down in golden spears through gaps in the high, vaulted roof.

Maybe Myrddin was right, and there were no such things as ghosts. But someone like Myrddin, long years ago, had built and dressed that place to make you think of ghosts, and gods, and the unknowable mysteries of the hot springs. The water stirred and bubbled; the mists swirled; birds sped through leafy holes in walls and roof and swooped above the water. On the far side there was space enough to stand, among the rubble where part of the wall had tumbled down. A statue of a woman in a war-helmet lay toppled off her plinth there, but I could not tell if she'd been knocked down by the falling masonry or by angry Christians. I tipped my head on one side to get a look at her face. She'd been painted once; you could see the flakes of colour clinging to her cheeks and hair. She must have been beautiful when she was new and bright, standing there in all that mist. A better goddess than I'd made.

"This is the heart of it all," I said. "The sacred spring. . ."

We weren't the first to go there, neither. I've never seen so many charms and offerings as hung from the branches of the saplings that had grown out of the walls, and lay glinting like fish-scales on platforms just beneath the water. It looked to me as if some people round about still trusted the springs better than their bishop's god, and I couldn't blame them. There was magic in that place.

Bedwyr threw a coin into the water with a plop that echoed off the old walls. "Now the goddess of the waters will watch over us when we fight the Saxons," he whispered. "She's on Arthur's side. She gave him Caliburn. I was there, that day. I saw the sword rise out of the water, all shining with light. I heard Arthur tell afterwards about her golden hair, drifting on the waters all about her face."

I would have liked to tell him different. I almost did. I felt close to him, standing there, just the two of us in those haunted ruins. I thought he'd keep my secret. But the look on his face was so strange that I hadn't the heart to take his story away from him. He believed it, see. He believed the old gods were on Arthur's side just as he believed that winter would follow autumn and the sun would rise tomorrow. And I thought that maybe that believing would make him strong and brave and lucky when the fighting came, and maybe without it he'd be killed, or turn and run away, which was worse than being killed. So I kept quiet, and the magic waters lapped against the sides of the pool.

"We'll smash the Saxons," Bedwyr said. "And Britain will be one land again, and Arthur will be our emperor."

And then something screeched, away in the ruins behind us, and we squealed and ran pell-mell through that maze of shadows and pillars and young trees, laughing and gasping and scaring each other until we found our way into a street where lights showed in windows, and staggered homeward, mocking ourselves for being scared of an old owl.

XVII

Two days later, in the grey of dawn, and I'm sat by my pony in a dripping wood. Around me, in the gathering light, the other boys of the war-band wait. Sometimes somebody speaks, but we're quiet, mostly. Good Christians among us pray, face down on the wet earth with their arms spread out, like fallen swallows. The rest of us finger lucky charms, and look for omens in the way the dew drips off the twigs above our heads. We all have weapons; not just our own knives and spears but old swords and rusty javelins that Aquae Sulis's cowardly mercenaries forgot to take with them when they quit. We can't stop touching these new toys; rubbing the worn leather bindings on the grips of swords, picking splinters off of spear-hafts, stroking the hide coverings of our clumsy, heavy shields. The horses snort steam and clomp their hooves in the beechmast and nose about vainly for grass to eat among the grey, still trees.

This is how I come to be here. The Saxon raiders,

according to farmers fleeing into Aquae Sulis, are close on a hundred strong. They're heading towards the town, but slow, distracted by all the farmsteads and villas that lie in their path waiting to be looted, and held to walking pace by the wagons of plunder and columns of slaves that they've gathered in their push from the east. They've heard that the citizens of Aquae Sulis have a treasure-house stuffed full of gold.

Arthur, who knew that his men and their horses were tired after their own journey to the town, had been all for waiting a few days and meeting the raiders at a place just a mile from the walls, where the old roads crossed the river. But my master had a better idea. He looked at an old map and saw which way the Saxons would be coming. The best route would bring them to a ford that lies beneath the Hill of Badon. What if Arthur could meet them there, where his father Uthr and Ambrosius Aurelianus won their great fight all those years ago? A new victory at Badon would add far more to Arthur's legend than a skirmish beside some fading town most men have hardly heard of.

Myrddin is not in the battle-line, of course. "My head's too valuable to have some Saxon axe-man use it for a whetstone," he said. He'll be watching from a safe distance, up on the wooded ridge west of the ford. He wanted me to stay there with him. I told him Bedwyr and the other boys would never let me forget it if I did not ride with them into the fight, but he said, "They are fools, and I need you by me. What if you were killed, Gwyn? What if you were wounded? What if someone found you on the battlefield afterwards and peeled your clothes off and found what's underneath, and what's not? No, boy; you stay with me, safe from harm."

But boys will be boys, even the ones who are only girls dressed up: that's one of the rules of the world. And another is that servants are always up before their masters. So in the dark before dawn, while Myrddin was still snoring, I crept away to join the others, a long line of us, riding silent as we could across the ford and up into the hanging woods on Badon's lower slopes. It was a fearful thing, to disobey my master, but not as fearful as facing the jeers of all the others calling me coward.

So here we are, in the wet wood, waiting. The battle-line is drawn up west of the ford, out of sight of us. There aren't many of them, for Arthur's hoping to make the Saxons think it's just a few men from Aquae Sulis come out to try and bar their way. Valerius, in his old Roman gear, has been put in command at the ford. But Arthur is waiting in the trees behind. Once the Saxons start to cross, his horsemen will come thundering down on them. And since the enemy are many, Arthur has decided to throw us boys into the fight as well. We may not be warriors yet, but the Saxons won't realize that when we come charging from behind them out of the trees, and our coming will push them back on to the swords of the real war-band.

The light grows. We stand as the hoof beats of a single horse come drumming uphill. It's Bedwyr; my friend Bedwyr, with a leather helmet on his head and straw stuffed in under the rim to stop it sliding down over his eyes. I feel my heart fill at the sight of him. You never love your friends more than when you fear they might be taken from you in the next few moments. I feel almost as much love for the other boys, for my pony, Dewi, for the trees, for the droplets which fall on my face as Bedwyr reins his horse in close by and spatters me with watery mud.

"They're coming." He's breathless. "Their scouts came at dawn. They saw our men at the ford and heard their challenges, and laughed when they saw how few there were. Now the whole band is moving up, wagons and everything. . ."

Through the trees behind him we catch distant shouts. Insults are bellowing back and forth across the ford. We strain our ears. We cup our hands around them to catch the drips of sound. We can't make out words, and even if we could, the Saxons speak a different tongue from ours. But we all hear the shouting blur into a roar as the attackers surge forward into the ford. It's that battle-noise again, that ugly music woven out of shouting voices and hoof-falls and the clang of swords. I start to wish I'd stayed with my master. Then we hear the high horns ringing, calling Arthur's hidden riders out of the woods.

"Mount up!" shouts Medrawt, who Arthur's put in charge of us. He feels ashamed at being left to lead this rag-tag army of boys, and he cuffs the heads of those who stand closest and bellows loud to make himself feel better. "Ride!"

There's no more time for fear, or prayers, or anything. We struggle into our saddles and dig knees and heels into our mounts' flanks and crash against each other as the animals turn and fret. But at last we're all moving, faster and faster, down through the trees with branches flailing at our heads like clubs, with twigs snatching at our caps and cloaks, with the whole world gone to a whirl of sky and trees and hooves and the hot stink of horses. I reach for my new sword, but Dewi is galloping so hard and the ground's so rough that I slip sideways in the saddle as soon as I take my hand off the reins, so I forget the sword and grab a handful of his mane instead, and a thick branch comes swiping at my face and I duck under it and suddenly there are no more trees and we're rushing out across open land, a water-meadow where the mist hangs in woolly ribbons above the drainage ditches, and the other horses are beside me, foaming, racing, and boys are shouting, and Medrawt ahead of us with a spear upraised, and ahead of *him* is a big crowd of men, white faces flashing under helmets as they turn to see us.

I have just time to think "Saxons!" before our charge carries us into the middle of the battle. Off to one side I see Arthur's red banner flying. The Saxons are bunched up on the road where it slopes downhill to the ford. We gallop past a wagon that has pitched sideways into a ditch and spilled out pots and cloth-wrapped bundles and a shrieking woman. Cows get in our way, white-eyed with terror, blundering across the line of our charge. Dewi rears up, and I lose my grip and slither backwards over his arse and down with a thump in wet bracken.

The battle wraps me in its noise and reek. I get up quick, not wanting to be kicked to death. Where's Dewi? This isn't like the battles Myrddin tells about, where brave warriors fight one against another. It's more like shoving through a packed marketplace. I blunder against friends and enemies. My ears fill with the sound of blades against shield-wood: a cosy thud, like someone chopping logs. My face gets shoved into a Saxon's side; I taste the hairy weave of his tunic, smell his sweat. Lucky for me he's too busy to notice, flailing with his sword at Bedwyr, who's still mounted. The edge of a shield catches me and pulls me sideways. A yellow-haired man is shouting something at me and waving a great big axe, which I suddenly understand he means to hit me with, but the blow never comes; the battle tugs us away from one another. A riderless pony sends me sprawling. I crash into the reeds at the edge of one of those drainage ditches, slither down into the water. The reeds are spear-high, with flags of thin, pale stuff at the top, waving. Between their stalks the water is brown and brackish, covered with a film of dead flies, their spread-out wings like tiny windows, hundreds of them, thousands. Beyond the reeds men are yelling and horses are shrieking.

Were they really Saxons? There weren't many of them; less than a hundred. How could such a small army have struck so deep into the British side of Britain? I think maybe they were no more than a gang of foreign *foederates*, mercenaries hired to protect some town up in Calchvynydd who had grown tired of waiting to be paid and turned to banditry instead. Saxons are hard fighters, I've heard. Saxons would have found high ground and formed a shield-wall, made a fence of wood and steel that Arthur's cavalry could not have broken. This lot just scattered when they saw the horses coming. Ran this way and that, pursued by horsemen. Rallied in small clumps, easily cut down. It was more like a hunt than a battle.

Later, when it's quiet, I part the reeds and scramble out.

I'm frightened that people will ask where I've been. I have worked out a lie to tell them, about being stunned and waking up in the ditch to find the battle over. But no one asks. They're busy in the piles of dead, digging out fallen friends or stripping the Saxons of the things they carried. Crows are circling. Up above, the green hill of Badon rises from its blankets of woods. I see Arthur on his white horse, and Medrawt among the knot of men around him. In the mud near the ford lies Valerius, and I can't help but notice that he's been speared in the back.

"Gwyn!" someone is shouting. "Gwyn!"

It's Bedwyr, leading Dewi, who he found wandering in the meadows eastward, where our men are plundering the Saxons' baggage-train. He runs up and hugs me. "We won," he says, but he doesn't sound triumphant. He says it like a question, as if he can't quite believe that any of us is still alive. "I killed a man. I killed him, Gwyn. We won."

He hugs me hard. He smells of sweat and other people's blood. And when my face presses against his I feel a prickling where his first, thin, boyish beard is starting to grow.

XVIII

Badon fight was a turning point. It was a change in the tide. Arthur and the people round him would talk often of the battle, and the men would swap tales of it whenever there was fighting or drinking to be done. It wasn't long before people who hadn't been there started to get Arthur's little victory over the robber-band confused with that other battle of the Hill of Badon, the big, important one that old Ambrosius had won. Which was exactly what my master was hoping for when he picked out the battlefield.

As for me, all Myrddin said when he saw me alive and whole after the fight was, "So you came through unscathed. Did you enjoy your battle?"

I nodded, of course, but he knew I was lying. "I am never, never, never going into a war again," I promised myself. And I felt sorry for Bedwyr and the other boys. They must have been as scared as me, but they'd be men soon, and would have to keep on plunging into fights like that until they got into one they would never come out of. I pulled out my sword and looked at it, and I wanted to cast it away. I'd not used it, but I knew that someone had, in the days before it was mine, and that there must still be dried traces of blood grained in the grooves of its hilt and the cracked ivory pommel.

Myrddin went stalking off to help tend to the wounded men who had been dragged from the field by their friends. He talked a lot about the great healers of times gone by, men with names like Hippocrates and Galen. He did his best, after the battles, binding wounds and applying poultices of herbs and cobwebs, lashing dead pigeons to the feet of men with blood-souring to draw their fevers out. I don't know if it did much good. It seemed to me that if a man had a wound that was more than a shallow cut, he'd most likely die, and if that was what God wanted for him then there was nothing my master's bandages and ointments and long words could do.

Down by the river Bedwyr and my other friends were wading about among the dead, pulling Saxons' boots and sword-belts off.

We pulled back from the ford and camped on Badon Hill, among the green slopes of an age-old fortress. That night, around the campfires, there was less talk of war than usual, as if the memory of the real thing was too fresh in everybody's minds for the old boasts and poems to work their magic. Even Arthur looked sombre and thoughtful, staring at the sparks as they danced up into the dark. We all kept close to the fires, wary of the ghosts that would be wandering in the dark beyond those circles of light. But when we had eaten, Myrddin took out his harp and spun the day's fight into stories, listing the brave deeds that each man had done, leaving out none of them, not even Bedwyr. He touched his story with humour, telling us how none of the enemy had dared face Owain, because he was so beautiful they thought he was an angel sent to help Arthur, and how they had fled before Cei, who was so ugly they thought he was a devil come to help Arthur. And slowly, as we listened, we started to forget how afraid we'd all been, and began to remember it as he told it: Arthur's shining victory.

And when the stories were done and we were winding ourselves in our blankets and settling down to sleep, Arthur and Cei came and found my master and they went away together into Arthur's tent.

I was a long time finding sleep. I lay on the hard ground and felt the bruises blooming on me where I'd been knocked and jostled in the fight, and all the while I could hear Arthur and Cei and Myrddin talking low. And I remember wondering what they were planning, and where it would take us to next.

Before dawn, my master's toe prodded me awake. I scrambled up quick and followed him between the turf ramparts to the horse-lines. There was a line of light like a tide-mark along the bottom of the eastern sky. I could see the curve of the river shining below us, and on the dark land beyond it I could dimly make out the heap of dead enemies we had left there for the crows and foxes.

"Where are we going, master?" I asked, as we saddled the horses.

"Back to Aquae Sulis."

"Just us alone?"

"The rest will follow later. Arthur is sending me ahead, with a message for the town."

"What message?"

"Was there ever a servant as impertinent as you? No business of yours, that's what message. Did you never hear of the boy who was turned into a stone because he asked too many foolish questions?"

We rode out of the camp before anyone but the

sentries were stirring. My mind worked all the way to Aquae Sulis, worriedly wondering what Arthur and my master were planning, and what it might mean for me. Was there to be another fight? Did Arthur mean to take Aquae Sulis for himself? I knew fretting about what was going to happen wouldn't stop it happening, but I couldn't help myself.

This was what my time with Myrddin had done to me. In the old days I'd never given a thought to the future, and not much to the past. I'd lived simply in the now. I'd been happy if I had enough to eat, and nobody was hitting me. I'd been miserable when I was cold, and frightened when I was ill, but mostly I gave no more thought than an animal did to what might happen tomorrow, or next week. Just an animal walking about on two legs, that's all I was till Myrddin changed me. It seemed to me sometimes I'd been happier that way.

The town greeted us uncertainly, not sure if we were good news or bad. People always expect news to be one or the other. Usually it's both, as the news we carried was. The *ordo* raised their old lizardy arms in praise of God when Myrddin told them how the battle had gone, and then set to groaning and looking downcast when they heard of Valerius's death. The servant-women who waited on the dead man's wife started to shriek and sob and pull their hair about, but the lady herself just stood there silently, her long face whiter than ever and her grey eyes fixed on my master, until they turned her about, and led her away.

"What is to become of us?" the chief magistrate

wondered as he watched her go. "This victory has come at a high price. With Valerius gone, who will be our defender. . .?"

"Arthur wishes to bring your town under his protection," said Myrddin helpfully. "In exchange for quite reasonable tributes he would be prepared to make Aquae Sulis his capital. Build up its defences and improve it in every way."

"But we pay our taxes to Maelwas of Dumnonia."

"Maelwas is as weak as a woman. Has he sent you any help in your present need? No. So how can he object if you turn to another lord, one who *can* protect you?"

"A half-heathen savage out of the western hills," grumbled the bishop, not loudly, but loud enough for all the rest to hear.

Myrddin ignored him. "Arthur would like a treaty. A sign of lasting trust between us."

"Gold," muttered another councillor. "He'll want gold."

The chief magistrate closed his eyes and ran his hand over his face like he was counting all the wrinkles. He wanted to be left alone to take in this news of Valerius's death. He didn't want my master standing here, pressing him for an answer that would seal the fate of his whole town.

"Valerius had a wife," said Myrddin lightly.

The magistrate opened a beady eye. "Gwenhwyfar?"

"Arthur is unmarried," said Myrddin. (I wondered about red-headed Cunaide, but Myrddin told me later she wasn't a Christian wife, so didn't count.) "I gather that the lady Gwenhwyfar's father came from the family of Ambrosius himself," he went on. "And that she is related on her mother's side to King Maelwas. That would be an auspicious marriage for our *Dux Bellorum*."

The other old men clicked their tongues and shook their heads, but the chief magistrate was snared. You could see the calculations going on behind his eyes, driving out whatever sorrow he'd felt for Valerius. If what he'd heard was true, Arthur might have all Britain under his command within a few more years. An alliance with a man like that might be most useful, and if all it took was a marriage with Valerius's beanpole widow. . .

He turned to a servant, sniffing delicately. "Call Gwenhwyfar here. We should talk with her, before the *Dux Bellorum* returns."

XX

Arthur's army arrived the next day, and fat black clouds came with them like a baggage train, drenching the town in rain. It ran in rivers down the street-gutters and waterfalled from clogged downpipes. It drummed on the canvas roofs of the plunder-wagons Arthur had taken from the Saxons. It drowned out the bleating of the women who ran to mourn beside Valerius's corpse. The dead man had been carried back in honour from the battlefield, wrapped in a cloak and laid upon a shield, a noble Roman fallen in battle. But the rain soaked him through and through, and by the time they reached the church he looked like he'd drowned in a flooded ditch.

The dead man's widow steps out into the rain to meet him. Gwenhwyfar has a striking face; too long to be pretty, but a face you notice. She has dark eyes, with secrets in them. Her hair is dark, too, ash-streaked with grey. It hangs low over her forehead, as if she would like to hide behind it. Her eyes and nostrils are red like she's been crying, but maybe it's a cold. Her body, what I can see of it under her woollen cloak, is all bony angles. Her name means "white shadow", and there *is* something shadowy about her. She looks as if she can't quite believe in herself.

The boys I run with could talk of nothing but Gwenhwyfar last night. They say she's bad luck. She was promised to Valerius's brother when she was young, but he was killed in a cattle-raid before they could marry. She wed Valerius instead, and gave him a son, but the child died and there have been no others. Now she has no husband either. We boys can't believe Arthur means to make a wife of this grey icicle.

She steps forward to kiss her dead husband's forehead, and the men carrying him lower the shield a little to let her do it, almost spilling the corpse into the mud. She looks at him thoughtfully. Her white fingers rest on his chest.

"There is no wound," she says, looking across the body at my master.

"He was struck from behind," says Myrddin. Her eyes stay on him. The question in them makes him shift awkwardly. I wonder about how Valerius died. Did one of our men drive the spear into his back? Did Arthur order it? Did my master advise that it be done?

"It is not unusual for a blow to come from behind in the turmoil of battle," Myrddin says, answering the lady's question as if she'd spoken it aloud. "Your husband was such a valiant fighter, Gwenhwyfar, that I doubt any Saxon dared meet him face-to-face."

Gwenhwyfar lowers her eyes and steps back into the company of her waiting-women. She can't press my master any further without insulting *his* master, Arthur, whose riders and spearmen pack the streets around. The question of her husband's death blows downwind, unanswered.

Arthur watches her carefully from the far side of the church all through the bishop's funeral prayers. He has the same look that he gets when he is thinking about buying a horse, or taking a new stretch of land.

Outside, in the skinny, driving rain, the men of Aquae Sulis dug a hole in the wet ground and bundled Valerius into it. Before they had finished filling in the grave, Arthur was making himself at home. Working men were ordered to repair the defensive walls and clear the rubbish from the ditches below them. What soldiers the place still had were set to drilling with spears and shields. We thought that when Maelwas learned of the bite Arthur had taken out of his borderlands he would send men north to take it back, and we wanted to be ready for them. We shod horses, and sharpened spears, and dragged felled trees across the places where the walls had tumbled down. We took turns to stand on the walls at night, watching the mist steam off the wet woods, watching the hills keep their secrets.

XXI

We watched and watched, but Maelwas never came. Maybe he'd heard tell of the great victory Arthur had won under the Hill of Badon, and didn't fancy meeting him in battle. He sent heralds instead, all in white on white horses, with green branches held up high to show they came in peace. They passed on to Arthur Maelwas's thanks for preserving Aquae Sulis, and asked that he send gold and cattle as a token of his loyalty. Arthur gave them half the gold they asked for, and none of the cattle, and the heralds went back to Maelwas's strongholds in the Summer Country, leaving the town in the hands of its new lord.

Winter set in soon after. The air grew cold. We lit fires to warm our quarters. Mist hung over the ruined temples at the heart of town. From the hill-tops, I thought, Aquae Sulis must look like a steaming stock-pot.

One morning we woke to find those hills all hoary with first snow. Parties of men went to and fro between the town and Arthur's western strongholds before the roads were buried. They brought back treasures to deck Arthur's new capital, and the women and hangers-on of some of his followers. Cei's wife and daughter rode in, but I noticed Arthur did not send for Cunaide. I felt sad for her, abandoned in that cold fortress, her place taken by Gwenhwyfar.

Arthur had wanted a quick marriage, but Gwenhwyfar made him wait till Easter, when her time of mourning for her husband would be done. Arthur asked the bishop to cut short her mourning-period, but the bishop refused. Arthur thought about killing the bishop, but Cei and my master reminded him it might be bad for his reputation.

To take his mind off killing bishops, Myrddin advised that a new hall be built for the wedding. "What is the difference between us and our forefathers?" he asked one night when the men were lounging around the big fire in Arthur's hall. "They built great palaces, while we are content to live among the ruins! Arthur should build here, to show that in him the spirit and the pride of old Britannia are come again! We'll build a round hall, with tiles upon its floor and painted garlands on its walls. And at the heart of the hall, a round banqueting chamber, where we who have fought at Arthur's side may meet as equals. . ."

"I've never seen you at my side in a fight, Myrddin," shouted Arthur. "You skulk safe out of danger's way with the women and the baggage-train." But you could see the idea at work on him, even as he raised his cup to acknowledge the gusts of laughter from his men. He'd never dreamed of building halls before, but now he was starting to see himself as a man who built; a ruler who left his mark upon the world in the form of splendid halls.

For the next week or so, my master pored over drawings in the smoke-fug of his quarters and took me out in the wincing cold to mark where the post-holes should be dug. "Here. And here. And here!" he ordered, walking a circle in the forum with instruments made out of willow-staffs and twine. The bishop and his priests and their wives looked on and muttered about witchcraft and conjurings.

But Myrddin's efforts conjured up nothing, and the snow kept falling to blot out the marks I made. It quilted the roofs and streets. It froze the water in the horse-troughs so that we had to smash it with stones and spear-butts of a morning before the animals could drink. In the after-Christmas dark Arthur lost interest in hall-building, and Myrddin's schemes withered like a flower in the frost. "It was only the seed of a hall," he said, rolling up the skins he'd drawn his sketches on. "We'll let it lie hidden till spring, then see what grows."

Arthur was tired of waiting for his wedding, and for fighting-season to come round again. He left Cei in charge and took his favourite companions off into the hills, hunting deer and wild pig down the same combes they'd hunted Saxons through that autumn. They took Bedwyr with them – he was almost one of them, since Badon-fight.

Myrddin whiled away the time by teaching me to write. So if you are following my story, you have

Myrddin to thank for it, and if it bores you, you have him to blame, for these crabbed black inky words that you're reading are built from letters that he showed me how to make, scratching them with a stick in the ash before a winter fire in Aquae Sulis.

One day, while the hunters were still away, I went down by myself to the waters, where I'd gone with Bedwyr when we first came to the town. The weather was warming, and the snow was gone from the streets, though the hill-tops were still speckled white. I was itchy and flea-bitten inside my clothes. I'd not had a chance to wash since Christmas, and even then I'd only splashed my face, too scared to even take my tunic off in front of the other boys. In the silent town the warm waters of Minerva seemed to call to me.

A couple of serving-girls from Gwenhwyfar's household were lingering near the pillared front entrance to the baths, the entrance the bishop had boarded up. I ducked along the building's side before they saw me. Bedwyr and the other boys were forever seeking out those girls, swapping stories about them and wrangling over which one was prettiest or friendliest, but they scared me. I thought they might not be as blind as Bedwyr and his friends to my smooth chin.

I crept into the baths through the same hole in the wall I'd found with Bedwyr, pushing my way through the twigs and the dangling charms. The big pool lay shadowed by its mossy, sagging roof, like a pool in a cave. I reached my hand down through the wreaths of mist and touched the water and it felt hot. It still smelled bad, but not as bad as me. I pulled off my leggings, unwrapped my breech-cloth, bared my whole white body to the shivery air. The water clopped gently against the old steps, and I walked down into it, grateful for its warmth.

Have you bathed in warm water ever? I never had. It was like a miracle, to be warm again after those months of cold. Not warmed by a fire that roasts one side of you and leaves the other cold, but wrapped and coddled in warmness. My skin tingled with pleasure as I ducked under, smoothing my fingers through the greasy louse-nest of my hair, imagining the winter dirt coming off me in a cloud. Old coins and tin charms slithered beneath my toes, and drowned holly leaves pricked my soles. Opening my eyes in the soft green dark I saw something glimmer on the mulchy floor, and reached for it. My fingertips closed on a moon-shaped slip of metal that some old Roman had thrown there as an offering to the sacred waters.

When I surfaced again, someone was watching me.

How had I not seen her before? It was dark in there, I suppose, and my eyes were not used to it. Gwenhwyfar was in the shadows, just her head and shoulders showing above the lapping water, watching me with her grey eyes. I didn't even recognize her at first. Her hair hung straight and wet around her face. I took her for the goddess of the place, and went under in a panic, snorting and gurgling.

She came through the water to me and pulled me up, looking intently at my face as I choked and spat. "I know you," she said. "The magician's boy."

She smiled. I'd not seen her smile before. Had she seen me naked on the pool-side? Or had she only turned at the splashings I'd made? I shrank down in the water till it hid everything except my hedge-pig hair and flat brown face. Wavelets lapped at my nose and made me sneeze.

Gwenhwyfar said, "Bishop Bedwin would be filled with righteous anger if he knew I came here. He says it is a wicked place, and full of pagan spirits. But I would rather risk meeting a spirit or two than smell as bad as Bedwin does."

I hugged myself under the water. My fists were clenched so tight that the moon-shaped charm I'd dredged up dug its points into my palm. "I won't tell," I promised.

Gwenhwyfar backed away from me in a swirl of water. "Turn your back, magician's boy."

So she still thought I was a boy! Or did she? I thought I saw an odd light in her eyes. Maybe I imagined it. I turned and bowed my head and shut my eyes, and heard the water shift and slosh as she waded to the far side of the pool to climb out. I stole one glance, and had a glimpse of her long body before she wrapped a square of woollen-stuff around her. White, she was, like a stripped twig.

She hadn't always lived in a town. When she was a girl
Gwenhwyfar lived in a villa on a green hill beside a
steep green cleave. The cleave was tangled with trees,
feathery with ferns, a secret stream slinking black and
gold through the oak-shadows. Gwenhwyfar went
riding there on her pony, or hunted along the wood-
shores with a little bow one of the servants made her.
She was as wild as a fawn.

At least, that's how I see her, when I make pictures in
my head of the life she led before.

But fate had laid a snare for Gwenhwyfar; set to trap
her when she reached the age of marriage. Her father
was a half-brother of Ambrosius Aurelianus. The old
general's blood ran well diluted in her, but still it ran.
You could see it beneath the skin at her temples, and on
the long, pale column of her throat. Those winding
veins, bluish under her white flesh, with maybe a hint of
imperial purple. She was a bridge between our time and
the happier times of Ambrosius, and the man who

married her would link himself and his sons with the great name of the Aureliani.

Valerius's brother was the first. He'd been chosen for her by her family and by her father's allies among the *ordo* of Aquae Sulis. Gwenhwyfar didn't mind. Marcus was handsome, light-hearted, kind; everything a girl could want. He brought her gifts. The seed of his son was already growing in her when the word came of his death in a cattle-raid.

After that, it was Valerius's turn. It's not uncommon for a dead man's brother to marry the girl he'd been promised to. Why spoil a neat arrangement just because the bridegroom had run himself upon some rustler's pike? But Valerius was a poor substitute. He was cold and stern. He'd grown used to being overlooked in favour of his older brother, and it had soured him. Now Marcus was gone, Valerius took the things that had been his with a sort of bitter triumph. It didn't please him to find that the baby in his new bride's belly was one of them.

It was a hard birth. The child was sickly, and soon dead. But in the few short days he lived, Gwenhwyfar loved him. Holding him made her happy. His little blue hands clutched fistfuls of her hair. She sang to him. When he died, the happiness went out of her for good. The cold old town they made her live in felt like a tomb. She dreamed her son was crying out for her, down under the cold ground, and she could not go to him. Her husband hated her. There were no more babies.

And now a new husband had come for her. However hard she tried to slow the approach of her wedding to

Arthur, the days kept slipping through her fingers. Her women made jokes about him. His strength. His manliness. All she could think of was the name his men gave him. The Bear. Sometimes it seemed to her that he really was a bear, poorly disguised as a man. His short, black bristling hair, his watchful eyes. The way he tore at his meat in the feast-hall. His snarls and roars when things displeased him. In the growing warmth of spring she shivered as she stitched her marriage-gown and imagined her wedding night.

I felt sorry for her. Poor old heron.

XXIII

We went travelling that springtime, my master and me, with Arthur and Gwenhwyfar's wedding-hymns still ringing around inside our skulls. "We'll let the Bear have some time alone with his new bride," said Myrddin. "He's a Christian lord now, with a Christian wife, and he doesn't need an old heathen like me about him." So we went south and west, into the Summer Country, and I found out why they called it that. There would be good grazing there in summer, the people said, pastures of lush green grass where their red cows grew fat and sweet. But when I was there with Myrddin it was barely land at all. Water covered acre after acre, leaving nothing dry except the hedge-banks and the causeways.

We'd come there with a purpose. King Maelwas of Dumnonia spent his year on a long round of travels from one of his holdings to the next. He was feasting that spring at Ynys Wydryn, the apple-isle which rises steep and green out of those wet levels, with a monastery balanced on its top. Maelwas was a Christian king. The monastery on Ynys Wydryn was his doing, and there was a fine hall there beside the wooden church where he and his sons and servants and his shield-companions could stay when he came to pray.

The monks who kept the place were wary of Myrddin, even though he took care to hide away his old charms and amulets before we crossed the causeway to their gate. They knew his reputation as a magic worker, and I think they would have turned him away, but someone went to tell Maelwas who it was who had come seeking him, and Maelwas sent a messenger to the abbot and told him to let us in.

Maelwas surprised me. I thought the king of so much country would be a man like Arthur, hard and scarred, forever sniffing the wind for fresh fights. But Maelwas was old, and spoke soft, and seemed gentle-mannered. I suppose he had been wilder in his youth, when he rode with Ambrosius. He greeted Myrddin, and asked after Gwenhwyfar, who was a kinswoman of his – his half-sister's daughter's daughter. "I remember her as a girl," he said. "A pretty thing. Your Arthur is a lucky man. I trust he'll treat her well."

That night in his hall Myrddin told his tales of Arthur. No enchanted swords or green men there. Just Arthur the soldier of Christ; how he'd driven back the Saxon army that tried to seize Aquae Sulis, and beaten the Devil in a rock-throwing contest out in the west somewhere.

Maelwas listened with a little smile about him always, as if to show us that he knew these tales weren't true, however pleasant it might be to hear them by the hearth.

We stayed a few days at Ynys Wydryn. On the

morning we left, when a booming wind was combing the grass flat and making cats'-paws on the flooded fens, Maelwas spoke alone to Myrddin. I heard them as I brought the horses close.

"I've had no tribute this year from your master in Aquae Sulis. Perhaps his wedding to my pretty kinswoman drove it from his mind."

"Arthur would like to pay you all he owes," Myrddin promised. "But he has an army of cavalry to feed. His warriors aren't untrained levies who can go home to their farms between fights and grow their own food. They are soldiers, who live for war. He must put their needs first if he is to keep them together, and strong enough to defeat the Saxon threat."

"But the Saxons have not troubled us since Ambrosius's time," Maelwas pointed out. "A few raids. More of a nuisance than a threat."

"They will come again," said Myrddin fiercely. "All the time we British fight among ourselves, the Saxons in the east grow stronger. They will drive west again one day, unless we smash them utterly."

"And is Arthur truly strong enough to do that?" Maelwas asked. "To drive them back across the sea? Can he really finish the work Ambrosius began? End the dismal partition of Britain and win back the lost east for Christ?"

"Not alone," my master said. "But if you would make him leader of your war-band in battle, and command all the lesser kings who pay you tribute to do likewise, he could be the new Ambrosius."

"Except that Ambrosius fought for Britain and the

Christian faith," said Maelwas mildly, "and I do not think Arthur fights for anything but Arthur. More robber than soldier, I've heard. A wild, roving man, like Uthr before him. A looter of churches. A cattle-thief. Only last summer he came plundering our westward lands, making men pay him tribute that was not his to take."

Myrddin shrugged. "A mistake. When a man is as strong as Arthur, he over-reaches himself sometimes. But your kinswoman Gwenhwyfar has tamed that wildness out of him. Her love of Christ has set him a good example. Arthur is God's strong man. Henceforward, he'll fight only Saxons. He would lead your war-band with honour and victory."

Maelwas was silent a moment, his eyes on Myrddin's, considering. The watching monks and warriors shuffled and stirred. Cloaks flapped in the breeze and a man coughed. I don't think they liked to see their master dealing so friendly-like with mine. There were men there who hoped to lead Maelwas's war-band themselves one day.

Suddenly Maelwas chuckled, and slapped Myrddin's shoulder. "Thank you for your stories," he said. "I shall consider what you say, and if it seems to me that Arthur is really all you claim, you will hear from me." Then, walking with Myrddin towards the place where I was waiting with the horses, he nodded at me, and said, "Why do you dress her as a boy?"

Myrddin must have been taken by surprise. Knowing him, I could see that he was startled. But he plucked a story from the air as calmly as another man might swat a fly. "She is my daughter," he said gravely. "But this travelling life leads us often among wild places and fighting men. For her own protection I dress her as a boy."

Maelwas smiled, looking me up and down. "It is a good disguise," he said. "But I don't think it will work much longer."

My master did not speak to me as we rode back across the causeway. I could feel anger coming off him like warmth off a fire. It had been bad for him, being found out in a trick at the last moment like that. I felt ashamed of myself for letting old Maelwas see the truth. Had it been my fault? Had I not been boyish enough? I'd let my hair get longer, following the same fashion as Bedwyr and the other boys. It hung below my ears, and maybe it showed up something girlish in my face.

I felt in the pouch on my belt and gripped the old moon-charm I'd taken from the baths that day Gwenhwyfar saw me there. When I found it I'd been thinking to give it to my master, so he could string it round his neck with all the rest, or hang it up outside his door to keep thieves out. But he would have wanted to know where I had found it, and I knew if I'd told him he'd have made me spill out the whole story, somehow: how I'd met Gwenhwyfar, and how she'd nearly found my secret out. Rather than face his anger, I had kept it hid. And now he was going to be angry anyway.

He didn't speak until we reached the old troop road. Then he said, "He's a cunning old fox, that Maelwas. He sees things other men don't." He looked at me a long while. Nodded, as if something had been decided. "The weather is set fair. We won't go back to Aquae Sulis yet."

"But you must tell Arthur what King Maelwas said. . ."

"I'll send him word. Arthur can cope without me for a season, I think."

And he turned his horse west instead of east, and what was there for me to do but follow him? He'd not been angry with me, but I couldn't help thinking, as I urged Dewi after him, that this was some sort of punishment.

Summer rolled us along like stones in a stream. Moridunum to Isca, Isca to Tamaris, and in between them all the little places, Caer this and Din that, which the Romans had never given names to, and had left with their old names and their old ways. And after Tamarisford there were barely any Roman names at all, just the long land of Kernyw under its wide sky. But wherever we went, people had heard of Arthur, and were glad to hear more. Myrddin scattered stories like sparks, and the brush-fire of Arthur's fame spread.

"One day Arthur will set up his standard, and the kings of Britain will flock to him like starlings," Myrddin said. "King Maelwas of the Dumnonii has as good as promised that Arthur will command his war-band come the fighting season. With all those warriors behind him, he'll be the new Ambrosius. He'll win the lost lands back, and the Saxons will throw themselves into the sea to escape him."

He was so sure that it would happen that I didn't think to doubt him. But it frightened me, the thought of all that war to come. Why did Myrddin want it so bad? Why did he seem so fierce, when he spoke about the Saxons? Sometimes I thought, why not let Arthur hold his territory and all the other kings hold theirs and leave the Saxons quiet in the lands they'd settled? But I didn't speak that thought, in case it sounded womanish.

At Din Tagyll, from the heights above the sea, I watched the ships go out on the evening tide. In winter Din Tagyll is too storm-threshed for any but a few mad monks to live there, but in summer King Cunomorus makes it his capital, and the steep headland's sides bloom bright with flags and awnings, and in the cove below the ships drop anchor. I watched their sails fill with the wind as they slipped clear of the cliff's lee, and they went out like swans over the wide ocean. Some of the men who sailed them had skin as black as coal. They were bound for shores I couldn't even imagine; lands of leopards and unicorns; harbours whose names burst sweetly in my mouth like ripe grapes. Alexandria. Antioch. Constantinople.

After midsummer we turned back. I'd hoped we'd go along the south coast, and maybe to Peredur Long-Knife's place. I would have liked to see what had become of Peri. But we stayed north, keeping to the shore of the Severn-sea, then striking inland towards the country I'd been born in; to Ban's hall, which was held for Arthur by the Irishman.

It was around then that I started to realize my master had plans to work a fresh enchantment on me. After so long on the road, my hair hung almost to my shoulders. One morning, as we were saddling the horses in a dell where we'd spent the night, I spoke of finding some shears to cut it.

He shook his head. "You'll not pass as a lad much longer," he said. "That old fox Maelwas was right."

I got frightened. I thought maybe he meant to leave me behind in those same soggy hills he'd got me from. I thought he meant to marry me to some shepherd, or one of the rough chieftains whose halls we'd been passing nights in. I went down on the earth and hugged his knees and said, "Please, master, let me come back to Sulis with you. I've been a good servant, haven't I?"

Myrddin smoothed my too-long hair. I wasn't looking at his face, so I don't know if he was smiling, but I like to think there was a smile about him as he said, "You've been a good boy, Gwyn. But you'll be a better girl. It'll be Gwyna who rides back with me at fall-of-leaf."

His words kicked the breath out of me. I suppose I'd always known it would have to come, but not yet, surely? "I don't want to be a girl!" I cried. "I'll never be able to go home. People will recognize me!"

"Of course they won't," said Myrddin. "Half a year will have gone by. Do you think they have statues of your head standing around Aquae Sulis as if you were some old emperor? You will go back in a woman's dress, with your long hair loose. You will walk like a girl and talk like a girl, and they will think, 'That maiden looks a little like Gwyn,' if they think anything at all. And I shall tell them you are Gwyn's kin, and they will think of you no more."

"But I don't know how to be a girl!" I told him. "I'll have to do the things that women do. . ." I gaped like a fish, groping about for examples. I barely *knew* the things that women did. "Sewing and stitching and spinning and brewing barley-beer. . . What will they think when I don't know how to do those things?"

"Then you must learn."

"I'll be no good at them. Slow and clumsy."

"Gwyna," he said. (His firmest voice, the one that brooked no replies.) "You will be a young woman soon. You'll look more out of place in Arthur's war-band then than you will fumbling your weaving-work in his wife's house."

"His wife?"

"Of course. Do you think *I* want a woman servant? You'll join Gwenhwyfar's household. Be one of her waiting-women."

I thought of Gwenhwyfar's house, which was a little small building, half hidden behind Arthur's big hall. I thought of the graceful, perfect girls she kept about her there, slender as withies. "She'll not take *me*."

"She will. To please Arthur."

"But I don't want to," I said, like a little child. I could feel the tears tickling my cheeks and creeping in salty at the corners of my mouth. "I don't want to leave you."

"Since when did it begin to matter what you *want*?" said Myrddin angrily, and turned away from me, stalked off with his shoulders hunched up like an old hoodie crow. Hid his face with one brown, bony hand like he was trying to rub the image of me off his eyeballs. Then turned and came back, kinder. "I have another purpose in this, Gwyna. When you are part of Gwenhwyfar's household you will keep your eyes open, and whatever you see you will bring to me."

"You want me to spy on her?"

"It would be wise for me to know what goes on in her mind. She is the wife of the *Dux Bellorum* after all. I should know what goes on in her heart, and who could tell me that better than one of her own waiting-women?"

I wiped my tears, and hiccuped, feeling glad that he did not want to cast me off entirely.

"Now come," he said, "I want to sleep at your old lord's home on the hill tonight. We have miles to go yet."

He kicked his horse's flanks and it trotted ahead, leaving me to follow. I didn't try telling him the other thing I disliked about becoming a girl again – that it would mean the end of my friendship with Bedwyr.

But riding on, I started to see that my friendship with Bedwyr was almost ended anyway. Those last few months in Sulis there'd seemed a barrier between us, like the horn pane of a lantern. He was almost a man, with a scruffy stubble of beard that he was vastly proud of, and a host of boastful tales about his skill at hunting. He'd ride as a warrior with the war-band when the next fight came. I remembered the way that he and the other boys talked about girls. They hadn't the courage yet to talk *to* girls, but they talked *about* them endlessly. They watched them at the marketplace. Their heads turned like the heads of watchful birds when Gwenhwyfar's handmaidens passed them in the street. They laughed, and scoffed, and compared one with another, and I couldn't join in that talk. It uneased me to hear the way they spoke. How hard they thought of girls' bodies, and how little of their feelings. Like women were just creatures to be used and traded. They respected horses better.

I was sure Bedwyr never guessed the truth about me, but I knew I unsettled him. My smooth cheeks, and my voice that had never cracked and deepened as his had. Perhaps he thought my master had put me under an enchantment, so that I would never grow.

We skirted the borders of the Irishman's country, and turned towards my old home up the river-road. In the afternoon, when the flies hung in lazy clouds above the water, we came to the pool with the waterfall where it had all begun for me.

My skull was filled up with a moil of thoughts. While the horses drank from the shallows I knelt down and stared at my reflection in the water, and tried to see something girlish in my sunburned face. "Gwyna," I tried saying. And it was like I was calling her back from the dead.

XXIV

The old farmstead where I'd grown up had been rebuilt, and roofed with thick, fresh thatch. There were red cattle lowing in a pound, and children playing in the river when we came riding past at set of sun. They followed us a little way, naked and shrieking with laughter, calling out to Myrddin to tell them a story, for they'd seen the harp among his saddlebags and guessed his trade. They didn't look at me, and if any of them were my friends from the old times, I didn't recognize them. A lot of water had flowed downstream since then.

The Irishman was summering at Ban's old holding. It was better than his own damp hall in the hills, I dare say. He had got an Irish wife from Demetia with red cheeks and a quick smile, and their children squabbled like puppies beside his hearth. He seemed a happy Irishman, though when Myrddin raised the matter of the yearly tribute he owed Arthur he was quick to say how hard his life was; how half his cows had died last winter, and Cunomorus of Kernyw kept sending raiding-bands to rob his tinners on the moors.

In return, Myrddin told him news from the east; Arthur's latest victories; the battle at Badon and the wedding to Gwenhwyfar. And when he had done he drew me forward out of the shadows where I'd been standing, and said, "This is Gwyna."

It was strange to hear my name made whole again after so long being Gwyn. "Yes," said my master, "I know she looks boyish, but she is a girl. Look closely. You see?"

They looked closely. They saw. My smooth face and slender fingers and the beginnings of my small breasts under my tunic. The Irishman gave a grunt of surprise.

"I brought her with me out of the mountains beyond Bannawg," Myrddin explained. "There is a dragon in those parts, and the people of the place make a sacrifice to it every year of three maidens."

The Irishman and his wife leaned forward, hooked. The cup bearers and the guards at the door pricked up their ears to listen, and even the children on the floor stopped pinching each other. I wondered what life my master was inventing for me, and did my best to look like I came from dragon-country.

"Well," Myrddin went on, "Gwyna's father swore he'd not let his little girl be breakfast for some worm. So when she was born he let it be known that his wife had given birth to a boy, and he dressed the child as a boy, and let her run with the boys of his place, and it is as a boy that she has lived ever since. But now that she is almost a woman, the ruse is wearing thin, and so I

132

agreed to take her back to Aquae Sulis with me, there to enter the service of the lady Gwenhwyfar."

The Irishman nodded, as if this was the only reasonable thing to do, where dragons were involved.

"Trouble is," Myrddin went on, looking into the guest cup and finding it empty, holding it out for a slave to refill, "the trouble is, she knows nothing of the ways of women. She knows about horses, and the hunt. She has fought against the heathen Scots who plague her country whenever the dragon rests. But of being a maiden among other maidens she knows nothing at all."

The Irishman frowned slowly, realizing that something was being asked of him. "Then let her stay here a while!" he said suddenly. It was Myrddin who had put the idea in his mind, of course, but he thought it was his own, and seized on it, and flourished it proudly as a sign of his loyalty to Arthur and to Arthur's friend. "Yes! Let her stay here with Nonnita! Nonnita will teach her everything! Weaving and . . . and . . . the rest of it. Yes! Anything to help Myrddin!"

And so I stayed there through the summer's golden end, with Nonnita and her ladies, while Myrddin went travelling off alone, carrying new tales of Arthur down into Kernyw.

At first I lived in fear of running into someone I'd known when the hall was Lord Ban's place, but all Ban's followers were dead, or fled, or scattered off as slaves across the world, and I was never challenged. I doubt they would have known me anyway, for I'd been an urchin then, and now I was a maiden, with a dress of wool dyed kingfisher blue and a russet cloak that did up

133

at the shoulder with a tin brooch. The clothes were faded, and had belonged to a girl who'd died of fever in the spring, but they fitted me. I was still enough of a boy not to care much about clothes.

The girls and women of the household didn't like me. They thought I was strange and clumsy and spoke too loud. But slowly I learned from them the things women do. They don't speak to the menfolk unless they're spoke to first, that's one. They don't tuck up their skirts and run. They sit for hours stitching and mending, which is slow torture, and embroidering, which is worse. They spin wool and linen. They weave cloth, singing in time to the clack of the clay weights which swing against the loom's frame. They steep meat in brine-barrels, and grind flour. They knead soft dough into loaves, getting flour on their arms and their cheeks and the tips of their noses. They make cheese, and butter, and cream, and buttermilk. They brew beer. They giggle. They whisper. They gossip.

It wasn't for me, that life. I missed Dewi and I missed my master. I promised myself I'd talk to him when he came back; plead with him, beg him, make him understand. "I tried being girlish," I'd tell him, "and it didn't work. I've been too long a boy. My voice isn't right. I don't move like the rest of them. My stitches don't hold. My yarn gets tangled. My loaves are soft as wet wool, or hard like river stones." And I told myself that Myrddin would see. He'd see his mistake. He'd find some other way, and I'd be a boy again.

"What was that dragon like?" they asked, every day or

134

so, until I cursed Myrddin for thinking up such a story. "Did you see it at all? Did you ever hear it roar?"

"I heard it once," I told them. "I couldn't not. It was loud enough to shiver rocks down off the mountainside. And I saw it fly over. Big as three horses it was, with bat's wings and bear's claws and a snake's tail."

"Was it red or green?"

I thought quick. "It was every colour. Red, green, all the colours of the rainbow. It *rippled* with colours. And in its jaws it carried a poor maiden from the village, as big as Rhiannedd." And I pointed at the plumpest of the lady Nonnita's girls, who turned pastry-coloured and began to twitter. The rest stared wide-eyed at me, like girls who would have nightmares later.

That night, like punishment for my lies, I woke with griping in my belly, and a sudden marshiness about the mattress under me. When I touched that damp and lifted up my hand into the moon-glow from the window my fingers were wet and dark with blood.

I thought I was dying. I'd not seen that much blood since Badon, and then it had been other people's, not spilling out of my own secret insides. My cries woke up the other girls, and they thought I was as big a joke as I'd thought them when I was scaring them with dragon-stories. It was only my monthlies, said Nonnita. It was the same for every woman in the world. We had tides, like the sea. The moon called forth our blood. Did I not know that?

Well, I'd heard something of it. But I'd thought myself too boyish to suffer it. I lay and snivelled while the others settled back into sleep. It seemed to me my own body had betrayed me, and sided with Myrddin. There'd be no way back into boyhood for me now. What would the war-band make of me washing bloody rags once monthly?

But later, when I'd learned to cope with it, as we have to cope with all things we have no hope of changing, later I thought, Myrddin must have known. The same craft that let him know when rain was coming, or a mist would rise, had warned him what would soon be happening inside me. If we'd turned east instead of west after Ynys Wydryn, if we'd gone back to Sulis in the normal way, it might have been Bedwyr and the other boys I'd woken in my panic when it started.

Halfway through apple-harvest Myrddin returned, and said it had come time to leave. I was surprised by how sorry I felt, to be saying farewell to Nonnita and fat Rhiannedd and the rest. But I packed up my few belongings, and the things I had learned, and set off behind him again, riding eastward through the first of the autumn's rain. Now I was a girl I rode sideways on Dewi, which felt awkward and unnatural. The colour seeped out of my blue dress and sprinkled off my toes in sky-blue drips. My shoes shrank and pinched my feet, and my newly long hair hung down in rain-dark rat's tails round my face. The west wind blew up my skirts and chilled my damp legs through. I hunched inside my cloak and consoled myself with daydreams where I was a boy again, and running after my brother Bedwyr towards adventures. There were no adventures in my future now, I thought, glaring bitterly at Myrddin's back.

Women don't have them. They just suffer when their men's adventures go wrong.

We went slower and slower as we drew near Sulis. Myrddin kept thinking of reasons why we should turn off the road and call in at scruffy settlements where he could exchange his songs and stories for a meal and a place to sleep and a few cups of watered wine. I think he was afraid of learning what Arthur had been up to in his absence. Like a father who leaves his children alone for the first time. But when we reached the crown of the hills that stand behind the town, and looked down, it all seemed much as I remembered. It was a day of sunlight and sudden, shining showers, and the red roofs of the old Roman buildings were as bright as the autumn woods.

A few miles from the walls stood a place that must have been a rich man's house in the olden times, with outbuildings and slaves' quarters and a smithy of its own. It was all fallen into ruins, but a part of the main house was still roofed over and Myrddin turned in at the gateway. A man and woman were waiting there, country people from a nearby steading. They fell down bowing at the sight of us. "Welcome, Lord Myrddin," the man called out. "It has all been made as your messenger commanded."

"This is my new home," he told me, leaving them to quarter our horses and taking me inside, into a long room smelling of fresh lime-wash. He'd sent word from the Irishman's place, and hired the man and woman to make the house ready, and bring his few possessions there from his old place in Aquae Sulis. He said, "If

Arthur is to lead the armies of Britain he must be seen to be a Christian lord, and keep magic and wizards at arm's length. The old ways still speak to his soldiers and the common people, and they will know I am close. But when he talks to Maelwas's envoys he must be able to deny me. He must be able to say, 'Myrddin? That old trickster? No, he has no place in my town. . .'"

I went through a pantry to a window at the back of the place. It had had glass in it once. Through the rusty frames I looked out on a garden, a few bean-rows fluttering with leaves and curved green pods, a cabbage-patch, a huge old oak rising among the scrubby younger growth along the wood-shore. It was a giant of a tree, but ivy had wrapped it round, and rot had hollowed out its trunk, and it held up only a few last golden leaves to the afternoon sun.

The servants brought wine and food and then went home to their own place, over the hill; Myrddin didn't want them living there with him. When he had eaten he rode on to Sulis, leaving me alone. He told me later what he found there, and so I'll tell you, for I did nothing that evening except pace about between the bean-plots trying to get used to the strange, flappy freedom of my new skirts.

Myrddin rode up to the gates of Sulis and announced himself and entered into the town. The walls had been repaired as he'd suggested, and the men who guarded them looked better trained. The town was as shabby and prosperous as ever, and old friends greeted him, and took his horse for him when he drew near the forum.

138

There, inside a cage of wooden scaffolding, the feasting-hall he'd planned with Arthur in the winter-time was rising, and he felt proud and then disappointed as he looked at it. For it was a great thing that it had been built at all, and yet it was not as he'd imagined. Its round walls bulged out-of-true. The big, glazed windows he had planned were crooked holes. Instead of baked clay tiles, it squatted under a hat of thatch. Myrddin knew without even looking inside that it would be dark, and stuffy, and earthen-floored, and that the smoke of Arthur's feast-fires would gather in a fog under the leaking roof.

He felt suddenly uneasy. He had been away too long.

Arthur was in the old amphitheatre, watching a white colt run circles on a rein. There was a knot of men around him. As Myrddin walked towards them he heard a familiar, silvery laugh, and there was Cunaide, Arthur's woman from the old days, standing at Arthur's side.

"I thought you had put her away," said Myrddin, when the greetings were done and he could talk quietly to Arthur. "What has become of your new wife?"

"The heron?" Arthur kept glancing at the colt, admiring its glossy flanks and the sharp tilt of its lifted hooves. "A cold nature she has. Why couldn't you find me a wife like Cunaide, with a bit of fire in her?"

"You need Gwenhwyfar. She's Maelwas's kin. Her sons will be descendants of Ambrosius."

"What sons? She's barren ground. Six months now, and no sign of a child."

That might not be Gwenhwyfar's fault. After all, Cunaide's never fallen with child in all *her* years with

Arthur. But Myrddin didn't voice that thought, of course. Instead he watched the colt go past, head up, mane flying, hoof-falls echoing from the raked stone seats all around.

"A beauty, isn't he?" asked Arthur, glad to turn their talk from wives to horses. "I took him in a raid last week."

"You have been raiding against your neighbours? Arthur, Maelwas will never give you command over his war-bands if he thinks you are a brigand!"

"Maybe I don't need Maelwas's war-bands," said Arthur, eyes on the colt. "This is good country. A man could live well here, without going fighting into Saxon lands." He glanced at Myrddin quickly, sensing his disapproval. "Anyway, it wasn't Maelwas's lands I hit. We rode north and east, into Calchvynydd."

Myrddin was too angry to answer. He'd worked hard to convince Maelwas that Arthur was the one, and now he would have to begin his work again. He'd hoped for an alliance with the lords of Calchvynydd, too, but they wouldn't want it now. He watched the stolen colt go round, running and running and getting nowhere.

"I brought a young kinswoman of mine back from the west," he said at last. "My boy Gwyn has returned to his family, but his half-sister came home with me. She's a good girl. I thought she might make a handmaiden for Gwenhwyfar. . ."

Arthur didn't even trouble to pretend to be interested. "Yes. Why not," he said. He turned away, shouting at his horse-handlers, "Give him more rein! Let's see him run!"

XXV

And so my transformation back into a girl was completed, and I entered the world of women, and the household of the lady Gwenhwyfar. I swapped my knife for a bone needle, and my shield for a sewing-frame, and my dreams of hunts and battles for . . . well, for nothing, for I did not yet know what maidens dreamed about. Husbands, mostly, if the chatter of Nonnita's girls had been anything to go by. But I didn't want a husband. I sat and listened in the winter evenings around Gwenhwyfar's hearth while Gwenhwyfar and the older of her women told stories about love, and men who did high deeds for their beloved. But I'd lived among boys, and I knew how men really thought of women, and I knew love hadn't much to do with it.

That hidden, bidden life was as big a shock to me as when I'd first become a boy. My time in Nonnita's place had given me a taste of it, but at least Nonnita's women had work to do. It wouldn't have been fitting for Arthur's wife to churn butter, or go laughing to the orchards with the harvesters. Arthur had slaves to do those jobs. For Gwenhwyfar and her women there was only a little sewing – new dresses for ourselves, an altar-cloth for Bishop Bedwin's church – and a lot of gossip. I was no good at gossip. I was so afraid that if I opened my mouth some rough, rude phrase from the horse-lines would slip out of it I kept it shut most of the time, and the other girls, hearing me say nothing but mumblings in my hilly accent and seeing how I was not pretty, nor well born, nor clever with a needle, decided I was simple, and left me alone. Some of them were a little scared of me at first. They knew I had something to do with Myrddin, and someone started a rumour running that he'd made me by his magic, out of flowers. But Gwenhwyfar came to my rescue, and gathered them together, and told them I was just a poor waif from over the sea who they must treat with Christian kindness. They weren't kind to me after that, but at least they stopped waiting for me to turn into a hoodie crow and fly off with their souls. After a while they didn't even bother making the sign against evil when I came near.

Arthur didn't often trouble himself to come looking for his lady Gwenhwyfar. It was enough for him to know that she was there, safe in her part of the house with her women around her, like a proper wife. Unless there were guests he wanted to impress, it was Cunaide who sat beside him in his hall at each day's end. He hadn't much time anyway for women's company. They none of them did. The worlds of men and women were as different as night and day, air and water.

And what was I? I'd lived in both those worlds. I didn't fit in either.

I missed Dewi. Myrddin had said my pony would be happy in the long paddock behind his new place where there was good green grazing. But I missed him still, and I thought he'd miss me. Who'd comb the knots out of his forelock now, and stroke and cuddle him, and bring him treats? I couldn't see Myrddin doing that. Couldn't see Myrddin keeping him long at all. What use would a pony be, with no boy to ride it?

I missed Myrddin too. Sometimes, when Gwenhwyfar sent me off on an errand, I thought I would keep walking, out of the town and along the track that wound beneath the green downs to his house. But I was not supposed to go anywhere alone, and none of the other girls would have gone with me. They were afraid of Myrddin, and convinced they would be cursed if they ventured through the fence of charms and skulls and knotted strings which he had hung across the entrance to his place. A spell woven into every knot. And what would Myrddin say if I showed up at his door? He'd done with me, and cast me off. He'd not be missing me the way I missed him.

That first winter I lived for the times when I saw Myrddin. When we were all together at a feast in the great hall, and he would get out his harp and tell us a story and his eyes while he was speaking would find me, singling my face out of all the watching faces round the fire. Or when I went to the marketplace with other girls and he passed by. Then the others would cross themselves and back away, but since I was supposed to be his kinswoman they could not stop me speaking with him, and him asking me how I did, and me telling him. I always expected him to ask me what was going on in Gwenhwyfar's heart, too. After all, that was the reason he had given for sending me to live in her household. He seemed to have forgotten that I was his spy. Or decided that Gwenhwyfar was not worth spying on.

I was glad. I'd grown to like my new mistress, and I didn't want to go passing on rumours about her loveless marriage, not even to Myrddin. Cold and shadowy she might be, but Gwenhwyfar was kind, in her vague, distant way.

It was like living with someone who was already halfway to being a ghost, but a pleasant ghost. Sometimes, when the right mood was on her, she would tell us stories. An old slave of her family, her father's tutor, had told her these stories when she was a girl. Tales of Odysseus and Aeneas and Queen Cleopatra. A better class of stories than we grow in our wet island. And when some of the girls were sick with the marsh-fever that first winter she gave up all her comforts and tended them herself, sat up beside their pallets at night and bathed their hot faces with cool water and sang to them although she was half dead herself with tiredness. They grew better, too, although the doctors said they'd die. My mistress might not have Myrddin's knowledge of the uses of herbs and the writings of men with old Greek names, but she was a better healer than he'd ever been.

Of course, I didn't tell Myrddin that, either.

Bedwyr was off with Arthur's war-band when I first became one of Gwenhwyfar's flock, so I had a week or so to fret about him, and to wonder how he could fail to recognize me. But when he came riding home I barely recognized *him*. He was a warrior now, with a warrior's windy vanity, and five notches cut in the edge of his shield to show the men he'd killed. He'd put his life as a boy far behind him, stuffed it away as if it shamed him, and the memory of his friend Gwyn along with it. He eyed up all the girls as he rode past, but he only saw the pretty ones. I heard them giggling about him, how handsome he was and what a fine husband he'd make, and wondered how they'd feel if they knew I'd beaten him in running-races, and picked prickles out of his arse the time he'd fallen in that gorse bush.

Only once, around Christmas, at the dark hinge of the year, he stopped half drunk in the marketplace while I was passing with two other girls. "I know you," he said, staring into my face, which was veiled by wind-blown strands of hair. "I know you. You look like Myrddin's servant, Gwyn, who rode with me at Badon-fight."

"Gwyn's my half-brother, lord," I said, shy as a cat, with my eyes on his boots.

"I can see him in your face. You're as ugly as him!"

I looked at the cobbles in front of him, speckled with small rain. The girls beside me, who'd gone taut with envy when he singled me out, relaxed when they heard him call me ugly.

"I heard he went home to his people," said Bedwyr.

"To Armorica, lord," I mumbled.

"He thought they'd all been killed. But I suppose they escaped? And sent for him?" There was a crack in his voice. I wondered if he was about to start weeping, the way soldiers do about old comrades sometimes when they've emptied one too many wineskins. But a couple of his friends came up laughing, calling out things that made my companions shriek, and they carried him off towards some wineshop by the walls.

I watched him go, stumbling away from me into winter twilight, his friends holding him up when he threatened to fall over. When there was no fighting to be done the days of the men were as dull as the days of women, but instead of needlework and gossip they killed their time with drink.

I would have given anything to be a boy again, and running races with him in the water-meadows.

Arthur's wars went on. Sometimes he rode way east into the borders of Saxon country, but most of his raids were closer to home, against soft settlements in the marches of Calchvynydd and up into Gwent. It was harder than ever to know the truth of it, now that I was penned up in Gwenhwyfar's house. All I know is that Myrddin's Arthur-stories grew and grew, painting him as the red dragon of the prophecies who would drive the Saxons back across the sea. Sometimes, when the war-band rode home, there were empty saddles, and I heard that men I'd known as boys had fallen in this fight or that. Sometimes one of the girls I lived with would be given in marriage to one of Arthur's companions and another girl would come to take her place in Gwenhwyfar's household.

So two years ran away like rain down a culvert. They were good years, mostly. Maelwas was slow about making Arthur *Dux Bellorum* over all his war-bands, but he seemed content to let him hold Aquae Sulis and the other lands he'd taken further west. And on the northern border scraps of country which had been loyal to Calchvynydd were coming under Arthur's rule one by one, and the store-houses of Sulis were filling with tribute that should have been sent to Calchvynydd's king.

For me, in Aquae Sulis, nothing changed. Except that one spring night, after weeks of rain, I was woken by a rushing, crashing, slithering sound and went out of doors to see that Myrddin's great round feast-hall had fallen down.

XXVI

The small lives of women don't make for good stories. That's why there were no girls in the stories Myrddin told, unless they were there as a prize for the hero to win at the end of his adventures. So I'll take you south from Aquae Sulis and tell you about something else. I'll tell you what had happened at that hall on the sea-strand, Peredur Long-Knife's place. I thought of it sometimes, wishing I was as graceful and girlish as young Peri, and dreaming back to the day when he and I had fooled that old drunkard saint into thinking he'd met an angel. But I never guessed the change that had come upon the place after I left it.

They called it Saint Porroc's miracle. Ever since Arthur's war-band came to claim a feast from Long-Knife's widow, the old saint had been on fire with the Holy Spirit. His monks processed about the ramparts, keeping everyone awake as they proclaimed the wondrous sign that God had sent them. For Porroc had been visited by the Angel Gabriel, who had commanded that he throw himself into the stormy sea. And Porroc had obeyed, trusting in the hand of God to buoy him up and keep him safe. No man could have lived in such a sea, they said. The great tempest of the world had been blowing, tearing the white tops off the breakers and driving fishing-smacks a mile inland. But the blessed saint had braved it and survived. Hadn't they seen with their own eyes his holy head bob on the long slope of the waves like a fisherman's float, hollering joyful prayers as each torrent of foam came curling down on him?

(What he'd actually been shouting was, "Oh, God! Help! Arrgh! Glug!" But I suppose that counts as praying.)

Saint Porroc grew more pious than ever. Crouched in that dazzling, sudden sunlight, in the gritty wind from the blown-open door, with the winged after-image of the angel seared on his squeezed-shut eyes, he had felt his soul reforged. His wallow in the icy sea had tempered it hard and true. The theft of the treasures of his church by the tyrant Arthur had only sharpened its edge. He was become a sword in the right hand of God.

He upended his wine-jars and let the sandy soil drink up his wine. He set free his pigs from their pens, and said a prayer over them before they went snuffling off into the woods behind the dunes, asking the Lord to grant them long lives. From now on he and his monks would live on water and cabbages. They would go each morning to the sea and cleanse themselves in the cold waves. If they were lucky the vicious undertow would carry them to Glory.

The monks weren't much pleased by the way things were going. Without meat and wine to warm them they shivered in their huts, which were no better than upturned baskets with the sea-wind blowing through them. The saint sent them into the hungry sea by day and by night. Their cabbagy diet caused great blatting farts to issue from beneath their robes like the trumpet-blasts of tuneless angels. One by one they slunk away, bound for places where God was served in less uncomfortable ways.

The saint's community took on a dwindling look, the empty huts rotting. But Saint Porroc never gave in to the sin of despair. He gave up his hermitage and went to and fro along the wind-scoured coast, preaching his miracle in the villages. The people set down their nets and listened. Their lives were hard. It gave them a strange sort of pleasure to hear that their troubles were their own fault. If only they'd been truer to the true God, and given up the old ways! The saint's words spurred them to a frenzy of smashing and breaking. Small shrines were battered into pieces. Decorations were torn off sacred wells. A wizened old sea-widow was found out to be a witch, and washed clean in the surf till she drowned.

And by way of reward God sent them bacon. The woods inland, which had never yielded anything more nourishing than a bramble, were suddenly home to pigs so tame it was simple to lure them close and stick a spear in them. A second miracle! Sick of fish, the villagers filled their bellies with roast pork and gnawed on the crackling, and agreed that the Kingdom of Heaven must be at hand.

From the walls of old Long-Knife's hall the girl called Peredur looked out, and saw the cook-fires burning. Sometimes the gusting wind brought snatches of distant, feverish prayers whirling through the gaps in the palisade.

The hall itself was falling into ruin. It had been a ruin really ever since Peredur's father died, but Saint Porroc and his monks had given it a semblance of life, like wasps rattling inside a rotten apple. Now that he had gone, and the monks' cells were coming apart like dried-out cowpats, the place felt empty. Spent.

Peredur's mother believed it was her own fault. Saint Porroc had told her before he left that she was a wicked woman for welcoming Arthur, that tyrant, that black she-wolf's whelp. She had fallen on her face and begged his forgiveness, but he'd not been in a forgiving temper, and stalked off, shouting curses over his shoulder. After that, she had retreated further into her own small world, whose walls were prayers. She spent whole days mumbling in her chamber. Her women lost patience with her. They grew tired of going hungry in that starveling hall, where the wind blew through the smoke-holes till the whole building hooted like a shawm. In ones and twos they went away. Some married fishermen. Some went to follow Saint Porroc. That girl who'd slept with Arthur on the night he visited ran off with one of the former monks. Only the old ones stayed.

Washed-out, ancient women with nowhere else to go. They rustled in the shadows of the hall like moonwort seeds.

Peri was changing, too. She'd grown even taller, and however often she altered her dresses they always looked wrong, stretched over her broad chest and strong arms. Her voice deepened. Flecks of beard began to show on her chin and upper lip and throat.

Her mother showed her how to shave, using the sharpened edge of a seashell. Peri noticed that none of the other women had beards. Did they shave in secret? "Hairiness is a blessing God sends only to a few maidens," said her mother wistfully. "It means that men will find you ugly, and you will never marry. You will stay here at my side always and always."

Peri wasn't sure how she felt about that. After the warband left, that girl who'd slept with Arthur and would run off with the monk had teased her, saying she'd fallen in love with one of Arthur's bright shiny riders. But Peri had known even then that wasn't how it was. The visitors enchanted her, and filled her eyes for weeks, long after the last glitter of their helms and harnesses had vanished into the haze of sea-spray on the road. But she didn't want to marry any of them. She wanted to be *like* them. She wanted to have a horse, and go riding far away into the wide world on it, and leave the lonely hall behind.

In secret, among the empty monks' huts, she sharpened a hurdle-stake into a spear and practised throwing it. Soon, from twenty paces, she could drive it through the heart of the drawing of Saint Porroc she chalked on the chapel wall.

Using her maidenly skills – her weaving and her needlecraft – she made herself a pair of breeks, and a man's tunic. She ventured into Saint Porroc's chapel and stole down the old curtain from behind the altar, which she turned into a cloak. Needing a helmet, she crept into the kitchen and took a cooking-pot. She took a kitchen knife to be her sword. The cook didn't miss them. The cook was so old that she barely remembered her own name.

Dressed in her makeshift man's clothes, Peri ran through the woods, chasing birds, hunting pigs with her wooden spears, fighting desperate duels against the purple-plumed thistles that stood guard in clearings. She used the kitchen knife to cut her beautiful brown hair short, thinking that under her head-scarf no one would ever notice.

One day, she came home and changed back into her maiden's clothes in the shadow of the rampart and went inside the hall and found that her mother was dead. The old moonwort women rattled and rustled, laying out the body on a table. Peredur wondered what to do. Sea-water tears ran down her face, and she licked them absent-mindedly when they reached her mouth. It had never occurred to her that her mother would die.

It was spring. Still a windy, salt-scratched time on that cold coast, but at least there were some flowers out in the burying-place below the hall. She fetched a spade and dug a hole and buried her mother, and the women stood round and mumbled prayers while she shovelled the earth back.

She was propping up a flat rock for a headstone when Saint Porroc arrived. Somehow, word of the widow's death had reached him. He brought a great rabble of his followers behind him. Peri saw them from the rampart-top, running along the sea-shore like an army of beggars. Some stretched their skinny white arms up, as if they were hoping to snatch a few angel-feathers from the underside of Heaven. Others waded and wallowed through the sea, heads bobbing on the steep swell like a flock of mews. At the front of the procession, on an old cob horse, rode the saint himself. What hair he had left stood out around his fierce, holy face like a white-hot halo.

Up the plank-road to the hall they came, dripping and sneezing and praising Christ. The women scattered. Saint Porroc climbed down off his nag and stood blinking at Peri, who waited beside her mother's grave.

"The Lord has delivered this place from the rule of that sinful woman!" he bellowed, pointing at the fresh grave with a quivering hand. Too much preaching on windy beaches had left him with a voice like a bull. Peri covered her ears. "Death has taken her," the saint boomed. "This house which was hers will be the house of God now!" (For he had grown tired of sleeping on nets and fish-scales, see, and had taken the news of the widow's death as a sign that his wanderings were over and he should settle down in her hall.)

"But she is my mother!" said Peri. "I thought you had come to say the burial-words over her. . ."

"And who are you?" The saint had not been blessed

154

with good eyesight. He squinted at Peri, alarmed at hearing a man's voice in this place of women.

"I am her daughter."

"Daughter?" The saint stepped nearer. "Daughter?"

The hard work of grave-digging had streaked Peri's face with dirt and sweat. She had pushed the sleeves of her dress up, baring her lean, strong arms with their hatching of dark hair. In the confusion of her mother's death, she had not thought to shave. There in the sharp, raking sunlight of the burial-place there was no mistaking her for anything but what she was.

Saint Porroc's wiry eyebrows waggled. He'd shouted his throat raw telling the fisher-folk about the ways of the sinful, but he'd never seen anything quite so steeped in sin as Peri. He grabbed the brocade bodice of Peri's dress and dragged her past him, displaying her to his ragged flock.

"Behold!" he bellowed. "See what wickedness lurks in this house! What unnatural things this roof has sheltered! Look at this youth, this boy so wrapped up in iniquity that he dresses himself in women's raiment! Can we plumb the depths of such wickedness?"

Boy? What boy? thinks Peri, looking round, surprised. A roar bursts over her like a great wave of the sea, and with the noise comes understanding. She – he – looks round at the ring of shouting faces. Righteous anger, mostly, but with a bit of hard laughter mixed in, for what could look more ridiculous than this tall, gormless young man dressed in an embroidered gown?

Saint Porroc rips off Peri's head-scarf, baring the

155

clumsily shorn hair. "Be gone!" shouts the saint. "Leave this place! Run, if you can run, weighed down with such masses of sin!"

Peri's fist catches him in the middle of his holy face. The crunch of his nose breaking is louder than the laughter. There's a gasp. Silence, in which the saint totters backwards and sits down hard. One hand to his nose. Blood squirting between his fingers. Everyone draws back, expecting fire from Heaven, or the opening of a burning Pit. They pull each other aside to let Peri pass. He glances back once at his mother's grave, then strides towards the gate with all the dignity a young man in a dress can muster. One of the saint's men lunges at him, but others tug him back. Maybe they're afraid of facing this angry, hurt youth. Maybe they feel sorry for him.

Peri ran into the shelter of the woods and, safe in a cage of young birch, watched the saint's army taking possession of his home. He felt no anger towards them. They'd done him a favour, in a way. Told him what he was. A boy. A young man. His man's name made him proud now. Peredur, son of Peredur.

He'd known it always, really. A long time, at least. He thought back to the angel-day, and the strange thing that boy Gwyn had asked of him, "*Why do you dress like that?*" He'd wondered sometimes what Gwyn had meant by that. Now he understood.

And thinking of Gwyn made him think of Arthur.

That night he crept back secretly to his mother's hall by the sea. Inside the hall he could hear the saint's followers at their prayers. From his hiding place beneath the ramparts he fetched out his breeks and shirt and travelling cloak, his kitchen-weapons and his cookpot helm. He knelt beside the fresh grave and said a prayer for his mother, wishing that she had lived long enough to give him the answer to Gwyn's question. Then he stole Saint Porroc's horse and set off to look for Arthur.

XXVII

A spring day stands in my memory, clear as a white stone. Blossom on the trees and a hundred hundred flowers in the long grass of the water-meadows. I'm about fifteen. My life as a boy lies far behind me, vague and half-forgotten. My hopeless hair reaches right down my back now, tied in two fat plaits. I wear a dress which was given me by my lady Gwenhwyfar, one of her own cast-offs.

I'm quite a young lady, you see. I gossip with the other girls my own age, and look after the young ones, and serve my mistress, and at the moment I am trying to catch the eye of the young man who has been sent out with us as an escort. His horse paces along beside us as we walk; its yeasty smell mixes with the scent of flowers, and the girls vie with each other to see who can walk closest to him. Unfortunately he has eyes only for Celemon. Celemon is Cei's daughter, but she has turned out nothing like her ugly father or her fat mother. She looks the way the rest of us look in our dreams. She has corn-gold hair, and grey eyes with flecks of gold and copper in them. She is wearing a wide hat, like a wheel of woven straw, because the sunshine brings her out in freckles, which she hates, but I think they suit her. And specks of sun come through the hat's weave and dapple her face with tiny patterns of light, so she is twice-freckled, dark and bright.

The little girls laugh, the bigger ones chatter. Even my lady Gwenhwyfar, going ahead of us, is smiling. We are going to picnic by the riverside.

Halfway there, someone spies a horseman coming down a hillside not far off. The girls clump together nervously. There have been rumours that the king of Calchvynydd has been boasting he'll take back the lands Arthur has scrumped from him. Is this the out-rider of a raiding-band?

Sunlight shines on metal as his distant horse brings him down through the trees. Our bodyguard kicks his pony in front of us and draws his sword, glad of a chance to show it off.

"He's alone," says Gwenhwyfar, in a warning voice, not wanting him to go and skewer some harmless traveller.

Through the wild flowers, glittering with light, the lone rider draws closer. His horse is the colour of sour milk. His cloak is a moth-eaten curtain. His helmet is a kitchen pot. One of the girls laughs, and the others lose their fear and join in as he swings his nag to a stop in front of us. His leather jerkin is too small, his boots are too big. An old carving knife is stuck through his belt, and the javelins bound to his saddle are just willow withies, sharpened to points and blackened in a fire. Under the shadow of the pot's brim his face is sun-browned, and his smile is big and brilliant.

"I'm looking for Arthur's place. Is that it there?"

It's Peredur. I'm so ashamed of him that I have barely time to feel astonished at seeing him here. I'm pleased to see that he's learned he's not a girl, but I wish he'd left that cooking-pot in the kitchen. He doesn't seem to know how dim-witted he looks. In fact, he sits there beaming at us as if he thinks he's the finest warrior in the whole island of Britain. I burn red, blushing for both of us.

Gwenhwyfar is well enough brought up not to join in her maidens' tittering. But even she can't quite keep a smile from her face as she goes forward to greet this newcomer. "Aquae Sulis is in Arthur's charge, and I am Arthur's wife," she says kindly. "And you – you have ridden far, sir?"

"Days and days!" Peredur can't stop grinning. He has *no idea* how to speak to a high-born lady! The girls hiss with shock, hearing him address their mistress as if she were a goose-girl. His pot slips over his eyes so that he has to tilt his head back to look at us. Is he a madman? Dangerous?

"A saint took my home, so I've come to join Arthur's war-band," he explains. "I'm Peredur, son of Peredur Long-Knife."

He looks from face to face, as if it surprises him that we haven't all heard of him, or at least of his father. His eyes go past me without a pause. Of course, he'd hardly be expecting to find his old friend Gwyn among the maidens, and as a girl I'm not worth looking at, specially not when I'm standing next to lovely Celemon.

He reaches up to hold his pot in place with a soft, womanish gesture, which makes the girls about me titter louder.

"Arthur does want warriors, doesn't he? They told me that's what he came looking for when he came to my mother's house once. And there were lots on the big road, riding towards that town. I saw them from the hill-top."

Warriors on the road? Riding to Sulis? What can he mean?

I still remember how the laughter stopped, and the sunlight seemed to dim. We turned to look towards the town, and there, like blood in water, we saw the reddish smoke lofting from kindled thatch.

XXVIIII

Those stories we'd been hearing that spring were not just stories. A war-band from Calchvynydd had threaded itself through the eye of the woods and into the vale where Sulis stood, and taken us all by surprise. Later, I wondered why no one had ridden in from the settlements they'd looted on their way to warn Arthur they were coming. But maybe the country people there were so sick of Arthur that they were pleased to see someone squaring up to him at last. Or maybe they didn't see any difference between these rival war-bands. They might as well let the raiders take their stuff as give it up in taxes to Arthur.

Whatever the reason, the raid came unexpected. The Calchvynydd men didn't breach the walls of Sulis, and twelve of them were cut down in the fighting round the gate, but they set fire to the great huddle of buildings in the wall's lee, and drove off a lot of cattle from the farms about. And as Arthur and his riders woke and buckled on their swords and spilled out to meet them, the raiders broke this way and that, and two of them came thundering out across the water-meadows to where we girls stood watching.

"What is happening?" Peredur kept asking, innocent as a child. "What's that smoke? Is someone's house a-fire? We should warn them! Look, here comes somebody!"

Here came somebody all right. A stranger on a great tall roan horse, scarlet his cloak and his tunic, scarlet his helmet and shield. Behind him, shouting vengeance, rode Bedwyr.

Gwenhwyfar stood watching as the riders closed with us, pounding across the meadows through a storm of flung-up turf and hurtling flowers. We girls hurried this way and that, half wanting to run to the river and hide among the willows there, half thinking that it would be safest to break back to the town and hope we met no more raiders on the way. And the red man veered towards us, scenting plunder.

The boy who'd come to guard us kicked his pony to a run and went out to meet the raider, swishing his sword about. He was brave, I suppose. The raider's horse crashed sideways against his pony, like two ships colliding in a surf of flowers, and the raider's sword went through his throat. A splurt of blood fell down the sky, poppy red. The riderless pony cantered off. The raider glanced back, and saw Bedwyr driving towards him. He sheathed his sword and drew a short stabbing-spear, turning his snorting horse to meet the charge. "Bedwyr!" I squealed, with all the other girls. I saw Bedwyr's red hair flap like a flag in the wind. He'd

163

not bothered to put his helmet on. I thought of the hardness of blades and the thinness of skulls. "Bedwyr!"

Bedwyr raised his shield as the spear came at him. The blade glanced from the shield rim and drove down, through Bedwyr's leg, nailing him to his own horse. He screamed. The horse screamed. They went down together, Bedwyr underneath. The raider dragged his own horse round and his hard eyes slid across our faces. Far away, more riders were speeding across the meadows. The raider's comrades, off to some safe place to count their loot and stolen cattle. I saw that he was scared. Scared to rejoin his friends without some stolen treasure to brag about.

I ran to Gwenhwyfar. I don't think she'd moved since all this began. She had one hand up to Peredur's saddle, as if to stop him spurring his old horse forward and trying to fight the raider with his kitchen-knife. I shoved her sideways as the raider's red horse cantered towards her. But he wasn't after Gwenhwyfar. He didn't know who she was. He'd seen a brighter treasure; pretty Celemon. I heard her screech as he leaned out of his saddle and swept her up. I saw her legs kicking as he dumped her across his saddle-bow and urged his horse towards the river. Her hat bowled down-wind.

I called her name. The other girls were scattering. "Celemon!" I shouted.

"I'll stop him!" called Peredur. "I'll save her!" He dug his heels into the flanks of his horse and was away, holding his pot on his head with one hand, clinging to the bridle with the other, a scared girl diving out of his path.

The red raider was pushing his horse hard, but it had been hurt by its collision with the pony, maybe lamed. I was afraid that Peredur would catch him up, and challenge him. I started to run. I stopped and bunched up my skirt and stuffed it into my belt, and then ran on. Thistles slashed at my bare legs. I slithered through a cowpat, startling up a storm of brown dung-flies. I ran till the back of my throat was one cold gasp, and I'd lost sight of the horses. Then I saw sunlit metal flash, away among the willows. The red man had reached the river, and was casting to and fro along the steep bank, looking for a place to cross. Peredur was galloping to cut him off.

I ran again, and reached them as they met. Peredur was lucky. The red man was encumbered by the squiggling girl across his horse's shoulders. He hadn't a chance to draw his sword. Instead, as Peredur came riding at him with one of those toy spears upraised, he caught it by the shaft and wrenched it sideways, tugging Peredur out of the saddle. I heard the yelp of surprise as he fell.

The sour-milk nag, indignant at being made to run so far, trotted off a little way along the riverside and started cropping the grass.

The red raider swung himself down off his horse and tramped back to where Peredur had fallen, pulling out his sword as he went. The boy lay face up. The pot had come off his head and rolled down the river bank, which was steep just there. I could see spreading ripples in the water where it had sunk. The red man lifted up his sword.

I wanted to shout out and tell him no. I wanted to beg him to take pity. But they don't have pity, those armoured, riding men. Even if he left Peredur alive, he'd still make off with Celemon.

So instead of words, I threw myself at him. Down the slope between the willows, across a few yards of short green grass. I can't have weighed half what he did, but he didn't know I was there, and didn't see me until I was almost upon him. He was turning towards me when we hit. I reckon I caught him off balance. He went backwards with me on top of him, and the river took us both.

I was all right. I felt safer in water. I swim like a fish, remember? But the raider had a helmet, and a belt with big bronze fittings, and a scabbard with more bronze on it, and a fat gold ring around his neck, and all those wanted suddenly and very much to be down in the soft mulch of the river bottom. A big bubble came out of his mouth as he sank. Squarish it was, and silvery, like a pillow of light. It wobbled past me to the surface, and I kicked free of him and went after it. Hauled myself out and sat shivering, watching the ripples spread.

When the water was still again I climbed back up the bank. The dead man's sword stood in the nettles, point down, still quivering, where he had dropped it as he fell. There was shouting from the water-meadows. More of Arthur's riders had come to save Gwenhwyfar and her ladies. Celemon was snivelling quietly, hung head down across the raider's horse. I left her to it, and went to

Peredur. He lay where he had fallen, looking dead, but when I touched his face and the water from my wet hair dripped on his eyelids he frowned and sat up, trying to look fierce.

"Where is he?"

"Don't you remember?" I said. "You fought him, and he's dead."

Peredur looked about for the body. He put up one hand to his head and ruffled his tangled brown hair. "My helm . . ."

"It went in the river," I said. "It smelled of soup, anyway. We'll find you a better one."

"And the red man?"

"He went in the river, too."

"He was Arthur's enemy?"

I nodded.

"And I defeated him?"

"Oh yes," I said, and nodded so hard that even I started to believe that it was true. And I turned and grasped the hilt of the sword and tugged it out of the earth, and gave it to Peredur.

XXIX

I was steeped in river water, but no one thought to ask me why as we tramped back across the fields to Sulis. I doubt they even looked at me. They were all too taken up with Bedwyr, who had been dragged out from under that wreck of horsemeat by two of his comrades and carried back to the town on a plank, trying hard all the way not to weep at the pain of his gashed and shattered leg. The girls praised his courage in a wistful way, knowing that he'd end up dead or crippled, and less handsome either way. They cooed and sighed about him, and saved their smiles for Peredur, who rode ahead on the dead raider's roan mare, clutching the dead man's sword and looking confused but happy to find himself so suddenly a man. Celemon, who was unhurt, was busy telling everyone how brave he had been; how he had challenged the man who'd taken her, and stuck one of those silly willow-spears clean through him.

A part of me was sorry that I'd given Peredur my triumph, and angry at him for accepting it so easily. But

Peredur wasn't someone you could be angry at for long. He was too open and smiling, and he looked too good. I stole glances at him through my wet hair all the way. Filled my eyes with him, and felt sorry, knowing that he'd be swallowed into the warrior-life, and learn to hide all his sweetness under bluster and ironmongery.

Arthur was red and shouting when we found him. Striding through the forum, past the rubble-heaps where the banqueting hall had been, demanding to know how the raiders had been allowed to come and shame him at the gates of his own place. Knocking down any man who tried to give him an answer. It was useless to tell him, as Cei was trying to, that only a few farmers and slaves had been killed, and a few huts set ablaze. The insult hurt Arthur more than the raid itself. The thought of men telling how he'd been outwitted.

But even he looked twice at Peredur. His anger faltered. "Who's this?"

Gwenhwyfar, kneeling before him, told him quickly what Peredur had done. Arthur looked at him, and put his anger aside, and smiled. "Peredur Long-Knife's son, is it? That mother of yours told me there were no men left in her fish-stinking hall. But you look like him, all right, and you fight like him too. You'll ride with us now, eh?"

In the ground behind the marketplace horsemen were mounting up, getting ready to ride out and cut off the raiders' retreat and win back the cattle they had stolen. Arthur heaved himself into his saddle and drew Caliburn and swished it about in the sunlight, bellowing some bloodthirsty oath. I saw Peredur clambering on to a fresh mount, and then lost sight of him as the riders clattered away.

I tried not to care. I thought if I didn't care, he might come back all right. It's the people you let yourself care about, they're the ones fate takes away from you. Look at poor Bedwyr.

They had carried him to the dingy, damp-smelling place which he shared with Medrawt and with Medrawt's wife and babies. Gwenhwyfar sent her girls home, and asked me to come with her, and went inside to see how he was being cared for. I thought she had asked me to go with her because I was the oldest, but perhaps she already knew we would find Myrddin there. He was stooping over the pallet where Bedwyr lay, his fingers parting the lips of a wound so deep that it made me feel sick and scared to look at it. It was like a red mouth.

"He'll not walk again," I heard Myrddin say.

Medrawt was there, at the head of the bed, cradling his brother, who was asleep, or unconscious. "Better to die than live a cripple," he said grimly. "Don't say it! God will heal him."

The wound in Bedwyr's leg filled with blood and dribbled it down on to the coarse sheets, which were already sodden. Medrawt's dogs nosed close, and Myrddin cursed them and kicked them away. I looked at Bedwyr's white face, and felt glad I'd drowned that raider.

"Bring him to my house," said Gwenhwyfar.

The men hadn't noticed her till then. She stood near

170

the bed with a corner of her mantle raised to her face, as if to shield herself from the smell and sight of blood. She looked pale, but she always looked pale. She said, "He won't heal in this place. He needs quiet, and air, and cleanliness."

"He needs splints and bandages more," snorted Myrddin.

"Then splint and bandage him, and bring him to my house," said Gwenhwyfar. "I shall tell my women to make ready for him."

Medrawt said, "Do it!"

My master glared past Gwenhwyfar at me, like he was wondering if I was part of this challenge to his doctoring. Then he nodded, and snapped at me to find a straight ash-stick and tear some linen for bandages, as if I was his servant still. But while we were working together, wrapping the wrecked leg in white cloth that kept soaking through red, he asked me softly if I was all right, and if I had been harmed or frightened by the raiders. As if it meant something to him. As if *I* meant something to him.

At last the bleeding slowed. Myrddin lifted Bedwyr's head and made him drink a cup of wine with stinking herbs in it. Then he was carried in the twilight across to Gwenhwyfar's hall, and I went with him, and looked back and saw Myrddin watching from the rushlight-glow in the doorway of Medrawt's place.

XXX

That was a summer of small wars. Arthur meant to teach Calchvynydd he was a man they should respect. Stories are all well and good, he told Myrddin, but if you want men to respect you, you have to show them strength. They burn one of your holdings, you burn two of theirs. Most days that summer, if you stood on the hill-tops above Sulis and looked northward, you'd see the smoke of torched thatch on the sky.

The cattle driven off in that first raid came home again, along with Arthur and his riders, flushed with revenge and carrying the heads of three dead raiders on spears. I saw Peredur ride in with them, still looking bewildered by it all. I think the world of men was not turning out to be quite as he'd expected. He was not quite what they'd expected, either. He didn't speak the language of men. He didn't know the rules I'd learned in my time among the boys. Cei and Medrawt and the rest treated him now as a simpleton; a sort of mascot. Medrawt made him the butt of the same half-friendly jokes he'd had flung at himself when he was younger. Peredur didn't ride with them again that summer, but stayed with the garrison in Sulis.

It wasn't that he was cracked, I tried telling Celemon and the rest. Just he'd been raised different, and come to things by his own road. He'd not grown up around fighting men, the way we had. That was why he stared so much at them, and took such a delight in polishing the fittings of the old shield they gave him till it shone, and thought it looked splendid to fit jays' feathers in his helmet and strut around the town like a dunghill cock. But the girls just teased him more, and laughed at the way he followed Celemon with his eyes, as if she was a lady out of one of Myrddin's tales that he listened to in the fire-hall of a night.

Peredur didn't seem to feel their cruelty. He forgave them everything. He was God's fool. He liked everyone. Well, almost.

When he'd first come my heart jumped up inside me. I remembered how glad I'd been of him when I first found him, just the gladness of knowing there was someone else in the world like me. I thought he'd be a friend to me, and one day soon I'd tell him (if he didn't guess) that that boy he'd met at his mother's hall that time was me.

I'd never told anyone my old secret, see. Even Celemon, who was my friend, would have been sure to think it strange or wicked that I'd been a boy, and she'd have told the other girls, and it would have spread all round Aquae Sulis, how Myrddin had disguised me. But telling Peredur would be different. We'd keep each other's secrets, and laugh about our strange pasts, my boyhood and his gowns. It would lead to deeper friendship and – who knows? I was so alone in my life. For a while I woke up every morning vowing that today would be the day I'd go to him. "Don't you remember how we scared old Saint Porroc?" I'd say. "Didn't you look a treasure, in your shift?" In my mind, I could already see his brown eyes widening, and his slow smile.

But it turned out Peredur, who liked everybody, didn't like me. I frightened him, maybe, or the sight of my face reminded him of his first and only fight; how scared and startled he'd been, and how doubtful his victory was. When he saw me his hand always went to the hilt of the red man's sword, which he wore on his belt, as if he thought I might take it away from him. When he saw me coming towards him in the town he'd go some other way.

Well Gwyna, you fool, I thought, what did you expect? And after a while I stopped trying to find excuses to talk to him. And sometimes, when the other girls were laughing about him, I'd join in.

Life in Sulis was good with Arthur off about his wars. The old buildings gave sighs of relief and let their shoulders sag, basking in the summer sun. Outside the walls, riders patrolled the margins of the ripening wheat. Cei, who ruled in Arthur's absence, made an easy lord. Nights in the feast-hall were full of laughter and stories of the old days, and sometimes he'd come to pay his respects to Gwenhwyfar, which was more than Arthur ever did.

He was a good man, Cei. In the stories Myrddin told

he was quick-tempered, violent and clumsy, but in truth he was none of those things. I think Myrddin made him that way in the stories because he was afraid that men might prefer him to Arthur if they knew what he was really like. Cei laughed off the slanders. "They're only stories," he would say. "What do stories matter?" But he wasn't stupid. He knew as well as Myrddin that in the end stories are *all* that matter. I think Myrddin's stories hurt him, and had led to a dying away of the friendship between them. At any rate, I never heard of him going to visit Myrddin at his new place outside the town. He visited Gwenhwyfar instead, and Gwenhwyfar liked him, and kept him talking often late into the evening, while we girls sat round yawning and dozing and wondering how they found so much to talk about, our fine lady and this rough old soldier.

Cei must have known who I was. He can't have forgotten the night he'd helped Myrddin turn me into a boy. But he never spoke of it, nor gave any sign that he knew, nor treated me different from the other girls. He was a good man.

Meanwhile, Bedwyr mended slowly. His sickroom was one of Gwenhwyfar's own chambers, which had doors that folded open to reveal a terrace and a tangled summer garden. A trickle of water fell endlessly into a cistern. There were foxgloves.

Bedwyr's fever left him pale and bony as his brother. The pain and shame of his bust leg left him bitter. He didn't think he'd ride again, or fight, and what good was a man who couldn't ride or fight? He snapped at the girls Gwenhwyfar sent to tend to him, until we hated going. He had a girl of his own he'd got in some raid the year before and grown fond of and given gifts and good clothes to, and she came into the house to be near him when he was first hurt, but he sent her away, as if it made the shame worse to have her there weeping for him. He cast her off, and after a while another of Arthur's men took her. After that it was just Medrawt, who would call in when he was not riding with Arthur.

We'd got off to a wrong start, me and Medrawt. You'll remember that business in the burning wood, how he waved his sword at me and sent me to seek shelter in the river. I'd never liked him since. But the way he was with Bedwyr changed my mind about him. He was a prideful man, and cold, and hard to like, but he wasn't all cruel, not by miles. He sat by his brother's bed, talking about old times with him and telling him he'd be up and running by fall-of-leaf, while I stood waiting, forgotten, clutching fresh sheets or the jug of watered wine they'd asked for, and saw a different Medrawt, a loving brother, a man who talked fondly about his wife and his children. I wondered if they were all like that, when you stripped the armour and the pride off them.

By summer's height, in the bright, bee-buzzing, flower-full days, Bedwyr was trying to walk. Gwenhwyfar went one afternoon to see how he was faring, and she took me with her. She had to take someone, I suppose, for Arthur's wife couldn't ever be alone with another man, even a poor cripple young enough nearly to be her own son, and I was about the only girl who would go near his room by then, he'd been so fearsome to the others.

176

While I spread fresh sheets on the bed, and smoothed the pillows, Bedwyr went leaning on a staff across the terrace, into the bobbing pinkness of the foxglove-filled garden. Each step tore a grunt of pain from him as he set his weight on his twisted leg. Watching him go, it was all I could do not to run and give him my arm to lean on. But I wasn't his friend Gwyn any more, and he was a man now. It would shame him if a girl offered him help.

"That's good!" said Gwenhwyfar kindly, from the terrace-edge. "That's good!" But she was lying. Bedwyr was as wobbly as a baby and as slow as an old, old man. Halfway to the cistern he fell, and knelt there, sobbing.

And Gwenhwyfar went to him without a word, and put her arms around him, and rested his head against her shoulder, and stroked his hair. And I stood in the shadows behind the folded-back doors, and watched, and didn't move or speak, because Bedwyr would hate it if he knew someone had seen him crying like a child. But I felt different about Gwenhwyfar ever after. I don't remember my mother, but the way she held him, the way she cuddled him close, that was the way I'd have wanted my mother to hold me if I'd had one and I was sad about something.

And after a little time Bedwyr's sobs stopped and he went still. And Gwenhwyfar kept her white hand moving on the red-gold of his hair. And there was something strange and new in her face when she looked up at me. And she said, "Gwyna – fetch us a little sweet wine, and some of those barley-cakes."

*

When Arthur came home for a few days, my mistress grew pale and thoughtful, and called Celemon and me to her chambers. We spent a long time dressing her in different gowns and mantles, and folding them away again when she thought something about them was wrong. When she was finally ready, she went alone to Arthur's hall.

I can see how it must have gone, that meeting, although I wasn't there.

Arthur is sprawled on a chair in his bedchamber, soaking his feet in a basin of water. He's just back from a fight. The cheek-pieces of his helmet have bruised the corners of his face.

He sends his slaves and servants scurrying away when Gwenhwyfar lifts the door-curtain. He would never admit it, but she unsettles him, his tall, quiet wife. She has a grace that speaks to him of old ways that he will never have, no matter how much land and treasure he can grab. In the first months of their marriage, when she was so cold towards him, he used to hit her. He would make the blood of the Aureliani bloom under her skin in purple bruises. She is his wife, after all, so he's a right to bend her to his will. But the more he hit her, the worse he felt. That's why he keeps his distance. Let her have her own life, her own household, her own women, so long as she's there to be displayed when allies and rivals come visiting. She's just one of the things that a powerful man needs.

She kneels before him. Bows low, and hopes he's well. Praises God for sending him safely home. He signals with his hand for her to rise.

"I have something to ask of you, husband."

"What's that?"

"The boy Bedwyr. . ."

Arthur twists his mouth sideways. Young men maimed make for bitter thoughts. Bedwyr had been a favourite of his once. He'd had high hopes. "It's evil luck. My own sister's son. He would have been one of my captains. But now. . ." He shrugs. "Myrddin says he'll die."

"He'll not die."

"Live crippled then, and what's the difference? But you needn't fear for him. He'll be looked after. His brother Medrawt will take him in. And I'll make sure he's got no need to beg. I don't forget my companions."

"He's a proud boy," says Gwenhwyfar. "He won't want to sit by his brother's hearth all his life, watching the women work."

Arthur's face darkens. He doesn't like to talk of things like this. Wishes Bedwyr had been killed outright. What's God playing at, sparing the boy's life but not his leg? Better a dead hero than a living cripple. "What else can he do?" he demands.

"He can guard me," says Gwenhwyfar, treading careful now. She knows how thin her husband's patience is. She feels like she's walking out across ice, with cold deeps of drowning-water under her. "He can guard me. Let him keep his sword and his place in the feast-hall, but instead of riding with you he can stay here to protect me and my ladies. It will give him a meaning. That's all he needs."

Arthur is surprised. Who'd have thought she'd understand so well what goes on in men's hearts? He looks at her, there in the rush-light dusk, and she's not unbeautiful. For a moment he wishes he loved her. Good, it would be, to ride home from battle to a wife like that. A woman his own age, instead of some chit like Cunaide who's just vanity and giggles and nothing but air between her pretty ears. He grins at Gwenhwyfar, suddenly shy and wanting to please her.

"All right, you can have Bedwyr for your bodyguard. Get a couple of those girls of yours to help him stand up if there's a fight."

"Thank you, my lord." Gwenhwyfar bows, showing him the top of her head, her neat white parting. She stands and turns to go.

"Gwenhwyfar. . ."

Looks back at him, a hand already on the door-curtain. Wary as a doe. "What, my lord?"

Nothing. He waves her away. Doesn't know what he was thinking of. What would his men say of him if he went soft over the old heron? "Go, go," he says, and takes his feet out of the basin, and starts shouting for his slaves and Cunaide.

Well, it must have been something like that. Because next day, she went to Bedwyr and told him he was to be her bodyguard – "Captain of my guards," was how she put it, though I don't know who those guards he was to captain were, unless it was us girls or the spearmen on the town wall. But it was as good as medicine to Bedwyr. He set about learning to walk again, and this time he would not give up. It wasn't long before you'd see him in the town, striding along stiff-legged, his face stone-white with pain and determination, using an old spear-handle for a crutch.

When I next met Myrddin he said, "Your friend has mended well. I didn't think he'd walk again on that leg. Your mistress has done good for him."

"They have done good for each other," I said. Gwenhwyfar was happier that summer than I'd ever seen her. Saving Bedwyr had made her feel useful, I thought. When she was with him, she was in a state of grace.

My old master scratched his nose thoughtfully. "It may be," he said. "Sometimes, on our way through the world, we meet someone who touches our heart in a way others don't."

He looked at me like he was going to say something more, but then he shook his head, and turned, and went away. He'd got a curly-headed boy of eight or nine who carried his bags and belongings for him. I think the boy was the son of that couple who'd made his house ready for him the year I came back to Sulis as a girl. For a moment, as I watched him follow Myrddin away, I felt envious. Gwenhwyfar's hall felt empty now with Bedwyr gone, and the emptiness reminded me again how thin the lives of women were beside the lives of boys and men.

XXXI

The Irishman rode in, bringing bad news from Arthur's lands out west. King Cunomorus of Kernyw had sent his warriors raiding across the Tamar again. They'd taken tin and cattle from the Irishman, and the Irishman wanted Arthur's help to get revenge. "Otherwise," he said, "how can I afford to pay Arthur the tribute I owe him? How can I pay him those three ingots of tin, those three loaves as broad as the distance from my elbow to my wrist, that tub of butter and the sow?"

His hill-country was so remote he hadn't heard of Arthur's quarrel with Calchvynydd. When he was told, his face fell. He knew he'd little hope of Arthur's help. Truth was, Arthur had all but forgotten him. And anyway, it was years since he'd sent Arthur tribute.

But Cei wanted to be polite, so there was a feast for the Irishman and his men. After, in the hot half-light around the hall-fire, Myrddin told us a tale of a young man who came to Arthur's court asking for help to win the hand of Olwen, daughter of Ysbaddaden, chief of the giants. He wove it full of quests and hunts, and the boar Twrch Trwyth was in there, and plenty of battles, to remind the Irishman's followers that Arthur was still a great battle-leader, who would deal with Cunomorus just as soon as he finished trampling the bones of the warriors of Calchvynydd into their own chalk hills. But what I mostly remember about that night was the way he spoke of the love of this young man for Olwen, and of Olwen's beauty, and how her hair was yellower than the flowers of the broom and her flesh whiter than the foam of the wave and her cheeks redder than the reddest foxglove. She was so lovely that four white flowers sprang up where she trod. And during these parts of the story most of the boys and the young men yawned, or laughed among themselves, or called out for their cups to be filled again by the lads who waited with the pitchers.

But Bedwyr, sitting with his bad leg stretched out stiff in front of him, stared into the embers of the big hearth with a look I couldn't read, a sort of shining look, as if there was wild happiness walled up inside him. And sometimes he seemed to be looking across the fireplace to where we maidens sat, in a neat cluster about Gwenhwyfar. I wondered if he had let himself fall in love with one of us now that he was on the way to being a man again, and if he would come back to our hall soon to woo Celemon. I even wondered if it was me he was looking at, and let myself think how it would be to be Bedwyr's woman. I would never have imagined such a thing in daylight, little dun-haired, brown-faced me, but in the kind shadows of the hall and the light of

Myrddin's story even I felt beautiful. As if four white flowers might spring up where I trod.

And the logs crumpled into ashes in the hearth, and the sparks went up out of the smoke-holes in the roof, and Myrddin's words went with them, out into the summer night.

Summer grew old and golden, each barley-plot a yellow-white sea. Season of tick-bites and fly-stings. Of salt-white sweat stains under the arms of my linen summer kirtle. Of walls and pavements hot as new-baked bread.

Gwenhwyfar decided to go bathing again, which I think she had forgot while she had Bedwyr to doctor. And since the girls she'd trusted to go with her in earlier years had husbands and children now, she looked about her for someone else to attend her on her evening visits to the baths, and she settled upon me.

"Me, lady?" I said, when she told me.

"You." We were alone in a quiet part of her house, the others busy somewhere. She said, "Bishop Bedwin would be angry at me if he knew I went near those old temples. So I must not have it spoken of. It will be our secret, Gwyna. And I know that you can keep secrets."

"I have no secrets from you, lady."

She laughed at that. "No? But you used to be Myrddin's boy."

I'd not expected that. Years it was, since that time I stumbled on her in the old pool. She'd never spoken of it, or given any hint that she knew it was me she'd seen that day. She'd stored it up, that little nugget of knowledge, till she needed it to buy my silence with. "You are fond of your old master, aren't you?" she said. "It might go badly with him if men ever found out about his trick."

"Trick?" I felt hot and cornered. There seemed no point lying, but I tried anyway. "I don't know what you mean. . ."

"Oh, Gwyna," said my mistress. "When Arthur has too much wine, he often tells that tale of his, how the lake-woman came up out of the depths and gave him Caliburn. But you and I know that there's no lake-woman. She's only a pagan superstition. The shadow of some old water-goddess, fading away in the light of the new God. So Myrddin must have had someone to help him when the sword was given to Arthur. Someone who could swim like a fish."

She'd worked it all out, see. She'd probably worked it all out that long-ago evening when we faced each other in the pool.

"Imagine how foolish Arthur would look if it became known that Myrddin had a girl to help him," she said. "And Arthur has no love for those who make him look foolish. So I shall keep your secret, Gwyna. And you will keep mine."

In the lavender-coloured, lavender-scented dusk I went down between the ivied houses with her, down to where the old baths waited, more crumbledown and overgrown than ever. I expected her to go into the building where I had seen her that other time, but instead she went round to the temple. A twisting, secret path wound through the furze-bushes that had grown around the gateway, leading to a gap in the planks that Bedwin's priests had nailed up there, and into the nettled courtyard itself. Gwenhwyfar threaded her way purposefully through the scrub, past old stone altars. I trailed behind her, wary, feeling suddenly afraid, and sure some danger waited for us in those ancient buildings.

"Lady, this is a haunted place!"

She looked back at me. "God will watch over us, Gwyna. I am not afraid of ghosts. But if you are, wait here. Make sure nobody comes."

She didn't go up the stairs into the pillared, roofless temple, but turned left to where an old grey building stood. Massive buttresses strengthened its walls. Stone nymphs with their faces knocked off still guarded an arched doorway. From the darkness inside I caught the sound of seething water, the hot mineral smell of the sacred spring.

"That water is too hot to bathe in!" I called. My mistress didn't look back. She climbed the three worn steps and went inside.

I waited. Birds hopped and fluttered in the bushes all about me. The white flowers of bindweed that had twined over the altars glowed soft, ghostly white in the twilight. The sounds of the town seemed muffled and far-off. A terrible stone face stared at me out of a tangle of vetch, round as the sun, with long hair and beard twirling out into stony flames and serpents. I kept telling myself what Myrddin had always taught me. There are no gods, no ghosts, no spirits. Nothing but our own fears. But my fears were enough for me. A blackbird started chittering in a clump of brambles and set me running like a deer, after my mistress, up the steps and into the soft, steamy dusk of the old shrine.

It was the chamber I'd looked into once with Bedwyr. Up there were the three windows we'd peered down through, opening into the caverny ruins of the big bath. The rest was greenish dark. I could hear the ferns stirring on the walls, the water simmering in its basin. I blinked, moving forward noiselessly, letting my eyes grow used to the shadows. I was about to call out "Lady," when I saw her in the shadows by the fallen statue of the goddess. There was someone with her, and he clung to her and she to him so tight, like if they let go of each other for even an instant they'd fall. I stared and stared, not understanding. I saw her lift up her face to his in that green twilight. Rapt, she looked. Her teeth showed pale as she whispered some smiling thing, drawing his face to hers, his mouth to her mouth, and her hands in his red-gold hair.

And then I knew it hadn't been me that Bedwyr had been gazing at across the feast-hall fire, nor Celemon neither.

Mouse-quiet, I backed out of that place. The ghosts in the courtyard didn't scare me now. I stood shaking, watching the nettles sway, feeling hot and stupid and ashamed.

That day in the garden, when Bedwyr tried to walk, and failed, and wept in Gwenhwyfar's arms. Had that been the start of it? "Gwyna – " she'd said. "Fetch us a little sweet wine, and some of those barley-cakes."

So off I'd gone to the storeroom. And I imagine her standing there, with Bedwyr in her arms. And he raises his head from her shoulder, and they look at each other, and they don't move, but still something has changed in the way that they are holding each other. And she knows that he is wanting to kiss her, this handsome young man. And he knows that she wants him to. And still they don't move, or speak, or breathe till they hear me coming back with the wine and cakes. Then, guiltily, they pull apart, each staring at the other's face. . .

I felt as huge a fool as Peredur. For not seeing what was in front of me. For not understanding what I had seen. And I felt frightened, because this fire they'd lit in each other would burn them both up one day, and burn me too if I wasn't lucky. Arthur had no love for those who made him look foolish.

XXXII

What is Bedwyr thinking? Why can't he see the danger? I want to grab him in the street, push him into a doorway and say, "Bedwyr, it's me, look, your old friend Gwyn." Say, "She can't be worth it. Don't you understand what will happen when Arthur finds out?"

But he does understand. He *likes* the danger. He's been trained for danger; lived for danger all his life, been taught to go and seek it out on battlefields and in the hunt. And this summer past it's all been taken from him. The best future he can hope for is to be a half-man, riding patrol along the field-banks, watching over Arthur's cows and barley. The pain in his bad leg always, souring him. Gwenhwyfar makes him feel like a man again. Arthur has no use for a broken warrior, but Arthur's wife has.

Each morning when he goes out to see the horses in their stable behind his brother's house he looks across the smoky slope of the town to her roof, and thinks of her asleep beneath it. The hope of meeting her is what pulls him through each day. Sometimes, if she is going out into the meadows, or to visit some friend who lives outside the walls, she sends for him. And he puts on his red cloak and rides out as her bodyguard, and there is something thrilling about being so near her and not being able to touch her or say more than the idle pleasantries that are expected between a young warrior and the wife of his lord. He can't even catch her eye, for fear her maidens will notice some glance, some glint. He does his duty in a daze, like a sleepwalker, knowing that when the twilight comes he'll slip away to meet her at the baths, and they'll say all the things they couldn't say by day.

Let's face it, he's in love. Like a hero out of one of those stories Myrddin tells in the feast-hall. He is in love with her hands; with her slender fingers and the creases of her knuckles. He is in love with the faint hair on her upper lip, which he can feel but barely see. He is in love with the downy hollow of the small of her back; with the hard jut of her shoulder blades, like the stubs of wings. He is in love with her eyelids. He is in love with her voice. He is in love with her kindness. He is in love with the soft sound of her breath when she lies drowsy in his arms. He is in love with the nape of her neck. He is in love with the girl she was before he was even born. He is in love with her because she's *not* some girl, some silly maid no older than himself who giggles and wants presents. Gwenhwyfar wants only him. She's *chosen* him. She watches him so intently when they are together. She takes him so seriously.

And isn't that what all boys want, and all men too? Just to be taken seriously?

XXXIII

Almost every night, while Arthur was away, Gwenhwyfar went to meet her lover. The year ripened into a golden autumn, the fruit heavy on hedge and tree. Apple harvest came and went, yet the weather held, and the war-band stayed gone. Day after day of blue sky and yellow sun and the fat white clouds sailing over Sulis from the west like ships, till it started to seem unnatural, and we grew edgy, waiting for the weather to break and Arthur to return.

And still, most every night, Gwenhwyfar went to meet her lover at the spring. And always I went with her. She knew I knew her secret. I think it pleased her, knowing someone knew. Sometimes she'd look at me with a proud, sly look that said, "I'm not quite as old or as cold as you thought, am I, Gwyna?" But she never spoke of it, except to say, "Wait outside for me," as she went into those warm shadows.

I never did wait, of course. I followed her. Crouched in the gloom just inside the doorway, tickled by ferns,

I strained my ears to sieve soft-murmured words out of the chuckling, bubbling, echoing sounds of the spring.

"What will we do when Arthur comes home?"

"He may never come home, Bedwyr. He may be killed. He may be cut down in battle, or murdered by his own men, the way he had Valerius murdered."

"Not Arthur. He's a great warrior. He can't be killed."

"No warrior is that great, except in stories."

"While he wields Caliburn he cannot be defeated."

"Because it came from the gods? You don't believe that, do you, Bedwyr? Do you?"

An awkward silence. Movements in the silence. The water laughing, and someone turning over on a crumpled red cloak.

"He cannot live for ever, Bedwyr. He might be dead already. He might be dying now, at this moment, while we lie here together. He may never come home. Then Cei would be lord of Aquae Sulis instead."

"Cei does not want to be lord of anywhere."

"That is what would make him a good lord. These men who want power, they're the ones who shouldn't be allowed to get it. They say they'll use it for good, but they only use it to make themselves more powerful still. Let Arthur die, and Cei rule us."

"But if Arthur *does* come home. . ." Bedwyr insisted.

"Then he'll kill me."

"I won't let him! I'll kill him first! I'll kill him and marry you!"

"And what will men say when they see you with your aged wife?"

"You're not aged. Men have older wives. I'll treasure you. He never did. I'll kill him."

Was that what she wanted? A strong young lover who would rid her of her husband? But why Bedwyr? Bedwyr wasn't strong. Bedwyr could barely walk. That wasn't it.

So was she in love with him?

Well of course she was. He had said he'd treasure her. Who doesn't want to be treasured? He'd gone to her head like honeyed wine.

It wasn't just me who saw the change in her. She smiled more, laughed more, was kinder to her girls. Or grew suddenly sad; wept for no cause, snapped at us, went walking by herself in the garden in the drizzling rain. The others gossiped about her, wondering what the reason was.

"She's in love," Celemon told me one morning while we knelt behind Gwenhwyfar in the church. "She has conceived a passion for Medrawt."

"That's nonsense," I whispered back.

"Well what would you know about it, Gwyna? What would you know about love? Medrawt is a better Christian than Arthur. I saw her speak to Bedwyr in the forum yesterday. And Bedwyr's Medrawt's kinsman. Don't you see? He was passing on a message. . ."

"Bedwyr's Arthur's kinsman, too," I reminded her. "Bedwyr has more sense than to betray Arthur."

Above my lady Gwenhwyfar's bowed head Bishop Bedwin waved his hands about, in that way God seems to like. I suppose God must have known her secret, but did the bishop? Bedwin had known her since she was a little girl. Maybe he was happy to see her happy. Maybe he couldn't bring himself to condemn her. Maybe he, too, was hoping Bedwyr might rid us of Arthur.

XXXIV

A secret's a weighty thing to carry. I wondered often if I should hunt Myrddin out and tell him about Gwenhwyfar and Bedwyr. After all, I was meant to be his spy, wasn't I? I couldn't decide. Sometimes I thought no, my mistress was kind to me, I shouldn't betray her, and I didn't want any harm to come to Bedwyr. But sometimes, when I heard him with Gwenhwyfar, I could have killed him myself for wasting all his love and gentleness on the old heron.

One morning, Myrddin surprised me while I was out buying saffron. His hand on my shoulder felt like a bird's talon. I hadn't noticed till then how thin he'd grown. He'd got a threadbare, abandoned look. He'd been travelling all summer, telling his stories of Arthur, helping people to imagine the day when Arthur would lead all Britain against the Saxons. Trouble was, now that Arthur had Aquae Sulis and his other little patches of land, he hadn't much interest in forging great alliances. He was happier raiding, and filling his hall with other men's treasure. Myrddin was wearing himself out for nothing.

Still, he had a smile for me. "It's been a while since I saw you, girl."

I asked him how he did. Well, he said, but he didn't look it. That curly-haired boy didn't look after him the way I used to. His clothes were dirty, and his hair long. A white stubble of beard showed on his cheeks, like mould on a cheese. He scratched his chin and looked sideways at me and said, "What news from the women's hall?"

I wondered, from the way he said it, if he knew something. He was clever, wasn't he? I remembered that thing he'd told me weeks back – how sometimes on our way through the world we meet someone who touches our heart. Had he guessed what was happening between Bedwyr and Gwenhwyfar, even then?

"Well?" he asked. "Does the old heron still spend as much time by her pond? Has she caught any fish yet?" He studied me while I tried to think of my reply, watching my face the way a cat watches a mouse-hole. "Something is troubling you, Gwyna. Tell me. Let me help." He smiled. His kindness was bait to tempt my secret out. He could see I needed a friend to help me bear the weight of it. He smiled, and I couldn't resist him.

"She has caught Bedwyr," I said, and looked round to make sure no one but he had heard me. I hadn't meant to tell him, but I was suddenly glad that I had. It all spilled out of me. "And she knows about me, master, and the sword from the water. She'll tell everyone about it if she finds out I've betrayed her. . ."

Myrddin looked angry. Quiet angry. He said, "When Arthur finds out what she is doing he will strike her dead before she can tell anything. Does she not know that? What is wrong with her?"

"It's love, master."

"Love?" He looked at me despairing, like he expected better from me. "She's not a girl." Then, softer, "Gwyna, you're not betraying her. This would have come out anyway. There are already rumours. Better that I know, so that I can decide what to do. Arthur will be back soon. . ." He groaned and pinched the bridge of his nose between finger and thumb, as if thinking on it all gave him a headache. As if I'd laid one burden too many on his shoulders.

"It's Gwenhwyfar who's the betraying one," he said. "She's betrayed Arthur. She's betrayed you. What right has she to make you part of her lies?"

"Will you tell Arthur?"

"I don't know. I must think what would be best. . ."

When I told him the secret I was hoping he'd say, "It's not so bad. It doesn't matter. It's nothing to fret about." Instead, he'd grown more distracted and grave-looking than I'd ever seen him.

"But Arthur doesn't care about Gwenhwyfar," I said.

"He cares about appearances, Gwyna. If he thinks his wife is false, a man like that, there will be blood. Arthur has this peculiarity: he cannot bear to be thought a fool. Tell your mistress that. Tell her he is only a day's ride away, and will soon be back. Tell her she must put an end to this."

Well, how could I? It wasn't my place to tell

Gwenhwyfar what she should do. But when I reached home with the saffron I went to her and told her that I'd met with my lord Myrddin and that he'd said Arthur might soon be back.

She blushed when I told her. I can see her now, standing in the garden in her robe of flame-coloured linen, turning her face away so that I wouldn't see the colour burning there. "And how does Myrddin know?" she asked. "Did some spirit tell him? Did he summon up his father, the Devil?"

I shrugged. It seemed to me that Myrddin was wiser than she reckoned, and that there were many ways he might know Arthur's movements. Messengers came in sometimes from the war-band, and not all the messages they carried were shared with her. But I had already said all I dared.

I imagine Arthur, next morning, sitting on his horse, somewhere where the round chalk downs are plump as cushions and the smoke of burned farmsteads makes shadows on the grass.

A messenger has come to find the war-band. As he waits for the man to draw close, Arthur thinks of home. It'll be good to get back, this time. He's not as young as he once was. Too many nights on his camp-bed, and too many days in the saddle. There's an old wound in his side that aches dull and steady. He thinks, for some reason, of Gwenhwyfar. When he gets home, he'll be a better husband to her. If he can make her happier, maybe she'll give him a son.

Perhaps this messenger brings good news, he thinks.

Perhaps Gwenhwyfar is already carrying his child.

(And perhaps I'm being kind to him. Perhaps I don't quite want to believe that what he did next was just out of hurt pride.)

But the man, pale, purse-lipped with worry, won't meet Arthur's eye. Men who carry good news don't wear that look.

"What is it?" Arthur says, and the messenger swallows hard and says, "I've word from Myrddin."

XXXV

I remember the sound her robe made, whispering as she wove her way between the thistles that had grown up around the baths. It was evening, the day after my meeting with Myrddin. Away in the redness of the west great clouds were massing, dark and sky-tall, as if some enchanter had cast spells upon the hills there and they were swelling into mountains. The autumn air was heavy with heat.

As we came into the courtyard I glimpsed Bedwyr waiting for us by the entrance to the spring. He vanished inside with a stiff-legged movement. It was careless of him, letting himself be seen like that. It felt like a bad omen.

"My lady. . ."

"One of the ghosts of the place, Gwyna," she said, trying to sound light.

"We should go home," I warned her.

But how could she? Arthur was coming. She did not know when she would be alone with Bedwyr again.

Maybe tonight was her goodbye to him. Oh, she saw the sense in what I said. It made her pause and look at me. A gust of breeze lifted the edges of her head-cloth. A smell of rain on the wind, and two dark blotches of colour high on Gwenhwyfar's cheeks. Then she turned and went into the shrine, and the first thunder grumbled in the west.

I waited outside this time. Since my talk with Myrddin I'd been edgy as a spooked horse. I was fearful we'd been followed.

The sky didn't help. It was lead colour, curdling, filled with wicked spirits. It wasn't a sky to be out under. A tree of lightning stood suddenly upon a hill-top westward. The temple precinct filled with a brownish, ghostly light, and the flowers of the bindweed showed white, white on the crumbled altars.

I heard shouting from the sentries on the wall, down by the gate. Then thunder again.

No, not thunder. That long rumble was the sound of Aquae Sulis's gates being dragged open, and hooves thrumming on the cross-hatch of logs which covered the muddy place between them.

I ran to the door of the shrine and looked into the darkness. A flash of lightning made all the dangling charms and wet ferns jink with blue light. I called, "Lady?" as loud as I dared.

Thunder. Horses in the streets, torches moving. Was it raiders? No, I'd heard the gates open. A shouted word whirled about like a leaf on the gusting wind.

"Arthur!"

I ducked inside. Storm light flickered off the water in

the pool. Lightning flamed on the white bodies of Bedwyr and my mistress. They looked like Adam and Eve, surprised in their garden by God.

"He's here." I said stupidly. "Arthur. He's back."

They were scrambling up, untying themselves from each other. I shielded my eyes from them. I said, "He'll go up to the hall first. He'll want food and stabling and clean clothes before he sends for you, lady. You've time to get you home. And if you don't want to see him we'll tell him you're sick. We'll say the thunder has given you a headache. . ."

Why did I have to make their plans for them? Bedwyr was a warrior. Gwenhwyfar was my mistress. Why couldn't they tell me what to do? But they just stared at me, numb, holding on to each other.

And Arthur wasn't going to the hall. I remembered Myrddin, and how he had watched me when we spoke in the marketplace. He knew everything. He'd known that if I warned Gwenhwyfar about her husband's homecoming she would be certain to meet with Bedwyr that night. He must have sent a messenger to find Arthur on the road somewhere, and told him to come home quick, and where to look for his wife.

I heard hooves on the old pavement outside the baths. I heard something batter against the planks that screened the entry-way. I heard Gwenhwyfar say "Jesu," as she struggled into her shift.

I ran out into the courtyard as the planks at the entrance gave way. Beyond them, rain, and tossing furze-bushes and men and firelight. Arthur and a party of his warriors, dismounted, some with torches, boys behind them holding the heads of their scared horses as the lightning flickered. The men looked confused. Maybe they were wondering why Arthur had ridden so hard to Sulis just to lay siege to this old temple. Arthur shoved past them into the courtyard, a black shape against another flare of lightning, hairy in his wolf-skin cloak. I'd forgot how big and broad he was. How tall. How like a bear.

Lightning flashed on Caliburn's blade. Rain, hissing on the flagstones.

He bellowed, "Gwenhwyfar!"

"She is at the spring, lord," I squeaked, running at him, like a mouse running out of the wainscot. "She only comes here to bathe. Give her time to dress, lord, and—"

A hard blow of his fist sent me sideways, spraddled me in a nettle-clump. I was lucky I was on his left side, or he'd have used the sword on me. What was I, to Arthur in his wrath? A mouse, that's all. I saw his face. The anger in it. Blood dark in his cheeks and the spittle blown white from his hollering mouth.

"Gwenhwyfar!"

He went past me, and I scrambled up to keep from being trod on by the men that followed him. Hands caught me from behind, twisting me round. Myrddin's black robes flapped at my face. I heard him say, "Come, Gwyna. This is no place for you. . ."

"You told him!" I screamed, trying to break away from him. I twisted my head and I saw Arthur climb the three steps and go inside, swiping down handfuls of the dangling charms. I heard Bedwyr in there shouting something. Later people said it was a challenge, but it didn't sound like a challenge to me. Arthur shouted back, no words, just a roar. There came scuffling sounds, a clatter of kicked stones, a noise like a hurt dog whining.

Myrddin's grip was weak. I broke free of him and ran. "Gwyna!" I heard Myrddin shout. Inside the shrine Gwenhwyfar was screaming. Arthur's men were bunched in the doorway, staring into the dark. One said, "Jesu, Christos. . ." as I squirrelled my way between them. Inside, rain spewed through the rotting roof, spattering into the spring. The torches lit up Gwenhwyfar, over by the felled statue of the goddess, half crouched, cowering, her hands up shivering in front of her. I thought she'd wrapped herself in Bedwyr's red cloak, but it was just her own white shift, splashed red. On the floor lay a red and white thing that jerked like a killed pig. Arthur stood over it. He raised Caliburn high and grunted as he hacked down.

"Bedwyr!" screamed Gwenhwyfar.

Arthur turned to face us, Caliburn red in his red hand, his whole arm red to the elbow. He held up some gaping thing for us to see.

"Jesu, Christos. . ."

"Gwyna!" my master shouted from behind me somewhere, angry sounding.

Hailstones hissed furiously on the roof. I ran past Arthur and round the pool's side to my mistress. "Bedwy-y-y-y-r," she was grizzling.

I picked up Bedwyr's cloak. I don't know why. Who knows why they do anything, at times like that? I wrapped it round her. It slapped wetly against her bare legs. Arthur was bellowing again, shouting at his men to look at what became of traitors. When he's finished, I thought, he'll come for Gwenhwyfar. For me too. Rage like his strikes anything it sees. I dragged her with me to a crack in the wall. "Bedwy-y-yr!" she sobbed, hiccuping.

"He's dead!" I said. And he was. I'd not believed it till I said it.

I shoved her in front of me like a bundle, through that crack and away along black nettly passages between the bath-houses, out into the pouring streets. While Arthur's men stood at the pool's edge and watched as Arthur swung Bedwyr's head by its hair and flung it from him – that tumbling, woeful, boyish, lightning-lit face, that red-gold hair like the fires of a falling star – and the waters took it with a feathery splash.

XXXVI

Where was I going? Just away. The animal fear that had set me running the night I first saw Arthur had hold of me again. Just get us away, me and my mistress, before he kills us too.

I steered Gwenhwyfar through the rain, making for the gate. Men barged past us, hurrying to the baths to see what the commotion was. The sky tipped water on us. Peredur came by, a straggle of wet feathers plastered over that helmet he always wore. I caught him as he passed. I yowled into his wide-eyed face. "Find Medrawt! Tell Medrawt that Arthur's killed his brother!"

I don't know why I did that either. I think I remembered the love Medrawt had shown Bedwyr when Bedwyr was sick, and thought he should know what had happened. Maybe I hoped he'd take his sword and come like an avenging angel and kill Arthur. Blood must have blood. Bedwyr's other kin might take Arthur's side when they heard what Bedwyr had done, but not Medrawt. You kill a man's brother, he's got to kill you, it's only natural. But as Peredur ran off with my message I realized that Arthur would know that as well as I did. He'd be expecting Medrawt's vengeance, and he'd likely have sent men to kill him too.

Then we were out of the town somehow. We were scrambling through wet fields. We were blundering through scratchy woods. Gwenhwyfar was so slow and stumbly I almost left her, for fear Arthur and his men were coming after her and would catch us both. Three times I ran on ahead. And three times I went back for her, because I couldn't bear to leave her lone and helpless. She was making a hurt, raw-throated noise that I could hear above the hiss of rain and hoo of wind-whipped trees. It was like she was a child, and I her mother. I held her hand and tugged her after me.

Where were we going? Just away. I think I had an idea of getting to the Summer Country, where Gwenhwyfar might beg her kinsman Maelwas to shelter us. But I didn't know how to find Maelwas, beyond just going south, and I couldn't tell which way south was, with no moon, no stars, and the wind coming from every way at once.

At last we came to a place where the track we were following sloped down into a flood. A swollen river filled the world ahead, glinting scaly under the lightning-flashes like a huge serpent winding its way between the hills. We turned back, shoving through alder and tussock-grass to a line of trees on a rise above a little lake, and we huddled on the wet grass in their shelter.

I'd been right to fear for Medrawt. When Arthur rode back into Sulis he sent his old companion Greidawl Widowmaker with a couple of men straight to Medrawt's house to kill him. But fate had better ideas. As Greidawl rode up through the streets that first great crash of thunder booming over the rooftops scared his mare so much she reared up and threw him backwards and he broke his head on a lead trough by the wayside. And since he'd not told his men where they were going or what they were to do there, they busied themselves getting him indoors and fetching doctors to him, and while they were about it Peredur went past them with my message.

"Arthur has killed your brother."

Anyone else, hearing those words from a bedraggled clown like Peredur, might have thought it was all some sort of joke. But maybe Medrawt suspected the truth about Bedwyr and Gwenhwyfar. Maybe he knew. For all I know Bedwyr had told him everything. At any rate, it took him only a moment to understand that this was real, and what it meant. He called for his sword, ready to go and get his vengeance, but while he was waiting for his man to bring it he thought again. He couldn't fight all Arthur's band. And he had his wife to think of. He could hear her voice in the next room, comforting their daughters, who'd been woken by the storm. More thunder broke over the house, so loud that it left no space in his head for his thoughts and he had to clutch his hands over his ears. His man came back, the sword-hilt flaring as lightning spiked in through the shutter-cracks. Medrawt ignored him, ran to the room where his wife was.

"Dress," was all he said. "Bring the girls and your women. We're leaving."

*

The storm tore eastward. It went away to throw its spears of light at Saxon men, and left us quiet upon our lakeside, my mistress and me. The moon came out, like a startled eye. She rolled dazedly through the wrecks of cloud. Stars showed. The wind grew gentle again.

All this time, and all this way, my lady Gwenhwyfar had said nothing. I began to think she'd left her wits behind. But in the grey before dawn, when the black shapes of the stooping trees were starting to show against the sky, she started talking. The creel of her ribs heaved and she retched out words. I wasn't in a mood to answer, but she didn't care. She was that wrapped up in herself she could hold a whole conversation without any need for me to say a thing.

She said, "It wasn't my fault."

She said, "Why did God let it happen?"

She said, "But I loved him so badly."

She said, "He needed me. I never thought anyone would need me."

She said, "Love made us mad." (Like it was something to be proud of.)

She said, "I will go to Hell."

She said, "I don't care. He was my man. Not Arthur."

She said, "He was so young! He was still a boy!"

She said, "Oh, what am I to do?"

She said, "Where am I to go?"

She said, "I cannot live in this world."

Myself, I thought she should maybe say "Thank you, Gwyna," or "You did well, Gwyna," or "God bless and protect you, sweet Gwyna, for saving my scrawny

209

neck." But she didn't. Didn't even know I was there, I reckon. Didn't think I was grieving over Bedwyr too. Didn't think people like me felt things as hard as a lady like her. Selfish, she was. What else had it been but selfishness that made her take Bedwyr as her lover? She must have known how it would end.

After a while I got so tired of her talk that I went off into a kind of sleep, cold and footsore and scared as I was.

When I woke I found Bedwyr's cloak laid over me. The cloak was as wet as me, and as wet as the turf beneath me, but I was glad of the thought. I looked sleepy-eyed at the tree I was lying under, and saw how the moss on its trunk had been combed all one way by the wind and the rain. But the rain was gone now. The sun was coming up, a brightness behind the early-morning mist. Down on the edge of the mere we'd settled by a heron stood in the shallows. It heard me stirring and took off, flapping away on its big grey wings, neck curled like a snake, legs trailing like winter sticks. I watched it go.

"We'll head south, lady," I said. "Maelwas ought to show you kindness, being your kin and all."

No answer. I sat up, and saw I'd been talking to nobody. Gwenhwyfar was gone, and not even a footprint in the soggy earth to show me where. All I could hear was the water drip-drip-dripping off the trees. "Not even a goodbye," I thought.

A hand rose from the mere, white, sequined with water-droplets. Pale fingers uncurled from their own reflections and seemed to beckon me.

*

At Aquae Sulis, rainwater and rumours gurgled in the streets. All round the town and for as far about as anyone had ridden trees were down, roofs gone, houses fallen, bridges washed away.

In Arthur's hall, in the dim, stunned dawn, Arthur and his captains meet. He looks at their faces, ringed round him in half-light, and sees doubt in them. For the first time they aren't sure where he's leading them, nor whether they want to follow. Even his own half-brother. Even Cei.

He spreads his big hands. "You saw how it was. You think I wanted to kill the boy? My own kinsman? My sister's son? But he betrayed me. When a man steals your own wife, what are you to do?"

The others shift uneasily, and won't meet his eye.

"What are you to do? Bedwyr and Gwenhwyfar. They were together. You saw them, Gwri. . ." He thumps the arm of the man beside him, urging him to tell the others, the ones who reached the spring too late to see more than the spilled blood and the boy's butchered body.

Myrddin, behind him, says, "I saw her. She was there. They were together."

Cei says miserably, "He was my kinsman too, Arthur. He brought death on himself, I know that. There's not a man in the world who'd blame you for killing him, after what he did. But it was the manner of it. You threw Bedwyr's head in the spring. Think how it looks. . ."

"I was angry!" shouts Arthur, growing angry again. "He betrayed me! My own kinsman! Do you stop to think when a red rage is upon you?"

Cei keeps talking, head down, like a man walking into a gale. "Think how it looks. As if you're some old heathen hill-chieftain who throws the heads of his enemies in a sacred well."

Owain says, "Bishop Bedwin and his priests are putting it about that you promised the old gods sacrifice in return for your victories in the north. They say Bedwyr was your gift to them, and the storm was the true God's tempest, sent to show us his displeasure."

Arthur curses. "Who holds this town? Me or Bedwin? And the storm had started already by the time I killed the boy."

"God's tempest makes a better story," says Cei. "That's what God-fearing men will believe."

Arthur strikes him across his doleful face with the back of his right hand. "Do you mean to stand here all morning moaning and drizzling like a woman? Get after Medrawt. Find him and finish him, before I have a blood-feud on my hands."

Cei's face is very pale in the smudgy shadows. One of Arthur's rings has gashed his cheek, and beads of blood show there. Arthur breathes hard, watchful. Some of the men who stand beside Cei, men who were Arthur's when he left them in Sulis at the summer's start, reached for their swords when that blow was struck. Just quick movements, quickly stilled when they saw that Cei was not going to fight. But they'd have been ready to back him, if he'd chosen different.

"I'll not go after Medrawt," Cei says carefully. "We don't know which road he took. And whichever it was, the bridges are gone, the rivers have broken their banks. My men are needed here, in their homes, in Sulis."

Arthur's nostrils flare. He's not used to disobedience. What Cei says has truth in it, but is it his only reason? Can it be that he's on Medrawt's side now, not Arthur's?

Myrddin says, "What of Gwenhwyfar?"

Arthur looks round. "What?"

"What of Gwenhwyfar?" asks Myrddin again. "What has become of her?"

"I don't know," says Arthur impatiently. "How could I know? That girl of hers spirited her away. Lucky for her, or I'd've had her head too."

"She is Maelwas's kin."

"Would Maelwas blame me for punishing an unfaithful wife?"

"Of course not," says Myrddin. "But it must be done properly, a high-born woman like her, your ally's kin. You cannot simply kill her. Maybe you should send her to Maelwas, and ask him to do with her as he sees fit. Show him you are merciful, and you respect his judgement. But first you must find her. Her and that girl of hers."

And I sat on the wet grass and watched that hand beckon to me from the shining middle of the mere. White as a stripped twig.

I was already wet as I could be, so I went down to the shallows and waded in. My torn skirts flowered out round me. The water was clear. There was grass on the bottom, neat and green and standing up on end, like it was startled to find itself under water.

Gwenhwyfar lay on the drowned grass. She had torn a strip off Bedwyr's cloak and used it to knot an old sodden log around her waist, to weight her down. She was on her side, and one arm had drifted upward, lazily, so her hand broke the bright surface. Her stained shift billowed. In the ruff of hair under her arm tiny bubbles were trapped.

Funny thing was, I didn't feel anything. I just stood there looking at her, and I couldn't find a feeling anywhere in me.

I sloshed back to the shore. What now? I asked myself. If I went back to Sulis, Arthur would likely kill me. He'd say I'd helped her betray him. I *had* helped her. There was no life for me any more with Arthur's band. So maybe I'd try for Maelwas's country myself, I decided. My feet felt as if I'd come twenty miles through the rain and the tempest the night before. I reckoned I must be already halfway to Ynys Wydryn.

I clambered up a hill that chuckled and shone with little streams. I looked out from the top, where the gorse grew thick. And I saw Aquae Sulis, not two miles away. Smoke was going up from the cooking fires as if nothing had happened. Closer, where the woods crowded down to the floody pasture-land, the roofs of Myrddin's house shone in the sunlight.

I was too tired to think. Too tired for sure to start out again for the Summer Country. So I went instead down the steep, slippery sheep-tracks to beg the mercy of my old master.

XXXVII

Myrddin wasn't there. The curly-headed boy – his name was Cadwy – was alone in the place. He was looking for eggs out where the chickens scratched. When he saw me squelching towards him he knew who I was, and let me inside. Said his master was still in Aquae Sulis. I asked for dry clothes, and he found me some to wear while he washed my soiled, soaked dress. I sat by the fire in his own spare tunic and a pair of old trews, eating bread which I smeared with sooty white fat from a skillet that stood on the hearth. The boy watched me like I was a spirit sprung out of the flames. Even with my hair grown I looked boyish in those clothes. Whatever I'd learned of grace and girlishness, the night had wrung it out of me. Cadwy couldn't tell what I was.

Later, he showed me a bed to lie down on. And I slept there till that day was near gone.

Myrddin was back when I woke. I heard his voice outside, talking to Cadwy, and went out to find him climbing down off his old black horse. My own pony Dewi came across the paddock to nuzzle me, and I hugged him and laid my face against his and wished there was a human being in the world who loved me as well as he did.

Myrddin looked strange when he saw me standing there. I'd have said he felt shy, if I'd not known him better. He came towards me cautiously, watching my face.

"You told Arthur," I said.

Myrddin reached out towards me, but didn't touch. He said, "Stories were going about, that Gwenhwyfar had a lover. I had to put an end to it. It would have been bad for Arthur's reputation."

"You knew she'd go to Bedwyr last night," I said. "You sent word and told Arthur to ride home quick, and where to find them."

"Something had to be done," said Myrddin. "The kings of Britain will never let Arthur lead them against the Saxons if they are laughing behind his back about his wife." He looked old, I thought, and ill. Kept kneading at his arm, as if it had gone numb. He said, "You should have come with me last night."

"My mistress needed me," I said, to make him understand I wasn't his any more. I don't know if he did. The mention of my mistress distracted him. "You know where Gwenhwyfar is?" he asked.

"Dead," I said.

That made him curse. Not because he cared about Gwenhwyfar, of course. "I told Arthur he must spare her," he said.

"Wasn't Arthur's doing," I said. "She drowned herself."

Myrddin's eyes went past me to the hills, the steaming woods, looking for ways to make a story of it. "That might work. She tempted Bedwyr, betrayed Arthur, and then, in guilt and remorse – but that makes Arthur seem weak. And will Maelwas believe it?"

Cadwy was leading the horse away, with Dewi following. I went after Myrddin into the house.

By Myrddin's fire I heard the news from Sulis. How Medrawt had fled in the storm's confusion, and how the slaves he left behind said he'd been making for Ynys Wydryn, to lay his sword at Maelwas's feet. The story was spreading of how Arthur had made sacrifice of Bedwyr and given his head to the old gods at their sacred spring. Bishop Bedwin had preached to a crowd in the forum, saying the tempest had been punishment for Arthur's sins, and warning the people to throw down their tyrant before God sent worse punishments. Arthur had him beaten, and let his warriors help themselves to the treasures in his church.

"And that has made those who hate him hate him more," said Myrddin, not talking to me really, just letting his thoughts pour out in words. "And there is Cei. The trust that was between them has soured. Cei may be Arthur's half-brother, but he's uncle to Bedwyr and Medrawt too, and a friend to Bishop Bedwin, and he had a liking for Gwenhwyfar. He's still loyal, but it's a grudging loyalty now. Arthur's afraid that there are men in the war-band who will try to throw him down and set Cei up in his place."

"Cei would never betray Arthur," I said.

Myrddin glowered, ignoring me. "And Cei knows about every trick I've pulled. What if he tells people the truth about Caliburn, or the other tales I've built Arthur's power upon? What if he tells them about you?"

"Why not help Cei throw him down?" I said. "Cei'd be a better lord. Or do you love Arthur so bad you can't see that?"

"Oh, Cei'd be a good lord," said Myrddin sourly. "He'd keep Aquae Sulis fat and calm and prosperous, right up until the day the Saxon hordes come west and burn it. Cei means nothing. Arthur's the one. He has to be. All those stories that I've sent out into the world – do you think I can just whistle and they'll come running home to me like hounds? Arthur is our hope. He is the hope of all Britain. One day the other kings will rally to him and he'll lead them in a war that will. . ."

". . .drive the Saxons out of this island for ever," I said wearily. I'd heard that tune before. Believed it once. Now it sounded staler every time.

Myrddin wasn't listening to me. He said, "Cei's a problem. Can't be trusted. I was a fool to let him in upon my secrets. The one thing worse than an enemy is a friend turned false." He set down the cup he'd been drinking from and rubbed his arm. "I must find a way to be rid of him, before more blood is spilled. Send him away so there is time for all this to blow over. Yes. But how? What reason could there be?"

And he looked at me as if he was expecting me to tell him, but he wasn't. He'd have looked at the wall for an answer if I'd not been in the way.

*

Next day when I woke he'd gone again. It was just me and Cadwy, and Cadwy was so nervous of me that he left me well alone, and I had time to think. I wondered if Medrawt and his family had made it to Ynys Wydryn, and what sort of welcome he would get from old Maelwas. The storm had washed away many things, and made others clearer. I saw now that Maelwas had never honestly meant to give Arthur command over his war-bands. He'd just been playing for time, afraid of this arrogant bandit who'd set up camp in his borderlands. He would be glad of the news Medrawt would bring, of strife in Arthur's gang, and God's displeasure. He would maybe think the time was right to move against Arthur, and give the holding of Aquae Sulis to a better man.

Myrddin came home in the late afternoon, while I was tending to Dewi in the paddock. If he had been thinking about Maelwas it did not show in his face. As he let Cadwy help him down from his horse he was smiling the old, sly smile that I'd first seen when he showed me Caliburn all those years before. A smile of simple delight at his own cleverness. "Well, Myrddin has mended it, as Myrddin always does," he said. "I had Arthur gather all his men on the steps outside the church. Had him remind them how the Irishman who is our ally has been insulted by Cunomorus. Now we've humbled Calchvynydd we must ride to the Irishman's aid and help him punish Cunomorus before he grows still more ambitious and land-hungry."

I blinked. So much had happened those past few days that it seemed an age since the Irishman had ridden in to ask for Arthur's help. "I'd forgotten Cunomorus. . ."

Myrddin chuckled. "So had they. So had Arthur. But I remember. A leader should always keep a few spare enemies to hand. You never know when you might need a good, far-away war to take men's minds off troubles close to home. If we let Cunomorus get away with the Irishman's cattle today, what will he try tomorrow? He must be humbled before he grows any bolder. That's what I had Arthur tell them. Some of our warriors must ride west at once, to join with the Irishman's band. Of course, Arthur can't lead them. He and his riders are war-weary, travel-sore. Cei and his followers will go in their place. By the time they return all this trouble will be behind us. And some may not return at all."

"What if they won't go?"

Myrddin scowled at me. "Have you forgotten all you learned about the lives of men? Of course they'll go. They would look like cowards, else. Anyway, Arthur promised them a good fight, and a share of the booty. Said he wished he could go in their place, but he must stay and guard their homes for them against the traitor Medrawt. And I told them about all the treasures they will take from Cunomorus's hall. A herd of red cattle. A golden shield. A miraculous cauldron, which is never empty – a drink from it can heal all wounds. . ."

"And does Cunomorus really have those things?"

Myrddin shrugged. "Who knows? Maybe. I made it up. But the promise of plunder will cheer Cei's men on their way west. They leave at dawn."

I could see why Myrddin was so pleased with himself. Cei's men were those who'd been left in Aquae Sulis while Arthur was off fighting that summer. For the most

220

part they were men that Arthur couldn't quite trust; Valerius's former comrades, the sons of the old *ordo*, men not linked to him by blood or long companionship. The very men who might rather have his brother as their leader. Now, thanks to Myrddin's cunning, they were all to be sent out of the way for a month or more. They'd return weighed down with plunder, with coin and cattle and magic cauldrons maybe. Plenty of reasons to like Arthur better.

Later, when we'd eaten, and the boy was outside cleaning the plates, and I was thinking about my bed again, another thought came to me.

"Peredur. He's not going?"

"Long-Knife's boy? Of course. Didn't I say? Cei's taking every man who didn't ride with Arthur this summer past."

"But you can't send Peredur to a war! He's too. . ."

"Stupid? Can't help that, Gwyna. He's not Arthur's man. I heard it was he who went to warn Medrawt. Maybe he's not as foolish as he looks."

"But he is! I know it's hard to believe, but he is!"

"So you say. All I know is, I can't leave him in Aquae Sulis, to plot against Arthur."

I wondered if I should confess that it had been me who sent Peredur to warn Medrawt. But it wouldn't have made a difference.

I went to bed, but I couldn't sleep. I watched the light of the dying-down fire lap on the roof-beams, saffron-colour. I'd been thinking about Bedwyr and Gwenhwyfar so hard I'd half forgotten Peredur, and how his open, silly face once made my heart catch, and how he'd been when I first met him, dressed up as a maid. My mirror-boy. I couldn't bear the thought of him riding off to that war. Not even a real war, but one made up to serve Arthur's purposes, a needless, reasonless war, spun out of lies. Either he'd not come back at all, or he'd come back changed. He'd change the same way Bedwyr had. The last of his girlishness would be gone from him, and he'd be just a man like all the rest.

I slept, and dreamed of Gwenhwyfar walking into the lake. She cradled her wooden anchor like a child, vanishing into her own reflection.

When I woke, I knew very clear what I must do. It scared me, but not enough to turn me back.

Myrddin was snoring in his bed-place. The boy Cadwy was curled up by the hearth. He stirred a bit as I crept round him, but I said, "Sshh, sshhh," and he settled like a sleepy dog.

I still had Bedwyr's cloak. It had faded in the rain to a tired brown, and the strip Gwenhwyfar had torn off the bottom made it about the right length for me. I had Cadwy's tunic and breeks, and in Myrddin's oak chest I found my own old belt from when I was a boy. There was a white bloom of mildew on the leather, which came off like chalk-dust when I rubbed it with my thumb. I had no shoes except my ruined buskins, so I stole Myrddin's boots. And I stole a knife, and a leather bag.

Outside, in the dark, old Dewi was sleeping, head down, one hind hoof tilted against the turf. He woke with a soft whinny when I threw the saddle-cloth across him. Turned his head and nibbled up the hunk of bread I gave him, and seemed glad that we were off again upon our travels, he and I.

XXXVIII

In dripping woods close by the Sulis road, I stopped and waited for the dawn. As the light gathered, pools of flood-water showed like glass among the trees. I crouched by one and looked down at my reflection and cut my long hair with the knife. Not too short. I left it shoulder-length, the way Bedwyr had worn his, and tied it back with a string I found in my pocket. I washed my face in muddy water to darken my skin till the sun could darken it properly. Then I stuck the knife through my belt and got me up on Dewi's back again.

Myrddin had told me they'd be setting out at dawn, but I didn't wait to meet the war-band on the road. I remembered too well all the snags and delays that beset armies setting off to war: lame horses and snapped saddle-girths, things left behind that had to be hunted for. Men waking late, stupid from too much mead or wine the night before. The lingering goodbyes. Anyway, I wanted to meet them further on, where they would not just have to take my word that I was a young man.

I rode west through the woods, crossed the swollen river at Camlann-ford and came late that afternoon to a place called Din Branoc. I remembered it from my journey with Myrddin two summers before. We'd stopped a night there on our way to the Summer Country, but passed it by when we were coming home. People there might remember a boy who had gone west with Arthur's wizard, but not the girl he had brought back.

It had suffered in the storms. The hall slumped on its low rise amid the flooded fields like Noe's Ark wrecked upside-down on Ararat. Men of the household were sculling across the fields in wicker boats, rescuing stranded sheep from knolls and hummocks where they'd fled to escape the deluge. As I urged Dewi through the knee-deep water on the track I felt a knot of fright grow in my gut. These people wouldn't be in any mood to offer shelter to a stranger.

But they were glad of me. It did them good to have someone to tell about the terrors that had overtaken them. They pointed at their landslip-scarred hills and torn-down trees like men who had seen wonders, and watched my face while they told me of the storm, making sure I was astonished.

I did my best. My time with Myrddin had made a good actor of me. I pretended awe, and never let on that the disasters they were so proud of had happened just as bad or worse at Aquae Sulis, and every other place, probably. For all I know they're still talking of their great storm in Din Branoc.

And when they asked me who I was I said, "Gwyn.

Servant to Myrddin. Don't you remember me?" And they nodded and welcomed me again, and said how I'd grown, and never thought to notice that I'd grown into a girl.

"What news from Sulis?" they asked.

I wasn't sure, at first, what I should say. And then I was. That night, sitting with them on the dais-planks in their mud-floored hall, while wet clothes and bedding sent up a fog of steam about me in the fire's heat, I told them the story of Bedwyr and Gwenhwyfar.

It didn't come out quite as I'd expected. I set out with good intentions, and I meant to stay on the road of truth, but somewhere along the way I strayed. Maybe I'd learned too well from Myrddin. I made Bedwyr older and finer than he really was, and told all the usual tales about his feats in battle, glutting the ravens and killing nine hundred enemies and such stuff. And I made Gwenhwyfar younger, and more beautiful, and less selfish. What harm could that do? These people had never seen her. She'd been kind to me at the end. She tucked me up in Bedwyr's cloak before she went into the mere. It was the least thanks I could show, to make her young again.

I couldn't tell their story's ending, neither. The Arthur my listeners knew was Myrddin's Arthur: noble, wise, and brave. So when I came to the part where Arthur found the lovers out, I made him sorrowful instead of savage. And I let them get safe away. Safe down the storm-lit roads to Ynys Wydryn they went, my Bedwyr and my Gwenhwyfar.

After that, I could never quite believe I'd seen them

both dead. It seemed so much more likely that they were safe together in the Summer Country.

Morning brought Cei's war-band. Twenty riders with shields on their backs and swords at their waists, and twenty more reflected in the wet fields as they passed along the road. Not many, even if you counted the reflections, but the Irishman would be grateful for them, and when they combined with his band they'd be enough to give Cunomorus some trouble.

The headman of Din Branoc came out with me to meet them. "My lords!" he called, as he waded ahead of Dewi through the flood. "You are welcome! Welcome!" I thought he was going to tell them all about the storm, but instead he pointed to me and said, "Here's Myrddin's boy, come to meet you on the way."

Cei, reining in his horse, looked at me hard.

"Gwyn," I said. "I'm kinsman to Myrddin."

Cei nodded. There was a smile hidden somewhere down behind his eyes. "I remember you. I'd not thought to see you again. Any news of your sister, who was in Gwenhwyfar's household?"

"Gwyna. My half-sister."

Another nod. "She came safe out of all this?"

"I left her yesterday, at Myrddin's place. Myrddin sent me to ride with you. I know that country west of Isca, see. I can guide you."

"You're welcome then, boy, and I'm grateful to your master. I've not been near those hills since we took old Ban's hall. The time the sword rose from the water." The faintest trace of a wink. Then his face set hard, as if

227

thinking on the old times pained him. He looked past me, taking in the sodden buildings and the drowned fields. "We'll press on. These people don't need us adding to their troubles. Besides, the sooner we reach the Irishman's hills the sooner we can finish this."

The column of men started to move again. Someone was singing a song. The swaying tails of the horses gave off a sweetish smell of old dung. I rode Dewi up on to the track and joined them, and looked for Peredur.

XXXIX

We rode west through the wreck of autumn. These things I remember of that journey. The ringing of metal cooking pots as they swung from the packs of the baggage-mules. The slither-splash of red mud in the deep lanes. Rubbing the horses down at day's end, blanketing them against the cold, seeing to their fodder before we saw to our own, the chores of the horse-lines coming back to me fresh as if I'd never stopped being a boy. The soft munching sounds of hooves on wet hill-tracks. Ambling, tuneless songs. Apples and bramble-berries. The hard, ashy-tasting rounds of bread we baked over our fires. The long detours around flooded valleys, flooded roads, washed-out bridges.

The men grumbling. Why couldn't Arthur have left Cunomorus in peace till spring? Arthur had lost his luck. He couldn't even rule his own wife. They wished they had a better man to follow. They looked hopefully at Cei. His sandy head was bare in the sunshine, hooded in rain, and he kept his thoughts inside it.

I hung behind the others. My old pony Dewi was sturdy enough, but slow. Anyway, I didn't want them questioning me too much. Most of them were lads I didn't know, men from Sulis, relatives of the *ordo* and the big local land-owners. But there were a few who might remember Gwyn, and wonder what he'd been doing in the years since he'd ridden with Arthur's boys.

Riding alone, listening to snatches of their banter blowing back to me on the breeze, I got to missing my life among the girls. I never thought I would, and never a day went by I didn't feel glad to be up on a horse and going somewhere instead of trapped indoors, but I wished I'd had Celemon there to tell some of my inward thoughts to. Girls tell each other things, in honest whispers, when the night is drawing on. Boys just brag.

Peredur was the only one I truly wanted to talk to, and he kept clear of me. He remembered me, I could tell, but he looked as if he hoped I didn't know him. He'd had sense enough to keep quiet about his girlish upbringing, and I suppose he was afraid I'd tell the others of it.

By night, around the campfires, or in the little shabby halls we stopped at, I would tell stories. Cei asked me to. "You're Myrddin's boy," he said. "Tell us some of your master's tales to make us forget our troubles and our poor cold toes."

Truth be told, it *was* cold, and I was as much in need of comfort as the rest. So I pitched my voice as deep as I could and paced my words to the tramp of the sentries patrolling at the edges of the firelight, and told them stories. I gave them old tales at first: the Green Man, and the Chief of the Giants. But slowly I got bolder. They all knew what had become of Bedwyr, but they'd not heard anything of Gwenhwyfar since the storm began. So I told them how she'd got away to Ynys Wydryn, with Medrawt. And though I couldn't tell them she'd been young, the way I had with folk who'd never known her, I made her kind and wronged enough that they started to think she had been beautiful, and not so old as they had thought. Sometimes, in the firelight, on one face or another, I'd see tears running down.

Peredur was one of the tearful ones. He never tried to hide what he was feeling, the way the others had all learned to. Once he came to me after a story and hugged me and thanked me for telling it. Looked at me strange when he'd said it, and said shyly, "You came to my home once, I think."

"That was me. We tricked old Porroc, you and I. You made a fair angel."

The smile lit up his face. "I thought it was you! I wasn't sure. . . You look so like that girl Gwyna. . ."

"My half-sister," I said quickly. The old lie came so natural to me now it felt like truth. "She told me she'd met you."

"She was there in the water-meadow the day I came to Aquae Sulis. It was she who gave me this sword, after I killed the red man. . ." His smile grew worried. "You didn't tell her about how I used to be before?"

"The dress? The hair?"

"I'd never live it down."

"It's safe with me," I said

He laughed. "I've never forgot that day! That was the

first time I'd seen men, real men. I was so jealous of you, riding off with Arthur. . ."

"And the look on Porroc's face when we. . ."

"I'd always known there was something not right about him, but till you came I couldn't see what a liar and a leech he was. . ."

And he sat by the dying fire with me while the others slept, and told me all the things that had happened to him since, which I've already told to you. It made me feel shamed, as you'll have guessed, to learn all the things my game with the angel led to. And as I sat listening, I could not help thinking what it would be like to hold Peredur's narrow face between my two hands, and say the sort of things to him that I'd heard Gwenhwyfar tell Bedwyr. To treasure him. I reckoned it was my bad luck that I could only come close to him by turning myself back into a boy.

We kept to the old road till we were near Isca, then veered north. Isca was loyal to Maelwas, and Maelwas might not look friendly on Arthur's gang any more.

"King Maelwas will want a new man to hold Aquae Sulis for him," said one of Cei's captains, Dunocatus. We were resting on a hillside-road, the smoke of Isca filling its wet valley a few miles south, the big river silver beyond. The horses cropped the grass with steady tearing sounds. Cei stared off westward at the Irishman's stony moors and said nothing.

"If a good Christian man was to challenge Arthur, and throw him down, and take his place, Maelwas might be glad of it," Dunocatus insisted. Other men, who felt the same but hadn't had the courage to say it, watched hungrily for Cei's reaction.

"Why are we fighting for the Irishman against Cunomorus?" Dunocatus asked loudly. "Why do we not ride back to Sulis and fight for Cei against Arthur?"

Cei turned and knocked him down into the grass and kicked him hard a few times and strode off, leaving him groaning there. "Arthur is my brother!" he yelled over his shoulder as he climbed back on to his horse. "We have promised to help the Irishman. Do you want your sons and your sons' sons to hear how you hadn't the stomach for that fight?"

We rode on, through steep-walled, thick-wooded valleys. Up the long shoulder of the moor we went, the road dwindling to a peat-track, climbing through knotted woods. Mossy boulders lay crowded between the trees, like sleeping beasts with thick, green fur. When we came up out of the trees at last there was nothing to see but the hills, folded one behind the next, all wrapped in fog and dragons'-smoke.

Cei had me ride with him up on to a hill-top where a great mass of stones stood, hooting and wuthering as the wind ripped round them. "You know this country," he said.

I knew a few of the high hills westward, or thought I did. I did my best. "The Irishman's place is over that way, where the moor slopes down towards Kernyw. Just north of here is Ban's hall. The river. . ."

"Your water-home, lake-lady," said Cei. He looked at

me wryly. "I've thought of that day often. What Myrddin had you do. It's a strange life he's led you."

I stared at the wind stirring Dewi's mane. I'd always known Cei knew my secret, but it still made me feel naked to be talking of it. I said, "I wish he'd let me be sometimes. Why didn't he? Why did he come back for me, that day at the waterfall?"

"He loves you," said Cei. "He never had children of his own. He had you instead."

"No! He sent me away. Made me be a girl again and gave me to Gwenhwyfar."

"He found you a comfortable living-place, one that might put you in the path of a good husband, just as I did for Celemon. The old man loves you, girl. Surely you can see that."

He wheeled his horse and rode back to the waiting column, shouting, "We'll camp here this night. Tomorrow we feast with the Irishman!" I was left on the hill-top with my thoughts. Cei had been Myrddin's friend, and should know what Myrddin thought. But I couldn't believe Myrddin loved me as a daughter. I couldn't believe Myrddin loved anyone, except maybe himself.

The naked feeling stayed with me as I went back down the hill. I began to feel that someone was watching me, out among the rocks and tussock-grass. But we had no enemies here. Cunomorus's lands were two days' ride away. This was the Irishman's country, and tomorrow we would reach his hall, and make ready for our raid into Kernyw. I shook myself to try to get rid of the feeling, and I told myself that men must always feel like that when they knew there was a fight coming.

That night around the fire the others wanted tales of battles won, and enemies cast down. They wanted to hear again about the treasure that would be waiting for them in Cunomorus's stronghold.

I wasn't sure what to tell them. If I promised them gold drinking cups or a jewelled throne, what would they say when they looted Cunomorus's hall and didn't find such things? Then the stories I'd spun might twist around like snakes to bite me.

"What about his magic cauldron?" said one, a man called Bodfan. "Myrddin told us once about a cauldron that was never empty, and in this cauldron every man could find the food he most wanted to eat, and the drink he most wanted to drink."

I nodded warily. If Bodfan hoped to find a thing like that anywhere outside a story, he was in for a disappointment. But Myrddin had promised us a cauldron, hadn't he? I said, "Cunomorus's cauldron's not like that."

"Like what, then?" someone asked.

"Shall I tell you the story of it?"

"Yes, yes," they said.

I hesitated, as if I was gathering my memories of the tale. Really I was stitching something new together out of scraps of other tales I'd heard.

"Back in the long-ago years," I said, "Cunomorus's grandfather was the finest of the warriors of the island of Britain. Tewdric was his name. And he came raiding with his war-band into these very hills."

(My listeners nod and mutter approval at this Tewdric's courage. A couple look round, as if they expect to see the ghosts of his war-band still sweeping across the moor. They'll be lucky. I just made him up.)

"Now in these hills are many lakes, and many rivers, and many pools of still, clear water, and the lady of the waters, the lake-woman herself, she looked out of one of them one day and saw Tewdric riding by and thought how handsome he looked, and how fine, and young, and strong, and a great admiration was in her heart for him.

"And one day, while Tewdric's men were hard pressed by their enemies, Tewdric was wounded, and parted from his band. Lost and alone, he wandered in the mazes of the woods, until hope deserted him, and he lay him down to die among the roots of a great thick oak which grew upon a lake-shore. But the blood of Tewdric's wounds fell into the lake, and the redness of it stained the clear waters until the lake-lady herself saw it, from the windows of her hall down in the depths, and she came up and found Tewdric laid there.

"Now the lake-lady thought it a very pitiful thing that such a fine young man should be left to die, so young and all alone, still in the flower of his beauty. So from her hall beneath the waters she brought this cauldron. . ."

(I spread my hands and curve them, like I'm holding the curved sides of a vessel.)

"A fine thing it was, made of beaten gold, with knots and swirls and fish and men and serpents wrought upon it. And the lake-lady knelt beside Tewdric where he lay, and told him to drink from it, and he would be healed. And he drank, and the pain of his wounds went from him, and his torn flesh grew whole again, and his eyes were made bright, and up he sprang. But the lake-lady had returned already to the waters, and whether she took the cauldron with her, or whether she left it and Tewdric took it home to his hall, I do not know."

My listeners nodded wisely. All of them were afraid of the wounds that might be waiting for them in the days to come. Now they had the hope of the healing cauldron to hold on to. "The lady of the waters has her favourites," I heard a man say. "Bedwyr was one. He saw her at the old springs once. He made a gift to her. That's why our luck turned sour when Arthur killed him."

They tugged their cloaks around themselves and settled on the grass to sleep. The sentries paced beyond the fringes of the firelight. A mule whickered, down in the horse-lines. I lay down too, pleased with the story I'd invented, and thinking already of ways I might better it when I told it next.

In the dark around our camp, all the gorse-clumps looked like armed men crouching.

XL

I come awake at first light surrounded by raw-throated shouts. "Attack!" "It's Cunomorus!" Scramble up, and fall again, still tangled in my cloak. Fall just in time, because arrows are winging out of the gorse on the hillside, whistling like curlews as they cut the air above me. Dunocatus catches one in his throat and curls round it, gargling. He topples into the embers of the fire, throwing up sparks and wood-ash. Other men are on their feet, running to and fro. In this dimsey-light I can't tell who are my friends and who're not. They are all shouting, and the arrows chirr among them, and sometimes someone falls. "The horses! The horses!" someone yells. There is a smell of burning hair. I get up again, groping for the knife in my belt. I run past our dead sentries, towards the horse-lines. Dark shapes spill like ghosts between the frightened, stamping beasts, cutting their tethers. Some horses are free already, running. Cei's bare-headed, bellowing at us to form a shield-wall round him. Then he's down on his knees, dropping forwards, a spear-shaft between his shoulders, and the man who'd stuck it there wrenching it free and pounding it down again and again, as if he's churning butter.

I know that spearman. I know his black spade of a beard, even in this light. The Irishman.

Groggy with betrayal, I blunder on. "Peredur! Peredur!" I'm shouting, and I trip over someone, and it's him.

He's down on his side, curled up, whimpering with fright and pain. One of those arrows is stuck through his shoulder. He turns a white face to me, eyes filled up with fear. "It hurts," is all he says.

Round us, the battle is falling apart into a dozen furious little fights. Screams, and smithy sounds. The Irishman's men yelling their wild, shrill war-shouts. Freed horses flick past us, trembling the ground, raining clods of earth on us. I can't think. I can't even breathe. Then I remember the thing I do best at times like this. I grab Peredur under his arms, and start to pull him downhill.

Not far from the campsite the gorse humps up thick. Peredur's heavy but the slope of the hill helps, and he struggles with his legs, half walking. The gorse drags sharp combs through my hair. The sounds of battle dim, but not enough. I go down on all fours. Gorse is thick in the crown, but underneath it's all woody stems, and bare ground brown with fallen needles. I shove and tug Peredur into a basket of twisty trunks. The wind hisses through the needles above us. A man is screaming smashed-bone screams away up the hill. Below us in the dark I hear the clatter of water.

I lie on top of Peredur. His heart hammers at my breastbone. His every breath comes out as a little sob of hurt. I cram my hand across his mouth and listen hard. Something rackets through dry bracken a few yards off across the steep curve of the hill. A loose horse, or a friend, or a foe-man who saw me creep away and has come hunting me? I lie quiet. My hip bones press against Peredur's. His blood is soaking through my tunic. I drop my head next to his and say into his ear, "Shhhh. Shhhhh."

Nothing moves. All is quiet. Whoever it was in the bracken has gone. We are alive.

We lay there a long time, till the sky above the gorse turned cheerless grey. Then, half walking, half sliding, we made our way down to the stream, and a pool under some alders where I struggled him out of his filthy tunic. I broke off the arrow's flight-feathers and pinched the smeared, shiny point which poked out of his back. He fainted when I pulled it through him. It had made a bruised hole under his collarbone, a red gash behind his shoulder blade. I washed the wounds with stream water. I pressed pads of moss over them, and ripped strips from my shirt to bind the moss in place.

I didn't want to have to look after him. It wasn't so long since I'd been forced to look after Gwenhwyfar, and I remembered how happily *that* had ended.

"I was afraid," Peredur kept saying, when he woke.

He was white and shaky. Too ashamed to meet my eye. "We ran away, Gwyn. We shouldn't have run. It was womanish."

"It's natural," I tried telling him. "You couldn't have fought them. They were too many. They caught us by surprise."

Of course he didn't believe me. He'd bathed too long in stories of heroes and battles. In the stories, running away is the worst disgrace. If ever anyone told the story of that morning's fight, Peredur and Gwyn would be remembered as cowards, who'd run like women. And being a coward is worse than being dead.

"Who were they?" he asked. "Cunomorus's war-band?"

"It was the Irishman. We were betrayed. He was waiting for us."

"But why?"

I hadn't an answer. I couldn't imagine. How could it profit the Irishman to murder Cei? "Maybe he means to oust Arthur, and his tale about strife with Cunomorus was just a trap to bring us here. Maybe he's gone over to Cunomorus's side himself. Or maybe Maelwas set him on us, to weaken Arthur."

"And what of the others? Are we all that's left?"

"We can't be. The others will be somewhere around. We'll find them. . ."

"I don't want to. They'll know we were cowards. We ran away."

I tied his bandages tight, but not too tight, the way Myrddin had taught me when we were tending to the war-band's wounds back in my boyhood. I thought there was enough blood left inside of him to keep him alive. But I kept thinking of something Myrddin had told me. When someone no longer wants to live, it's beyond any earthly doctoring to save them.

XLI

Downstream I found an old building. Just a heap of stones really. Two low walls standing, a wedge of sheltered grass between them, roofed with holly-trees. It was not a good hiding place, for close by it the stream fell whitely into a narrow black pool, and the noise of the water would drown out the sounds of enemies creeping close. But I found nothing better, so that evening I moved Peredur into it. At least it was out of earshot of the crows at the battle-place.

Peredur was weak and feverish, inclined to sleep. Bad dreams kept waking him, and he would jerk his eyes open and say, "I was so afraid. I should have stayed a girl."

So should I, I thought. I hushed him, and soaked my neck-cloth in stream-water and bathed his face with it. By morning he was worse. Some ailment was working in him, and I was afraid he hadn't the strength to fight it. It was the shock, I think, as much as the wound itself. Since that day Myrddin had come to his hall Peredur had lived in stories. He'd expected war to be the way it was in stories: banners and glory and brave deeds. He'd not expected defeat, or pain, or fear.

I sat with him all through that day. I tried telling him that there might be other endings for his story. Maybe this was just a setback. Something to make the listeners gasp and draw closer to the storyteller and think, "It cannot end like this!" before the hero gathered himself up and went on to triumph after all. "You'll get well soon. Then we'll go and fight Cunomorus, just the two of us, if we must. Or creep into his hall by stealth, like Odysseus at Troy, and steal some plunder from him that you can take back as tribute to Arthur."

Peredur smiled. "The lake-lady's cauldron," he said. "That will heal me."

"Of course it will," I said.

And then I thought, why shouldn't it? He'd *have* to find the strength to live if he had something like that to carry home to Arthur. Something wonderful. A new gift from the otherworld.

"Sleep, and be strong," I told him. "Tonight I'll go and find where the others are. Where *we* are, come to that."

The day was cold. I risked a little fire, praying that its smoke wouldn't show among the moor mists. There were speckled brown fish in the pool of the stream and I leaned over the water until one came near enough and I snatched it out. I slit its belly with my knife and cooked it in hot ashes at the fire's edge. I fed Peredur on baked fish and brambles under the pinkish smears of the evening sky. Afterwards, he slept, and I piled bracken over him to keep him warm and then scattered wet earth on the fire.

Then I left him there and climbed back up the hill, not knowing if he'd be alive or dead when I came back.

 XLII

I climbed past the battle-place. The heap of our dead was so high it made me think Peredur had been right, and none of the others had escaped alive. I told myself to stay calm, but the thought of ghosts got inside my head, and set me running, fearful that dead men were running behind me, angry at me for being still alive. I imagined cold hands reaching out to snatch me by the hair. That's the trouble with this story-telling life. Stories start creeping into your head unbidden, and not all of them are good.

By the time I stopped myself, a lopsided moon had come out from behind the clouds. It showed me the road we had been riding on the day before. Hills whose shapes I knew stood black against moonlit clouds. I followed the road, down through trees, off the moor's edge. An eye of fire winked at me. Ban's hall. The woods, bare-branched, making the hillside below it bristle like a hog's back. Beneath it, out of sight among the riverside trees, my old home. I left the road and pushed through cages of young birch towards the smell of the river.

Halfway there, a noise in the underbrush brought me up short. A rippling shiver, a scraping metal sound like a dragon unwinding itself, ready to strike.

I drop down in the moon-shadows. The wood-floor between the birches is made of rocks and water. Big tumbled boulders, and little pools between. Twigs and windfall branches everywhere, but all too wet to crack, thank Christ, as I creep crabwise to a place where I can see bare sky between the branches.

A snort. A white smouldering of smoke in the dark and a huge head up-reared, black as a raised hammer on that moony sky. My heart stops, and my bladder empties, drizzling warm piss down my legs into the puddle I'm crouched in. But then, as the thing swings towards me and shambles into a spill of moonshine, I let out my pent breath. I even manage a shuddery laugh.

For it's my own Dewi. Of course, the Irishman's boys who ran off the rest of our horses wouldn't have wanted a stocky old plodder like him. His dangling harness drags over another rock, making that dragony clitter and chink that had sounded so fearful a half-minute before. But I'm not scared now. "Dewi," I say, and I go forward gently, shushing and calming him, hands out to catch his long head, rubbing his nose, laying my face against his face. It's a stroke of good luck, plain and simple, but in my nervy state it's hard not to see it as more. Maybe it's a sign that God or the lake-lady is looking after me, and has sent Dewi into my way.

I lead him to a place where the trees grow dense. Knot

his broken reins around a birch-bole. Whisper goodbye and promise I'll be back soon. Then, feeling braver and luckier than before, I go fast as I can to the river. Fight my way out of the clutch of the birches a quarter-mile shy of the homestead I was birthed in.

My first idea, when I left Peredur, was to climb to the hall on the hill-top. My lady Nonnita has a bowl there, which I filled often and often for her with water from the spring, and sprinkled rose-petals in for her to wash herself. An old, gold bowl from Rome or Syria or somewhere fine like that, leopards and hares chasing round its rim. Peredur would easily believe a bowl like that was the lake-lady's magic cauldron, and even if he didn't, it would be fine tribute to carry home to Arthur.

But now I'm here, my mind's changed. My fright on the hillside and my meeting with Dewi have left me feeling thin on strength. The hill looks steep, and at the top there's a ditch and a rampart and a wall of logs to get through before I can even start creeping into the hall to find Nonnita's bowl. I'm not Odysseus. I decide to set my aim on something I can maybe reach.

I cross the first big field. Cattle stand sleeping, hairy backs steaming in the night cold, breath smelling of sweet grass. Over the turf wall into the yard. Pigs snuffling in their enclosure. The dwelling-place quiet under its loaf of thatch. Moonlight pales the crossed paws of a dog asleep in its kennel by the door. I creep round to the back, to the place where the spring purls up. Good-luck offerings are balanced on the stones around it, to show the people here aren't yet so Christian they're ready to forget the older gods. And next to the spring, just where it stood in my childhood, a wooden cup, waiting there ready for any weary one who needs a drink. I pick it up. It's carved from cherry-wood, worn smooth by many hands.

I stuff it inside my tunic. At the front of the house the dog starts to bark, woken by some small sound I've made. But I'm over the wall, running along the field-boundary, into the eaves of the wood where the soot-black shadows lie beneath the trees like hides pegged out to dry in the moonlight.

Peredur slept. Fevery dreams of home drifted inside his head like smoke. The arrow-wound in his shoulder was a sick throbbing. Sometimes he thought Gwyn was with him, and sometimes he remembered that Gwyn had gone. He hoped he would come back soon. He was afraid, alone here. The bracken rustled and the stream belled. The night wind whispered words he couldn't catch.

Then, in the grey of early morning, he came dimly awake. He was not alone.

She stood on the far side of the little fire that Gwyn had made the day before. She was quite naked, and her limbs and her body were white as milk against the dull rusty colours of the autumn bracken. Behind her the hillsides were ghostly with mist, and she herself seemed ghostly, her shape wavering in the shimmer of heat from the smouldering fire. Sometimes the thin trickle of smoke veiled her completely.

Peredur started to move, to pull himself upright. He

tried to remember his prayers, but his mind was empty. Pain poked through his shoulder and his chest like another arrow hitting.

She came towards him. Her white body dripped riverwater. Her face was half hidden by the hanging-down strands of her wet hair, but he felt he knew her and he was suddenly not scared.

In her hands she held a little bowl. Just a cup, really. Made of wood. Dark, and much used. Clear water filled it to the brim. He held his breath as she crouched in front of him. The water in the cup was a trembling oval of light. He glanced past it at her white breasts, her nipples dark against the white, like old coins. He started to raise his eyes to her face, but she pushed the cup towards him and said, "Drink from the cup, and you will be healed."

So he drank. The water was cold going down. The rim of the cup jarred against his teeth. It trembled with the steady trembling of the hands that held it.

"Shut your eyes," she said.

He didn't want to. He wanted to look at her some more. But he knew from stories that the creatures of the otherworld are fickle. If he didn't obey she might turn him into an owl or a log. He shut his eyes tight.

Her wet hair tickled his face. Her cool mouth touched his. He heard her shivery breath; felt it against his face.

Nothing else. The bracken rustled. He opened one eye. She was gone. On the grass at his side lay the empty cup.

Peredur stood up. He was giddy and his wound seared him, but he didn't care. He stumbled through

251

the bracken and looked down into the stream. There was a deep pool overhung with trees. She crouched at the edge among mossy rocks, and though he called out she did not look at him. Just tilted forward and went in with a splash. He saw the white shape of her flatten and dim as she went down deep. Autumn leaves were scattered on the water. The leaves bobbed on the ripples that she'd made. They turned like fish, beneath the surface. Red-golden beech leaves and the paler leaves of oak. Peredur waited and waited, thinking that she'd come up for air. But she did not come up.

At last a noise behind him made him turn. There was Gwyn, coming down a path behind the old shelter, leading Dewi.

"Gwyn!" he shouted. "Gwyn!" Crashing through the bracken, forgetful of his pain. Waving. "Gwyn! She was here! The lake-woman! She was beautiful! She. . ."

"You've been dreaming." Gwyn was looking oddly at him. A flush of colour on that flat, honest face. A straggle of dew-damp hair hanging down from under his felt cap.

"No, no," said Peredur, eager to share the good news. He snatched up the cup. "Look! Look! She left this! The water in it, Gwyn, it tasted better than wine. It made me better, Gwyn. I feel strong again!"

He swayed, light-headed. Gwyn dropped the pony's reins and ran to catch him as he fell. He had been going to tell Gwyn about the lake-woman's kiss, but, falling, he decided not to. It would be his secret. He sat in the wet grass, laughing. "It wasn't like you said, Gwyn. It wasn't a golden cauldron. Just a wooden cup."

And Gwyn shrugged and said, "Well, you can't believe everything you hear in stories."

XLIV

It was only river water, really.

I was afraid he'd guess. I thought he'd think back to Saint Porroc's miracle and guess his lake-lady was only me, up to my old tricks again. I planned to leave the cup upon a river stone, and work out a way for him to find it there.

But when I got back to the ruin before dawn I found him sleeping, a little feverish still, and I thought he'd be weak and dreamy enough when he woke to believe whatever I wanted him to. So I tethered Dewi in a holly-clump uphill, and left my clothes there too. Crept to the stream and ducked under water. My hair would look longer and straighter and darker wet. I combed it with my fingers, tugging it forward to hide my face. There wasn't enough to really hide behind, but I wasn't worried. I had spent enough time around boys to know it wouldn't be my face he'd be looking at.

The dawn air was chill on my wet skin. I had gathered some birch bark and some of the thin red twigs from the branches' tips, and I stooped and cast them on the half-dead fire without waking him. Added some wet oak leaves to make a smoulder. I put the fire between myself and him. The wind blew the thin smoke in his face and he woke.

"Drink from the cup, and you will be healed." I whispered it, so he wouldn't know my voice. And when he'd drunk I made him shut his eyes and left quick as I could. I hadn't planned on him coming after me, but I was glad to see he had enough life in him, even if it did mean I had to take another bath in that corpse-cold stream. From under the water I could see him, all ripply-looking, black against the sky. I let the water pull me away from him. Branches hid me as I slipped down into the next pool, and the next, and then I was out and haring round between the trees to find the place where I'd left my clothes and Dewi.

As for the kiss, you can't blame me for that, can you? He was so lovely, and so easy to fool. Sitting there with his eyes shut, all surprised. Just a quick warm touch of our mouths together, over in a heartbeat, but I felt glad to have the memory of it.

All the way back to Sulis he talked of nothing but the lake-woman. And every time he spoke of her she grew more beautiful, and her speech to him grew prettier. He wasn't lying. He really thought he remembered her dark blue eyes and her lips as red as rowan berries. Sometimes he filled the wooden cup at a spring or a well, but the water never tasted as good as the water *she* had filled it with.

I tried telling him my own tale; how I'd found Dewi wandering in the woods. But it couldn't compete with his miracle.

We found our way home along back-roads. Down drift-lanes and sheep-paths and half-forgotten tracks through the deep woods. Slow going, mostly, for the ways were poor, and Peredur still weak. His wound hurt him, and his fever rose and fell but never quite left him. I made him ride, and trudged along at Dewi's side until my feet wore through the bottoms of my boots. I listened out always for the Irishman's riders coming after us, but they never did. Sometimes we passed small settlements where the men looked slantwise at us, but we had knives in our belts and nothing else worth stealing, and they let us go by.

Around first frost we crossed into Arthur's territory, and reached Din Branoc. The people were surprised to see me back, with only one companion. I asked if any others from Cei's war-band had passed that way, and they just stared. Save me and Peredur, none had returned from the Irishman's hills. The only traveller they'd seen since I stopped there was a messenger from the Irishman himself, who passed through like thunder, pausing just long enough to ask the way to Aquae Sulis.

"We offered him shelter," said the headman, as he welcomed us to his fireside, "but he would not stop. Said he was carrying news Arthur would be glad to hear. Said he'd eat well in Sulis that night."

That threw me. What word could the Irishman have sent that Arthur would be glad of? I wondered for a moment if Cei was alive after all, and the Irishman wanted Arthur to pay ransom for him. But my own eyes had seen the Irishman kill Cei. His messenger would not have been so sure of a welcome at Arthur's fireside if the message he had carried was only, "Your brother and his companions are all dead."

Would he?

I tried to think like Myrddin, remembering the reasons he had given for sending Cei and Cei's closest followers west. Some may not return at all, he'd said. As if that was a good thing.

So wouldn't it be an even better thing if none returned?

I imagined a messenger leaving Aquae Sulis, two days after Bedwyr died. Speeding west, outpacing Cei's warband. One of Arthur's trusted companions, Owain or Gwri, with a message from Arthur for the Irishman. "Twenty warriors are riding to your hall. Meet them on the road. Kill them all."

I told myself I was wrong. I told myself I'd lived too long with Myrddin, and it had made me see tricks where there were none. But I still could think of no other reason for the Irishman's messenger to be riding up to Arthur's hall.

And if I was right, and Cei and his men had been meant to die in the Irishman's hills, what would Arthur make of me and Peredur coming home, with our tale of wonder and our wooden cup? We'd be dead within a day, I reckoned. Arthur would have us snuffed out, for fear we knew the truth about the others.

While I stood there, silent, thinking those thoughts,

Peredur had fetched the cup out. The men of Din Branoc passed it around reverently while he told them how he came by it. "It's a sign from the lady of the waters. Just like the sword she gave him. She's on his side still. She gave me this cup, and I'll give it to Arthur."

"May it change his luck," said the headman, shaking his head. "Arthur's fortune's turned foul. A score or more of his companions have sneaked off to join Medrawt."

"Medrawt's raising himself an army down in the Summer Country," another said. "We heard Maelwas has promised him lordship of Aquae Sulis if he'll rid the place of Arthur."

"What about Myrddin?" I asked. "What news of him?"

The men looked sour. I saw a couple cross themselves at the mention of Myrddin's name. One said, "That old heathen."

"Myrddin was took bad, a month back or more," said the headman, and leaned over to spit into the fire.

"There was a girl at his place," explained one of the others, pleased to be sharing good gossip with one who'd not heard it yet. "She was some kinswoman of his, who'd been Gwenhwyfar's handmaiden, and after Gwenhwyfar ran off she got took in by Myrddin. I reckon she must have turned his head, for when she left him he fell down in a fit, and now he can't walk nor talk. He keeps to that place of his, with just a boy to look after him."

"Nothing so foolish as an old man running after a girl," said the headman.

"She enchanted him's what I heard," put in another man. "She wove spells round him to make him love her, so she could learn his secrets."

I let them talk. It was strange, meeting my story-self in their tales. How much of what they'd said was true? Was Myrddin really ailing? If he was, it was no more than he deserved. Yet I felt troubled at the thought of him sick, and none but the boy Cadwy to look after him. And I thought, if I could see him, talk to him, he'd tell me whether what I feared was true, and whether it would be safe or not for Peredur to go back to Sulis.

Lulled by the voices and the fire's warmth Peredur fell asleep, leaning against me, his head on my shoulder. I lowered him gently on to the straw-covered boards, and brushed away a strand of hair that had fallen across his angel face. His brow was hot. His fever was worse again.

"Can you care for him?" I asked the headman. "He needs food and warmth and shelter till he's mended."

The headman nodded, the others too. They were good people. The headman's wife, who'd sat silent till then, said, "I'll nurse him. You've done your best, but nursing's woman's work."

"You leaving us, Gwyn?" someone asked, as I stood and pulled my cloak about me.

I nodded; told them I'd be back in a day or so with a horse for Peredur and not to let him leave before I came.

"It's an ill night for travelling," the headman said. "Snow on the way, maybe."

"Myrddin's my kin," I said. "If he's sick, I must go to him."

And if he isn't sick, I thought, going out into the cold to saddle Dewi, I shall have some hard things to say to him.

XLV

I reached my master's house soon after sunrise. Tethered Dewi outside in the slanting, orange light. Quiet as a grave it felt, as I pushed in past the dangling talismans. Dead birds and knotted twine. An armour of hoar-frost on everything. When I spoke into the silence my breath made steam in the cold air.

"Master?"

The boy Cadwy was curled on the floor by the embers of the kitchen fire. I left him sleeping and went into Myrddin's bed-space. A sickroom stink came out at me as I lifted the curtain at the doorway. My nose told me the story I'd heard at Din Branoc was true, even before my eyes got used to the curtained gloom and I made out Myrddin lying on the bed.

I couldn't believe a man could have shrunk so, aged so, in the time I'd been away. I felt like the prince in the story, the one who sails away to see the Blessed Isles, and comes home after a month at sea to find a hundred years have passed on land and everyone he knows is gone to bones and ashes.

Myrddin wasn't quite a corpse yet. He looked like one, shrunk as he was, yellowish, with his mouth twisted sideways and his eyes sunk deep. But he was breathing, and when I leaned closer he grunted and his eyes came open.

I don't think he knew me. I pulled off my cap, let my dead-bracken hair hang down. "It's me, master."

He frowned. His breath came harsh and rusty. It sounded like fate sawing at the thread of his life with a blunt knife. When he spoke, he didn't make words, just grunts and growlings. It took me a while to understand that he was trying to say my name. One hand flapped on top of his blankets, trying to reach for me. The angry questions I'd been saving up for him all night drained out of me and I sat down on the edge of the bed and pressed his hand against my face.

"Gwyna?" he asked.

Cadwy appeared in the doorway, his hair flat on one side where he'd lain pressed against the warm tiles by the fire.

"It's just me," I said. "Gwyna. I'm back."

I washed Myrddin's blankets and changed the straw in his mattress. With Cadwy's help I scrubbed down the walls of his chamber, trying to get rid of that stale sickroom smell. I fed him bread softened in goat's milk. The day deepened round us, fat snowflakes dithering past the windows like goose-down. Myrddin talked, and slowly I learned to fish words out of the badgery growls and owlish hoots he made.

He said, "That fool Arthur came here. Said I should go into Sulis, to the surgeons' care. As if I'd trust those butchers, bleeding and poisoning me."

He said, "Arthur wanted some trick that would defeat Medrawt. I told him I'm too old for tricks. No more tricks. When the time comes, he'll have to fight Medrawt the old way."

He said, "Ah, but you remember the sword, Gwyna? The sword from the water. That was a thing! What a tale!"

It was time to be a girl again. I itched to be gone, to ride back to Peredur. But Peredur would be safe at Din Branoc, and someone had to nurse the old man. Cadwy had done his best, but nursing is woman's work.

I looked in the chest I'd found my man's gear in, and there I found my old dress laid, pressed between sheets of linen and sprinkled with dried lavender.

"Master done that," said Cadwy, watching me take it out and hold it up against myself. "That morning we woke up and you were gone, he went chasing off to Sulis to bring you home. When he came back, it was liked he'd aged ten years. He said you'd not been seen there. Said you'd ridden to join Cei's war-band, and would be killed for sure. Said he had to go after you. Said it would be his fault if you died. He sent me outside to saddle his horse, and set about folding up your things neat. When I came back in I found him lying on the floor there by the chest. All he could say was Gwyna at first. Not even that very clear."

263

I felt like I was dreaming. Had Myrddin really cared about me so much my running off could strike him dumb and cripple him? Or had he just been angry that I'd disobeyed him? It was easier to believe that. But when I sat by him he didn't seem angry. He held my hand and said, "Gwyna."

All that night and the next and the one after I sat by Myrddin's bed. Sometimes he slept, but mostly he talked. He talked and I listened. By the end, his voice was almost the last thing left of him.

"You shouldn't have gone with them, Gwyna. When I thought of you riding off with Cei's band, and death waiting for you in the hills, something in me broke."

I didn't like that. What did he expect? Pity? I'd used up all my pity on Cei and Gwenhwyfar and Bedwyr. I pushed myself backwards, away from the stench of his breath. "And how did you know death was waiting for me? You'd had Arthur tell the Irishman to betray us, that's how!"

Myrddin turned his head a little, looking at me. "You were always sharp, Gwyn."

"Not sharp enough, or I'd have guessed your plan and warned Cei what he was riding to!" My shadow was huge on the wall behind his bed. It raised its fists, like it was getting ready to smash his eggshell skull.

He said, "It had to be done. Men were talking of Cei as a rival to Arthur. He had to be removed. At least if the Irishman did it Arthur wouldn't be left with the blood of another kinsman on his hands. Arthur's our hope, Gwyna. He's the hope of Britain."

I spat on him. I turned my back and flung myself to the far side of the room and hit the wall hard with both my hands. "Some hope!" I shouted. "Arthur? You've wasted your life building him high and wrapping him up in stories, but Arthur hasn't cleaned the Saxons away. They're still sitting on their stolen lands, growing stronger and stronger, and laughing at us while we fight among ourselves. Arthur doesn't care about anything but making his own self fat and rich, and he hasn't even managed to do that very well. And all you can do is make up stories, make up lies, try and turn him into something that he isn't. And your stories won't last any longer than Arthur does. When he dies, the stories will die with him, and he'll be forgotten. And so will you. And so will all of it."

Long silence after that. Wind lifting the roof-tiles. I wouldn't look at Myrddin for a time. When I did I saw a silvery line, like the trail of a snail, shining on his face. I looked closer. His eyes were tight shut, the yellowish eyelids wrinkly like the skin of an old apple. Tears seeped out from under them. He was weeping.

"Master?" I asked, softer. "Why did you keep me? After the waterfall, I mean."

He didn't answer. I thought he'd fallen asleep. His eyes stayed shut and the tears kept coming. But after a minute he spoke again. Still not an answer, exactly. Just another story. But at least it was one I hadn't heard before.

XLVI

Out east somewhere. Out in the round green downs behind Noviomagus. So many years back the Saxons hadn't quite settled there yet. But this summer night one of their war-keels has slid out of its shelter in the coves of Vectis and come to drop its crew of fighters in the riverside woods. They come fast up the white roads in the moonlight. Flames leap from kindled villas.

And suddenly a boy is running and running, with the smoke of his home going up into the sky behind him. And behind him, running faster, comes a Saxon raider, reaching for him, catching him, flinging him at the chalk ground.

"I grew up a slave," said Myrddin. "I grew up like a beast, shoving a plough for my Saxon master through some piece of Britain that he'd stolen. But I listened to my fellow slaves telling stories, about how the Saxons had come, and how it had been before, back in the days of Rome-in-Britain. Civilization. Peace."

And as soon as he was old and strong enough, he

started planning his escape. He watched the men and women around him, Saxon and slave alike, and learned the ways their eyes and minds and hearts worked, till he knew how to deceive them. He watched the seasons and the skies, making himself weather-wise. One night, when he knew a fog would rise, he ran off, leaving behind him a litter of clues that set his Saxon owners searching for him in every direction but the one he'd really gone. They hunted for him for a night and day, and then decided that he'd been a magician, and had turned himself into a vapour and blown away on the wind.

Safe in the ancient forests, he fled west, always west, keeping the sunset ahead of him till he reached country where there were no Saxons. He'd picked up a few handy conjuring tricks from travelling men he met upon the road, and he remembered stories he'd heard, and spun better ones of his own. Tall tales and hedge-magic paid his way from town to town, until at last he came to Urbs Legionis, where Ambrosius had his headquarters that year. He wasn't a fighter, but he hung around the fringes of the army, sure that Ambrosius was the man who'd smash the Saxons and bring back the light of better days. And when Ambrosius died and the war-bands of Britain took to fighting each other instead of Saxons, he chose the one he thought the strongest, the armoured cavalry of Arthur, Uthr's son. Oh, he wasn't stupid; he could see that Arthur only wanted what the others wanted: power and land. But maybe, if Arthur could be made strong enough, that wouldn't matter. The Romans only wanted power and land, and they ended up uniting half the world. So he tried to use his wits and stories to make Arthur great, in the hope he'd finish what Ambrosius began.

And all those years he never had a wife. Never had children. Never wanted any. Said he was too busy. Said they'd have slowed him down when he was travelling. He'd already lost one family. He couldn't live with the fear of losing another. He still remembered the night the raiders came, and how the screams of his mother and sisters had sounded among the dark downs, calling out to God, who took no more notice of them than of the cries of the owls in the woods.

And then, one wintry night, out in the wild western hills, below a place that Arthur's men were burning, he stopped beside a river-pool to watch a girl claw her way out of the water. He'd learned not to let himself feel pity for the waifs that Arthur's wars left homeless. He told himself, as he watched her dry out beside his campfire, that he had only rescued her because she would be useful. But something about her touched his heart. Afraid and all alone, she put him in mind of himself.

He meant to let her play her part, then leave her be. But afterwards, riding away from the river with Arthur's band while they talked about the miracle of the sword from the water he found that he could not forget the girl. How bright she was. How brave. Just the same age as he'd been when the Saxons took him. Abandoning her was like leaving his own self behind. As soon as he could he crept away from Arthur's victory feast and went back to the waterfall, and found her.

At first she'd been a worry to him. He'd dressed her as a boy and called her Gwyn, but there was always a fear she'd be discovered, that the truth would come out, and Arthur would smell some insult in what he'd done. But months went by, and the girl seemed well able to play the role he'd put her in.

He started to enjoy travelling with her. Liked waking to her tuneless singing as she made up his fire, or readied his breakfast. Liked answering her endless questions. Teaching her things. Watching her learn, and grow. Her high seriousness as she picked the yellow-white specks of flies' eggs from her pony's coat. He started to feel proud of her. The way she'd exposed that old fraudulent so-called saint down on the sea-coast that time! And kept quiet about it after, as if she'd thought Myrddin hadn't the wit to go and ask among the monks and work out for himself what she had done. . .

He started to see why even hard, strong-headed men like Cei went soft when they spoke about their children.

And when she grew older, and he couldn't keep up the pretence that she was a boy, he made a girl of her again. It had cost him dear, to go away that year and stay away while she learned women's ways. If he'd been in Aquae Sulis to keep Arthur in check, things might have gone better afterwards. But at the time, the girl had seemed more important. He was starting to fear that Arthur was not the man he'd hoped. Arthur couldn't unite the greedy, squabbling Britons, and maybe no one could. But if the girl could grow up happy maybe that would be enough. Enough reward for one life's work.

He found her a place in the household of Arthur's

wife. He was startled by how much it hurt him to let her go. When she stood weeping on that road in the west and said, "I don't want to leave you," he had had to hide his face from her in case she saw his tears. It would have been so easy to give in to her and let her stay. But she deserved better than a life used up in serving an old man. He wanted her to have the company of other girls, and the hope of a good marriage one day, and children of her own. So he made up a story to save her pride, and to give him a reason to see her sometimes. Told her she'd be his spy in Gwenhwyfar's house.

He half hoped Bedwyr might take the girl, after Bedwyr was wounded. No man could have asked for a better wife, and he knew the girl's upbringing had made her impatient with the settled, cow-ish ways of women. She would be happier with a husband who needed her help.

Then she told him of Gwenhwyfar's betrayal. A double betrayal, it seemed to him, for not only was Gwenhwyfar deceiving Arthur, she was making the girl part of her deception. What would happen when Arthur learned of it? What would he do to a girl who had helped his wife insult him?

He'd had to tell Arthur, of course, before Arthur found out for himself. He'd thought he'd be able to control Arthur's temper. Thought he'd snatch the girl safe out of the storm that followed. But she'd grown headstrong. He'd *taught* her to be headstrong, and he felt sorry for it, for it made her put herself in danger's path. Made her go riding off to her death.

He had folded her dress with his own trembling

hands. Folded and smoothed it and pressed it in linen, and scattered lavender on it to keep the moths and mould away. And all the weeks since, in his sickness, he had prayed to the God he did not believe in to send her back to him. And now, at the very end, here she was, leaning over his bed, watching him talk, a little small frown between her eyebrows, and her hand holding his.

"Gwyna," he said. "You've been a good daughter to me. And a good son, too."

XLVII

Well, I didn't feel like a good daughter. I felt angry at him. If he loved me so, why had he never said? Why had he never said something till now? Why had he never told me till it was too late? I could have done with a father, but I'd always thought him just my master. I'd thought I was a servant, and a feckless one at that. I hadn't realized that love was part of the arrangement.

I wasn't even sure I believed his tale. I wanted to. But what if it was just another story, one to make sure I stayed by him, nursing him? That's the trouble with a story-spinner. You never know what's real and what's made up. Even when they are telling the truth, they can't stop themselves from spinning it into something better; something prettier, with more of a pattern to it.

And as I sat there, thinking on all this, I started to notice how quiet it was in the room. How even the rusty saw of Myrddin's breath had stopped. And I looked at him, and I saw that death had stolen him away from me.

I felt flat and quiet as the sand when the tide goes

out. I knelt beside Myrddin and held his hand until it was quite cold, wishing my hard words of earlier could be unsaid. "I didn't mean it," I told him. "About the stories. They'll last, even if nothing else does. They'll be like a light in the dark, and they'll burn as long as the dark lasts and go on out the far side of it into the morning."

Which I didn't believe, but I thought his ghost might be lingering close by, and I didn't want it to linger in a foul mood.

Morning came. Snow on the hill-tops. I woke the boy Cadwy and told him what had happened, and together we set out to dig a grave for our master. In the overgrown gardens the dead grass was grey with frost, matted and shaggy like an old badger. The ground beneath was frozen stone-hard. I broke a spade on it, and blistered my hands on a mattock shaft, and didn't make a scratch.

So I carried Myrddin to the woods, which clustered closer to the house each year. Light as a linnet he was, with all the words gone out of him. I took him to the great old oak, the ancient oak which had stood outside his house before it *was* a house, before the Romans even came to Britain. Its trunk was hollow, and the deep loam inside had been sheltered from the winter winds and had not frozen. I used my hands and the broken spade to shovel it out. While Cadwy watched, I laid Myrddin inside, and wrapped my own cloak round him, and I piled the loam back over him, heaping it over him with my hands and whispering what prayers I knew.

And there I left him, in the hollow oak. Littler trees will have grown up round it now, and the brambles tangled thick, and the nettles and the dock grown deep and green. And I suppose he lies there still, and will for ever.

XLVIII

That was the last I saw of Cadwy. He went home to his own people, to tell them about the girl who'd buried his master in a tree. Alone, I haunted that empty house like a ghost. The day was already dying. I hadn't the heart to start out for Din Branoc. I found Myrddin's old harp, and rubbed the mildew off it, and carved new pegs to replace the ones which had broken, and tuned the strings as best I could, and made it sing again, after its own crack-throated fashion. And that night, which was long and lonely and full of strange, small noises, I told over the songs and stories I'd heard Myrddin tell, making sure each one was fixed firm in my memory like a stone in a wall. It was something to do, and at the sound of my voice and the harp the ghosts of the place drew back and left me safe.

"Myrddin!"

I came awake thinking the voice was in my head. Just my dreams forming words out of the roaring rush of the trees. The creak of branches. It was full daylight. I'd fallen asleep with the harp on my knees by the dying-down fire.

"Myrddin!" A shout outside, louder than the wind in the oak-tops. Other sounds too. Harness-jingle. Putter-thud of hooves, like fingers tapped on the drum-skin of the earth. I stumbled to the gateway, rubbing sleep from my eyes. Arthur and a half-dozen of his men waited outside the house on their white horses, looking warily at the talismans and spells Myrddin had hung about the entrance. Strange, I thought; these men would charge shield-walls, but not one would venture in through Myrddin's flimsy fence of charms.

Arthur rode closer when he saw me. Came and looked down at me through a smoke of hot horse-breath. He was all in armour, fish-scales gleaming, Caliburn at his side. His eyes considered me through the gap between the cheek-guards of his helmet. Either he didn't recognize me as his wife's companion or he didn't care. He said, "Where's Myrddin, girl?"

"Myrddin is gone, my lord," I said.

"Gone? I need him."

"He is dead."

Arthur looked hard at me a moment, then sniffed and started to turn his horse away. "I was afraid so."

Beyond him, on the road, a whole line of riders was passing. Spear-points and shield-fittings shining like candle-flames as the sun came up out of the bare woods. Arthur started to ride back to them, and the men who'd left the road with him turned their horses and galloped away to join the rest. But Arthur, maybe thinking I had some of my master's magic about me, hesitated, and looked back at me while his horse danced nervously.

"Medrawt is coming," he said. "We had word last night. We ride out to meet him."

I said nothing. It seemed to me that this was a strange time of year to make a war, with winter just closing its grip on the world. In Din Branoc they'd spoken as if Medrawt was raising an army and would wait till spring before he tried to overthrow his uncle. But then Medrawt had always been impatient. Medrawt couldn't wait the months it would take to gather a proper warband round him. He'd attack with whatever men he could muster. I imagined him hurrying them towards Sulis, his face set in that look of furious longing I'd seen on it the night I first met him.

If Arthur had been hoping for me to tell his fortune or weave a spell to help him, I disappointed him. He sniffed again – I think he had a cold – and kicked his horse and went off quick towards the road, galloping to the head of the passing column.

I watched them go. I watched their banners swim through the morning mist and pass into the west. And then I ran back inside and hunted out my travelling clothes. Because I'd worked out, see, that if Medrawt's band was coming to Sulis and Arthur's band was riding out to meet him, one or other of them would be passing Din Branoc. And if Arthur found Peredur there he'd want him silenced before he could tell of Cei's betrayal, and if Medrawt found him he'd press him to join his war-band, and either way it would end up with Peredur dead.

Which is how people mostly seem to end up when I try to look after them.

So I wasn't going to let it happen this time.

I put away Gwyna's dress for the last time, and pulled on my worn old breeks and tunic and my master's cloak, and saddled poor, patient Dewi and set off after Arthur's band. It was midday. The sun had gone, hidden behind a lot of lead-grey clouds. More snow started falling, whitening the road and making the winter trees look even starker. It was bad weather for fighting in. I thought that if Arthur had had Myrddin with him Myrddin would have read the sky-signs and told him snow was coming, and he'd not have gone.

Aiming to outpace the war-band, I turned Dewi off the miry roads and went over the heads of the downs. But I'd not gone more than halfway to Din Branoc when I heard a sound like a great wind down to my right where the road lay. I knew it too well, that sound, though I'd heard it only three times in my life. The bellowing of men, the clash and thud of weapons. The scream of a horse rising clear above it made Dewi's ears go up like two knives.

I reined him in and sat listening to the noise as it rose and fell, surging between the hills. Whatever was happening was happening out of my sight, beyond a spur of downland. I remembered the place: a ford in a gorse-speckled valley where the road from Sulis crossed a river. If Medrawt's army had reached it then they must have passed through Din Branoc the day before. I hoped that Peredur had had the good sense to hide from them. But good sense and Peredur were not things that went together. I could see him taking on Medrawt's whole war-band, sure that the lake-lady's cup would protect him.

I went west. A river barred my way, fat with autumn rain. I went north. A bog stretched across my path, too wet to pass. I wasted a while, searching for a crossing place. Itchy with worry. The battle noises grew fainter, rose up, died away. There was nothing for it but to risk the ford. Hope the battle there had finished, or at least moved off.

I followed the line of the river, crashing through dead bracken, alders, seeking paths through masses of gorse. After a time I started to pass wounded men dragging themselves away from the fight. Some lay moveless, dying or already dead. Others sat with their heads hanging down, too hurt to even bother glancing up as I went by. One shouted out to me, challenging me or begging help, but I kicked Dewi to a canter and went past. Then there was only silence, and my own sharp breathing, and the beat of Dewi's hooves. Snow coming down again. White patches on those drab ochre tangles of winter grass between the gorse. On the red sky, ravens wheeling.

And me on my tired pony coming around that shoulder of the hills at last and riding out on to the battle-place of Camlann.

XLIX

The river made a turn there, bent round a low hillock that stood above the ford. All the land from the river to the hillock's crown was sewn with spears and swords and fallen horses and dead men. Over my head the ravens went, their wings' black fingers combing sighs out of the air. Others hopped about among the dead, walking with careful, prissy steps. Arrows jutted out of the grass at all angles, like last year's thistles. On the slope of the hill a dying horse was struggling to stand up and falling back and struggling to stand up and falling back. . .

I brought Dewi to a halt and climbed down off him. Don't ask me why. It was a place that needed looking at, however much I didn't want to. I went along the riverside, then up the hill, setting my boots down carefully on the patches of bare ground between the dead. The further I went, the harder it was to find ground that wasn't squelchy with blood or covered with heaped-up bodies and fallen shields. Here and there men stirred, or moaned, or called out for God, or for their mothers. There was that shit-smell of ripped-open bodies. Two jackdaws squabbled over a drabble of gut, so blind with greed they didn't see me till I was almost on them, when they took off with flat tearing wing-beats and indignant cries. Arthur's dragon banner slapped at its staff, which poked sideways out of a snow-drift of dead white horses.

"Myrddin!"

It was the second time that day that voice had hailed me.

"Myrddin!"

Right at the hill's top he was. Arthur himself. As soon as I saw him I knew that it was him I'd come here looking for. I'd wanted to see him dead. But he wasn't. He was dragging himself across the smeared grass, reaching out towards me with one hand, parched voice cracking as he shouted at me.

"Myrddin!"

I suppose it was the cloak. The black hood I'd pulled up against the wind. And he probably couldn't see me too well. One of his eyes was gone, and the other was covered with blood that had spilled out of a gash in his head. There wasn't an inch of him had not been splashed with his own blood or some other man's, and where a gleam of his fine scale armour did show through that showed red too, reflecting the fat red sun that was going down into the mists and flood-waters of the levels westward. There was a great ragged hole punched right through that armour of his. An ordinary man would have been dead long before, and even the

281

Bear was failing, his strength slopping out of him into the grass.

I went closer.

"That girl," he said. "She told me you were gone."

I swallowed, and wondered about making a run for it, back down the hill to Dewi. Arthur looked finished, but there was no telling with a man like him. He might take it amiss if I deserted him, or explained I wasn't Myrddin. There was no shortage of spiky things laid round about that he might snatch up and hurl at me with his last strength.

So I said, "I have come back."

He beckoned me close so I could hear the words that he hissed out through his clenched teeth. "Take Caliburn. Cast it into the waters."

The sword was in his hand. I took it from him. After all, it's a woman's job to tidy up after the men. Caliburn felt smaller than I'd remembered. Stickier, too. Arthur grunted at me to hurry.

I've regretted it since. The gold on that sword would have kept me for a year. But there in the dusk with the mist rising round me, I felt the tug of a story. Arthur was right, for once. Things needed finishing.

I went slither-scrambling down the steep west slope of the hill, scattering the carrion birds. At the hill's foot were reeds and alders and the dark swirl of the river. The sun was wedged in the bare branches of the trees on the far bank. I paused and steadied myself and drew back my arm, and I flung Caliburn as far as I could out across the shining water.

Which wasn't very far. A sword is a heavy thing. It fell

a few feet from the bank. Hit the water with a flat splat like the sound a collop of dung makes dropping from a cow's arse. Went under with barely a ripple, and the river rolled over it.

Back up the hill I went, cursing its steepness, grabbing at tussocks of stiff grass for handholds. Arthur was watching me as I picked my way through the corpse-field to him. Not moving any more, but still not dead.

"Did you see her?" he asked, when I sat down beside him.

I could have told him a lie, but I was sick of them. So I shook my head, and said, "I saw nothing. Just the wind on the water."

People will tell you Arthur isn't dead. They'll tell you how he was borne away to lie in enchanted sleep under a hill, or on the Isle of Glass. But don't you believe them. I heard his last breath rattle up his throat. I watched his thick fingers dig into the soil as if he was clinging on to the world with all his might. And when he'd finished dying it was me who helped myself to his rings and his belt and his boots and the old gold cross he wore round his neck. I thought I'd earned them.

I left that place, and I rode hard, and I came to Din Branoc under a bleached-skull moon. A door banged in the wind. I walked Dewi up the muddy track, expecting to find more dead men. But I found no men at all. In the hall the women waited, cautious, wary, the way women wait when their husbands and their sons have gone to war. Medrawt had come through the day before, and made the men of fighting age join his war-band. By now they were either dead in the mud of Camlann-ford or in Aquae Sulis, taking for themselves the things that had been Arthur's.

"What, even Peredur?"

Not Peredur. When he heard word that Medrawt's crowd were coming the headman told Peredur to run and hide in the deep woods, for fear they'd know him as Arthur's man and do him harm. But Peredur had been too weak to run, and so the headman's wife had hidden him instead at her own fireside, among the women. Thin as he was from his long fever, pale and big-eyed, he made a pretty girl.

He wouldn't meet my eye when they took me to him. He hung his head, face down-cast, like a shy young maiden. He felt ashamed. He thought I'd laugh at him. But if I laughed, it was the laughter of relief, at finding him alive still. And when the women let us be I went to him, and hugged him, and whispered him my secret.

It felt good to tell it. People had sometimes found me out – Maelwas, and Gwenhwyfar – but I'd never *told* anyone before, "Gwyn and Gwyna, we're one and the same."

How he stared, when he began to understand me. I thought his understanding would carry him further and he'd work out it had been me beside the river, giving him that cup. But he never thought to. In his memory, the lake-lady was beautiful, and I was hardly that, with my flat round face like a barley bannock, and dressed up as a boy. I had to explain that, too.

"But I *saw* her," he said, struggling to make my face fit his remembering.

"You saw *me*. You were fevery. Half in a dream. . ."

"She kissed me."

"Yes," I said. I suppose I should have been shy about it. Maidenly. But I didn't feel maidenly. I felt like I'd ridden a long way, through battles and bad country, and he was my girl, waiting for me at journey's end. "Yes," I said, "she did." And I kissed him again. And we held each other, and it seemed to me he was pleased to find his old friend Gwyn was Gwyna after all.

"And if there's no lake-lady," he said, "is there really no magic? Is there nothing but tricks?"

"All tricks and stories, angel," I told him. "But that story's over now. It's time to start another."

Time to go, before winter tightened its grip so hard we could not go at all. We kept off the roads. Stuck to the woods and the quiet places. Just a young harper and his travelling-companion heading west, taking turns to ride our single pony. Soon we were across Tamar, out of the lands where Arthur had been known, and riding into country where he was just a story.

I paid our way with that story. It bought us food and warm beds and shelter from the winter's snow. All down the long tongue of Kernyw, where Britain narrows south and west into the grey ocean, in high halls and cow-warm herdsman's huts I told my tales of Arthur. For was I not Gwyn, son of Myrddin? And didn't I alone know the truth of it? And couldn't my beautiful young friend coax such songs from that cracked old harp that my words took flight upon the music, and wheeled about like swifts under the roof-beams?

I didn't tell what really happened, of course. At first I felt ashamed to be telling lies for a living, and it stung me that I could not tell the truth. But as the year ripened and our road wound west I came to see it didn't matter any longer what the truth had been. The real Arthur had been just a little tyrant in an age of tyrants. What mattered about him was the stories.

So I told stories of the high deeds of Arthur, and that last great battle where he and the traitor Medrawt fell. I put Cei in that fight, too, at Arthur's side. And I told how Arthur, as he lay dying, commanded Bedwyr, the last and bravest of his men, to take his sword Caliburn and throw it into a pool of still, clear water. But when he reached the water's edge Bedwyr could not bring himself to cast the sword away, so he hid it there among the reeds and went back to Arthur. And Arthur asked him, "What did you see?" And Bedwyr said, "I saw nothing but the wind on the water."

And then Arthur knew that he was lying, and he lifted himself up in that last red of the dying day and said, "Do as I ask, Bedwyr."

So back went Bedwyr to the water's side, and he took Caliburn and threw it out far, far across the mere. And a white hand, jewelled with water-drops, reached up out of its own reflection and caught the sword, and held it for a moment, and then drew it down beneath the waters.

And always at the end someone would ask, "Is it true he's not dead? Not really dead? Will Arthur return?" And I'd think, "Christ, I hope not!"

But they weren't thinking of the Arthur I'd known. It was Myrddin's Arthur they wanted back, the story-Arthur, the wisest and fairest and best king they had ever heard of. You can't blame people for wanting to believe there'd been a man like that once, and might be again.

So I'd say, "A ship came for Arthur as he lay on the field of Camlann. Away downriver it took him, to the sea. And on an island in the west he lies sleeping, healed of all his wounds. And he'll wake one day, when our need of him is bad enough, and he'll come back to us."

Then, if the hall was rich, and the listeners friendly, I'd unwrap the things I carried in my pack and say, "Here. This ring was Arthur's. This cross was the one he wore through all his battles." And I got enough in exchange for those relics that by the time we found our way to Din Tagyll in the springtime, my Peri and I, we had enough to buy passage with a trader, outbound for somewhere better.

So I'll end my story the way stories of Arthur always end. A little ship is setting out on the evening tide. Further and further from the land she goes, out beyond the breaking surf, out away from the cliff's lee and the chough's cry and the deepening shadows of the land, out to where the sun lies silver on the western sea. And the ship gets smaller and smaller as she goes away, until at last the faint square of her sail fades altogether into the mist of light where the waters meet the sky.

And the name of that ship, the name of that ship is called, *Hope*.

AUTHOR'S NOTE

Here Lies Arthur is not a historical novel, and in writing it I did not set out to portray "the real King Arthur", only to add my own little thimbleful to the sea of stories which surrounds him.

Very little historical evidence survives from fifth and sixth century Britain. The last Roman legions left around AD 410, but we don't know how long a Roman-style government went on operating after that, or who took power as it collapsed. There are references to states like Dumnonia and Calchvynydd, but we can't be sure where their borders lay, or who their rulers were. Nor do we know whether there was a major war between the Saxons and the native British, or whether Saxon settlement was a more gradual and peaceful process.

As for Arthur, we know only that he is mentioned as a war-leader in records compiled some centuries later. He is associated with a British victory at the battle of Mount Badon, which some traditions place near Bath (though dozens of alternative sites have been suggested). Some historians have seen him as a

Romano-British general fighting against the Saxons, some as a sort of emperor of Britain, and some claim he lived much earlier. Many would argue that he never existed at all.

The names of Bedwyr and Cei are associated with Arthur from some of the earliest stories. Bedwyr is remembered as Sir Bedivere, but his strength and heroism seem to be transferred to Lancelot in the later tales. Cei becomes Sir Kay, Arthur's brother or step-brother, who is often presented as a rather rude, boorish customer.

Peredur is the hero of one of the stories in *The Mabinogion*, a collection of Welsh myths and legends. In later mediaeval romances he becomes Perceval, the most human of Arthur's knights, and finds the Holy Grail. (And, yes, he really does spend his childhood dressed as a girl in several versions.)

Myrddin, the prototype for the Merlin of later stories, may actually have existed; there seem to have been two poets of that name in the late sixth century.

Gwyna, like Saint Porroc, is my own invention.

Anyone interested in learning more about the historical background and the development of the Arthurian legend will find that there is a vast array of books on the subject. Paul White's *King Arthur – Man or Myth?* (available from www.bossineybooks.com) might be a useful starting place, as it's fair, thorough, well written and only forty pages long! Kevin Crossley-Holland's *Arthur* trilogy, published by Orion, is a great modern reworking of the mediaeval Arthurian romances.

As usual, I'm indebted to my editors at Scholastic, Kirsten Stansfield, Amanda Punter and Katy Moran (who also came up with the title). Tim Wright, whose knowledge of the subject (and most others) is far deeper than my own, was a source of much useful information, as was George Southcombe. Lu and Tizzy Palmes helped me with the horses. Needless to say, any mistakes are my own silly fault.

My interest in Arthur began on 5 July 1981 at about two o'clock in the afternoon, when I wandered into the ABC cinema in Brighton to watch John Boorman's film *Excalibur* (cert. 15). Brilliant, beautiful and barking mad, it's still my favourite modern retelling of the legends.

Philip Reeve, Dartmoor
2006

NOTE ON PRONUNCIATION

Due to the very different sound systems of English and Welsh, many of these are approximate rather than exact representations of the Welsh pronunciations. Italics show that the syllable is stressed.

NAME	PRONUNCIATION
Bannawg	*ban*-owg
Bedwyr	*bed*wirr
Cadwy	*kad*wi
Calchvynydd	kalckvanith*
Cei	kay
Celemon	*kel*emon
Celliwic	keth*lee*wick
Cunaide	*koon*-eyed
Dewi	deh-wee
Din Branoc	deen *brannock*
Din Tagyll	deen *tagihl*
Greidawl	*grayd*-owl
Gwenhwyfar	gooenn*hooee*varr
Gworthigern	goo-or*theegern***
Gwri	*goo*ree
Gwyn	*goo*inn
Gwyna	goo*innah*
Gwynedd	goo*inneth***
Kernyw	*kerr*nioo
Maelwas	*maeel*wahss
Medrawt	*medd*r-out
Myrddin	*marthinn***
Peredur	*perre*dirr
Powys	*poh*wiss
Rheged	*hreh*gedd
Rhiannedd	hrree*anneth***
Tewdric	*tao*-drick
Trwch Trwyth	toorckh *troith*
Uthr	*ithirr***
Ygerna	ee*gerr*na
Ynys Wydryn	*un*-niss *widrinn*
Ysbaddaden	uss-bad*athenn***

* In these words, "th" is pronounced as it is in the English word "then"
** In these words, "th" is pronounced as it is in the English word "thin"

With thanks to Dr Mari Jones of the University of Cambridge

MY WORLD
JONNY WILKINSON

headline

First published in 2004
by Headline Book Publishing

First published in paperback in 2006
by Headline Book Publishing

2

ISBN 0 7472 4278X

Printed and bound in Great Britain by Clays Ltd St Ives plc

Headline's policy is to use papers that are natural, renewable and
recyclable products and made from wood grown in sustainable
forests. The logging and manufacturing processes are expected to
conform to the environmental regulations of the country of origin.

Designed by Perfect Bound Ltd

HEADLINE BOOK PUBLISHING
A division of Hodder Headline
338 Euston Road
London NW1 3BH

www.headline.co.uk
www.hodderheadline.com

CONTENTS

Acknowledgements   7

Introduction   8

The Journey   20

The Final   46

Celebrity   76

Integrity   108

Heroes   140

Setbacks   166

England and Lions   192

The Future   224

ACKNOWLEDGEMENTS

In putting together this book my thanks go to my mum and dad for their constant unconditional love and support, and to my brother for his humour and for always being there for me. Thanks also to Steve Black for his amazing dedication and ambition and to Tim Buttimore, Simon Cohen and Brendan Sargeant for their professional and selfless approach to organising me, as well as to my ghost, Neil Squires, for his effort and friendship. Finally, thank you to all my team mates and coaches who work tirelessly to fulfil the dreams of Newcastle and England, and to all the England fans for their incredible support and impeccable behaviour.

INTROD

UCTION

'It is the game that has dominated my life. And I am proud to feel a small part of its history'

Jonny Wilkinson

I don't mind training alone, in fact I like it, but when you are your own boss as much as I am it is so easy to take a short cut, to knock off early. When the rain is pouring down on another cold Newcastle night and the wind is howling around Kingston Park, the temptation is always there to pack the bag of balls in the back seat of the car, head home from the training ground and put my feet up. After all, who would know?

I would. Cutting corners is not my way. I reason like this: if I train harder and better than anyone else, I will come out on top. Others might get lucky every now and again but the way I look at it life has to provide a reward for all the effort in the end.

This approach means I have to forego pleasures many twenty-six-year-olds take for granted but if I want to be true to myself and my team mates I have no choice in my mind. To be the player I want to be for Newcastle or England or the Lions I need to be sure the foundations for success are all in place. If that entails making sacrifices to spend more time on the training field so be it. Preparation is power.

I cannot accept that the drop goal which won the 2003 Rugby World Cup final was just some random bolt out of the blue. It was the result of years of practice. Before the tournament England put themselves through the most demanding fitness programme the squad had ever undertaken. I did the same with my kicking. I have always worked my hardest, but ahead of the most important tournament of my career, I wanted to find a way to do more.

At the end of a light day's training – and I use the term relatively – I would work on my place kicking, grooving my routine for when it would be tested under the most severe pressure I have ever known. There was no time limit on the sessions – some lasted for three hours. After a heavy day's training, I would work on my drop kicks. I would kick at least twenty with my left foot and twenty with my right. Then I would practise my

I play the odds – the harder I work, the more likely I am to succeed

restarts. The process would be repeated again, and again, and again until I was happy.

All the kicking took its toll. My boots are specially made from casts of my feet so they fit like slippers but I had to keep having new casts made because my feet changed shape with the constant battering. When the squad went home for days off, I would go through the process each day on my own at Newcastle United's indoor training facility at Darsley Park. Bang, bang, bang. Ball after ball aimed at a three-inch-wide metal bar, doing my best to make sure that if the moment came in the World Cup I would be ready.

During the tournament itself, I made sure I hit forty drop goals every day, twenty off each foot, so by the time of the final, I had probably kicked something like

It's like an equation – what I get out has to match the amount of energy I put in

7,000 drop goals in four months. Obsessive? Maybe. Necessary? Definitely.

I play the odds – the harder I work, the more likely I am to succeed. All the practice doesn't guarantee success – against Australia in the final I missed with my first three drop goal attempts – but the scales have to balance eventually. It's like an equation – what I get out has to match the amount of energy I put in. The fourth one, with my right boot, went over. You may have seen it.

That kick didn't change the way I approach rugby but it did change the way people approach me. Even now, two years on from that November night, I am still coming to terms with the fact that my life will never be quite the same again.

So where did this all begin, this dedication, this passion, this love of the game of rugby?

I was introduced to rugby very early on. My brother started minis when he was four. I was three and I'd go and watch, and my dad used to pass me a ball on the side of the field. Four was the acceptable age for getting on the under-eights circuit, according to the Wilkinson family, so at that age I got in there and started playing. I soon realised that I had a great love for the game.

A good example of this was an under-eights game when I was about five. I used to play at full-back. I'd be the last line of defence, and I used to love tackling. I still do, although some commentators have tried to suggest I change the way I play to avoid some of the injuries I've suffered. I can't do that. To change the way I play would be to change myself, my integrity out on the pitch. That's not me.

Back then I'd almost enjoy the challenge of when someone broke through the line. It would be like them versus me, and I'd have to make the tackle. In one game, we were playing against a young team which was famous for being the only side we played which had a girl. In the game, this under-eights girl, probably not a dissimilar age to me at the time, sprinted round the outside winger. She was very good, and I went running across the field with no hesitation thinking, 'I'm gonna smash her.' She sprints up the touchline ... and then off the pitch. 'Where's she going?' I think. Then all of a sudden, she goes around the outside of the corner flag, comes back into the field of play and puts the ball down. The referee, who isn't exactly the fittest person in the world, is a bit far behind play. He doesn't see the infraction so he gives the try. I immediately burst into tears.

I was starting to understand that it wasn't just about winning, it was more a way of life. We were up by quite a few points, so the score didn't really matter. It's the way I viewed it that's important. I wasn't able to go 'Oh come on ref. She ran off the pitch.' It was actually the pure heartbreak of 'No. This can't be happening.' That was at age five, more than twenty years ago.

I've never really been able to understand why some people might laugh at the situation, when the first thing that I thought was that it was the end of the world. It's just the way I am. Nothing's really changed. The smallest thing still means that much, but now instead of bursting into tears on the field, I take that feeling home with me and I lie there in bed and it takes me a long time to get to sleep because I'm thinking, 'I know I can do better than that.' I certainly felt that during the two Lions Tests I played in the summer 2005 tour, as did the rest of the team, although a lot of that disappoint-

I expect to be a big part of my team and help them win

ment comes from not feeling as though we had a fair opportunity to express ourselves. It's all about expectation. At the age of five I expected to make that tackle, to stop the try. I still feel like that now. If I know I let one attacker get past me in a game, it eats me up inside. That is not what I am expecting to happen. I also always expect to get my next kick over. That's a good thing. A positive mental approach. And I expect to be a big part of my team and help them to win. That's my attitude.

Is there something specific about this game that has allowed it to get under my skin? It's hard to pinpoint exactly what it is that I love about rugby. I think it's a lot to do with the game itself – the different skills required and the physical side of it all. A contest

I was starting to understand that it wasn't just about winning, it was more a way of life

between two players. Two teams. And there is an honesty to rugby that I like. Pride and determination certainly, but also the honesty of responsibility, of putting your body on the line, placing yourself in dangerous situations for other players.

There are other values of the game such as respecting your opposition and discipline which are commonly mentioned, but for me they all fall under the honesty category. You prepare as much as possible for the next game. It doesn't matter whether it's England vs. Australia, whether it's Lions vs. New Zealand, whether it's Newcastle vs. Gloucester, you always prepare like it's your last game and you must give your best show. I love that side of things. That's respect for your team mates as much as it's respect for your opposition.

I also think rugby helps bond friendships deeper than you can possibly imagine. When you're in the changing room five minutes before the game, and everyone's nervous as hell, and you're all there for each other, each one of you gives the next person a little bit more strength, because you're there sharing the tension, and that sort of thing does carry a lot of weight when it comes to friendships off the field. And there are so many shared experiences – the adulation of winning, the disappointment of losing, the nervous tension late in the game when there are only a few points in it, the relaxed feeling in the last ten minutes when you're twenty points up, that sort of thing. All this you share at the time, but also relive together afterwards.

That sharing of emotion is one of the things I love most about being able to play with my brother. We hang around so much anyway, but being on the same side, to be training on the same team, to come home and to be able to share those feelings and to be able to talk about what's been happening is a real honour. It all contributes to making rugby a truly brilliant game.

It is the game that has dominated my life. And I am proud to feel a small part of its history and I'm excited at the prospect of playing an even bigger role in its future. I want to work hard to be the best I can be in this world. Because it's My World.

THE JO

URNEY

'Destiny is no matter of chance. It is a matter of choice.'

William Jennings Bryan

I thought I understood the intensity of international rugby until the 2003 World Cup. I believed I had reached a level that could not be surpassed in the quarter-final of the previous tournament against South Africa which England lost. All the hype, all the tension – the sheer scale of the event surely could not be eclipsed? I know better now. The knockout matches in Australia left that quarter-final for dead. They were more than rugby experiences, they were life experiences.

The defeat in 1999 by the Springboks proved England weren't ready to win a World Cup. That point was underlined in the years of squandered Grand

Slams which followed. Yet all the time we were learning, filing away the knowledge gained from the
disappointments and setbacks and using it to become
a side that could win a World Cup.

The game against South Africa in Perth was again
deemed our critical match in 2003 because it was the
pool game which would logically send us along what
was perceived to be the easier path into the knockout
stages if we won. If results panned out as expected, we
would avoid New Zealand in the quarter-final. The
stakes, and the expectations engendered by our 53-3
win over a weakened Springboks side at Twickenham
the last time the sides had met, made for a horribly
twitchy build-up. The two squads met at a World Cup
launch in Perth and largely ignored each other. We all
knew what was resting on the game.

Our preparations were disrupted by injuries, with
Richard Hill and Matt Dawson ruled out and Kyran
Bracken doubtful all week because of a back spasm. He
came through in the end and so did we. It was an
extremely tense, incredibly physical contest, the equal
in intensity of that game four years previously, but this
time we won 25-6.

The Springboks' fly-half Louis Koen, a fine goal-
kicker, uncharacteristically missed three chances in the
first half which allowed us to go into the break level. We

were fortunate to be in that position – we had created little and made too many mistakes – but from there we took some semblance of control, riding out the South African storm and easing ahead as they ran out of steam. Will Greenwood touched down for our crucial try seventeen minutes from time after Lewis Moody had charged down Koen's clearance kick, I kicked my goals and we defended like our lives depended on it. Job done. It wasn't pretty but it was pretty effective.

Coming on top of our opening victory against Georgia, beating the Springboks put us in the position we wanted to be in and there was a brief but tangible feeling of relief within the squad. But it was like reaching a false summit. Far from conquering the mountain, we found that it just went up and up even more steeply from there.

The subconscious notion that we could relax a little after South Africa before the heavy-duty tests later in the tournament was smashed to smithereens by Samoa in Melbourne. There had been controversy before the World Cup over the absence of some of their top players like Trevor Leota, who had stayed to play for Wasps instead. The no-shows might have left them weak, some critics thought. They reckoned without the fact that the Samoans are the most natural rugby players on the planet.

The Samoans stretched us every which way with their break-neck-speed rugby

We had a fair idea of what was coming from them and in training before the game the management asked the shadow squad to play as we believed the Samoans would – fast and furious. It was quite embarrassing. They gave us the runaround, with Mike Catt pulling the strings with his long passes and Trevor Woodman running like an outside back. We consoled ourselves with the thought that the Samoans wouldn't be as good and that the ball could never come back from the breakdown as fast as in that session. They were bound to drop some balls. Fat chance. They spilled so few they were 22-20 up with twenty minutes left.

There was an omen that all might not go well beforehand. The last thing I do before heading for the dressing room for our final team talk is to line up one easy confidence-boosting kick at goal from in front of the posts. I had to take three before the Samoa game because I was so unimpressed with the first two. Lo and behold I missed for the first time in the tournament early on in the game with a 50:50 long shot and then failed with a penalty from just to the left of the posts. I couldn't even blame the wind – the Telstra Dome's roof was closed. I knew from the moment of impact that the ball was heading for the upright; it was just a question of whether it would take a lucky ricochet. It didn't.

I could hear the murmur of the crowd afterwards – I couldn't pick up what they were saying but I could imagine. 'The pressure has got to him – he's bottling it.' It was just a simple technical error which was to blame but for all the crowd knew I was imploding. The neutrals in the Telstra Dome loved it. They were revelling in seeing us have our backsides bitten by the underdogs. The miss seemed to sum up an evening which was not going to plan for England to say the least.

We found ourselves chasing shadows. Samoa's stand-off, Earl Va'a, was magnificent, varying the play with kicks, breaks and long passes and the athleticism of some of their forwards was more like that of backs. The Samoans stretched us every which way with their break-neck-speed rugby. I was hurtling across the pitch from one side to another to try to provide defensive cover outside the forwards and I felt heavy-legged. I had so little left that I couldn't fully impose myself in attack. I was having to grow a third eye to avoid Brian Lima, known affectionately as The Chiropractor for his bone-rearranging hits, who was trying to blow a hole in me. I didn't know what I had missed out on until I saw South Africa's Derick Hougaard turn a full somersault on the receiving end of one of his beautifully timed one-way collisions the following week.

The force was with the Samoans and our World Cup was slipping away. Crucially, though, we clung on to our composure and hung in there. Gradually we hauled ourselves out of an almighty hole. It wasn't easy when the rope was fraying so badly but our resolve pulled us through. Iain Balshaw picked off a cross-kick of mine in full stride to go in for one try, Phil Vickery stepped his way over for a cracker and we were safe. The final whistle, when it came, was a blessed relief.

Coming back in those circumstances, when it felt like the world was against us, to win 35-22 should not be underestimated. Given how much trouble we were in, I would rate England's comeback as better than when we overhauled a twelve-point deficit to beat Australia at Twickenham the previous year. Nevertheless, we had been forced to dig deeper than we could have imagined against Samoa just to keep on course and that

Coming back in those circumstances, when it felt like the world was against us, should not be underestimated

was a big concern. Far from the job being done by beating South Africa, the game against the Samoans underlined that it had hardly started.

A crunch meeting was called ahead of our next game against Uruguay, one that was to shape the rest of our World Cup. It was held at our base at Surfers Paradise on the Gold Coast. Clive Woodward, all the coaches and the key decision-makers – Martin Johnson, Lawrence Dallaglio, Will Greenwood, Phil Vickery, Neil Back, Matt Dawson and I – were there. We sat around tables on three sides of the meeting room while our coach, Andy Robinson, noted everything down on a flipchart at the front.

We were honest with each other. We had beaten South Africa and Samoa but had looked nothing like

Clive was publicly supportive but he was concerned about the strangulating pressure I was under

the England side we knew. We weren't thinking cor-
rectly. We use key words and phrases in the England
set-up to dictate how we want to play. Nothing earth-
shattering – words like 'ruthless', 'direct' or 'possession
control' – but terms which, combined with coaching,
are brought together to produce a style of play. People
were not responding to the language and the result was
that the game plan was staying behind in the dressing
room. The responses needed sorting out.

We were attacking too narrowly and cutting down
our range of options. A lot of it was down to over-
keenness. This tournament was the culmination of four
years' work and our anxiety to perform was proving to
be self-defeating. Players were clattering into rucks all
over the place and joining blind-side attacks out of a

heightened desire to get involved, leaving us short of numbers to attack in the open spaces when the ball came back. This left us predictable and therefore vulnerable to aggressive defence and turnovers.

I was guilty of it myself to a degree. Clive felt I was over-committing myself clearing out rucks when I should have been leaving those duties to the likes of Backy. He stressed that as the play-maker I was of no use to the side trapped under a pile of bodies at the bottom of a ruck. I could see the logic in what he said but it is difficult when you are right beside a tackled colleague – your first instinct is to go in to protect him and the ball. If I could be of use in a physical sense I wanted to be in there. It didn't come naturally to let others do the work.

I was aware from my press conference appearances in Australia that people had been critical of how I was playing but since I went out of my way not to watch any of the television coverage or read any of the newspapers this hadn't had much impact. Sometimes, if a team mate was reading a paper at breakfast, I would catch the odd headline by mistake but I would just go to sit somewhere else. In any case I was only really bothered about how my peers viewed my performances. Clive was publicly supportive but he was concerned about the strangulating pressure I was under, pressure that I was largely creating myself. I wanted to win the World Cup so much that I could think about little else.

Fatigue was a problem. I had never felt so tired playing rugby in my life. On top of training, I was kicking every day for up to three hours, as well as attending all the meetings. And when most were thinking about turning in for the night I would return to the team room to analyse our opponents on video over and over again. I made page after page of notes, detailing which foot every opponent preferred to step off, which arm they carried the ball under, everything I could think of. The rainforests took a real hammering. I was over-analysing everything in my head, but I believed it would make the difference if it could help me make a try-saving tackle. Rooming on my own, I was becoming a recluse. What spare time I had was spent watching trashy television. I was glad when October changed to November and with it the film selection in my hotel room. I'd watched all of them. Even the guitar sessions with the maestro Paul Grayson, which I had come to use as an escape, weren't quite working any more. I couldn't let go.

Locked inside my tunnel, the worries mounted up and from the most unexpected of sources. After our regulation victory over the amateurs from Uruguay in Brisbane in the next pool match, we sat on the bus on

Locked inside my tunnel, the worries mounted up and from the most unexpected of sources

the way back to the team hotel and listened on the radio to Wales's game against New Zealand. What was going on in Sydney was unbelievable. The Welsh, who had struggled through their pool matches, had suddenly come alive and were threatening the shock of the tournament.

We had banked on a quarter-final against Wales since we had beaten South Africa but with fifteen minutes left they were ahead and we were staring at a knockout game against New Zealand in a week's time. We had worked so hard through adversity to get past the Springboks and Samoa and now it seemed our best-laid plans were going up in smoke, with us unable to do anything about it.

I couldn't bear to listen to the commentary – I felt

The long-range drop goal with which I finished the game was undoubtedly my favourite one of the tournament

so helpless – but I was outvoted forty to one so I had to sit there and hear our fate being decided hundreds of miles away. At least when things were going wrong against Samoa I could take an active part in trying to sort things out. Now my hands were tied and that was a horrendous feeling. In the end New Zealand prevailed but Wales had served notice of what they were capable of and they were to give us another agonising examination in the quarter-final.

The way the Samoans had played against us had served as a warning of what was to come – we thought Wales were bound to employ the same tactics, and it came as no surprise to us when they did. Not that we did much about it. Riddled with anxiety, our response was equally inadequate in the first half and at the interval we were 10-3 down. It could have been more – Wales had given us the runaround.

We were blowing hard in the dressing room but Clive and Andy sat us down and calmly reiterated their confidence in us, spelling out the way we were going to play and how we were going to re-take control of the game. 'If we play the game in their half and take care of the ball when we get hold of it we will break them down and win,' was the message and to a man we all knew it was true. There were no dire warnings of what would happen if we didn't, no panic, just a professional measured response to the crisis that faced us. Those words were so important. We were on the ropes at the time but after the break the confidence seemed to seep back into us, and with Mike Catt coming on to help dictate the play, we hit back again and won 28-17. Jason Robinson set up a great try for Will just after half-time with a superb piece of counter-attacking and Wales's propensity to give away penalties under pressure allowed us to pull clear. The long-range drop goal with which I finished the game was undoubtedly my favourite one of the tournament. It was my sleeping pill for that night.

I'm convinced we would have lost that match in previous seasons. The impetus, like in the Samoa game, had been with Wales and in those Grand Slam defeats we had been unable to find a way of reversing it. However, by the World Cup we had become an extremely experienced side – the starting fifteen against Wales had a world-record 689 caps – and we used every last bit of that combined knowledge to adapt and adjust under severe pressure.

Allied to our response against Samoa, the way in which we reacted in the quarter-final underlined to me that we had within us what it would take to win the World Cup. It was still going to take a mighty effort, of course, because we weren't playing with the freedom we wanted. The matches to come and everything which surrounded them would be colossal but I just felt we had been through too much at the tournament to fail. The game in Brisbane against the Welsh added another coating of steel around us and I don't think we looked back after that. When the critics judged another narrow squeak a sign of fallibility they misread the tea leaves. The more important fact was this: we had come through the examination – our third towering challenge of the tournament – intact and were still afloat, heading for the semi-finals.

The Australian media made a big issue of the fact that Wales had outscored us in tries and labelled us boring. I was asked about whether penalties should be worth fewer points. It was ridiculous. If teams stop you playing by giving away penalties, you kick them. I was just baffled to hear people talking about whether or not the laws were correct in the middle of a World Cup tournament.

When we reached Sydney, one of the papers even printed 'stop boring rugby' T-shirts and conned me into posing for a photo to back their campaign. The T-shirts featured a picture of me goal-kicking with a diagonal red line plastered across it. Their reporter held out his hand for me to shake on the way out of a press conference and, not wanting to appear off-hand, I did. The telltale click of the camera and a quick glance at the T-shirt told me I'd been had, good and proper. I could just imagine him exchanging high-fives with his photographer as I walked off, nervously anticipating what tomorrow morning's edition would bring.

What this all showed, as well as a good imagination, was that the Australians were worried. Clive, who had lived out in Australia for five years, warned us what was coming from the local media and lapped it all up. When I sat alongside him at the press conference after the Wales victory, he confronted the sniping head on. He just stated in plain and simple English that we were going to Sydney to play France in the semi-final and that we would beat them. End of story. It is terrific

The support was both inspiring and terrifying. Seeing all those England flags and jerseys was a great lift

when someone has that level of belief in you and when you know that he means it. There were no mind games here.

Arriving in Sydney meant diving into the epicentre of the World Cup. It had been a superbly supported tournament, embraced enthusiastically everywhere we had gone across Australia but this was where the mercury shot out of the thermometer. When a giant rugby ball lights up the Sydney Harbour Bridge, you know you are in the middle of something special.

The huge number of English supporters had swollen further, meaning our hotel, looking out through the pines onto the beautiful Manly Beach, was besieged. I had as much chance of a dip in the sea as Clive did of becoming Australian Prime Minister.

Richard Hill was back to fitness for the semi-final. He and I take great pleasure in sharing an inconsequential afternoon together a couple of days before a match, just strolling to a café or a clothes shop and chatting about anything other than rugby. Unfortunately that was not possible in the circumstances – we would have been buried in the crush. Not even my unofficial minder, our scrum coach Phil Keith-Roach, who had taken to accompanying me in public because I was so useless at saying no to autograph hunters, would have been any use.

The support was both inspiring and terrifying. Seeing all those England flags and jerseys was a great lift a long way from home, after six weeks away, but it also gave us an inkling of just how many people we would be letting down if we lost. For a side that had exhibited signs of tension throughout the tournament that was a heavy burden to carry.

What helped us a great deal, though, in a one-off match where we lived and died by the result, was the way France were being talked up. They had become the darlings of the media during the tournament, throwing open the doors of their hotel overlooking Bondi Beach at all hours to all comers. That same media, we were told, were making them favourites on the back of our struggles and the great rugby France had played in sweeping aside Ireland 43-21 in the quarter-final. Some bookmakers had followed suit.

Our aim had always been to travel to Australia as favourites because that meant we were, in theory, the best team there but the label had put us in straitjackets. There is no doubt we were feeling inhibited. It is curious that a side sometimes plays differently when they are expected to win. They tend to try not to lose with risk-free rugby, placing more emphasis on making the right decisions than just playing naturally. That had been the case with England.

But with the weight of expectation lessening a little on the back of France's billing, there was a noticeable change in the atmosphere in our camp as the week wore on. It was reflected in training – the team runs were shorter and sharper, the minds less woolly. The nerves were still a constant companion hammering away at me – this was a World Cup semi-final after all, a forbidding place I had never been before – but I had such faith in the men around me that I felt like I could face my fear.

I had also discovered a temporary escape from all the suffocating anxiety. Steve Black, my fitness conditioner at Newcastle, sent me out two detective novels by Michael Connelly and I lost myself in the cases of

We knew what we had to do and we went and did it

private investigator Harry Bosch. I am not a big reader usually but in the claustrophobic situation I was in, unable to escape from the hotel except for training, I cherished my time inside the pages of *Angels Flight* and *The Black Ice* with an irrational passion. They were my comfort blankets. I used to lie in my room and allow myself to be taken away by the words, away from all the madness building up outside the hotel and the responsibility, away from rugby itself. Occasionally I would glance at the clock. You would not believe the joy I experienced from seeing I had lost half an hour in the book and still had half an hour spare to indulge myself before a team meeting or dinner. A big part of international rugby is about being comfortable. It is such an unnatural and demanding environment that anything you can grab hold of to make you feel calm and relaxed is helpful.

Some critics have said France were beaten by the weather in the semi-final, but I was just as disappointed

The conditions were bad for kicking – there was a strong swirling wind as well as rain – but I had encountered worse in Newcastle

as they no doubt were when I pulled back the curtains and saw the rain coming down. We had trained to explode onto the pitch that week and to know we would now have to play a limited game was deflating. No matter. We knew what we had to do and we went and did it.

The conditions were much the same as at Murrayfield in 2000 when we had blown a Grand Slam. People said we tried to play too much rugby that day – an argument which grossly over-simplified the problem and that I never agreed with – but we had developed to the stage where we knew what was required in the wet.

The forwards were magnificent – their strength and investment were phenomenal – and if you needed a visible illustration of what was to come from them, the sight of tears streaming down Lawrence's face during the anthems said it all. We had worked on our set piece ahead of the game, knowing the threat the French scrum and line-out posed to the basics of all our ball winning, and we countered it superbly. Every piece of possession the French backs received seemed to be on the back foot which made life very hard for Frederic Michalak, their young fly-half who had enjoyed such a fabulous tournament. In contrast, when we got hold of the ball we were going forward, so it was that much easier for either me or Catty to drill them back. Even though we conceded an early lead again, this time to a Serge Betsen try, we were able to put ourselves in the positions to keep the scoreboard moving and we eventually got out of sight.

The conditions were bad for kicking – there was a strong, swirling wind as well as rain – but I had encountered worse in Newcastle. I trusted my technique and it held up. Likewise with the three drop goals – any method of keeping the scoreboard moving and of rewarding our forwards for their relentless toil was valuable. Putting France in the position where they

It took all of about two seconds after the semi for me to start thinking about the final itself, the biggest game of my life

needed to score tries to win in those conditions was our aim and we managed it. In the end they ran out of ideas. Having established a 24-7 lead, I was actually able to enjoy the last five minutes of the semi-final, to bask in pressure-free rugby played out in front of a fantastic wall of English support. Aside from the Georgia match, they were about the only five minutes of the tournament in which I felt able to relax. We knew at that point we would be back in the Telstra Stadium the following weekend.

One of the great motivating factors for me in winning that semi-final was reaching the World Cup final but there was another bonus to be had from beating France – not playing in the third-place play-off. We had watched Australia beat New Zealand in the previous day's semi-final and as the All Blacks had traipsed off disconsolately at the end it had occurred to me what an appalling sense of anti-climax taking part in the play-off would have brought. I would have preferred to have gone straight home if we'd lost.

The Wallabies had headed off on a lap of honour after beating the All Blacks, but even though the stadium was bathed in white for our semi-final and our magnificent fans probably deserved a wave or two after being drenched by the rain, the thought never entered our heads. We had come to Australia to win a final, not a semi-final. The management called a 1 a.m. meeting after the game to reinforce that point but they need not have bothered. It took all of about two seconds after the semi for me to start thinking about the final itself, the biggest game of my life.

THE

FINAL

'There's **35** seconds to go, this is the one. It's coming back to Jonny Wilkinson. He drops for World Cup glory...'

Ian Robertson

The journey – South Africa, Samoa and France

I am always nervous before a rugby match. I always have been. When I played mini-rugby as a ten-year-old I would go to bed the night before a game happy enough because I had the barrier of sleep between me and what I had to do the next day. I always slept well. But once I woke up, the anxiety would sweep over me. I would suffer panic attacks, the tears would flow and I would be consumed by a strong urge not to go through with it. To try to alleviate the symptoms, I used to set my alarm ridiculously early – 5 a.m. – so that I could turn over and go back to sleep, putting off the reality for another precious couple of hours. Waking up again at 7 a.m., the anguish would have subsided to a degree. By 8 a.m., after turning over for another hour, it was possible for me to contemplate going to the match. The tension would rise to the surface again on the way there. Dad would often have to stop the car for me to be sick. The condition wasn't physical fear – my favourite part of rugby, then as now, was tackling. Instead, it was the thought of losing and letting myself down at something which meant so much to me. The stress levels which that brought on were almost paralysing.

Fourteen years on, I woke, for the second time, at 8 o'clock on the morning of 22 November 2003, in the England team hotel feeling the familiar dread. My thoughts were a mixture of excitement, tension and a raging desire to run away from it all. I have sat in stadia the world over before games, thinking to myself, 'Do I really want to do this? Wouldn't life be so much easier if I didn't show up?' World Cup final or not, I didn't feel any differently. Overcoming the instinct to pull the duvet over my head and hide was hard. It had been a crazy week. The theme from the management had been to treat the match as just another game of rugby but all the other indicators were suggesting it was anything but. Everything surrounding the match was unreal.

The support had gone crazy. There were swathes of England fans outside our hotel at all hours. *The Times*,

I have sat in stadia the world over before games, thinking to myself, 'Do I really want to do this? Wouldn't life be so much easier if I didn't show up?'

for whom I was writing a newspaper column, wanted me to pose for a picture by the sea a few days ahead of the game. The photographer took me to a beach he assured me would be quiet. I had my reservations, given that 50,000 Englishmen were in town, but, hidden by shades and cap, I dutifully went along. It was packed. A quick snap and you couldn't get me out of there fast enough.

The hotel fax machine was in danger of burn-out with all the good luck messages from home. Jack Charlton, a World Cup winner thirty-seven years before, sent

The hotel fax machine was in danger of burn-out with all the good luck messages from home

his best wishes, as well as the Welsh and Irish teams. Most numbing of all was the weight of words from ordinary people.

The media interest had gone through the roof too. Hundreds of journalists, photographers, radio and TV people turned up for press conferences, not all of them maintaining objective neutrality. One Australian television crew decked out their camera with a big poster of the Wallabies for Clive to stare at as he answered their questions. The country's most down-market paper urged patriotic Australians to keep us awake the night before the final by making a racket outside the hotel. The same rag printed a cut-out-and-keep voodoo doll of me for people to stick pins into. Classy touch.

The media scrum had become so unwieldy when we

left the hotel for training that we had taken to coming back via an underground car park in an attempt to side-step all the camera crews. They soon got wind of it. On one occasion we ended up sprinting off the bus to the lift at the back entrance but because it took an age to descend they got plenty of footage of us hanging around awkwardly waiting for it. Best-laid plans and all that.

We trained lightly, not cutting corners but reflecting how much our quarter-final and semi-final had taken out of us. We had a day less to prepare than the Australians and we tried to conserve our energy. The forwards didn't do any scrummaging and we walked through a lot of our moves. The hard work had been done in pre-season and before the other matches. We had to trust that it was safely in the bank. We needed to be fresh for the challenge that lay ahead. After kicking, I rested as much as I could in my room, reading Harry Bosch. He had provided such comfort that when I finished the last page two days before the final, I seriously considered re-reading it. In the end I begged a book off Dave Reddin, our fitness coach. It didn't quite hold the same hypnotic power though.

On the night before the game we gathered together, as we always do, to watch an England 'greatest hits' video – big tackles and great tries set to music. Clive spoke to us with passion about what was to come and as I left the room the nerves were jangling. In my pocket were two pieces of paper.

One was from Matt Dawson – a list of five key words for me to shout at him during the match to keep him on top of his game – and the other was the game plan. It was scribbled on a small piece of hotel notepaper. Part of it related to me, part to the team. This is what it said:

Eng–Aus, Jonny Wilkinson, 52nd cap
Defence
Alert, stay bouncing, head up
Make 100 per cent tackles – focus low, drive the legs
Incredible work rate – non-stop, get off the floor
Destroy someone – embarrass them

Attack
Direct – go forward
Kick on front foot when appropriate – turn wingers
Sailor and Tuqiri
Use short sides
Build a score
Drop goal routine

There were words of advice and encouragement too:

Play my game
Nothing changes
Be the best
Get what you deserve

Around these bullet points were the names of the team plays and the calls I planned to make early in the game.

The bare bones of the game plan were to play the game in Australian territory and then keep the ball when we got there. The Australians had an outstanding defence but we felt we had the edge in the front five and that we could wear them down by building phases and moving them around. Our general kicking game revolved around turning the Wallabies' wings to receive our kicks, thus making it more difficult for them to run the ball back at our defence. It was aimed at giving our kick/chase time to organise itself. Neither Wendell Sailor nor Lote Tuqiri, who had both come from rugby league, were motivated to kick the ball and we backed our defensive system to cope with their counter-attack. Australia's full-back Mat Rogers had also come from league but while he was a good kicker off his left foot we thought we could reap rewards by forcing him to kick off his weaker right foot.

With these instructions safely tucked away, I went to bed knowing exactly how I would feel when I woke.

So it begins. On the morning of the final, I reluctantly leave the safety of my room and wander down to breakfast. I make small talk with my team mates over cereal, toast and egg-white omelettes. I used to be silent on the morning of a match, wrapped up in what lay ahead, but I have improved to the extent that I can manage to converse with the outside world a little now. After breakfast, I go to the training ground in Manly with Dave Alred, the kicking coach, for an hour's 'nudging'. In amongst the punting and the place-kicks I practise twenty drop-kicks off each foot. The session goes well, although I still can't properly feel my feet on the floor because of the tension in my legs.

Back at the hotel, we have a team meeting to run over the weather forecast and check everyone is fit and healthy. Clive has taken no chances. On the day of the 1995 World Cup final, several All Blacks were affected by food poisoning so he has brought over our own chef, Dave Campbell, to keep an eye on things behind the scenes. We are all OK.

Johnno takes the forwards off for a word and I have a chat with the backs to run through our tactics. I stress the importance of communication. I tell them it is

I used to be silent on the morning of a match, wrapped up in what lay ahead, but I have improved to the extent that I can manage to converse with the outside world a little now

going to be noisy in the Telstra Stadium so we have to talk loudly and constantly to each other even though it will still be virtually impossible to hear a thing. Mentioning this is to state the obvious with 80,000 people there but the point behind it is to emphasise to the players that we will have to react almost by instinct to help each other out under the pressure of the occasion that awaits us. When we arrive at the stadium we cannot afford to be surprised by the atmosphere.

Before the quarter-final against Wales, the match twenty-two had gone for a stroll to loosen the muscles but, hemmed in by the wall of supporters, it is impossible this time. So after a light lunch, I return to my room and pack my bag. In go my shoulder pads, two kicking tees and three pairs of boots. Two are studded and one bladed. Then I try to relax on my bed. The 8 p.m. kick-off, Sydney time, leaves a lot of hours to fill but I like to watch the minutes tick by. It is preferable to the relative rush of an afternoon game.

I surface for my usual pre-match ritual of a shave and shower before settling down to listen to a mental rehearsal CD. The script is prepared by myself and Dave Alred but read by him – I don't want to doze off and miss the bus listening to myself droning on. This visualisation technique is a sort of clarified daydream with snippets of the atmosphere from past matches included to enhance the sense of reality. It lasts about twenty minutes and by the end of it I feel I know what is coming. The game will throw up many different scenarios but I am as prepared in my own head for them as I can be. If you have realistically imagined situations, you feel better prepared and less fearful of the unexpected.

Finally, before leaving the privacy of my own space, I dig out two faxes from Steve Black. The first one, which came during the knockout stages, encourages me, World Cup final or not, to go with my instincts. If it feels right, it is right, is his message.

'Go with your instinctive gut feeling and reasoned response – it hasn't let you down before. Have total belief in yourself and your internal guidance.'

It is almost like Blackie has been reading my mind. This is not a conversation we had ever had together but the words hit the nail on the head for me. Trusting your instincts is an integral part of feeling confident. I needed to know that the way I had been preparing was correct for me – from reading a book in the afternoon to kicking on the training field. I was worried about letting others down and I was concerned that if I blew this opportunity I would find it hard to live with the regret.

The other fax from Blackie arrived at the start of the tournament. It is one I have read on the day of each game at the World Cup. I read it through again. It is a speech delivered by General George S. Patton, the commander of the US Third Army in Europe, during World War II. I almost know it by heart now.

'Today you must do more than is required of you. Never think that you have done enough or that your job

'Fill yourself with the warrior spirit – and send that warrior into action'

is finished. There's always something that can be done, something that can help to ensure victory. You can't let others be responsible for getting you started. You must be a self-starter. You must possess that spark of individual initiative that sets the leader apart from the led. Self-motivation is the key to being one step ahead of everyone else and standing head and shoulders above the crowd. Once you get going don't stop. Always be on the lookout for the chance to do something better. Never stop trying. Fill yourself with the warrior spirit – and send that warrior into action.'

I head down for our pre-match meal – chicken breast, mince and a couple of sandwiches for the carbohydrate levels. I burn energy very quickly, so, for all the nerves, I've never had a problem eating before a match. Even this match.

Andy runs through a few points with the squad before a final word from Clive and then we are off into the frenzy. There must be close to 1,000 people waiting for us, cheering us, applauding us. We are given a tumultuous reception – everywhere I look there are English flags – but I don't allow myself to acknowledge anyone. I want to show myself that I am not going to be distracted by anything, good or bad, ahead of this game. I think the fans would rather be given a World Cup than a smile.

Safely on the bus, I sit in my usual place, halfway back, and idle away the forty-minute journey to Homebush, picking the labels off my energy drinks. It is a subdued trip, through largely deserted suburban streets, before the storm to come. A special CD accompanies us en route. It has been compiled by Mike Tindall and is intended to finish with an inspirational tune as we arrive at the ground. Before the semi-final somebody fiddled with it and we pulled in to the stadium to the strains of 'Rock The Casbah' by The Clash. Close, but no cigar. This time the choreography is perfect and as the Telstra Stadium climbs spectacularly into view the England bus arrives to the strains of 'Lose Yourself' by Eminem.

I change quickly and, as always, have a brief flick

through the match programme then head out onto the pitch to kick. When I return the tension is eating into every pore. I try to sit down but it's impossible. My legs won't keep still. I pace the changing room, talking to the backs, checking out how they are feeling and spelling out again what I need from them. I re-read my sheet of paper, over and over again.

The coaches do their bit and then we're out onto the field for the team warm-up. The atmosphere is building all around the stadium but it barely registers. I'm into it now. I am reassured by the knowledge I will have trained as hard, and in my mind harder, than anyone else on that pitch. I also know that when the whistle blows, a switch will flick inside me. Suddenly I will become incredibly competitive and ultra-aggressive. I will be inwardly driven to do anything to win this match. I put over my final kick and then return to the changing room. I check my piece of paper one last time, then spray glue on my hands to combat the evening dew.

It's just the players now. Johnno pulls us into a huddle. He talks passionately, telling us to look around at each other and remember the experiences we have been through together. This is our time. In the last year we have beaten everyone and overcome every challenge. It is this thought that we hold onto at this

I try to sit down but it's impossible. My legs won't keep still. I pace the changing room, talking to the backs, checking out how they are feeling and spelling out again what I need from them

moment. Man for man we believe we are better than Australia, we have worked harder than they have for this moment and we are stronger – physically and mentally. It is the game of our lives and there must be no regrets afterwards. No ounce of effort must be left behind. Lawrence Dallaglio and Phil Vickery chip in. Beneath the expletives key points are being reinforced – it isn't just 'let's kick the hell out of them'. Nobody

He has the capacity to shock us and intimidate opponents with his venom and aggression and I wonder what he is going to say

is punching or head-butting anyone. The fury is controlled. The aggression lurks just below the surface. It is there, though – I can feel it – and the adrenaline from that provides the last piece of comfort I need to go out there and attack the game. The thought of facing Australia in that furnace is frightening but exhilarating too.

Then it is time to go, time to leave the sanctuary of the changing room and time to face our destiny. We are held in a line, feet from the Wallabies, waiting for the signal to take the field together. In this situation, before every match I have ever played with him, Johnno has turned around and offered one final call to arms. He has the capacity to shock us and intimidate opponents with his venom and aggression and I wonder what he is going to say. The Australian players will hear it as well as us and with all the tension it would not take much to light the blue touch paper. Johnno turns around, fixes us with that beetle-browed stare and begins to open his mouth. But for the first time he does not say anything. That silence counts for a thousand words. He can see in our eyes that we are ready. I still wonder what that must have felt like for Australia.

We run out into a tumbling wall of noise thrown out by the vast banks of gold and white. It takes your breath away. The anthems follow – a very personal moment in a highly impersonal setting, with all those people looking on and a camera up my nose. Although I'm singing the words to 'God Save The Queen' loudly in my head they come out of my mouth as a quiet mumble. I am thinking about the important people in my life, about those who have helped to put me in that line. I am thinking about how fortunate I am to be playing for my country in a World Cup final. Most importantly, I'm thinking about the first play of the game. The music finishes, the crowd roars and after one final huddle with Johnno we are away. Steve Larkham puts the ball into the sky against a backdrop of exploding flashlights and instantly all the nerves and all the anxiety melt away, just as they did when the whistle blew when I was a ten-year-old. I am just a rugby player playing in a rugby match again. I don't feel sick any more.

The game plan I have taken such care to memorise is more a starting point than a strict doctrine – you have to play what is in front of you on the pitch – and that point is underlined when the Wallabies take the lead. A brilliant cross-kick by Larkham puts Lote Tuqiri in an aerial battle with Jason Robinson and with a six-inch height advantage there is only one winner. Five-nil Australia.

We gather under the crossbar. There are no recriminations. It was a great play by the Wallabies and there is not much we could have done to prevent the try. We can hear the noise of the crowd but it doesn't affect us. I try to imagine what the stadium will sound like when we score. Within minutes we have done, with a penalty. Then another. Then another. We are into our stride.

Just before half-time comes a big moment. Mat Rogers kicks long, Jason runs the ball back and from the ruck in midfield suddenly everything opens up. Lawrence bursts off it and I hare after him, screaming for the pass back on the angle because, for the first time in the game, we have the Australians stretched and I

I try to imagine what the stadium will sound like when we score. Within minutes we have done, with a penalty. Then another. Then another. We are into our stride

can see a big hole opening up. He delays too long and goes into contact but with his strength he manages to get his arms out of the tackle and the ball away to me with one hand. I am one-on-one with Rogers, the last line of the Australian defence, but I can sense English support runners arriving on either side of me. In the tumult of the crowd, I can't hear Ben Cohen calling on my right or Jason on my left. It wouldn't matter if they had loudspeakers – in these situations peripheral vision has to take over. I have only a split second to make the decision. Twenty metres out, Ben has the ideal line to go between the posts but I reason that with the Australians' fantastic scramble defence a covering wing or George Gregan must be tracking him so I go for Jason. After delaying for a fraction to try to hold Rogers, the pass is delivered, he takes it and, with his pace over a short distance and low, scuttling running style, there is simply no-one better to finish in that situation. Rogers can't get there and Jason slides over for the try. The place goes mad and so does Jason, punching the ball heavenwards.

The move in itself hadn't been planned – they rarely are – but neither had the try simply materialised out of nothing. It came late in a half when we had tired the Wallabies by draining them in the set piece and dragging them around the field. The success came from the whole team's understanding and reaction. It was a good effort for either side to have engineered a try. The defences were so strong, the desire so great, that even in an elongated game there were only six line breaks in a hundred minutes of rugby.

Half-time comes – keep it going boys, don't stop playing, let's win the second half. Except Australia have other ideas. They chip away at us, punishing us for giving away silly penalties while keeping their own discipline superbly. I don't have one shot at goal in the second half. Elton Flatley pulls the score back to 14-11 but the clock is running down and we are keeping them out of range. We are within touching distance of the Webb Ellis Trophy. Then, disaster. Referee André Watson blows his whistle at a scrum. Penalty to Australia. Don't ask me to explain why – I don't know what goes on in a scrum. What is frustrating is that there is nothing us backs can do about it. In fact, despite being in the scrum, I think the forwards feel the same. The Wallabies have an escape route and up steps Flatley. One kick to keep his side in the World Cup.

I would have done anything to have won that World Cup final in eighty minutes, to have spared myself the agonies of extra time but as Flatley lines up the ball I find myself thinking as a fellow kicker rather than an opponent. This is the kick we all train for, the one we visualise over and over, alone on the practice field. And under all the pressure in the world, he nails it. 'Fair play to you, my friend,' I mutter under my breath. If anything deserves to take a game into extra time, that kick does.

So extra time it is – uncharted territory for everyone. Part of me wants to go over to the Wallabies and offer to share the cup but we've come too far for that. There must be a winner. And a loser. The rules are twenty minutes of extra time, followed by ten minutes of

We are awarded a penalty almost immediately, right at the limit of my range. Johnno asks me if I think I can get it. I tell him I'll have a go.

I make it.

sudden-death rugby and then, God forbid, a drop goal shoot-out. I can't face that. Lining up a drop goal with defenders running at you is all very well in a match but in the sterile environment of a shoot-out, with the cup on the line, it would be totally unnerving. And how could I face myself if I missed?

As we mill around the pitch, thinking these thoughts and regrouping ourselves for one last push, it all feels strangely surreal. Standing there, out in the middle, waiting to go again, it's a bit like we're at some inconsequential sevens tournament rather than the World Cup final, if it wasn't for Revenge of The Nerves, Part Two. I half expect Clive to bring the oranges on. As it is he makes a beeline for me. He starts going on about us needing points to win this game – penalties and drop goals. 'No kidding Clive,' is my instinctive reaction but I bite my tongue. 'Kicking,' I'm thinking. 'I need to practise my kicking.' And I go off with a ball towards the posts. Clive is left standing there, talking to thin air. Not very polite, I know, but I'm aware of the score. If it will be a penalty or a drop goal that wins the World Cup, then I want the chance to check how I'm looking.

Johnno gathers us in again and exhorts us not to dwell on the last eighty minutes but to put everything into the next twenty. I've never been here before but the trick in situations like this must be to get two scores up and, unbowed by the disappointment of being pushed into extra time, we are awarded a penalty almost immediately, right at the limit of my range. Johnno asks me if I think I can get it. I tell him I'll have a go. I make it. Paul Grayson tells me afterwards that he could tell from the sound of the strike that it was over and he let the bench know way before the ball reached the posts. It is my best goal-kick of the tournament and gives us a three-point lead.

However, we cannot pull clear and spend our time trying to keep Australia out of penalty range. We know the referee has an itchy finger. We reach the break intact but, with the tension almost unbearable in the second period, Australia are awarded another penalty. Flatley does it again – 17-17. There is pandemonium in the stadium.

Near exhaustion and despair, I look up at the clock. We have three minutes – one shot, one opportunity.

Field position is everything so we make a quick decision to kick-off long, knowing Rogers will clear his lines and that we will have the line-out throw inside their half. I call 'Zig-zag' to Matt Dawson and he relays the code word to Ben Kay who will then call an appropriate line-out to enable us to activate the move. 'Zig-zag' is a move we have rehearsed many times, setting up the ideal position for a drop goal. It has been in the back of my mind all through the final; now it is right at the front.

We need a secure set piece – by no means guaranteed in a final where neither side have been able to dominate their own ball. Steve Thompson hits the button, picking out Lewis Moody at the tail, the hardest part of the line-out to find but obligatory for this attack. It allows us to launch Catty onto the ball and immediately over the gain-line. Australia know what we are

I know it doesn't have to go far; just straight. When I connect it feels good

planning and concentrate on getting up fast to charge down the drop goal but in doing so leave a hole for Matt Dawson to burst through the ruck. He is hauled down having made a crucial twenty metres – an awesome run for the team but don't mistake the fact that he was trying to score himself! He has put us in range and, back in the pocket, I scream for the ball thirty metres out, readying myself for the kick. I'm to the left of the posts so I line it up with my right foot to open up the angle and to avoid the charge-down. But Daws is buried and Backy is waiting to deliver the pass at scrum-half. Johnno sees this and, critically, takes the ball up one more time, making the Australian forwards defend again and allowing Daws to return to his station. The Wallabies go offside in their keenness to come through but the referee only warns them. Then I see Daws picking up the ball. I lift my hands to receive it and he fires back the perfect pass. This is it.

The knack with a drop goal is to connect with the ball as it makes contact with the ground, turning it into a place-kick in effect. But when I drop the ball it lands slightly off-centre, bouncing fractionally towards me as I strike it. This reduces the power I can put through the ball but it actually makes accuracy easier. I know it doesn't have to go far; just straight. When I connect it feels good. Phil Waugh tries to block the kick but he can't get there – it's up and away into the sky. I look up, I see the posts and I know it is going between them. It does. After all the pain, all the sacrifice and all the hardship it might just be that England are going to win the World Cup.

Then I am seized by a moment of panic. Can the referee deny us again? I look over at André Watson. He raises his arm and signals the drop goal. Everything is OK. We still have to deal with the kick-off but Trevor Woodman catches it and the ball is fed back to Catty to deliver the laziest yet most beautiful touch-kick in the history of English rugby. Then it's over. We've done it. My head is spinning like a tumble dryer. I jump up and down with Will Greenwood, shouting like a mad man,

'World Cup, World Cup'. In the emotion of the moment I am unable to come up with anything more profound. It does say it all, though – we are world champions.

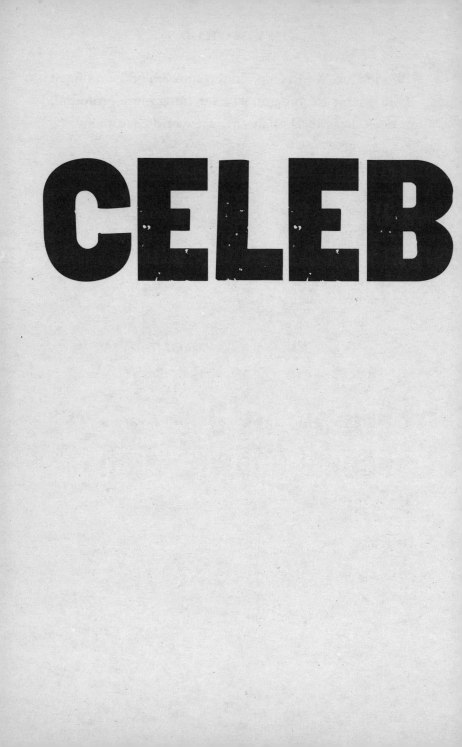

RITY

'A celebrity works hard all his life to become known, then wears dark glasses'

Fred Allen

Am I famous?

I look at myself differently now than I did perhaps a couple of years ago. I understand more now about how society works. How people get put in the spotlight. Two years ago I wouldn't have answered the above question with a 'yes'. Now I have to accept that people do take an interest in what I do. Truthfully, I sometimes wonder why. Especially as fame was the last thing on my mind when I first started playing the game.

Two aspects of the reaction to our World Cup win flummoxed me. Firstly, I didn't anticipate how big it was going to be – for all the hype and support in Australia I don't think any of us did – and secondly, I had no idea the all-consuming hype would last as long as it has for me. I hadn't looked at an Australian newspaper, let alone an English one, Down Under so I had no real idea of the impact our World Cup adventure had had back home. I soon found out.

I had looked forward to the journey home and I slept soundly on the flight all the way from Singapore, so I had some of my faculties about me when we landed at Heathrow at 4.30 a.m. Until I stepped out of the plane. To find 8,000 people waiting for us scrambled my mind completely. I was told afterwards I looked shocked and bewildered by the throng – that was because I was shocked and bewildered. I was excited about seeing my friends and family again but I hadn't expected the rest of the country to turn up as well.

Walking through the doors into a teeming arrivals hall at that time of the morning was astounding and a little bit frightening. The situation felt almost out of control. It took twenty minutes to force our way onto the team coach. Even when we were safely inside people stayed to cheer, many from the upper tiers of an adjacent multi-storey car park and one group from the roof of an unattended police car. As the bus pulled away into the deserted roads beyond, escorted by eight police motorbikes, I thought maybe that would be the end of it. Wrong. It was only the start – that much became abundantly clear when I walked through my front door back in Northumberland.

England might have enjoyed a great World Cup but my postman hadn't. I came back to a pile of letters as high as a house and the volume intensified in the days afterwards. They were coming in at four hundred a week at one stage.

A lot of people simply wanted to share their World Cup experiences. There had clearly been some tense sitting rooms on the morning of the final. There was one letter from someone whose priest turned up late for confirmation class because he couldn't pull himself away from the game. There was another from a surgeon telling how he and his anaesthetist had delayed an operation to make sure they caught extra time. The patient made a full recovery, he assured me.

Others wrote to offer advice. I should smile more, said one; I should drive a British car rather than a Mercedes, read another. There was even a letter from a vicar saying that I should become a man of the cloth.

The letters came from places as far afield as Finland and Fiji, Malawi and Luxembourg; there were even a few from Australia – including one from Elton Flatley. He congratulated us on our win, said we deserved it but that the Wallabies would be out to get us next time. They did.

He congratulated us on our win, said we deserved it but that the Wallabies would be out to get us next time. They did

Many children wrote to say how they had started playing rugby after watching the World Cup which was gratifying, although one seven-year-old said he had been sent off for trying to tackle like me in a non-contact game. At the opposite end of the scale was a lovely note from an 87-year-old lady who was about to emigrate to South Africa a happy woman to 'pop her clogs' alongside her family.

It gradually began to dawn on me that the World Cup victory was an achievement that had crossed the boundaries between sports and gone beyond sport altogether. Somehow, by doing our jobs, we had touched people's lives. Wrapped up in the middle of our own little world in Australia we had had no conception of that. A common theme ran through much of the correspondence and it was extremely humbling. It was that we had inspired people and made them proud of their country, not only by winning but also, apparently, by how we had carried ourselves through the tournament. That made me want to go out and do it all over again.

If there was one event which illustrated the extent to which the country had been affected it was our victory parade. Looking at everyone from the top of the bus on that freezing December day was an incredible experience. It was an assault on the senses. Seeing three-quarters of a million people lining the streets of London and hearing the choruses of 'Swing Low' in Trafalgar Square was absolutely mad. If England won World Cups in major team sports more often it may have been different, but it had been a long wait since 1966.

I would probably have been more at ease watching than being watched but I tucked myself away as best I could at the back of the players' bus, next to my day-release partner Hilly, as we set off from the Inter-Continental Hotel at Hyde Park Corner just before midday. The parade began properly at Marble Arch and it soon became obvious that we weren't going to be accompanied by tumbleweed down deserted streets as we had joked when the idea had first been suggested. The numbers just swelled and swelled and by the time the parade reached Oxford Circus it was a full-blown street party. We all looked down on it open-mouthed for the most part, exchanging comments of disbelief. All this for a rugby team?

There was red and white confetti in the air and flags everywhere, there was even one up on the platform of a crane high in the sky. People were on top of bus shelters, clinging to lampposts, all yelling their support. One guy even climbed up a set of traffic lights to shake our hands. People hurled cameras up onto the bus for players to take pictures of each other. We then had to throw them back from thirty yards down the road as the bus moved on. They were all returned in one piece – apart from the ones Thommo threw!

As for the scenes in Trafalgar Square, they were amazing – a sea of smiling faces and a bottomless pit of warmth on the coldest of days. It was a country and a team saying thank you to each other. In amongst the faces was one very familiar one – my granddad. The police had let him through in front of the barrier so I could see and wave to him. It was an emotional moment for both of us. My grandma had passed away while I was in Australia.

A sea of smiling faces and a bottomless pit of warmth on the coldest of days

The clamour and the euphoria were staggering, yet one of my clearest memories of it all is of turning off the procession route at the end and suddenly no-one being there. It was similar to the feeling after a match when you leave the ground, head home and close your front door behind you. Welcome back to real life. Except on this occasion, life became even more surreal afterwards. Hearing from the Queen how she had watched all bar one of the games, then visiting 10 Downing Street and finding the Prime Minister's son Leo in the England shirt he had worn throughout the tournament, brought home – if what we had just seen hadn't – how everyone had been caught up in the drama. No-one, it seemed, had been immune.

Tea and scones at Buckingham Palace was quite something. Inside it was just how you would imagine

Some very important people had trodden those floors – a lot more important than the England rugby team

a fairytale palace would look. Everywhere there seemed to be masterpieces or wonderful sculptures. We were received in a suitably opulent room, dripping in chandeliers and with Rembrandts on the wall. I was quite taken with the history of it all. Some very important people had trodden those floors – a lot more important than the England rugby team. We passed an edgy few minutes drinking in all the tradition and splendour while we waited for the Queen. After what seemed an age the magnificent doors opened and in came… nine corgis. It was a slight anti-climax. Mark Regan whistled them over.

Eventually we did meet the Queen and posed with her for a picture with the trophy. She talked about how she had listened to the final on the radio and then watched the game on video later that evening. She said she was glad she didn't have to go through the tension of watching it live. I told her that she sounded like my mum who went shopping instead of watching the final. After she admitted she was in Tesco during extra time, the supermarket ran a full-page advert using a picture of her in some of the papers. The caption read: 'She shopped until he dropped.' Mum rarely watches me play. She just waits for the phone call from my dad afterwards to say I'm OK. I think she would prefer it if I played a non-contact sport like tennis.

A few days later Mum was able to meet the Queen when I collected an MBE back at the Palace. The different categories of honours recipients were roped off from each other, giving the inside of one of the stateliest buildings in the world the look of a nightclub. We were strictly drilled on how to address the Queen and how to approach her to receive our honours. The choreography was so exact; the whole performance had the feel of a complex backs' move. Fortunately I didn't knock on.

The Queen has a definite aura about her. Obviously she was quite a lot smaller than a bunch of international rugby players but she had this presence which seemed to fill the room. Being used to life in the public eye, she asked me how I was coping with the attention. Prince

We swerved into a ditch and the front of the car hit a tree and crumpled but fortunately we both walked away without a scratch

William was at Buckingham Palace and we also chatted about life in the spotlight. It seemed to be a recurring theme. When we headed off to Downing Street, that was the topic with the Prime Minister too. Nice to know so many people care.

Walking through that famous black front door was a lot less like stepping into another world than entering Buckingham Palace. No 10 Downing Street is not your average house – it seems to go up and back an awful long way inside – but it is still a family home. There was a huge number of staff inside – you could hardly move for them all – and with the whole squad in there too it was quite crowded. Security was understandably an issue too. We were asked not to bring any unnecessary hand baggage and to leave cameras on the team bus.

I had quite a long chat with Tony Blair and he came across as a decent guy. It must be difficult being PM – you have to be so careful what you say or people like me will repeat it all in a book. He made a few pertinent points about the team, in particular the inner strength which had prevented our heads dropping even when Australia took the final into extra time. Charles Kennedy, the Liberal Democrat leader, was there as well and he was also good company, despite the personal disappointment of Scotland's quarter-final exit.

That wasn't the end of the fun and games. After an extraordinary few hours, I said my goodbyes and left Downing Street early in order to be ready for training in Newcastle the next morning. A car and driver were kindly provided to take me home. As I relaxed in the back, we made our way north. We were almost home when the driver lost control on black ice just before Scotch Corner at midnight and we ended up veering across the A1 at seventy miles an hour. We swerved into a ditch and the front of the car hit a tree and crumpled but fortunately we both walked away without a scratch. I completely forgot to mention it to the Newcastle lads at training. I'd had a lot on the previous day.

The recognition for the England team continued in

many different ways afterwards. While I could accept all the fuss in a team context, I felt very uneasy about being fêted personally. I naturally squint in the glare of the spotlight anyway but after what was the ultimate team triumph it was all the more awkward to be singled out so often.

I know I kicked the winning drop goal but other players were equally valuable, if not more so, to our success. Just take that kick in extra time. If Steve Thompson hadn't found Lewis Moody at the back of the line-out and Lewis hadn't caught it, we would never have had the ball. If Mike Catt hadn't held onto possession when he took the ball up so strongly in midfield and Matt Dawson hadn't made that crucial break, we would never have been in position. And if Johnno hadn't taken the move through one more phase, the Australian defence might have been able to close me down. So there were all those people who contributed directly. And that is without including the line-out lifters and every player who cleaned out the rucks to win the ball, stopping Wallaby hands slowing it down.

I was made a Freeman of the City of Newcastle in February which was great except my Falcons team mates took time out to turn up at the ceremony. They even wore suits. These were the blokes who had helped me break into the England team in the first place –

I naturally squint in the glare of the spotlight

without them I wouldn't even have been in Australia –
and there they were joining in the applause as I was
handed a framed piece of music written in my honour.

I also felt somewhat uncomfortable at the Sports
Personality of the Year awards in December 2003. Here
was a programme I had watched religiously with my
family every year when I was growing up. So many
legends had stood there, with that famous music
playing at the end, holding the trophy with the camera
on it. When my name was read out I felt like a fraud.
Don't get me wrong, I was incredibly grateful to receive
the award from Princess Anne, but when Johnno – the
man who had led us to the World Cup – was standing
behind me in second place it didn't feel right at all. I
felt a lot happier accepting the team award. He
deserved that individual award as much as anyone ever
has in all the years I've been watching.

I am genuinely embarrassed when people chant my name or crowd around me just because they have seen my face before on TV

There was some criticism of the whole squad and the coaches being honoured in the New Year's list because of the numbers involved but I thought that was exactly right. It wasn't just the odd individual who had won the Webb Ellis Trophy.

As the goal-kicker and fly-half, I am always going to receive a lot of scrutiny – good and bad – but it does not equate to deserving it. I am genuinely embarrassed when people chant my name or crowd around me when I get off the bus just because they have seen my face before on TV as I line up a kick. I mean how can I look someone like Hilly in the eye and say I deserve it more than he does?

I was able to laugh off some of the more ludicrous individual attention – the haircut of the year award, for instance. The Wilkinson 'look' was created by Ian Morrison at Salon 66 in Newcastle, a great bloke, chosen less for his international styling credentials than the fact that he has cut my Falcons team mate Dave Walder's hair since he was four. Cost to the public, with wash, £11.50. I choose to have it cut at Ian's house to avoid the self-conscious, uncomfortable feelings that plague me when people stare in the barber's. The setting is hardly what you might imagine for an award-winning cut – the kitchen of a cosy house in Gosforth. You could not wish for a more down-to-earth back-drop. Dinner on the go, kids racing around pretending to be David Beckham, telly on in the next room – it is not a swanky King's Road hair artiste's. If I want my hair rinsed, I have to put my head in the sink with the washing-up.

Being voted the country's most fanciable male also amused me. The whole concept of being a pin-up does not fit in at all with the person I know I am. Although I'm learning to overcome my shyness, I'm still not that confident in social situations and I spend very little time on my appearance. I didn't have women falling all over me when I was unknown so I don't see what should have changed just because of one drop-kick. Who in their right minds would be interested in someone who spends most of his life booting an egg around muddy training pitches and the rest of it locked inside his house? If you're after lifestyle, I'm not really your man.

However, I could not simply shrug off other aspects of the outside world's interest in me. I found I could not go anywhere anonymously any more.

Things were already changing before the World Cup. The recognition rate was increasing at the same speed as rugby's popularity was growing. Even before the tournament I tried to avoid going to places where I knew there would be rugby supporters, but that was where I drew the line at altering the way I lived my life. I still more or less did what I wanted to do. I can't any more. The World Cup's success in touching so many people has opened up millions more to the game, which is something I feel genuinely proud of. But it has also closed off just about every avenue for relaxation I had outside my own home. I used to enjoy shopping in New-castle; now I wouldn't do it unless I had to. Visits to the cinema, a favourite release for me, are also a no-go unless very carefully planned. And this is Newcastle – the football hotbed. After the World Cup I can see why, but the recognition factor still applies today. And I

The World Cup's success in touching so many people has opened up millions more to the game

haven't been in an England shirt for over two years now.

When I'm out I feel I can never really relax. When I was injured last season I went to watch Newcastle play at Leeds. It wasn't a cold day but I togged myself up in hat, scarf and coat so I could stand on the terraces behind the posts without anyone spotting me. Only one guy did and he asked for an autograph without drawing attention to me so there was no problem. But as I trailed away at the end of the game, staring at my feet so no-one would do that double-take look at me, I found myself feeling a little sensitive. Why should I have to go through all of this to watch a game of rugby with my dad?

I find myself wondering if the world will ever spin normally for me again

I have always been a very shy person. From an early age, I found it difficult to mix with others. I was a quiet child and liked keeping myself to myself, getting on with my own things and spending time with my family. When I first started to play professional rugby, I had to become much more confident because of the nature of the position I play. If I hadn't been able to find the strength to put myself in the limelight a bit more I would never have made any of the teams that I've been fortunate enough to be in. I had to make that change, and I think this has helped me to deal with being under so much public scrutiny. I try to separate my rugby self from my individual self. To be the centre of attention as an individual rather than as a rugby player terrifies me. I'm just not an extrovert. I'm susceptible to mood swings. I like to spend time on my own and if I don't I can get quite edgy. I'm very self-critical and analytical and I spend a lot of time thinking about things and worrying. That's who I am, and it doesn't fit with what people expect from my public persona.

I have various sponsorship commitments which I am very proud to fulfil, but when they involve being in front of the camera it generally terrifies me. When I'm filming adverts and have to give off a certain image or pretend to be doing something or show emotions, I get terribly self-conscious. I think I'm useless at that kind of thing and I get very embarrassed. Doing these ads has been an eye-opening experience for me. It's got me more into my films and has made me appreciate what an incredible skill acting is.

It was a different story, though, when I was filming Jonny's Hotshots, a CBBC programme aimed at kids who want to improve their game. That was an amazing experience. I loved coaching in front of the camera and I found it very easy. Scarily easy. I think the reason I felt so comfortable was because I really believed in what I was doing. It's a major ambition of mine to share what I've learned throughout the years with talented young-sters who love the game as much as I do. I want to pass on my knowledge and help others to cope with all the things I've experienced – the injuries, the disappoint-ments, the highs, the lows, the adulation. I find talking about these things comes very naturally, even in front of a camera. I would love to get more into coaching; there's a real opportunity to make a difference and give something back to the game. I'm sure there are many equally qualified people with invaluable experiences to share, but I think, because of my high profile, I would be able to make a bit more of an impact in this area.

I do sometimes find myself wondering if the world will ever spin normally for me again. I find it depressing to think it never will. I realise completely that the vast majority of people do not want to cause me any sort of discomfort. Most are just wanting to give their support and ask for a picture or an autograph. And most say lovely things to me. It is nice to know you have people's support and that makes me feel stronger. But I am a private individual and that privacy is very precious to me. I never asked to be famous. I just wanted to play rugby. If there were one man and a dog watching I wouldn't care – I would still play the game. I am not a performer on a stage. The crowd and their reaction can make for a marvellous atmosphere, provide a vivid backdrop, and can be incredibly inspiring – anyone who watched our World Cup semi-final against France would acknowledge that – but it is the game that attracts me, not the adulation.

Celebrity, for want of a better word, has exposed me

I want to pass on my knowledge and help others to cope with all the things I've experienced

to what I perceive to be some of the negative sides of society. There are a fair few con-artists out there that want to take a ride on the achievements of the England side. I have learned to be careful who I sign items for. I do not sign any England shirts any more because so many of them end up on internet sites being sold for profit and they, in turn, lower the value of the ones being auctioned for good causes. Actually, it doesn't seem to matter if I sign them or not – people just forge them anyway. I've seen them out there with Jonny spelt wrongly. Having to try to pick out these bad apples that are out for a quick buck is a nightmare. I hate having to be suspicious and say no to requests but some of the fabricated stories I've had to put up with would turn a saint into a sceptic.

If there were just one man and a dog watching I wouldn't care – I would still play the game

What is wrong with your life when you make up a disabled relative to try to scrounge some autographed kit? And what possesses somebody to send a baby-grow, complete with a picture of baby wearing it, to be signed, only for it to end up on a selling site a fortnight later? I just do not understand where these people are coming from. We all worked so hard to achieve what we did, something which made a lot of people in our country proud, and these individuals try to hitch a lift on the back of it with no regard for right and wrong. The lengths they are prepared to go to are incredible. It angers me, not least because it will always mean that some of the loyal and genuine fans miss out on the respect they deserve because of the actions of a few individuals.

Experiencing the flip side of fame since the World Cup has made quite an impact on my life. It has created negative energy out of what should have been an entirely positive experience.

More negative than anything else have been my encounters with the paparazzi. I never thought I would question whether achieving rugby's ultimate goal was worth it but in my dealings with this separate species I have done.

I used to love holidays. Still do, but I have had to grow to accept, or at least understand, some of the more negative aspects. A few days in the sun would be the carrot that pulled me through the weariness of end-of-season rugby. Some time after the World Cup I thought I would get away with my girlfriend to Mauritius. Thanks to deliberate information leaks at airports and to the sneak photographers, a few days in paradise turned into hell. What should have been the perfect week to start my professional recovery had to be cut short by two days because of them.

They operated from boats at sea and took pictures of us on the beach. It was so intrusive and I felt so helpless because there was nothing I could do about it. The beach was private but the sea was public property, so people in boats could do what they liked. It got to the stage where we had four or five boats shadowing us.

As we walked, they followed. If we stopped, the boats stopped. If we turned and went the other way, they did a U-turn in the sea. Everyone else on that beach had their freedom, yet ours was taken away. What had we done wrong?

I thought winning the World Cup was a good thing – why did it feel like we were being punished? I felt uptight, angry, depressed and vowed not to go near the sand again. But the pictures they had already taken appeared in three of the British tabloids which was like having our privacy invaded all over again.

It didn't stop when I returned home. I landed at Newcastle Airport to be confronted by another snapper who had his lens so close he ended up in the same section of the revolving door. He even had the cheek to ask me for another picture when my father and I had clearly told him that he was intruding. I used to read about people punching these characters and be astounded at how they could lose their cool so badly, but being on the other side of it I can understand their reaction now, if not condone it.

I don't know how these people can look at themselves in the mirror. The more intimate and private the moment, the more valuable it is to them and the more willing they are to intrude. These people find what they do acceptable, but I don't. I know everyone

When I play for England I understand I am public property. But when the rest of my life is opened up to comment and judgement that is a totally different scenario

has to put bread on the table for their families but there are choices to be made in life. No-one is forced to do that job.

This sort of thing happens to me all the time. More than eighteen months after the World Cup final I went with my brother and some mates on a much-needed holiday after the Lions tour. It was the best holiday I have ever had. We managed to get away in the sun for a couple of weeks (Sparks joined me on the second week) and it gave me an opportunity to clear my system

If all your existence amounts to is chasing fame for fame's sake, it is a life built on sand and is liable to come crashing down around you.

after a year of injuries and then the build-up to the New Zealand games. I came back fully recovered and raring to go.

On the holiday, however, I did find it a bit difficult feeling that all eyes were on me. The friends I was with were able to go off and have a great laugh, do exactly as they wanted without a care in the world. For me, it doesn't feel I can do that because people notice everything I do. So if I want to do something a bit daft, try a funny dive off a rock for instance, I think, 'Oh, people are going to see this,' whereas others can just go for it and no-one pays any attention. Of course, I understand why and I am not complaining. It just makes things a little awkward. But I fully accept that a lot of my quality of living comes from being recognised.

As I have said, the only aspect of this recognition factor that really gets to me is when it invades my private life. And I think photos of me relaxing come under that banner. Again, on the same holiday, pictures of me having a laugh by the sea appeared in the newspapers back home. That annoys me still – but maybe after all these injuries I have a different perspective which helps me deal with it mentally.

When I play for England, I understand I am public property. I know everything I do will be examined in pictures and words. That is absolutely fine. Everyone is entitled to their own opinion of me – whether I am playing well, whether I should be in the team – that's part of the deal. But when the rest of my life is opened up to comment and judgement that is a totally different scenario.

Other sportsmen, like David Beckham, are better at handling the whole media circus. He deals with all the attention – positive and negative – fantastically, although not in a way I could ever manage. Accepting it will always be a part of his life, he is more pro-active and uses it to his advantage. I think you need a certain kind of outgoing personality to carry that off which I don't have. I have a group of very good sponsors but I try to represent them in the way I prepare, perform and behave on the rugby field, rather than by joining the celebrity circus.

I am very uneasy with the whole idea of a celebrity culture. Fame may be a spin-off of success in the sports and entertainment world, but if it turns your head you can lose sight of what helped you reach that position in the first place and then you have problems. Just because an actor gets his big break in a hit film, it doesn't mean he should ease off in his next role. If anything it should spur him on to give an even better performance. It's the same with sportsmen. Look at Beckham. He doesn't allow himself to be distracted despite all the madness around him. It is the core which is important, not all the peripheral flannel.

Not everyone recognises this and for some people their whole life appears to revolve around becoming a celebrity and then maintaining that status by increasingly desperate means. If all your existence amounts to is chasing fame for fame's sake, it is a life built on sand and is liable to come crashing down around you. It is short term and empty and certainly not the life for me.

GRITY

'I want to make sure that if young people are looking up to me, they are looking up to the genuine me, not a fake. The way I live cannot be an act'

Jonny Wilkinson

have been accused of being an obsessive. I used to shy away from that description because of its connotations – someone kindly described me as a 'basket case' at the World Cup. However, in the case of training, at least, I feel more comfortable with the term now.

When I go out onto the pitch I want to look at my opposite number and feel as if I am stronger, quicker and better than he is. I need to believe that whatever he throws at me I will be more than equal to it. For that to happen, I have to prepare obsessively.

I don't view the sacrifices I make as a pain. They are my choice. Once I get something in my head that I need to give up or change, after the initial battle to forgo it, I will forget about it completely. If something does not help improve me as a rugby player, I'll bin it. Simple as that.

I don't drink alcohol. I used to indulge in the odd binge to let the lid off the pressure cooker but gradually the gaps between the big nights out grew and grew until I stopped drinking altogether. I no longer feel it is part of me. Although we all probably deserved one, I didn't even have a tipple the night we won the World Cup. Instead I drank a couple of Diet Cokes as we celebrated in a nightclub in The Rocks. The last time I touched alcohol was when England beat Australia in Melbourne in June 2003.

I eat healthily. All the benefits of a hard training session can be lost by munching the wrong food afterwards so I choose not to eat sweets, biscuits or chocolate. People have given up buying me Easter eggs because I just pass them on. I have a real complex about giving in to this sort of temptation – even if I took a single bite, which would have no consequence whatsoever for my fitness, I would feel guilty and regard it as mental weakness on my part. There is that obsessive streak again.

I also steer clear of fast food. In fact I have taken its avoidance to a new level. I refuse to go into a fast-food

If something does not help improve me as a rugby player, I'll bin it. Simple as that

outlet – to use the toilet even – in case anyone got the wrong idea and thought I was sneaking in a quick burger.

England have a nutritionist, Adam Carey, who provides dietary advice and keeps me up to speed with what I should and shouldn't be eating. He also recommends the supplements I take, a necessary part of professional rugby life if not always the easiest to stomach. I love good food but it has to be healthy.

As for smoking, it is my pet hate – it always has been. When I was younger I used to have nightmares that someone was pinning me down and forcing me to smoke. I would wake up feeling like something was terribly wrong, only to realise I had been dreaming and my non-smoking record was still intact. I don't ever want to smoke a cigarette.

Rugby has been everything to me for so long and my family has always been there

I try to be consistent. Because I don't drink and try not to eat unhealthy food, I would never tell others to do so. When a fast-food chain approached me after the World Cup to endorse their product, I turned them down. I hadn't been in one of their outlets since I became a professional rugby player – it doesn't fit with the lifestyle – so it would have been hypocritical. A snack-food company also approached me but, again, it wasn't a product I would eat myself or encourage prospective sportsmen to eat so I said no.

People tell me I am in the position of being a role model to young people so I want to provide a good example. If I have achieved a position of influence, then I want to use that power wisely. I remember walking into the Newcastle changing room as an eighteen-year-old and seeing legends like Inga Tuigamala and Pat Lam. I instinctively gravitated to them and the way they went about things. Fortunately they were great examples of how to live your life. Inga talked in great detail about using his time playing rugby to build his reputation as a person and player. He told me that will be all that is left when the boots are hung up.

I want to make sure that if young people are looking up to me, they are looking up to the genuine me, not a fake. The way I live cannot be an act. Image is a buzz word of our times and central to the celebrity culture which prevails at the moment but the only image you can truly portray without fear of being exposed is that of the person you are.

I am not, in the practising sense of the word, religious. My parents are not really churchgoers so I wasn't brought up that way but they did give me, through my upbringing, the means of determining my own black-and-white picture of wrong and right. I'm not quite sure where I stand on organised religion but I like to believe in judgement from a greater power. I live my life as if a twenty-four-hour surveillance camera is trained on me, which is ironic as over the past two years or so it has felt as if one has been. At the end of my days, I want to be able to hand over and sign away the video, happy that its contents accurately reflect the person I am.

I also believe this is a way to pay back my parents and brother who have been so supportive of me and my career. It boils down to respect. Rugby has been everything to me for so long and my family has always been there. Dad has thought nothing of driving me to matches, Mum has washed my kit and made me the correct food, and now they both look after so much of my life around the game. And as for my brother, Sparks, whenever I've asked him to kick with me, train with me, tackle with me, outside a regular session, he is always up for it. No matter how tired or drained he is. And I'd do the same for him. It may sound selfish, but what I haven't been able to do, because of the way my life is, is to repay them with my time. So much of my day is taken up by commitments to the game and to others. And so I hope I do pay them back with respect – in the way I lead my life. That is very important to me.

There are boundaries which I set for myself and do not want to cross. I won't take my clothes off for pictures, for instance. My reticence is partly to do with appearances. I don't find images of people without their clothes on all that attractive – I prefer to leave something to the imagination because mystery is a very appealing part of a person. But it is also to try to preserve what remains of my privacy. I don't want

I earn a good living in a wonderful job so I am in the fortunate position of being able to pick and choose what I do

everyone else owning all of me. During the World Cup, England spent some time at a water park relaxing. I'd have liked to join in but there were photographers waiting to snap the players without their shirts on. I kept my top on and watched instead – so did Jason Robinson. We both found the idea of being picked off half-naked by the snappers a bit grubby. I did take my top off for a picture once when I was very young for a health magazine. I had my arm twisted after forty minutes of trying to say no. It is something I learned from but still resent very strongly.

None of us is perfect. I can be grumpy and fractious to the people I care for the most, particularly before matches. If I'm not training well, I am not the best person to be around. There are times when I become

Each time I've been sidelined I've determined to come back even better

too obsessed with trivialities and fall below the standards I set myself but that should not stop me trying to reach them.

After the World Cup I also rejected an approach to take part in coffee adverts – I don't drink the stuff – and a spread in *Hello!* magazine. A million pounds or not, that was a non-starter. After working so hard protecting what little privacy I had left, the last thing I wanted was to invite a photographer in to show the world my 'tastefully decorated' bathroom.

Aside from the promotional work I was committed to with my five existing sponsors, I said no to virtually every commercial opportunity or public appearance after the World Cup. I thought it would be seen as cashing in.

I don't want to come across as some sort of martyr. I earn a good living in a wonderful job so I am in the fortunate position of being able to pick and choose what I do. I don't judge others for making their own decisions over what constitutes a reasonable offer. It's just that you give a part of yourself away when you take money off people and I want to feel happy with where that part of me is going. I feel I've been very lucky with the companies that have taken an interest in me.

That's not to say there weren't some corking offers. The chance to be immortalised inside a glass paper-weight or to feature on a pair of tiny rubber boots attached to a key ring was tempting. But not that tempting. The ideas for Wilkinson board games, pens and models were no-nos too, especially as the dolls didn't even look like me. There was one strange grog-like figure, which bore a closer resemblance to Jude Law, and a hand-made plaster sculpture of me whose head unfortunately fell off.

I was inundated with requests from charities, which meant having to make some difficult decisions over which I felt I could support. Raffling off one of my World Cup final shirts was a practical way of doing so once I had made my mind up. I chose the raffle ticket idea because I didn't want it simply to go to the highest bidder at an auction, as is usually the way with sports memorabilia. I wanted to give fans the chance to win it.

I try not to short-change anyone. When I'm conducting a kicking clinic I will always give more time to the kids who are there than I promised. A chain of frustrated parents who have waited shivering on the touchline will confirm that what is supposed to be an hour's session usually snowballs into something longer. It does when I'm on my own so I might as well give them the authentic experience! Besides, it is a professional duty not to mess with the dreams and ambitions of someone who is there to learn. I know how disappointing bad teaching can be. One of the team's sponsors in Australia threw a golf day and after finishing my kicking, I turned up late but excited about the prospect of a golf lesson. I live right next to a course and play occasionally so I was keen to iron out one or two of my long list of faults. The instructor took a little time out to just confuse me and then walked away. It was the perfect example of how to discourage someone from ever picking up a golf club again. The worst thing was that I was really looking forward to it, even if he wasn't. It is a useful reference point for me for when the boot is on the other foot. The experience the children have may well contribute to whether they stick with rugby or not.

You have to put the hours in. There are no short cuts

If I do promotional work, I will always catch up the time on the training field, even if it means an evening kicking session alone on my local football pitch. I kick six days a week. How long for depends on how well a session goes. The minimum is probably an hour and a quarter, the maximum – well, there is no maximum. I am trying to taper down some of the kicking to give my life more balance but I am finding this very difficult. This is especially so after the string of injuries I've suffered since the World Cup. Each time I've been sidelined I've been determined to come back even better – stronger, faster, fitter and with more skills in my armoury. For kicking, indeed for all the core skills of rugby, that takes practice and training. You have to put the hours in. There are no short cuts.

I sometimes become frustrated that others do not share my all-consuming approach to my sport. I can't rest until I have tamed the devil in my head and if that means kicking until all hours, then it just has to be done.

I complete each session with six kicks at goal from different positions. I have to make every one before I can go home. If I don't, the sequence starts again. My conscience doesn't allow me to stop before the set is complete. My record, and it is not one I'm particularly proud of, stands at five hours, set when I was seventeen.

There are certainly drawbacks to having this mindset. Personal ones. I am really into Australian rugby league and one of my ambitions is to go and see the State of Origin live. A few of the guys, when England have been in Australia in the past, have had the chance. But not me. Because of all the kicking and practice I do I've never been. Not that I'm complaining really. Sacrifices have to be made, and they are worth it.

I have come to realise, however, that my way is not for everyone. Not only is it weird to keep going for that long but I know now it can also be counter-productive. There's nothing I can do to stop myself but I do at least recognise the danger. The point of all the hours on the training pitch is to enable me to feel satisfied. Other players can manage that with half the effort. For me, it just wouldn't work. Understanding this was a huge step forward for me.

The one person I take notice of when he tells me I

am overdoing it is Blackie. Well, usually. Sometimes I will slip in a crafty kicking session while he's not looking.

I might kick with my brother or one of the Newcastle Academy lads and occasionally Rob Andrew will appear out of his office to relive his distant youth and kick the balls back. For quite a lot of the time, though, I train alone at Kingston Park. I think having to go and fetch the stray balls that have bounced into the stand in order to repeat the exercise adds mental toughness.

If you were to come along to watch, you would hear me talking to myself as I go along. More persuasive evidence to back the basket-case argument on the surface, but there is a sane point to the cries of 'sweet', 'great kick – that's the one', 'concentrate – hard foot' and 'if I do that again I'm going to punch myself'. In technical jargon this is called self-talk. I use it in matches to re-enforce my confidence. If I'm telling myself I'm doing well, it will help me to do so. Telling myself that it's not so good is also important as long as the criticism is underpinned with technical coaching to help correct the next one.

I like to compare the perfect kick to a jigsaw puzzle. Every time I am away from the training ground, the box the jigsaw is in is shaken up, so when I go back to kick

The cupped hands were voted the most irritating sporting trait in the world. But it works for me, so I'll stick with it

the next day it doesn't quite fit together any more. The aim of every session is to reassemble those pieces to make the complete picture again.

I didn't understand the mechanics of how to do so until I started working with Dave Alred when I was sixteen. He was Rob's kicking coach at the time. The beauty with Dave was that he was able to call on all sorts of influences from a varied playing career which incorporated both codes of rugby and American football. He basically ripped apart my technique and reconstructed it so that as many of the variable elements as possible were taken out. It was difficult for me at first but as I practised I could see the improvement with my own eyes. The most important thing Dave has taught me is how to be my own coach. I know I will make mistakes but I also know why, so I can put things right.

There are probably people who look at my kicking stance now and think it must be uncomfortable, what with my hands cupped in front of me. Exactly the opposite is true. This is the position in which I feel at ease, shielded against all distractions. It has evolved over many seasons.

When I kick I try to blot out the outside world by employing a yoga technique. It is called centring and involves channelling all my inner energy from a core point behind my navel. As I prepare to strike the ball, I concentrate on the energy surging down my left leg and into my left foot. This creates an explosive contact with the ball. That is the theory anyway.

Subconsciously, as I worked on doing this, my hands took up their prayer position. When I started out they were a lot further apart but the style has changed over the years until it has become something of a calling card. I even had it trademarked after the World Cup. Not everyone warms to it. The cupped hands were voted the most irritating sporting trait in the world, ahead of Tim Henman's clenched fist, in one magazine. But it works for me, so I'll stick with it.

Oddly, my hands remain apart if I use my right foot to kick at goal. I do this in practice sometimes as it helps with the drop-kicking. When I was sixteen I used to take goal-kicks in matches with both feet, using my right from the left-hand side of the pitch and vice versa. I gave that up when I realised how much time would be needed to perfect the art with just one foot. However, I stuck with the two-footed approach with the punting and the drop-kicking.

Maybe my way of doing things comes from having a dad who was left-footed and an elder brother who prefers his right. As a right-handed five-year-old I used to find it an interesting challenge to try to pass a ball equally as well off my left hand. It was the same the opposite way round with kicking. A lot was made during the World Cup of me targeting the unfortunate Doris behind the posts in kicking practice, an imaginary lady holding a copy of *The Times*. It's nothing personal. It is just a means of narrowing down the zone I'm aiming for. So if I'm slightly off, the ball should still go through the middle of the posts. Doris came into my life in 1998, in the week leading up to the Test against Australia. I was struggling badly to hit through the new Summit rugby balls and nothing I tried seemed to help. Eventually Dave suggested we forget about technique and imagine trying to hit an empty seat in the stand behind the posts. As we narrowed the margin of error the seat became a lady (Dave's idea), then the target became her newspaper and finally her ice cream. It really helped me with my confidence and accuracy.

Being a kicker obviously involves extra practice compared to the rest of the team but I try to do more fitness work too. When it comes to conditioning, there is no escape from the basics of running and lifting weights but I try to train more efficiently and often in a different way to other players to gain an edge. There are so many good young players coming through that to stay still I have to keep moving ahead.

I trust Blackie's guidance in this area implicitly. From day to day I never know what he has in store for me. I have turned up for sessions and found badminton and short tennis rackets waiting for me. My brother Mark is my usual training partner but Blackie has provided everyone from karting drivers to a Hollywood actor who was filming in the north-east, all with the idea of keeping training fresh and interesting. The programme changes each session and my challenge is to react positively to whatever he throws in front of me and be ready to give everything I have.

If you peered into the breeze-block gym under the West Stand at Kingston Park, with its weights machines and running track, you would be as likely to find me

I could probably hold my own in a boxing ring, although wild horses couldn't drag me into one

with a football or a punchbag as a rugby ball. Like Dave Alred, Blackie is a man of many parts, having trained Newcastle United in the past and been a professional boxer, and he imparts the knowledge and self-confidence he has accumulated in these fields.

The boxing is not designed to help me in the event of a fight on the field, but it is incredible for explosive power and fitness. The punching can also replicate a strong hand-off and the footwork is useful for getting myself in the right position for a tackle. The spin-off of regularly pummelling a punchball or a drunken sailor is that I could probably hold my own in a boxing ring, although wild horses couldn't drag me into one.

Equally, the point of the football work is not to stop me looking like a fool in adverts like the one I did with

Everyone needs heroes

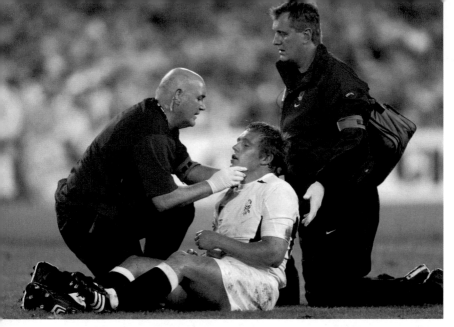

Setbacks

David Beckham or to recall my glory days in the Farnham Town under-elevens defence, but to work on co-ordination and concentration. Blackie will often demand a football skill, like continuously volleying a ball against a wall without it touching the floor, when I am already dripping in sweat from my exertions. The act of performing a precise skill under extreme stress simulates what happens in every rugby match, even if at Twickenham I rarely flick a rugby ball onto the back of my neck and balance it there.

I use a lot of football training techniques because foot-ballers generally use their feet and evasive skills more often than rugby players. When I set about improving my footwork a few seasons ago, Blackie used drills Kevin Keegan had employed as a player to spin off defenders. Blackie tells me there was no-one better. You learn from the best, whichever sport they happen to play, and I do like football. I suppose I am an adopted Newcastle United fan these days but I have a soft spot for Norwich City. My granddad, Phil Wilkinson, has a season ticket and used to take my brother and me to Carrow Road for Boxing Day fixtures.

The sessions with Blackie, which can last a couple of hours, are extremely intense. The exercises are sharp and there are few breaks. Although England's pre-World

Cup training was tough, I had endured worse before with Blackie. I have got to the stage where flogging myself is second nature. I wouldn't say I relish the thought of training but it is something I know I have to do and I also know how good it will feel afterwards. The thought that I have moved myself on is a comforting one. I gain a perverse kick out of the agony I am putting myself through. I train to the point where my shirt is drenched, my body is screaming at me and I feel like I'm going to be sick. I often have to lie flat out to recover because I feel light-headed and dizzy. The secret of dealing with the pain is not to look to the end of the exercise but to concentrate on what you are doing at that precise moment. If you let your mind think of the torture ahead it will try to persuade you that you cannot face it.

Blackie keeps a benevolent eye on what I am doing, occasionally barking out instructions, but always encouraging me rather than chastising me. He takes a lot of time to befriend and get to know well every member of the Newcastle squad, assessing their physical and mental strengths, limits and weaknesses. He knows me inside out so he does not ask me to carry out a specific number of repetitions or spell out how long I should work for; he just keeps me going until he decides I have endured enough. This is incredible for

You learn from the best, whichever sport they happen to play

mental toughness. It is impossible to save yourself for the latter part of a session if you haven't a clue what you will be doing or for how long. The only answer is to go at it hammer and tongs from the start.

There has only been one occasion when I have failed a test he has set me. It was at the gym at his house and the challenge was to complete a session consisting of a nasty set of exercises on a cross-aerobic system. Only four members of the Newcastle squad had managed it but because I was one of them I expected to be able to do so again. When I didn't, I was livid. I had been ill the previous week but I refused to recognise this as the reason why I had failed and I was so upset I stormed out, roaring in frustration, past this startled

Some people have observed that my approach would be ideally suited to an individual sport. However, a crucial part of what drives me to go that extra mile is a reluctance to let down my team mates

bloke waiting outside to use the gym, and kicked Blackie's garage doors. The bloke turned out to be Paul Gascoigne.

Some people have observed that my approach would be ideally suited to an individual sport. It is something I have considered myself. However, a crucial part of what drives me to go that extra mile is a reluctance to let down my team mates. You have to have more to lose than just the game.

If I have achieved certain standards then they have every right to expect me to reach them in every game I play. If you play well one week for England and put in the big tackles, your club colleagues have every right to expect you to match those standards the next time you play for your club.

I have no respect for players who do not prepare to give their all every game and those who pick and choose the matches to peak in. If an individual only puts maximum effort in for his country and cruises through run-of-the-mill club games, he needs to examine his integrity. There is no such thing as a great England player and an average club player. He is just an average player with a poor attitude.

We are all well paid and we owe it to our team mates, fans and families to commit everything totally in every game. It is inexcusable not to. It means you are not a team man – and in my book there are few more powerful insults in rugby than that.

I don't deny that a lot of what I do, I do for myself. All the practice is aimed at self-improvement. But part of that is a desire to show my team mates what I am capable of and, if possible, to surprise and please them.

If I flatten someone in a tackle and hear one of my colleagues chuckle at the outcome, as has happened once or twice, then the thrill of doing so is heightened.

Life is not something that is best lived alone. A team sport like rugby offers the opportunity to share your pleasure and pain with people who you grow extremely close to. I would say winning the Cup with Newcastle in 2001 was the equal in terms of satisfaction to most of my England achievements because of the guys I shared it with. These are individuals I have been to work with every day for years and shared a lot of time with off the pitch. They are my friends. We embark on a journey together every match. The destination is not always the one we would like but there is a bizarre pride even in a losing dressing room if you have given everything. Even sharing disappointment is a communal act worth treasuring.

Rugby, to me, is the ultimate team sport. Its physical nature and requirements of courage and bravery, as well as skill, develop a camaraderie which sets it apart. I often compare how we feel together in those moments before kick-off to how a soldier might feel before a battle. Your heart is pounding like a hammer, your mouth as dry as a desert, your stomach knotted with nerves. You are willing to put your body on the line for

There is a bizarre pride even in a losing dressing room if you have given everything

your comrades, to do whatever it takes to achieve victory. Aggression is coursing through your veins yet your head is calm, your mind detached. The difference, of course, is that we are all going home at the end of the game.

I like to think I play rugby as it should be played – there are no yellow or red cards in my collection – but I cannot say I'm an angel. If you class slowing the ball down in a tackle as cheating then I would have to hold my hand up and say I've done it before and would do it again for the sake of the team. If it means giving a penalty away to save a try and taking a 'shoeing' in the process I'll do it. That is part of the game, if not part of the laws.

Where I draw the line is with the physical stuff. If I hit someone hard in a tackle, perfectly legally, then fantastic. Rugby is an intensely physical combat sport and I love making big tackles but it never crosses my mind to throw a cheap shot. If you feel the need to punch someone when they're on the floor after a tackle to make an impact, then you need to look at why you're playing the game. Knowing how I've felt being out of the game with injuries, if I felt I'd caused an injury because of something I thought I shouldn't have done, I'd be very disappointed in myself to say the least.

I have only been involved in two fights in my career and I was a reluctant participant on both occasions. The first was against Harlequins as a nineteen-year-old. I was playing centre and, as Quins kicked through, I blocked John Schuster who was trying to chase the ball. What I did was just about within the laws but he took exception to it and threw a punch at me. I never thought about retaliating. All I was concerned about was rejoining our defensive line so we weren't a man short and so I didn't have to answer to Dean Ryan! I set off towards play with Schuster having to aim at the back of my head.

I did actually swing my arms in the other incident against Bristol a few years ago but it was more for self-preservation than to cause any harm. I went in hard to clear out a ruck and accidentally caught Matt Salter in the nose with the back of my thumb. It must have hurt because it certainly drew blood and he lined me up for some retribution. I avoided the first two punches but I reckoned the chances were I would cop a haymaker eventually if I stayed in range so I put my head down and flailed about in front-crawl fashion until the referee stopped the fight in round one.

I become very, very aggressive on the pitch and hit rucks and tackles as hard as I possibly can but I could never do something against the laws to hurt someone. It just isn't in my make-up. When I clatter someone with a heavy tackle I like to see them go down quickly but I don't like to see them stay down. There is no satisfaction in injuring an opponent. If you tackle with the correct technique there is no reason why anyone should end up hurt – you or the guy who ends up on the floor. What I don't like to see is the sort of cowardly stiff-arm tackle which you can do nothing to protect yourself from and which can end someone's game or career. That is a disgrace.

With all the cameras that are around at professional matches these days, the dirty player has all but disappeared. Those that do indulge generally use cheap shots to try to put opponents off their games rather than hurt them. It is the same idea with sledging. The bulk of the exchanges on the field are good-humoured but there are one or two characters who like to dish out the verbals.

I've never quite managed to crack the art of sledging – I only ever got myself into awkward situations through being cocky. Breaking into the Newcastle side as an eighteen-year-old gave me a higher opinion of myself than I should have had and I basically tended to get a little over-excited, telling opponents how well I thought I was doing or how badly they were faring.

I remember Rob Andrew getting involved in some pushing and shoving in one match against London Scottish while Newcastle were scoring a try, and I came over to offer my wisdom. 'No, no, stop this – you go and stand under the posts while I kick this one over,' I said. After delivering my knockout line, I suddenly realised the try had been scored in the corner and that there was a fair chance of me looking even more of an idiot by missing. As it was, the conversion went over but there was certainly no crowing on my part. I was just relieved to have saved face after putting myself under a whole load of unnecessary extra pressure. I decided after this incident to quit while I was ahead.

I have grown up since then and I now limit the verbals to geeing up my own side or occasionally acknowledging an opponent for a good kick or a big hit on me. If I have any breath left.

ROES

'Genius is one per cent inspiration and ninety-nine per cent perspiration'
Thomas Edison

Everyone has heroes. As a sports-mad kid, it was natural that mine would be sportsmen. Being a great ambassador and humble person is all very well but when you are growing up those aren't the main prerequisites for choosing your idols. The common link between the individuals who fascinated me was that they were winners – not only that, but they dominated their sports to a staggering extent. Despite the fact that they were all performing in incredibly competitive environments against many other great athletes, they still managed to stand head and shoulders above everyone else. I didn't know then, but I understand now, how much toil that must have taken. All the talent in the

143

world will get you nowhere without blood, sweat and tears. These guys had class but they welded a ferocious work ethic to their natural ability.

WALTER PAYTON

Channel 4 introduced a whole new sporting world into the Wilkinson sitting room in the eighties with their coverage of American football. I was fascinated. This strange sport from across the Atlantic seemed to have everything – power, pace, spectacular collisions and, above all, Walter Payton. The dynamic Chicago Bears running back used to light up my Sunday evenings. He seemed to spend every weekend defying gravity to leap over defences or run straight through them for improbable touchdowns. I was head of his Farnham fan club. While everyone else sported their football tops, I used to wear this white T-shirt with his name ironed on in black felt letters.

Payton held the NFL's rushing record for eighteen years. He broke it in 1984 and when he retired after the 1987 season he had extended it to 16,726 yards. That's almost ten miles through some seriously heavy traffic. They called him Sweetness but there wasn't much sweet about running into him. He was 5ft 10in of pure

He seemed to spend every weekend defying gravity to leap over defences or run straight through them for improbable touchdowns

power. He wasn't the quickest running back around but he was incredibly destructive. 'If I'm going to get hit,' he once said, 'why let the guy who's going to hit me get the best shot? I explode into the guy who's trying to tackle me.' He talked about beating the opponent to the hit, a statement that has made many an appearance on my game-day preparation sheets in both attack and defence. It wasn't all a case of bang, crash, wallop, though – his footwork was fantastic too. What a centre he would have made if he had been introduced to rugby instead of gridiron.

I can see a day when the USA make it to the top table of world rugby

Despite all the contact, he only missed one game in thirteen seasons for the Bears, which is an incredible record of durability in a sport like American football. And he wasn't just consistent, he was consistently brilliant. Between 1976 and 1980 he led the league's rushing stats every year. He was part of the famous side that won the Superbowl in 1985 and was held in such high esteem by the Bears that when he retired they retired his No. 34 jersey as well. Sadly, he died in 1999 at the age of just forty-five.

American football holds a fascination for quite a few rugby players – Martin Johnson is another big fan. As a self-confessed statto, he, along with my brother, is my information source for anything I want to know about the game.

The sports are close cousins with their base blocks of running, passing, tackling and kicking. Clive went over to the States soon after taking over as England coach to study the setup at the Denver Broncos. Their model of specialist coaches for all areas of the game was one he transplanted successfully into rugby. I use an American football in practice sometimes. It is harder to kick than a rugby ball because it has a smaller sweet spot, so I know if I am punting that well then it should be easier when it comes to the day job. But while I enjoy knocking a ball about with my brother and watching gridiron, I'm not sure I would want to play it professionally. The specialist nature of the sport means that a kicker – which is what I would presumably be – does not get to take part in the other areas of the game and without the running and tackling I'm sure I would end up frustrated. The only time the kicker gets to throw his weight around is on a punt return and most of them seem to keep out of the way when it comes to tackling. A notable exception, whose example I think I'd have to follow, would be Darren Bennett of the Minnesota Vikings. Mind you, he is 6ft 5in and 17st and a former Aussie Rules footballer.

I can see a day when the USA make it to the top table of world rugby – the Eagles gave a glimpse of their potential at the 2003 World Cup. They beat Japan and gave Scotland a scare with one of the biggest packs at the tournament. And they pushed a good French side to the limit in Connecticut last summer, losing 39-31 after leading the Six Nations champions at half-time. The sky is the limit for them if they can persuade some of those gridiron guys to get rid of the helmets and padding. Even if rugby just took the unsuccessful NFL guys, the USA would be some force.

MICHAEL JORDAN

Basketball may not be all that big this side of the Atlantic but the one American player every British sports fan will have heard of is Michael Jordan. His performances transcended any cultural divide.

Whenever I watched an NBA match, it seemed pre-ordained that the following script prevailed: a see-saw match goes into the final few seconds with one score between the teams. Everything hangs on the last play. The ball finds its way to Michael Jordan who has one shot to pull the game out of the fire. He makes it. Every time. I can't think of any sportsman who has struck so many significant shots under pressure. In rugby terms, he would be the man to make the kick from the corner to win the game. Only he would do it every week. There

I can't think of any sportsman who has struck so many significant shots under pressure

was his hanging jump shot which decided the 1989 playoff for the Chicago Bulls against the Cleveland Cavaliers. And then there was his three-pointer with just twenty-five seconds left on the clock that won the 1997 finals.

He would pull it all off with such style; he seemed to find basketball so easy. In fact, when he had mastered it, he briefly turned his hand to baseball to challenge himself in another environment. The flirtation did not last long and he returned to basketball to continue his domination of the sport. His record speaks for itself – five times the NBA's most valuable player, the leading scorer in the league ten times and the star of a Bulls side which won the championship six times. In his eleven full seasons with the Bulls he was top scorer ten times, averaging over thirty points per game. It may have been his showmanship which amazed everyone but he backed the flash stuff up with results. He would graft as hard as anyone for the team in defence.

I have Michael Jordan's autograph. This is a scandalous piece of name-dropping, but it was Daley Thompson who obtained it for me. Daley was another performer who left clear water between himself and the rest of his sport but, more importantly, he is also a friend of my manager, Tim Buttimore. Tim asked Daley to beg, borrow or steal Jordan's signature and he did. So, thanks to one of the greatest athletes Britain has produced, I have a personally signed photo of perhaps the greatest athlete in history. It is addressed to Johnny with an 'H'. You can't have everything.

BORIS BECKER

It is one of my great regrets that I never saw Boris Becker play at Wimbledon. I used to go along with my mum every year but we only ever had tickets for the outside courts. And Becker was a man destined for the show courts.

He was always centre stage, right from the time he swept through the tournament to become the youngest

He just seemed to have this swagger which told everyone else he wasn't afraid of them

winner in 1985 as an incredibly powerful seventeen-year-old. He was still at school at the time. He must have been remarkably mature, physically and mentally, to beat the best players in the world at such a tender age.

He is on record as saying he found instant fame difficult to cope with – something I can relate to – but he had the sort of personality which seemed to enable him to grow as a player when the spotlight was on him. Like Andre Agassi, I suppose. He just seemed to have this swagger which told everyone else he wasn't afraid of them. They might have been older but they weren't better. The tennis world must have wondered what had hit it when this big German arrived on the scene. Becker went on to win two more Wimbledon singles titles in 1986 and 1989 and overall reached the final six times in seven years – an incredible record.

As well as being a precocious talent, Becker was a great entertainer who people really warmed to. He was

I turned around, spread my arms wide and looked up into the crowd, inviting their adulation like a Cantona or an Ian Wright. I couldn't hold it. within a second I was jumping about

self-assured – on the brink of cocky – but he had the talent to carry it off. I remember him creaming a return past David Wheaton in the 1991 semi-final to win the match in straight sets at Wimbledon. Before the ball had even passed Weaton on his way to the net, Becker was walking forward, hand held high in triumph.

I can't help loving that sort of stuff. I have a basketball video at home featuring Larry Bird, the Boston Celtics legend, in a shoot-out contest. With the clock running down fast Bird, who up to that point had struggled, needs the last four balls from the corner – the toughest part of the court – to beat his rivals. The first hits the target, quick as you like, and as he launches the fourth ball, with two and three still in the air, Bird knows straight away he's made the pressure shot. He just strolls away with his finger in the air. Sure enough, plop. Straight into the back of the net they all go. Can you imagine if the last one hadn't gone in? I can't either. He was just too good.

I wish I could carry this sort of thing off, but I can't. When England beat Australia at Twickenham in 2000 with Dan Luger's injury-time try, I had the conversion from the touchline to finish the game. We knew we had already won because the referee had said it would be the final kick so, for once, there was no external pressure. I hit it well and through the middle it flew. It was the perfect chance to showboat so I turned around, spread my arms wide and looked up into the crowd, inviting their adulation like a Cantona or an Ian Wright. I couldn't hold it. Within a second, I was jumping about, doing the worst type of sporting celebration imaginable, with any pretensions of style shattered. Maybe one day.

It was a thrill to say hello to Becker at the 2003 Sports Personality of the Year awards and I probably came across as a bit of a nerd, telling him how I'd watched him as a kid and thought he was great. He may have heard it before. Actually, it felt like I had met him before. My brother Mark was always Becker when we re-enacted Wimbledon on the local tennis courts as kids. It was Sparks, as everyone calls him, who got to ape Becker's rocket serves and his aggressive volleying. I particularly loved his diving volleys. I tended to be Agassi – or the breathtaking Miroslav Mecir, the mystery man who could beat the best in the world on his day without breaking sweat.

There will always be detractors who say Becker was too much of a grass-court specialist to be considered an all-time great. People said he couldn't play on clay and it is probably true to say his power game didn't really suit it, but to me tennis was Wimbledon and Wimbledon was Becker.

ELLERY HANLEY

Even though he existed in another world north of Watford, Ellery Hanley was part of my life from a tender age. Knocking around at home on weekends,

He could be relied upon to create something out of nothing in almost every game

rugby league always seemed to be on the TV and the distinctive tones of Ray French always seemed to be saying one word – 'Hanley'. He was constantly doing something special.

What a player he was. Strong, fast and entirely dependable, and not in a boring sense either. He could be relied upon to create something out of nothing in almost every game. He had phenomenal power, which made him a nightmare for defenders, but also a great rugby brain, seeking out gaps for himself and his team mates. His try-scoring record was amazing – almost one per game.

As a schoolboy in Hampshire I had a soft spot for Wasps because they weren't too far away and my chemistry teacher Steve Bates played for them. My true love, though, was Wigan, a rugby league club 200 miles away, whose posters adorned my walls. I've grown out

League was ahead of union as a game when I was growing up. It seemed to have so much more flair than union, which was very dependent on the conditions and over-technical by comparison

of that sort of thing now – I have a framed Wigan shirt up at home instead.

Back then, Wigan were a sporting dream team, winning the Challenge Cup every year with a side dripping with talent. Kevin Iro, Brett Kenny, Shaun Edwards, Henderson Gill ... fantastic. At the centre of it all, though, was Hanley who managed to eclipse even stars like these.

After his record £150,000 transfer from Bradford, where he had already become a superstar, he won medal after medal at Wigan. He was routinely great, but absolutely breathtaking in the 1989 cup final against St Helens when he won the Lance Todd Trophy.

Hanley was renowned as a consummate professional and what I loved about him was that, having reached the top in this country, he didn't just sit back and take the easy option, he pushed himself even further by taking on the challenge of playing in Australia. He won their respect, taking Balmain Tigers to a grand final in 1988 and in the same year led Great Britain to a 26-12 win over the Kangaroos in Sydney – the last time we won in Australia. The Australians were a big influence on English rugby league, and on me too. I enjoyed watching creative half-backs like Ricky Stuart and Brad Fittler, as well as the power players such as Mal Meninga, Steve Menzies and Steve Renouf. With talent like that, it's no wonder Great Britain have generally struggled against the Kangaroos in Ashes series.

League was ahead of union as a game when I was growing up. It seemed to have so much more flair than union, which was very dependent on the conditions and over-technical by comparison.

Times have changed now, with some of the best league players like Jason Robinson and Henry Paul switching codes in Britain, and Sailor, Rogers and Tuqiri playing union for the Wallabies. But even stripped of some of its assets, I still like league and watch more of it than union on television. I don't necessarily find it a better game any more but I do find it more relaxing viewing. Tuning into a union match, however gripping, can seem like a busman's holiday. I end up analysing the play rather than enjoying the action.

I've always said I would love to try league – following in the footsteps of someone like Jonathan Davies would be quite a challenge – but as I go further down the union path it becomes less and less likely. Not many players go from union to league now both are professional.

My heroes are drawn from four different sports but you may have noticed a glaring omission – there is no-one from rugby union. That is not to say it did not throw up players I respected – there were loads – but the individuals who captured my imagination came from other sports. For a young boy obsessed with playing the game, rugby union did, however, provide influences and role models.

In terms of goal-kicking the first person who held my attention was Grant Fox of New Zealand. Later it

He wasn't the biggest guy in the world but he was fearless and fearsome in equal measure

was Neil Jenkins who fascinated me. The reason was the same – they never seemed to miss. While I was pulling tickets out of a hat on the training pitch, fluffing one shot, kicking the next, these guys were relentless. They could win a game for their team almost single-handedly, games their side should by rights have lost. Jenks did it to us in the Grand Slam game at Wembley in 1999. Having such a quality kicker in a side was inhibiting and depressing for opponents. They knew they could not be negative because if they conceded a penalty anywhere in their own half it was three points. I've been desperate to reach a level where I can have a similar effect.

In terms of tackling, the dynamic Frank Bunce, the New Zealand centre, stood out. He wasn't the biggest

Music has grown to play an increasingly important role in my life

guy in the world but he was fearless and fearsome in equal measure. When he smashed an opponent, they stayed smashed. I have tried to model the way I attack tackles on his approach. Again, I'm not the biggest player on the pitch but if I can intimidate opponents it provides a lift for my side. I know people have advised me to tone down the physical side of my game for the sake of my health, but if I stepped back from making big hits it would take a lot of the enjoyment away for me. Whenever I watch a match, the thunderous tackles are the incidents I like best.

It's the same with cricket. If I watch a Test match, I will happily skip most of the day's play but I am absorbed by the quickies sending down the short stuff and making the batsmen duck and weave. In summer my brother and I re-enact this by watering a patch just short of a good length in the back garden and letting fly at each other or other willing victims like Ian Peel, the Newcastle prop. If there's not enough life in the mossy track, we head for the drive where steep lift is guaranteed. The gladiatorial element of any sport is the part that instinctively attracts me.

Perhaps this is why, outside sport, Arnold Schwarzenegger was my hero growing up. As a kid who was fairly small for my age I was keen on the idea of growing big and strong and no-one seemed to be bigger and stronger than Arnie. I wasn't particularly fixated with his acting – although when I gave up counting, I had seen the film *Predator* thirty-seven times – it was his power. He had muscles on muscles and won seven Mr Universe titles. He might not have been Sir Ralph Richardson but he could deliver a line, which I'm sure comes in handy in his political career now that he is Governor of California.

I never really had rock heroes but music was always there in the background at home and it has grown to play an increasingly important role in my life. The first band to make an impression on me was The Beatles. They were what my parents listened to and I picked up on the genius of John Lennon because of them. Later, I got into bands like The Verve and Coldplay in a big way too. I'd like to meet Chris Martin.

However, if there is one musician I would have at my fictional dinner party it would be Noel Gallagher. Obviously I would need to stock up on the alcohol first. Oasis have provided the soundtrack to a lot of my adult life. 'Wonderwall' was the song I sang (badly) on the team bus after my England debut to continue the tradition of all first caps and it was also the first tune I learned on the guitar. As for 'Married With Children', well, that song played a part in England beating New Zealand in Wellington ahead of the World Cup.

I had been learning it on the guitar on that trip and for some reason I couldn't get it out of my head. Everywhere I went the song came with me, including onto the pitch that night. I was even humming it in my mind as I went through my goal-kicking routine. It is odd the way you can react to these pressurised situations. I had become so fixated with the song that my brain wouldn't let me take a kick until I had finished the chorus. Each time I lined up a penalty, I had to wait at the end of my run-up until I had completed it in my head. The kicks probably took longer than usual but the process helped to relax me. On a windy night at the Westpac Stadium I kicked four out of five, plus a drop goal. The song finishes with the words 'Goodbye. I'm going home.' England went home happy. We won 15-13.

'Wonderwall' was the song I sang on the team bus after my England debut ... and it was also the first tune I learned on the guitar

In the summer of 2005 I had the opportunity to see Oasis in concert in Newcastle. It was an awesome experience. I'm not one of those people that would travel around following bands wherever they play, but to be able to say I saw Oasis live is fantastic. It really triggered something in me. I've spent my whole life just wanting to play rugby and suddenly, for a while, at the age of twenty-five, I was walking around thinking I'd love to be able to be on stage, performing music I'd written.

The concert was definitely one of the high points of the year and it inspired me to start playing my guitar

There's nothing I enjoy more when I get home than having a session on the guitar or piano with my brother on the drums

solidly. I first picked up a guitar with my Newcastle colleague Jamie Noon a couple of years ago to try to find a way to switch off from rugby. As I have progressed I have become more and more engrossed in it.

I recently acquired a Roland piano and I'm determined to learn to play that properly too. Or a bit better than the England squad's resident pianist Joe Worsley anyway. I've found it's incredibly important for me to have hobbies. It keeps me fresh and there's nothing I enjoy more when I get home than having a session on the guitar or piano with my brother on the drums in our makeshift studio at home. I'll never master either of these instruments – something which is all too clear to those who have to listen to me play! – but I love having something new to learn and strive to improve at.

ACKS

'Challenges are what make life interesting; overcoming them is what makes life meaningful'

Joshua J. Marine

If you get knocked
down make sure
you get straight
back up again

I remember sitting in my hotel room in Brisbane after England had lost 76-0 to Australia in 1998 and crying my eyes out. I was on the phone to my dad, telling him what a nightmare the whole experience had been. My first game at fly-half for my country and a record Test defeat – what could have been worse?

I was only eighteen and it was still early in my career. In time I would realise that watching Australia go about their business brought home to me that I still had an awful lot further to go to become as good as those Wallabies. They were where I wanted to be and I resolved to use the experience of seeing the level players like Tim Horan were operating at to develop.

If you get knocked down, make sure you get straight back up again

But in the immediate aftermath of the thrashing I just felt desolate.

Dad waited for the sniffing to stop, then encouraged me not to let the disappointment beat me but to get up the next day and come back stronger. I had heard the advice before. It was exactly the same thing he said to me when, as a fourteen-year-old, I didn't get picked for Surrey's age-group side.

Different stage, but equally valid. If you get knocked down, make sure you get straight back up again.

That county setback felt like the end of the world at the time. When my dad passed on the bad news in the car park I was very upset. But after I had settled down, I resolved to show them what they were missing. Living on the county border, I also qualified to play for Hampshire so I went along to their trial a few weeks later and got into their side instead.

Hampshire wasn't the most fashionable of counties, and when it came to selection for the England Schools setup at under-sixteens level I was put on the bench and left there for the entire course of both games. So I rolled up my sleeves and fought my way into the under-eighteens 'A' side the following season, a year early. But when it came to England under-eighteens the next year I again missed out. In the end, an injury opened the door for me and I ended up playing alongside a big centre from Yorkshire called Mike Tindall and a whippet from Lancashire by the name of Iain Balshaw, but my experience of the trials system left a bitter taste.

The level playing field of professional rugby, where it didn't matter what school you had gone to or how well-connected you were, gave me what I wanted – the chance to prove they had got it badly wrong. Everyone has similar facilities and opportunities; it is up to each individual how hard he works to make the most of them. I resolved to work harder than anyone else and, with everyone at Newcastle's help, made my way into the full England side. In hindsight, I think having what I perceived to be a rough ride was good for me. A lot of players who achieve success early find it hard to maintain their inner drive at senior level. Because I wasn't handed the chances I thought I deserved, I fought all the more to earn them.

Having made the England side, I wanted to make sure I kept the jersey. The worst part of the 76-0 drubbing was not the actual defeat but what happened afterwards. When the England squad for the autumn internationals that year was announced, I wasn't in it. There wasn't so much as a phone call from Clive, so I was obviously a long way away from his thoughts. Perhaps I just wasn't ready for Test rugby then but I felt I had let myself and the people around me down. After all, I was in the England squad before the tour and clearly my performances in the southern hemisphere hadn't been good enough to make me indispensable. Grabbing every opportunity that presents itself is extremely important to me and this was a bad setback.

Faced with a punch in the guts you can either take the easy option in response or the hard one. My knee-jerk reaction was to hit club rugby at Newcastle with renewed venom and show Clive I was worthy of a place in his squad. It paid off. When the 1999 Five Nations' squad was announced two months later I was back in.

Since then I have only been dropped once by England – for the 1999 World Cup quarter-final. I was on the bench and I still had an important part to play in the second half when I came on for Paul Grayson, but Clive's decision meant he couldn't trust me when it mattered most. I understood his point, but I thought he

Faced with a punch in the guts you can either take the easy option in response or the hard one

was wrong. I had to persuade him to have more faith in my ability to control a game. I had to shed the 'inexperienced' tag which dogged me and the only way to do that was to play more matches. Fortunately, Newcastle was invaluable in terms of my learning. Playing outside Rob Andrew when I first arrived at the club gave me an insight into the ruthlessness with which he went about the job. He called the shots and the rest of us obeyed. With Rob's help and the wise guidance of Steve Bates I improved my level of influence on the field.

While a player can do something about form and therefore, to a degree, selection, there is nothing he can do about injury.

I have been relatively lucky with injuries in my career. That might seem an odd thing to say now, but

I mistimed a tackle, banging my head and neck against an opponent, and this led to an alarming tingling sensation down my right side

for a long time I thought I was invincible. My body seemed to absorb the blows and remain intact. The biggest inconvenience I suffered was a perpetual cut to the top of my left ear which I have had stitched several times and now smear with Vaseline before every game to stop it reopening.

Rugby union is a high-impact sport with combatants that are growing bigger and more powerful by the day, so I suppose it was inevitable that sooner or later I would have to spend some time on the sidelines. But even when the injuries did come, they generally did so at the right time. I underwent a groin operation in the off-season in 2000 and spent six weeks of my summer break off my feet after damaging my ankle in the last game of 2002 against Gloucester.

My first experience of a prolonged lay-off came after the infamous battle with South Africa at Twickenham in 2002, when I was late-tackled by Butch James. He popped my shoulder out of joint and dazed me in the collision too so that, with my senses scrambled, I rejoined the line and threw a long pass out to Will Greenwood which made the injury worse. While Will scored and celebrated, I was left staring at nine weeks out.

And then along came the neck injury.

It was really the final instalment in a series of injuries I have suffered from since I was fourteen. I first felt what was to become the familiar 'stinger' sensation down my arm playing for Hampshire. I mistimed a tackle, banging my head and neck against an opponent, and this led to an alarming tingling sensation down my right side.

A 'stinger' is caused when a nerve is banged against something it shouldn't be in contact with – in my case part of a small bone growth off the spine. It transpired I was particularly vulnerable to this sort of injury because the canal which transports the C5 nerve from my neck and down my shoulder to my arm was unusually narrow.

It is not an ideal ailment for a rugby player but it is something I have had to live with. When it happens, the arm feels very hot and heavy and difficult to move. Most stingers don't tend to last that long – a minute or two – then pins and needles replace the heaviness in the arm as the disturbance subsides. After rest, I could go for six months without a recurrence if I didn't take any bangs on the wrong spot. The problem was that the weakness worsened when I took repeated blows there, and from time to time it threatened to get out of control. I had stingers down my left side, then down my back and down my front when I played against Wasps in my first professional season for Newcastle. In 2000 I had six in one game against Harlequins in a European Shield tie as a result of a series of blows in previous weeks. On each occasion a summer off settled everything down again and I was able to carry on playing. Until the 2003 World Cup.

I suffered my first stinger of the tournament against Samoa in the pool stages. It was no great problem, and neither was the minor one I picked up against Wales in the next game. However, there was a more severe occurrence against France early on in the semi-final. I lined up Imanol Harinordoquy for a big tackle after

It's not an ideal ailment for a rugby player but it is something I have had to live with

Neil Back had half-held him and hit the No. 8 hard, setting my neck off in the process. The impact sent a buzzing sensation down my arm and I knew that a repeat would set it off properly. I suppose I was fortunate I didn't take another bang, or I might not have played in the final. As it was, I was receiving regular physiotherapy for my neck ahead of the game to get me fit. It wasn't something we advertised at the time for obvious reasons.

When I tackled Matt Giteau in the first half of the final it went again, this time badly. I wasn't sure at first if I could continue. I stayed down for a long time because I couldn't move my arm. The paralysis brought temporary panic but as it eased off and feeling returned I was able to get up and get on with the game.

I took a few weeks off when we came home. An X-ray showed I had a fracture in a bone in my neck. It

I knew there was a problem. The pain was much worse than before

was an old injury which was healing and a red herring to the root cause of my stinger problem.

By the time I made my comeback for Newcastle, three days after Christmas 2003, I thought the condition had settled down. However, when I tried to tackle John Clarke, the Northampton wing, fifty minutes into the game, I came off second best by a considerable margin. As I lay on the ground with play continuing downfield, I knew there was a problem. The pain was much worse than before. It was like a siren going off in my head. The familiar burning sensation down my right arm was hotter than I had ever known it, coming in great pulsating waves. I couldn't move my arm at all. Because I had taken a bang to the head in the tackle as well, I wasn't all there for a while. I was concussed and I couldn't think clearly. I was very concerned. After five minutes I was helped off and gingerly made my way round to the dressing rooms but it wasn't until well over an hour later that I regained feeling in my arm.

Even when I had recovered, I couldn't move it in certain directions and as the days went on matters worsened. Three of the smaller muscles in my arm just died on me. There was nothing there. The nerve that transmitted the message to them to tell them to grow had been damaged one too many times and now refused to work at all, shutting down completely. I sat and watched the muscles disappear in front of my eyes and there was nothing I could do about it.

I had two choices – to wait and hope the nerve would sort itself out or to have an operation to free it up to grow again. The problem was I couldn't wait forever for nature, not just because I would be missing more and more matches, but because the longer the delay the greater the chance of the nerve never recovering.

However, the operation carried elements of risk. The nerve might be irrevocably damaged by the procedure and because it was to take place so close to the spinal cord, the surgery carried a tiny risk of permanent paralysis. It was a one in a thousand chance but the surgeon was duty bound to tell me.

This scared me, but the decision was a no-brainer in the end. The improvement was coming far too slowly and I didn't know when it might stop for good. I had to go for the operation. Having made the decision I never really considered the paralysis outcome but I did worry

Because it was to take place so close to the spinal cord, the surgery carried a tiny risk of permanent paralysis

that the operation would not work properly and that somehow I would have to modify my game to account for the fact that I would have no muscles on my right side. I thought about how I might change my tackling and passing techniques but I couldn't imagine hitting an opponent with any other motivation than to knock him into next week.

The operation left a neat, inch-long vertical scar down the back of my neck. As well as removing the bone spur, the surgeon widened the canal along which the nerve runs so there would be less chance of it jarring against anything in future.

The operation was a success, but it doesn't mean I'll never get another stinger again. I've got two arms, after all. Proof of this fact came in the second Test of the Lions tour in summer 2005. I got two stingers. The first came after a tackle on Tama Umaga. The pain went straight down my left arm (thank goodness it wasn't my right – I'd have been really worried then) accompanied by the familiar burning sensation and the feeling of my arm being a dead weight. But it passed and I played on, although I knew a second was a real possibility. And so it happened. I tried to go in too hard on Daniel Carter and got it a bit wrong. Head in the wrong place and mistimed. Cue the stinger and a little concussion to go with it. The pain flared and faded again and I wanted to play on but our doctor, James Robson, quite rightly advised otherwise. Twice was more than enough. And it wasn't as if we were short on cover. Stephen Jones was on the bench.

After I had that neck operation in 2004, I was back training within a few days – but the nerve stubbornly refused to grow back as fast as I wanted it to. The weeks grew into months and the Six Nations' absence I had been told to resign myself to spread into a summer tour off as well.

Not playing does odd things to your head. It is funny how quickly you can begin to doubt yourself. When Newcastle contested the 2004 Powergen Cup final against Sale, it had only been five months since I had played against Australia at Telstra Stadium. Yet I had completely forgotten what it felt like to be involved in a final in front of thousands of people. I was as tense as if I had been playing, but whereas I would normally have channelled all that nervous energy into my own performance, I could find no outlet for it. As I watched from the side, ready to bring the water and messages on for the boys, I found myself marvelling at how well they were handling all the pressure and wondering whether I was capable of coping with it again. I was so relieved when we won a helter-skelter final I nearly exploded. When the boys set off on their lap of honour around Twickenham I watched them go with a great deal of pride but also with sadness. I wanted to have earned the right to go on it with them. I found out that being a squad member but not being involved in a big victory is very hard. It only adds to the enormous respect I have for the guys in the thirty at the 2003 World Cup who did not play in the final.

I hooked up with the Newcastle team for the celebrations in a London hotel afterwards but I made my excuses and left early. I was still feeling a little down and in any case I had to be up early to start the London Marathon in the morning. There were three more very clear clues that it was about time to go:

1. Mark Mayerhofler and Epi Taione were doing a Haka on the dance floor without any shirts on.

I found out that being a squad member but not being involved in a big victory is very hard

2. Steve Black was performing an 'erotic' dance on his own in the middle of the dance floor.

3. Stuart Grimes and our young flanker Ed Williams were literally ripping the shirts off each other's backs. It wouldn't have been so bad if it hadn't been taking place a matter of feet away from the sponsors who had kindly supplied the Hugo Boss shirts and suits to the squad for the final.

I worked hard over that summer and was finally ready to make another comeback, but disaster struck once more after a pre-season game in Ireland in August 2004 against Connacht. During the game I hurt my arm slightly, but it wasn't giving me much grief and I played on, thinking it couldn't be anything too serious. However, after two or three further games I was in a fair amount of pain. My arm had swollen up, which I later found out was due to the fact that my blood had started depositing bits of bone in my right bicep. It sounds

I'd needed that break to give me a chance to review how I'd been playing and allow me to rethink my strategy

gruesome, I know, but it was still more of a niggle than a muscle-tearing thing. In the end, though, I had to make the decision to stop and get it sorted out. This might have been the most frustrating of all my injuries, because it was the only time I had to make the decision to stop. With my other injuries I knew I had no choice, but with this one I sometimes felt that I could play on. But I was losing form and was unable to do anything aggressive or physical on the field, so I resigned myself to yet more time on the sidelines.

I was off for about eight weeks this time, letting the injury settle down. I had to go for numerous scans and blood tests and was put on medication - two or three different drugs that were cooling down the bone and relieving some of the pain. I missed the autumn internationals, which was as bad as it got, especially as I had been named captain. Watching those games live was unbelievably frustrating. Despite this, when I was ready to play again, I found that I was much more relaxed than I had been. I think maybe I'd needed that break to give me a chance to review how I'd been playing and allow me to rethink my strategy and approach my next comeback in a slightly different way.

I felt like a more mature, wiser player and my game was much improved. I benched in two games and came on in both, and I really felt that I was making a difference. My first full game was Sale at home – I got thoroughly involved and managed to cross the line for a try in the last minute to win the game. But another terrible blow was just around the corner.

During a game against Perpignan in the European Cup in January 2005, I twisted my knee and tore the medial ligament. So there I was, lying on the physio bed yet again, knowing that something was seriously wrong. I was facing the possibility of having to endure knee reconstruction surgery and a further nine months out of the game. I was to have the scan that very evening that would tell me what my fate would be. I'm not ashamed to admit that the frustration came out in the form of tears as I waited with my brother and the physios.

We headed off for an MRI. The Perpignan medical team kindly opened up the local facility specially so I could get my scan done right away. To my enormous relief, it showed that, while I had torn the medial ligament, it hadn't fully ruptured and there was no damage to the cruciate. No reconstruction was needed and I would make a full recovery in eight or nine weeks. Again, I tried to stay as positive as possible and I was actually able to do some good work during that period.

Thirty minutes into my comeback game, I went down again. I heard a popping noise and felt the same pain in the same knee. I signalled over to the physio bench from the bottom of a ruck and was carried off for tests. Again I was pretty sure that I'd snapped the entire ligament. This time there were no tears. I was very very quiet. It felt unreal and I couldn't believe it was happening again. I just sat there and took it on the chin and said, 'Well this is obviously what someone's got planned for me.' I don't think I could have done things any better. I'd rehabbed properly and I couldn't have been more ready to come back. I'd had all the help I'd needed from the physios, especially in Newcastle. So I was quite calm because I knew I'd done everything that I could.

I went to get a scan the next day which showed that it was the same sort of injury as before. Another relief. I went straight into the rehab process and within a week I felt that I was firing on all cylinders again. I was off for about a month and it could have been less than that had

It wasn't a case of 'Hey, come back and see how you go.' I had to perform in order to make the Lions tour

there been certain games to play in.

Again, I was very positive about my comeback. I benched in a game against Northampton. I really got stuck in, kicking 11 points, and I couldn't feel the knee at all. Then I went into a London Irish game at home, which we won, and played a game against Gloucester. The only worry now was that we were coming up towards the Lions tour and there was so much riding on these games. It wasn't a case of 'Hey, come back and see how you go.' I had to perform in order to make the tour, I had to show I was good enough. I really felt the pressure of having to perform when I'd played in only nine games that season. But in the end things went pretty well and I was happy with the way I played.

The tour might not have been what I had hoped in terms of success, but I was very proud to be on it and

You have to treat the injury as a challenge, something to overcome

part of the team. But my series of misadventures wasn't quite over yet. Following a much-needed and highly enjoyable holiday after we returned to New Zealand, I went on a Falcons trip to Japan. Part way through the tour I began to feel unwell and was admitted to hospital for five days. Not a rugby injury this time – but an inflamed appendix!

Obviously I couldn't play any further part in the tour, but after being well looked after I was released from hospital to come home. But it wasn't just me who was grumbling about being sidelined again – my appendix was as well. So much so that three weeks or so later, after just one half of rugby against Sale in our first Premiership game, I had to have an operation to have it removed. That put me out again, until I came on as a sub in the Anglo-Welsh Powergen Cup, ironically again against Sale, at the beginning of October.

Things didn't go quite as well as I would have hoped. It almost felt like the Fates were conspiring against me, attacking my enjoyment of the game. I've already mentioned how I dwell on things and in this game I had a kick on the touchline to win it. I missed.

I go over moments like that in my mind - moments I feel can define careers and are supposed to be looked back on with joy and satisfaction. After the game I thought, 'Did it happen because I've been taking things a bit more loosely in terms of trying to enjoy the game?' That's what I've been trying to do. Missing that kick forced me to make a choice of whether to carry on with this new ethos or go back to being a player that fears failure. I'm going to stick to the former.

My new approach was again tested a few weeks later when I suffered a groin injury which required further surgery. It's been important to me not to think about all these injuries mounting up and why they are happening. I've told myself that it's unfortunate, but that I need to get back to the game soon and back to my new ethos.

I'm obviously disappointed that I've managed to acquire a new injury. Having had the operation, though, and having found out there were several tears around my groin, I realise that it had to happen. I also realise I have to look at my work ethic and respect my body and get that balance right. I know that what I put into the game is what I get out. The groin injury has come from the shearing forces of constant kicking, training and running. So it's my responsibility and I'm accountable for it, and I need to make a positive change for the better in this respect. It's not a case of saying, 'Oh well, I can't do anything about this.' Instead, I'm going to put as much into my game as ever, but I'm going to distribute that energy more to take the pressure off my legs a bit. It'll be interesting to see how that pans out in the next few years. It's a change that had to happen and one that could make a big difference.

The key thing I learned from my series of injuries was the importance of rehabbing properly. You have to treat the injury as a challenge, something to overcome. It's almost like someone taking you on in a tackle, running at you with the ball and asking you questions like 'Can you hit me backwards?' or 'Can you make this tackle? Can you deal with this? Do you have the strength to never give in?' If you look at it this way, the road to recovery is much easier to deal with. Each time I have a setback, I try to come back from it physically fitter and stronger. I think I've achieved this. The injuries allowed me to get into better shape than I'd ever been in before because of the amount of training I was able to put in without having to taper down for games. I feel I'm mentally stonger now too because of these enforced changes. I'm not the same person I was after the 2003 World Cup.

My injuries have made me realise the importance
of enjoying the game in the time that I have left. You just
never know when you might be faced with a career-
threatening injury. It always seems to happen to
someone else - one of your friends or someone at
another club - but this is just not the case. I've always
been told to prepare for such a thing, to have something
to fall back on and in the past I'd think, 'Yeah, that's
great, but that's for other people.' But now, having
become one of those 'other people', I have a new perspective on things. After my neck injury I got more
intense and was so determined to come back a better
player that I forgot to enjoy myself out on the field.
While I'm always going to give my all, I now realise that
sometimes I need to ease up a bit and put more confidence in my natural ability as a rugby player. In the past
I think I put too much into the idea that everything that
happens on a rugby field comes from the work you do
in training. Now I realise that a large part of it comes
from being the person that you are as well.

What I've learned is that there's always something to
be positive about. Even in my darkest moments I've
tried to look on the bright side and learn lessons from
my experiences. That's what makes you a stronger
person. There's no better feeling than overcoming a
seemingly impossible challenge.

ENGLA
AND
LIONS

'I will be fighting as hard as I can to be back in the England squad. You can be sure of that'

Jonny Wilkinson

I haven't played for England since the World Cup final.

That is a hard thing for me to write. But it is true. The series of injuries I have suffered since that night in Sydney have kept me from pulling on an England jersey for two years.

And what is even harder is that in that time I was appointed England captain. Andy Robinson had taken over from Clive as coach and he made me captain in October 2004, for the forthcoming three autumn internationals.

It was a massive honour. Being as into my sport as I am, and having always wanted to succeed in the game

195

I was following Lawrence Dallaglio and Martin Johnson. Very big boots to fill

and play for my country, being asked if I would like to be captain was something I couldn't refuse. Not that I wanted to, but it is important to consider all the ramifications of taking on the role. Can I benefit the team as captain? Will it affect my own game and therefore be detrimental to the team's success? Am I the type of person who can help other team mates, on and off the pitch? Can I inspire when it is most needed? And I was following Lawrence Dallaglio and Martin Johnson. Very big boots to fill. You have to think about all these things. But of course, when Robbo asked me, I didn't hesitate.

I am a very proud person and just the thought of becoming England captain was a massive excitement. (I was lucky enough to have experienced it once already.) It was something that I had always wanted to do. And when it was announced officially at the end of a squad meeting everyone was so encouraging and supportive. That meant a lot to me, especially as up to that point I'd been sidelined with my injuries for a while. As I've said, it wasn't a case of wanting the job of captain, but I've always believed if you're doing something, why not do it to the best level you can and reach your potential. I think the opportunity to captain your country is that top level.

Unfortunately, because of the injury to my arm, the opportunity never materialised. I never ran on to the field as captain. I never ran on to the field at all. That was disappointing. But the honour still remains. It was difficult for me, during that year and a half, to even believe I was England captain. The time I spent with the England squad over that period was when Jason Robinson was captain, and then Martin Corry. They were both incredible players in their own right, both incredible leaders, and they could both quite happily have been picked as captain themselves before me. You just need to look at that fantastic game against Australia in the 2005 autumn Test series to see how effective Martin is in the role.

Despite my recent groin injury I feel fit and hungry. My focus is on playing the very best I can for Newcastle and, like anyone else in the Premiership, I hope if that continues it might lead to other opportunities. I will be fighting as hard as I can to be back in the England squad. You can be sure of that. But the truth is, international selection is beyond my control. And that is as it should be. Making sure I put the hours and the effort in to be able to play at my full potential is what I can do. For the rest, we'll just have to see what happens.

Watching England on the television can be hard. Even though watching a couple of the Six Nations games earlier this year, with my dad, took me back to my childhood, I was too close to it all to revert to being an armchair fan. I found myself living the match without the ability to alter the outcome. Horrible. Playing for England can be stressful at times and tough to deal with but I know now it isn't half as painful as not playing for them.

I miss everything about being involved with the England team. It is a fantastic environment to be involved in, both in terms of the professionalism and the people. Every aspect of our preparation is catered for, from the physical and nutritional side to the technical analysis of our opponents and ourselves. Every training session is videoed and a computer logs every step we take on the field.

The attention to detail is superb. For instance, when

Playing for England can be stressful at times and tough to deal with but I know now it isn't half as painful as not playing for them

Clive was coach he sent Richard Prescott, the RFU's communications director, along to the ground with the kickers when we practised to ensure we weren't disturbed. For someone like me, who doesn't enjoy saying no to people, having someone on hand who does this for a living makes life so much easier. Richard's brief also included looking out for any suspicious camera-wielding opposition spies. He still found time to fetch the balls for us.

With the RFU's backing, Clive provided everything we could possibly want, from great hotels and facilities to specialist coaching in all important areas – some that we had never even considered. Sherylle Calder, a

I've always believed if you want to do something, why not do it to the best level you can and reach your potential

visual awareness expert from South Africa, worked with us on improving our peripheral vision so we could pick out colleagues and space more effectively in the hurly-burly of a Test match. We spent at least twenty minutes per day when we were with England on computers, exercising our eyes. This was innovative and people are instinctively cautious when it comes to new ideas, but if you think about it, we use our eyes all the time in matches so something that makes them better makes us better. We are always looking for that edge.

Then there are the shirts. One of the more bizarre sights in the England dressing room is the rigmarole involved in helping people in and out of the streamlined jerseys. They are so tight that it takes two or three people to do the job. The idea is to stop opponents grabbing a trailing shirt. I can't wear the ultra-tight one

– it is just too restrictive. I prefer the flared version, which is still almost like a second skin.

Even though it is an ultra-professional setup, the social environment is extremely relaxed and friendly. The England squad is a much more welcoming place now than it was when I made my debut. Playing international rugby is a serious business, but the tension which surrounds it needs a release and often laughter is the answer.

Dave 'Otis' Reddin, England fitness conditioner and a former non-league footballer, was my keepie-uppie partner. Early on in a Test week, or the day after a game, we would take over one of the dining rooms in the swanky Pennyhill Park Hotel and re-assign it for indoor football trick shots, each of which was given a code name. It was quite warm in there. Quite what the waiters thought when they poked their heads around the door and found two sweaty men lying on the floor trying to flick the ball into the air with their backsides – the hitherto unachievable Northern Soul – I don't know.

Anyway, at the World Cup, Otis was at the centre of a disciplinary storm when England were discovered to have briefly put sixteen men on the field against Samoa. It was a serious matter. Clive had been summoned to fly to Sydney from Surfers Paradise to answer the charges and there were even calls for points deductions. Otis was the man who had given the instruction from the touchline for Dan Luger to go on and become the notorious sixteenth man and this had led to an altercation with the fourth official, Steve Walsh from New Zealand, in which Walsh reportedly called Otis a '****ing loser'. When we met to draw up our defence, every time Otis's name was mentioned so was the insult. Without fail, on hearing it, we all collapsed like kids in a playground.

Before our World Cup warm-up match in Marseilles in 2003 we had some light relief at our French training camp with some backs against forwards football. The backs cruised to victory, of course, due to the appalling work rate of the forwards – idleness that was only matched on our side by Will Greenwood. To compound our justified sense of superiority we also cantered clear in the penalty shoot-out which followed. Two penalties each and the forwards did not score a single goal. However, that didn't matter to Phil Vickery who pulled off a remarkable, and I have to stress totally inadvertent, save from my second penalty. Having gone for the top right-hand corner with the first one but curled it just over the bar of the five-a-side goal we were using, I decided to go for pure power with the second. I really connected. The ball smashed into the post just

We are always looking for that edge

below the bar and, with Vicks cowering away, ricocheted across square onto the top of the shaven noggin. He's a big bloke but he went down like a sack of spuds. For a moment I thought the ball had knocked him out but he looked up with a big smile because the ball had stayed out of the net.

This was vaguely reminiscent of an incident that occurred two days before we played South Africa in 2000. We were attempting to perfect the cross-field kick to the corner for Ben Cohen and Richard Hill, a move that was to pay rich dividends for England. The lineout had been set fifteen yards further back than the move was suitable for so, to put the ball into the in-goal area with time for them to arrive and catch it, I had to give the ball everything and put plenty of height on it. Unfortunately, the sun was directly behind me as I hit what is still the sweetest punt of my life. Hilly arrived and was temporarily blinded. The ball came down with snow on it right on top of his head and cannoned back into the air. It was then that Ben leapt beautifully to take the ball above his head and touch down, much to the delight of Dave Alred, who doubles as our catching coach. Five points, one man down and an outbreak of mass hysteria – even Clive was bent double.

You can't beat slapstick. The bizarre backdrop to the successful World Cup campaign was a spate of trouser attacks by our reserve hooker Mark Regan. 'Ronnie' started an unfortunate trend by whipping down the shorts of Josh Lewsey at Perth Airport as he was trying on a pair of sunglasses. Unfortunately, Josh hadn't got any pants on.

As we moved on to Brisbane other people started to get in on the act. A training session in a school gymnasium ended in disaster for Dan Luger when he put his arms in the air to line up the perfect swan dive into a deep foam-filled pit, giving Cohen an opportunity to take advantage of his vulnerability and take down his shorts. Dan sported the same underwear as Josh – i.e. none – and as he scrabbled about to restore his dignity, Ben shoved him over onto the crash mat with his shorts still round his ankles. Unfortunately, the gym was also being used by some schoolchildren and a couple of irate mothers, watching the high jinks from the balcony, gave Ben a severe ticking off. Incredibly, Dan copped one too.

Ronnie was untouchable as the master of the clandestine assault, though, and as the tournament progressed he peaked magnificently. He pulled off a spectacular attack on the team doctor, Simon Kemp, in full view of all the photographers, during a training session before the semi-final. He finished the assault by slapping the doctor's exposed backside. Alert to the danger and aware that the odd lens might be on me, I pulled my drawstring so tight it was in danger of cutting off the circulation to my legs. As if there wasn't enough tension around.

Ronnie's *pièce de résistance* came after the final when we were doing our lap of honour around Telstra Stadium. You would have thought the distraction of winning the World Cup would have kept anyone's mind off the potential for trouser comedy but that reckoned without the dedication of the man. Down came the shorts of Simon Shaw in front of a global audience of countless millions.

Playing rugby for my country is what being with England is ultimately about but to me guys like these are England. Turning up at our team hotel on an international week and seeing close friends like Hilly and Catty sets off the unique tingle of Test rugby – all the hype, all the planning, all the tension is embodied in those people. Even running into them as opponents at club level brings the same instinctive surge of electricity. When we've retired and we meet up we'll probably still feel it.

I think England were victims of the expectations which surrounded them as world champions

Looking in at England from the outside was made worse by our defeats in the past two Six Nations and on the summer tour in 2005.

England cannot win every match, however much we'd like to, and the losses to Ireland and France left us third in the final Six Nations table in 2004. It was a desperately difficult tournament so soon after the World Cup. I know what I went through and I wasn't even playing. As some familiar faces stepped aside, I can only imagine how difficult it was mentally for those who remained to switch from the adulation that followed the World Cup win to the task of facing our European rivals with points to prove. Facing huge ovations before matches rather than after them is an awkward position to find yourself in.

Australia and New Zealand in the summer was hardly a picnic either, especially when you consider our guys had been at it solidly for twelve months, while the southern hemisphere's season had ended after the World Cup.

More than the physical exhaustion, I think England were victims of the expectations which surrounded them as world champions. The experiences Down Under will have underlined how hard it is to live up to them if you take your eye off the ball even for a second.

Australia and New Zealand are difficult places for European sides to go in June at the best of times, and the three defeats only served to emphasise what an achievement it had been winning in both countries two years before.

I watched the matches at home and spoke to guys like Hilly, Mike Catt and Ben Cohen to find out how they were doing and how they were feeling. It seemed a tough tour. I think England were very unlucky with Simon Shaw's sending off in the second Test against the All Blacks, which had a big influence on the outcome, but in the first Test against New Zealand and against the Wallabies it was hard going and we were beaten very fairly.

Our defensive standards slipped – letting in fourteen tries in three Tests is very unlike England – and we didn't create as much as we would have liked to in attack. If it proved anything, the tour probably showed that we have to be prepared to speculate to accumulate and take risks. Both New Zealand and Australia had attacking threats in every back-line position and players in the forwards who could do real damage with the ball too.

The 2005 Six Nations didn't see us fare any better. Or not on the surface anyway. Three defeats (Wales, France and Ireland) obviously isn't good. But remember, the losses were all very narrow and the Welsh, Irish and French all had exceptionally good teams. I could sense things were beginning to come round in that tournament, odd as it may seem if you look at the bald statistic of the final table – England fourth.

In the long term I believe these experiences have definitely not done England any harm. As with individuals, it is not the victories but the setbacks which truly shape a team and provide the biggest avenues for improvement. Those harrowing Grand Slam defeats at Wembley, Murrayfield and Lansdowne Road in 1999, 2000 and 2001 were the making of England. We learned from those experiences and that is what made us the side we were when it came to facing Australia in Sydney in 2003. This new England side is starting down the same road and the next stage of the journey, which has already begun as far as I am concerned.

Travels

Falcons

It is not the victories but the setbacks which truly shape a team

I feel that the England side has a fantastic balance to it right now. There's a huge amount of youth. Under Andy Robinson and the other coaches, the last two years have not been wasted at all. There's been a rebuilding process after the World Cup and this has been put into place very effectively. It's been a tough period at times, but it is what has been needed – players coming into the side, others deciding that they want to retire, experience to be gained, lessons to be learned. It's all been a success as you can see from looking at the internationals in autumn 2005. We beat Australia, which is no mean feat, then Samoa and then we nearly beat New Zealand, who have been rightly rated so highly. Winning two of the three games shows that the forward-dominance is the platform needed. The creativity is there and will build and build. The players are getting to know each other more on and off the field

Clive has changed the oval for a round ball and he will bring a lot to football

and it will only get better from now on. So England are in a very positive place at the moment.

Clive is now gone, of course, and inevitably things have changed slightly. Andy Robinson takes on the role in his own special way - a very committed way I am certain. Unfortunately, I haven't yet been there to experience it, but I know the setup will be very focused, very selfless and very honest. Robbo, being a rugby player himself, a forward, knows how the game works – by putting your body on the line and by sacrifice and respect and confidence – and that will no doubt form the basis of his leadership to come. He will gain the respect and trust of the players, because he has that honesty and is willing to make those sacrifices.

There is also enormous ambition to move forward. I think the Lions tour helped to illustrate how important having that ambition is. That will be a massive part of the next few years, with the players being given the opportunity to prove themselves with a new freedom to perform and express themselves when they are sent out on to the field. It's going to be an exciting time. I am looking forward to hopefully being part of it.

Clive has changed the oval for a round ball and he will bring a lot to football, I am sure. Certainly an enormous ambitious edge. He sets stretching goals and makes changes for the right reasons to achieve those goals. And he won't just tinker with the tip of the iceberg. He'll look to address fundamental issues. Not necessarily the skills, or the way people do things, or the training times. It'll be more things like mental approach, preparation, lifestyle, a sense of team, trust, humility, honesty, loyalty, respect, winning behaviours. Things like that will have an enormous effect on the game he's going into. With the amount of skill there is in football and the number of participants of all ages in the sport throughout the country, he has a chance to make a real difference. And knowing the way he is and how driven he is to succeed, I can see it being a fantastic relationship.

Clive may no longer be with England and I might not have run out with the national side for two years, but of course we teamed up again in summer 2005 for the Lions tour. That was a huge, huge honour. For a while it looked like I wasn't going to make it. But I never gave up hope, even when, in March, I damaged my knee again in the game against Harlequins and the headlines were all 'Wilkinson Out for 10 Weeks'. Then I wasn't in the squad when it was announced in April, but Clive had made it clear to me what I had to do to get back in. And I worked incredibly hard to make sure that happened.

It wasn't just my injury, of course. I never took my place on the tour for granted for a second. How could I when I was up against players like Stephen Jones, Ronan O'Gara and Charlie Hodgson, who had been playing all season and playing very well. So to make it on to the tour was an immediate bonus, I suppose, but, as with all things, there's absolutely no achievement in just getting there. It's about trying to make a success of it.

I suppose the high point for me was being part of the Lions tradition. Getting to know a lot of the guys, especially some of the Irish and Welsh guys who I hadn't known so well, was fantastic. Catching up with the likes of Brian O'Driscoll again after so long was brilliant. The Irish guys were just easy to mix with. I got on very well with Denis Hickie, Shane Horgan and Shane Byrne. The Welsh guys too, like Stephen Jones, Martyn Williams and Dwayne Peel, were very easy to talk to and have fun with and they produced a lot of smiles out

The high point for me was being part of the Lions tradition

of a very difficult trip. This was particularly important after the first Test when we knew we'd let ourselves and a lot of other people down. It is easy to be despondent after a defeat like that, but getting bogged down doesn't help anyone. So the lifting of the collective spirit with jokes to lighten the atmosphere was very important.

Those were the good bits, but the trip was hard for me. For everyone. It is difficult to pull any high points out of the rugby side of things because I didn't think the games that we won, we won with enough conviction against teams we should have been beating by more. The New Zealand teams played well, but even so we didn't do ourselves enough justice. I don't think we played with full comprehension of each other or what we were trying to do. We didn't play with our heads up enough. I think we were a little naïve as a group of players in the way that we made life easy for the New Zealand teams, and especially the All Blacks.

The low point would obviously have to be losing the

Test series. That and any time on that tour when I felt I wasn't able to perform at my best or give a good account of myself as a person or a player. That ultimately marred the tour for me. As much as people might like to criticise it for various reasons, I thoroughly enjoyed the 2001 Lions tour because we had certain degrees of success. And, as Clive himself said, a successful tour comes out of winning the Test series and winning games and playing well. We didn't do enough of those things this time round.

Something that I would do differently would be not to put so much pressure on myself. I wasn't really able to enjoy the experience fully. I would certainly try to relax more and try to be a bit more natural. The fact that I wasn't either of these things also meant that I wasn't able to do myself justice in training. I was always trying to catch up and I don't think that was what should have been on my mind. Instead I should have trusted in my ability more. I found the whole thing a little too nerve-wracking and maybe that was to do with the lack of game experience in the run up to the tour. I would have liked to have taken my time and found my way in.

In terms of my own performance, I never really felt I had the opportunity to really show what I can do. Or perhaps more accurately, what I should say is that when the few opportunities did come along, I don't think I did myself justice in taking them and making them work for me. I never came off the field feeling like I'd exhausted myself or shown the different elements of my game now. I'd been working on so many things which never saw the light of day and that was maybe the most disappointing thing of all.

What I can say, however, is that I held my head up high. I prepared as much as I could and gave as much as I could on the field. It's a difficult feeling, and one that I've never got completely used to, when you go into a game and feel like, after a certain amount of minutes, everything that you're doing is making very little difference to the outcome or to the grand scheme of things. It certainly felt like that for the two Test matches I was involved in.

For the first Test I played at No. 12. To make the side was a fantastic feeling. I was very proud and I just wanted to get out there and perform. But we didn't really win much ball and became a little bit defensive. I see myself as an all-round rugby player and so playing No. 12 has never been something that I've complained about. I see myself as a No.10, for sure, but I am not so rigid I can't adapt and I would like to think that I'm able to bring a certain quality to the No. 12 position. Playing there is different to playing No. 10, certainly defensively. Attacking-wise it's actually sometimes quite a nice change to be a bit further out from the pressure, giving you more space and time to make better decisions, but then again the pressure's never been something that I've been desperate to avoid. Playing as a No.10 with a good No. 12 is always a fantastic experience and makes life a lot simpler.

I've had a frustrating run of injuries for sure, but I am now looking forward to playing more rugby. With that in mind, I greatly appreciate everything that I learned from the Lions tour. Before I came back after my initial neck injury, I said that it felt like it was a brand new start for me. Not dissimilar, if you like, to the start of my international career when I was eighteen, when I went through a big learning experience out in Australia and New Zealand. New Zealand, Part 2, has been another one. After those experiences when I was eighteen I like to think that things went forward from that moment. Similarly, I will make sure things take another leap forward now. I want to use the lessons that I was taught out there and absorb them and turn them into a positive.

Pulling on the Lions jersey and the England jersey you get a very similar feeling. It's a massive honour and a great deal of respect and responsibility goes into it. Believe me, you see it on the players' faces before a

Pulling on the Lions jersey and the England jersey you get a very similar feeling. It's a massive honour

game, after a game, during the week. The tension's there, but the pride brings on an excitement, an enthusiasm and so it is difficult being part of a tour when things aren't going so well. In New Zealand it's true to say it was harder to build on the excitement and enthusiasm that comes with the pride, certainly after the games when there was immediate disappointment. But the Lions is still a very special thing, as many people have said. It only comes around every four years and it has the potential to be incredible: but it also has the potential to not quite work. This was one of those times. It's a tradition that needs to be respected and continued and I'm sure it will be, and there will be many people who will go on to more tours. Hopefully I'll be one of them and see the brilliant side of the Lions that has been shown so many times in the past.

New Zealand were a very talented side. I've never been one to comment on tactics particularly, but I think they prepared the game brilliantly and went out there and played to their strengths. To an extent, we made life a little bit too easy for them in several areas and I think they relished that and fed off it, showing what a ruthless edge they have.

New Zealand has this ethos – they take the game to the limit. By that I mean they understand how to make the rules work in their favour. They attack the rules and play right to the edge of them and therefore become very effective. That can be when they're challenging the ball on the floor or getting on to it very quickly. By employing such tactics it allows the individuals to flourish as exciting and individual players. Adopting this ethos can sometimes mean you give away penalties, but at other times you need to take the chance and tread the line a bit. Sometimes it felt like they had a couple more extra players than us. Maybe that says something about how we were defending and the decisions we were making at the time. But they have an amazing amount of players to choose from - good, powerful players, natural players. The squad showed the ability, even with injuries, to bring players in that made such an enormous difference. We saw that during the Lions tour and in the 2005 autumn internationals against the home nations. New Zealand is a rugby-dominated country and they have the potential when they're on their game to beat anybody in the world by a huge number of points. They will continue to be a leading light and I think they've shown that by never really being too far from the top. They've never really had a period where they've fallen too low or lost too many games in a row. They're always there or thereabouts.

The most controversial moment of the tour happened, of course, in the first minute of the first Test. I didn't really see the Brian O'Driscoll tackle, and it's not something I really want to watch, for obvious reasons. Knowing Brian as I do, it's really unfortunate that he wasn't able to play in all three Test matches, not just for his own desires and dreams, but also for the team. It's not my place to apportion blame or not, but I do believe you have to have a certain trust in people and know that events do happen on the pitch and if there's accountability people will own up to it. It's a case of having respect for your team mates and the opposition and accepting that things can happen. I don't believe the incident would have been deliberate, even though I haven't seen it.

Obviously the tackle was an unfortunate event. Brian should have been leading the team. But he's had the

I gave everything to the Lions tour. Everyone did. Players and management

opportunity to recover and I'm sure he's going to move on fantastically. Whatever happened, New Zealand deserved to win.

The things that I learnt from New Zealand would be their ambition, their desire to play the game to the full and to play with a passion to do something special. On the field they read situations as they saw them right there and then, as opposed to playing with a fear of failure or a fear of being shown up individually or letting their team mates down. They were able to play a situation as it unfolded, as opposed to playing the game thinking, 'We're five points ahead, we've got to hold on,' or, 'We're two points down, we've got play down there, we've got to kick the ball.' They play the game as they see it, in a very natural way.

They have a great understanding of each other and the way each individual plays the game and wants to play it. For instance, when one of them was looking to play a disguised pass, a team mate was expecting it. So when they tried the move, it tended to come off. I've often been involved in situations where we talk about offloading a pass out of a tackle and we describe that pass as a 50:50 if it's a tough pass, i.e. there's a fifty per cent chance that it will go to ground. And we talk about not making these 50:50 passes. I think the way New Zealand are doing things is that when someone looks for that pass and makes that pass, with their natural evasive ability to break tackles, or certainly to weaken tackles, that ups the percentage of the pass being successful. So now you're talking 60:40 or 70:30. But the fact that the next person is expecting that pass, and therefore is switched on and in the right position and ready to scoop up the ball wherever the pass goes, means you increase the odds again, say to 80:20 or 75:25. Now you are talking possibilities you really need to go with.

They were also very effective and efficient around the ruck area, never over-committing numbers to lost causes, but always ready to attack a ball that's open on the floor. By playing effectively like this, they were very economical with their numbers around the ball, never leaving their outside defence in trouble because too many people that didn't need to be there had their heads in a ruck.

They always have a big defensive line, which is capable therefore of making two-man tackles and turning the ball over. What it boils down to is being dominant in defence and very aggressive. A team's aggression is stripped, as I think the Lions found out, when it's been made to feel insecure, with space around it on all sides. It's very difficult to be aggressive if you're trying to cover holes. It becomes a bit of a bluff really and it's very difficult to make offensive tackles if someone can move around you in so many different ways.

So there was lots to learn. The speed at which they played was fantastic, as was the enjoyment on their faces, which was plain to see. It seemed to me that the special abilities of each player, which were all very different, flourished. You saw the power of some players, and footwork and passing ability from others. Decision-making around the ruck was another skill that was on display – especially from some of the very clever ball players. Players such as Daniel Carter.

The reason all this worked so well for them, I think, is that they were given the opportunity to enjoy themselves on the field. The players were working with each other, unselfishly helping those around them to find the environment on the field that was best suited for them to prosper in.

I gave everything to the Lions tour. Everyone did.

Players and management. We contributed an enormous amount to the cause and never stopped trying, never stopped working, never stopped thinking about it. We were all very honest – rugby players tend to be – and when things were going wrong we held our hands up and admitted it. It's easy with hindsight to say this, I know, but I think everyone could have spoken up a bit more and maybe could have changed things when we still had a chance to. At the time I think everyone was fully committed to the way we were going, and every-one believed that was the right direction. But with hindsight we could see that maybe it wasn't. Maybe we needed more time to develop as a team. Maybe we needed to look at things from a different angle. But it's easy to say that with the knowledge we have now.

Above all, the most important thing I learned from the tour is that however long I have left in the game for the things I want to achieve, I cannot afford to be doing it without a smile on my face. I didn't manage that in New Zealand. The sacrifices I make for the game of rugby won't always bring success, I know. But whatever happens on the pitch, I realise there is no point to these sacrifices if you are not playing the game.

UTURE

'A person who aims at nothing is sure to hit it'

Anon

Winning the World Cup fulfilled a promise I made to myself when I was ten. Most children write out Christmas lists for Santa – I wrote out a list of goals I wanted to achieve as a rugby player.

I began to think about what would come next about an hour after the World Cup final. While the celebrations continued in the changing room, I found peace in the physio area. With ice on my neck and elbow, I went through in my head what had enabled me to be part of a team that had just won a World Cup. I thought about everything that had gone into that game, what we had achieved and where I wanted to go next. More importantly, I began to work out how I was going to get there.

It would have been so easy to bask in the reflected glory of what the team had done and take my eye off the ball – maybe to train a little less intensely or skip a few kicks at the end of a session. I didn't want to view 22 November 2003 as an end point. I'm guessing it will form the background noise to the rest of my career, my life maybe, but I want it to be a stepping stone to further achievements.

The injuries and the operations since then provided an unwanted detour from the path I had begun to set down, but at the same time they supplied a clear dividing line between the past and the future. During the flight to Mauritius to start my recuperation after my neck injury, I wrote down a new list of goals in a black notebook. These still hold true today. It is a more detailed, clearer look at my future than ever before, covering my club and international rugby and also my life. Here are a few examples.

Short-term goals:
To come back physically stronger, more powerful and in better shape than ever before, making myself the fittest player in world rugby.

To improve my defensive technique and communication.

To improve all my skills by a large amount, specifically

my passing and kicking.

To improve my quality of training to ensure I get the best out of my effort.

To make sure my diet and nutrition is as effective and professional as it can possibly be.

To enjoy playing the game of rugby a great deal more.

My operation after the World Cup gave me a lot of time off and I could have switched off from rugby completely. Mentally, I suppose a break would have been refreshing. However, I know that if I had taken the time off, I would have looked back and regretted it. In rugby's crowded calendar, there are so few opportunities to work on your conditioning that the time away from playing matches was actually a godsend. In the past, I had merely maintained my levels of strength and fitness because there was no time to do anything else. The off-season, such as it was, meant a couple of weeks' holiday and then straight back to pre-season work. The enforced breaks from playing I have faced since November 2003 through to the Lions tour in summer 2005, and again for a few weeks after that with my appendix and groin operations have meant I have been able to drive myself up to a new level. To maintain some balance, I have made sure I train hard but relax even harder in the evenings.

The nerve damage I have suffered means I have had to come to terms with the fact that my right side will probably always be slightly weaker than my left. I have had to modify my technique a little in some of my skills to take account of this, but this is just another challenge for me to embrace.

Overall, physically I am way ahead of where I was pre-World Cup. I now weigh fourteen stone and my body-fat levels are down to nine per cent. I can lift heavier weights, I can recover more quickly after pushing myself to the limit – every aspect of my conditioning has improved.

This is going to help with my tackling. It is an important part of my game and I want to make myself more effective in this area. I have set myself a target of five big hits per game. I won't always reach it – the overriding aim for me is to finish each match with a hundred per cent tackle success rate – but the heavy collisions are the ones that can really lift a team.

I think I can kick better too. I was really disappointed with my punting, particularly from my left foot, at the World Cup – my right was probably thirty per cent better – so I have set out to try to rectify the disparity. During my time off, I have put myself through more sessions than I would have done if I had been playing. When Newcastle took the posts down at

Kingston Park at the end of last season for an event on the field, I asked them to leave one up so I could carry on. Like a mechanic in a garage, I stripped down my goal-kicking technique and gradually built it back up again. I enjoy the process of self-analysis. If I kick nine goals out of ten, I will devote all my time to working out why I missed one, rather than why I was successful with nine. Some people might find this approach negative but the aim is to try to eliminate as many mistakes as possible for next time. For me, playing sport at a high level is largely about handling the mental side and the only way I can do this is to have a routine I can trust. Only robots aren't affected by tension. I've faced kicks when the anxiety has been so great I could actually see my heart beating through my shirt. I've been at the end of my run-up and felt like my legs had dissolved under me. But if I've put the hours in I know the chances are that I will be able to confront and control the demons. I firmly believe practice makes you luckier on the pitch.

I do a lot of practice – it is what my whole game is based upon – but having done so I have come to realise that I should try to get something more out of rugby than just winning. While I don't intend to drop my concentration and intensity levels, I want to embrace the experience more. I no longer want to feel relieved to come off the field; I want to enjoy actually being out on the pitch. If I can smile when I'm out there, express myself better and come out of myself then I believe I can unlock more of what I have to give.

Since coming back from the Lions I have adopted a new outlook on my game. I'm going out on to the field now to make a difference, to try to fulfil my potential as a player – as opposed to trying to hang on to what's gone on in the past, to my reputation I suppose.

So in my mind I'm going out there to play a little bit like I'm eighteen or nineteen again, but with the benefit of the experience I've picked up in the past seven or eight years. I don't want to play with a fear of failure or with an attitude that asks, 'What happens if…' I want to approach the game as if it is a blank canvas and regard it as an opportunity to do something very special.

I want to look back on each game as a chance well taken, a stage on which I expressed myself. What matters to me is that I show the elements I've been working on and how much I care about the game; and also that I demonstrate to my team mates how importantly I view my relationship with them. I'm aiming to impress myself and know that the things I have been working on have been worth the effort.

In the games I've played since the New Zealand tour I feel I've been making some very positive moves forward to embrace this new ethos – but it is not always

I've faced kicks when the anxiety has been so great I could actually see my heart beating through my shirt

easy. There are pressures that build up which can impact on the way I approach the game, and my enjoyment of it – pressure from the goals I've set myself that I want to achieve before I finish playing; pressure from my desire to get back into the England set-up, having been out for so long; pressure from Newcastle being at the wrong end of the table.

The situation with the Falcons is a factor of the professional era, where the threat of relegation is so dominant. There is always a fight for survival that brings with it a 'win at all costs' attitude. If you let that get to you there is a possibility that it will make you narrow your horizons and play a safe, tight and unambitious game which gives very little enjoyment.

Despite these factors, I'm enjoying my rugby now and I'm enjoying my new approach – even though it's not necessarily working all the time. But it is a way of moving forward rather than standing still or going backwards.

Talking of the targets I set myself, back in 2004 I also wrote down a set of long-term goals. Here they are. As you will see, they weren't all quite achieved, but it is important to have goals to aim at.

To win the World Cup again with England and be a major influence in the side that does it.

To be selected for the British and Irish Lions tour to New Zealand in 2005 and to have an influence on a successful trip.

To play as many games as possible for England, injury allowing.

To win more Grand Slams.

To be the best-prepared rugby player in the world.

To play at my very best in every match – not just the big ones – so as to be a leader in consistency as well as performance.

To train at my very best in every session. Never to accept that bad days just happen. To make every day a good day.

To help my brother develop into the player he wants to be and play with him regularly in the Newcastle team.

As I've said, the series of injuries I had to overcome and the Lions tour have taught me that I need to strive to get the most out of the game, in terms of my own enjoyment of rugby. I was putting so much pressure on myself and giving myself such a huge extra workload that I wasn't relishing my time on the field. This is up there on my priorities list alongside kicking, passing and tackling. If I don't get it right I won't move on as a player.

Personal milestones, like points tallies and numbers of caps, aren't really important. People make a fuss about them, but if records come along they are essentially spin-offs of training and playing to your best. One leads to the other. They would be good to look back on when I have retired, but that's about it. When Jason Leonard broke the then world record for international caps against France in the World Cup semi-final we presented him with a ball and a shirt numbered 112 after his record number of caps. It was an incredible feat, after all, for a guy who had had part of his pelvis grafted onto his neck to save his career a decade before. Jase was quite embarrassed about all the hullabaloo. What mattered to him was that we had reached the final. I want to look at records the same way. The individual achievements are only important in so much as they mean I have contributed to the side's success. A man of the match award in a losing team is utterly worthless. Even in a winning side, they do not mean much. The point of the exercise is not the physical prize but the inner satisfaction of knowing the goal has been achieved. I have a few awards at home – unopened champagne bottles, that sort of thing – and I feel very honoured. I have no idea where my World Cup winners' medal is, though. My dad put it somewhere for safekeeping, I think. I must ask him.

The long-term goal that would mean the most to me is the one involving my brother. He has always been there for me and I want to be there for him as he continues to carve his own professional career at Newcastle.

We are unusually close. His abstract take on life and bizarre sense of humour make me laugh. We chuckle at a lot of the same things, whether that is the weirdly amusing Garth Marenghi's Dark Place, the wise-cracking Simpsons, the slapstick of an old Young Ones episode or a Fantasy Football Phoenix From the Flames skit. I know people probably regard me as quite earnest and older than my years – and I do take my job and everything that surrounds it very seriously – but when I'm at home with Sparks it is a pathetically juve-nile environment. There's a non-stop stream of banter flowing between us which we find incredibly funny.

To win a trophy in the same side as Sparks would be as special a moment as I can imagine on a rugby field

That's just as well because no-one else does.

Unlike most brothers, we don't really argue. Perhaps that is because, although we train together, we never play games against each other – not even computer games. When we were growing up we might have knocked up on a tennis court for three hours at a time, working on serve and volley or passing shots, but there was never a match. Perhaps we feared the consequences. We are both fiercely competitive. The last time we took each other on was on the computer when I was ten. Sparks is seventeen months older and used his extra experience to give me a sound beating which I reacted to by storming off to the rhubarb patch at the bottom of our garden and sulking there for forty-five minutes.

I've forgiven him now. To win a trophy in the same side as Sparks would be as special a moment as I can imagine on a rugby field.

For that to happen, Newcastle have to develop as a side and as a club. My goals for the Falcons, which I also wrote down in the black book, are as follows:

To win the Zurich Premiership.
To win it again.
To win the Powergen Cup.
To win the Heineken Cup.
To dominate the game in England and Europe for several years.
To lead the club in our quest.

If you shoot for the moon, even if you miss you'll land amongst the stars.

Perhaps because of where we are geographically, on the far reaches of the professional circuit in England, Newcastle is a very close-knit and friendly club. We have a great time together. At the end of a season, all the players who are staying on club together to buy mementoes for all those who are leaving. They receive them at our end-of-season get-together at Kingston Park. In 2004, Garath Archer, who was forced to retire because of a back injury, went up to collect his award and gave an incredibly moving acceptance speech. Naked.

I want more than just laughs from my club career, though; I want Newcastle to become winners. We have a decent team, a stadium at Kingston Park built from scratch and a great crowd filling it. What we haven't yet created is a winning mentality and a winning habit, and at present, as I've said, we're at the wrong end of the table. It does seem unfortunate that we seem to have come out on the wrong side of too many close games. That's when you start to lose that winning habit. There have been four games this season, for instance, that could have been won with the last kick. Dave Walder did a fantastic job to win one of them, but the other three were lost – and one of those missed kicks was mine.

It's disappointing and shows how ruthless the league is. You fight really hard against Leicester away from home, for instance, and end up with a draw even though one of their conversions didn't seem to go over. Other times, it's been a kick in the last minute against you that has been successful or a miss-kick right at the end that does the damage. Suddenly you're down near the bottom of the league rather than the top.

Regardless of this, however, what is most important is to move forward as a team – we want to play the style of rugby we believe in, which is an exciting game, and we respect the commitment we have made to ourselves.

We're dedicated to make rugby a better sport and we know we can make that work. It is important not to narrow the game because you are desperate to hang on. Instead we aim to build for the future, turning players into specialists and helping the younger mebers achieve their international dreams. So in that respect we're doing okay. We're aiming to be one of those sides that people want to watch – and to be consisitently winning both here and in the European competitions.

In performance terms the most important area we have to improve on is our defence. We've had seasons where we were a top four side in the number of tries we scored but near the relegation zone in the number we conceded. I want our defence to equal that of a world-class international team by raising the levels of understanding, enthusiasm and technique.

But that is only part of the challenge. What won England the World Cup was not how well we played – we performed better in a physical rugby sense nine months earlier in beating Australia and New Zealand away – but our mental strength. The whole team had supreme confidence that we would win those one- or two-point games. Our killer instinct was unparalleled – we had pretty much forgotten how to lose.

People ask why it is that other English sports teams or sportsmen have not won many important titles. Not

We have set of teamship rules with England, drawn up by the players, which govern our conduct and help to set standards

being involved directly it is difficult to say. From the outside it looked as though England's football team had prepared well enough to have gone on and won Euro 2004, only for them to lose the penalty shoot-out against Portugal. But while penalties are a lottery, I would just point out how important the confidence that comes from having won big games like that previously can be. If you know you can do it and trust your team mates implicitly, there is almost a feeling of inevitability that you will come through. You cannot buy that reservoir of reassurance, that knowledge that even if the opposition opens up a lead you have the know-how to claw it back. The England football team had a good

I've chosen a narrow passage through life, trading my youth to challenge myself to become the best rugby player I can be

record prior to the tournament. While they were not quite able to build up enough of a winning habit for Euro 2004, if they continue the way they are going there is no reason why they cannot win the World Cup in 2006. They qualified top of their group and the way they fought back to beat Argentina in November 2005 shows they are developing the mental toughness to succeed.

Part of the reason the England rugby team were able to do so was down to the personalities involved and the quality of the players, but also the environment we existed in. It was a no-excuse environment. We have a set of teamship rules with England, drawn up by the players, which govern our conduct and help to set standards in areas such as punctuality. On time for a meeting means ten minutes early, for instance.

I want to mirror that with Newcastle. The resources might not match those of the RFU but there is no reason why the approach cannot be the same. The winning habit has to be created from within and that impacts on all areas of preparation. Everyone at the club has a responsibility to be accountable for everything they do and how it affects the team.

I recognise not everyone is like me – it would be a particularly boring world if they were – but we all share the same desire for success. It's how far we are prepared to go to achieve it that will decide whether we get there.

I have been through a lot with Newcastle, both good and bad times. We have enjoyed great one-off success – the title delivered by the team of superstars Sir John Hall bought in – and two cups in the space of four seasons. We have also endured some challenging lows – when we nearly folded before Dave Thompson stepped in as chairman and a horrible flirtation with relegation in 2002/3.

Loyalty is a big part of my make-up and I have been at Newcastle since I left school. I want to be part of building something. To me the end goal is only rewarding after strife and struggle. With all my injuries, I haven't been able to give as much to my club as I would like, but now things are back on track I'm planning on giving it my all. I want to be involved with a team that has great success which will be remembered long after we are all finished and have moved on. That will always be my goal with Newcastle. As long as I still think it is possible for the Falcons to reach the heights I am aiming for, I will give everything I have to the club to help us scale them. I passionately believe we can.

I have to chase goals. I have a lot of energy which needs channelling in a positive direction and ambitions are a key part of keeping me sane. I had a summer off a few years ago and without specific aims I found myself becoming bored. I was doing too much thinking and became too insular. I ate away at myself and became very gloomy. It was a paradox, but without something to strive for I couldn't relax. I began to wonder whether rugby had stopped fulfilling me and whether my all-consuming approach to it was the problem, when in reality it was the absence of rugby which was killing me. Once the new season arrived, I was fine.

Out of rugby following my various injuries, I could easily have gone the same way. Mapping out a set of goals I wanted to achieve and training towards them stopped that.

I widened the goal-setting approach beyond rugby. These are the personal aspirations I wrote down in my black book:

To become a better, more mature and developed person.
  To work with charities and make a difference to the causes that are closest to me.
  To learn the guitar and piano.
  To become fluent in French and Spanish.
  To stay true to the ideal of being able to sign off the video of my life.

I've chosen a narrow passage through life, trading my youth to challenge myself to become the best rugby player I can be. I haven't missed the hangovers – they're not really me – but there are things I regret not doing.

I found myself standing outside Newcastle University last summer, thinking how different my life would have been if I had taken up the place at Durham I was offered. When I was eighteen, I didn't feel I could combine my studies with rugby, and with my myopic approach I was probably right, but I know I passed up a life-enhancing opportunity. University would have been a wonderful experience, socially as much as anything. Forming a circle of friends away from rugby is something I haven't been able to do. I have so many great mates in rugby, but I suppose they can sometimes be like office colleagues. I know I can't recapture that time now – if I went back to uni to study when I was thirty-two it wouldn't be the same.

Travelling is something I wish I could do more of. Playing rugby for England you fly around the world and stay in top hotels but all you tend to see are the insides of meeting rooms and training pitch after training pitch. I know it won't happen for a while but I'm looking forward to the day I can go exploring New Zealand and be treated exactly the same as every other English backpacker. That's a country I would like to see more of.

I can only get away for short periods of time at the moment, and I relish the few holidays I can squeeze in here and there. It was great to be able to get away in the summer of 2005. It was one of the best holidays I've ever had. After the Lions tour I realised that I needed some time off, and I really bought into it for once rather than thinking I was cheating myself and damaging my game by taking a much-needed break. Two weeks wasn't really enough and I now understand the necessity for more balance in my life. I'm going to try to take more holidays, give myself a chance to see things from a different perspective. This will improve my quality of life and thus, hopefully, the quality of my performances.

I did have a rare chance to see some of the world in July 2004 on an adidas promotional tour to the Far East. The trip was an eye-opener in many ways. It was the first time I'd experienced an earthquake for a start. There I was, minding my own business, in my hotel in Tokyo, signing a few bits and pieces, when everything in the room started rattling.

'What's that?' I asked Duncan, the cameraman who was with me, alarmed.

'That would be a tremor,' he replied. It turned out he had been on the receiving end of one before in Mexico.

'How did that turn out?' I asked.

'Pretty badly,' he said.

The room, which was on the ninth floor, began to sway and shake. The walls seemed to be bending in front of my eyes.

'Should we head downstairs?' I asked.

'That would be probably be best,' he said.

Even though I was in a potentially bad situation, where time was clearly of the essence, I found myself searching for my trainers and the lid to my pen before we evacuated. Sometimes I despair of myself.

By the time the door had shut behind us, the strange, shifting sensation had died away. In the corridor I had with me the pen lid and my trainers but not my room key. We had to head down to reception for another one to get back in.

One of the locals estimated the tremor to have measured three on the Richter scale, nothing special by Tokyo standards but quite enough for me. Oddly, the same thing happened to me the following year. This time I was with the Falcons on a pre-season tour. My brother and I were in our room on the 12th floor when the hotel started swaying and the pictures on the wall started rattling. I, of course, played it much cooler than Sparks, having experienced something similar before. Only kidding, Sparks. It is a strange and incredible experience to be a part of.

The cultural differences are what immediately strike you when you travel but sometimes it is what we have in common which can cause the problems. I was due to have dinner with senior adidas management in Japan. I needed to visit the gents beforehand but was confused by what I came across when I got there. The toilet had a button on the side, which I presumed must be for flushing. I pressed it and in a classic piece of slapstick it squirted water at me. Drawn like a rabbit to a car's headlights, I had another two or three stabs at the same button and soaked myself in the process. Only then, as I prepared to meet my sponsors dripping wet, did I see the correct button on the top of the toilet. Exactly where you would find it at home, of course.

Singapore was wet too, for a different reason. The humidity. Walking along the street was like taking a shower. I tried washing away the sweat but it was almost counter-productive. I sweated even more after taking a shower. In the end I simply gave up and turned up at the airport for my flight after a moist game of basketball looking like I had been swimming. Not great for my fellow passengers. The basketball – a head-to-head dunking competition with an adidas guy called Dave – had ended in high drama when he pulled off the hoop and the glass backboard by mistake mid-shot and it ended up crashing down around him.

Rather than ruining local basketball facilities, the idea of the tour was to carry out kicking clinics for youngsters. Hong Kong was memorable. Fifty children from local clubs had been rounded up to take part, and in front of them and around 500 spectators I went through a training drill with them. I was wired up to a microphone throughout so the kids could hear what I was saying. Despite some wind, the punting went off OK, but there was a marked lack of response from them as I told them what I was trying to do. They just looked blank. I thought I was maybe being too technical so I toned it down as I went into my goal-kicking routine. Still nothing. 'Tough audience,' I thought. By the time it came to my last kick, a shot at goal at a very narrow angle, I knew I needed a top one to win them over. I hit it perfectly and through the eye of the needle it went. Triumphantly, I looked across – at the same sea of impassive faces. Only later did I find out that they didn't speak English.

A translator was provided to help out in Japan. I did the same routine for a group of very talented players from the Waseda University team in Tokyo. I had generally kicked well out there but for some reason the radar had gone haywire for ten minutes in my own two-hour session that morning. It put me on edge a little as the kicking clinic, the real reason for me being there, approached. The presentation went well and when it came to the big finale the first kick I lined up from a tight angle five metres from the goal line scraped the post. The next three all went through the middle.

However as I lined up my penultimate kick the wind speed increased. 'When the wind picks up,' I told the students through the translator, 'it's important to aim for a spot to one side and to stick to it rather than trying to bend the ball in. The wind will do that for you.' Message conveyed, I promptly struck a ball which never deviated an inch straight into the far post. 'However sometimes the wind drops,' I added. After a nervous wait for the translation, it transpired my line had gone down OK.

I coached some five- to eight-year-olds in Tokyo as well. They were fantastic - all decked out in their white or red scrum caps. They did this drill where they all lined up around a basket and kicked balls into it. I found out where the scrum caps came in when they overshot and peppered each others' heads with stray balls. None of them batted an eyelid.

From what I experienced of Japan, it would be a good place to host a future rugby World Cup. The Japanese love the game and are exciting and skilful players too. As a country to visit it would be great for the fans as well - a vivid and memorable experience. I loved the place. One of my most prized possessions is now a Waseda University shirt signed in Japanese symbols by the team.

I studied languages at school and I have started to revisit my French textbooks of late. France is another place that interests me – it's so close and yet the approach to life seems so different. I'm quite envious of guys like Dan Luger who have gone across the Channel to play and who are picking up the language and getting to understand the country and its people. I've recently read *Running Man* by Stephen King in French. It's my favourite film and I know the story well which made reading it easier and I found I didn't have to keep consulting my dictionary all the time.

Africa is another part of the globe I'd like to spend some time in. I have this dream of going off to work in a game park when I finish playing. I'm used to the outdoor life but I imagine it would be so different to the regimented lifestyle I have chosen for myself, being woken by the chatter of the monkeys and the distant roar of a lion. There's something thrilling and basic about the idea of living amongst animals in their own environment. The nearest I get is visiting Mike Tindall's room with England. A cheap shot, I know, but I owe him for claiming on television that he was standing in for me at an awards show because they couldn't afford my appearance fee.

Post-rugby, I know I'll have to find something to do which satisfies my need to achieve. I couldn't imagine doing a job which did not make a difference. Coaching may be one avenue worth exploring. My brief taste as Newcastle defence coach while I was injured was an experience I found interesting, if worrying. You can't really practise defence properly without physical contact and I was scared stiff in case anyone was hurt and missed a match. I must admit I did really enjoy seeing the penny drop on the occasions I managed to get my message across. I know from the other side of the fence how helpful it is when you are struggling with something and a coach comes up with the answer. I also did some kicking coaching a year or so back with a couple of very good students – Paul Gascoigne and Peter Beardsley. They were playing as celebrity goal-kickers in a charity match at Kingston Park and were unjustly worried that they might make fools of them-selves, so we did a little work together at Darsley Park. We aimed at a post from twenty metres away for one training drill and Gazza hit it three times in a row. When it came to the match, Gazza landed five out of six while Peter managed nine out of ten including the last one with his left foot. What a teacher! In fact they were just naturals.

More recently, as I've mentioned, I've been involved in coaching young kids through the Hotshots TV pro-gramme. I found myself being able to talk very naturally to the children, even with the dreaded cameras present. It was immensely satisfying to have the opportunity to pass down some of the invaluable lessons I've learned from the likes of Dave Alred, Steve Black, Clive Woodward, Rob Andrew, Andy Robinson, Steve Bates and my brother Mark. So I do think coach-ing will play some part in my future, but to what extent I don't know. I would like to experience more things in life than rugby and see life from another angle. I'm beginning to think that just going with the flow and seeing where my life takes me is no bad thing.

When my body tells me it is time to give up and I am no longer moving forward as a player, I will go

Maybe I could do something charity-related. I was honoured to be made an ambassador of the NSPCC. Family is hugely important to me – one day I would like to have a big family of my own – so trying to help children who are less fortunate is something I care deeply about. Kylie is also an ambassador. I haven't met her yet but I do need a word. There is a vocalist spot going in the Wilkinson band which she might want to audition for.

How long will I play rugby for? I remember talking to Inga Tuigamala about this. In his last season at Newcastle he was still a thundering force, but it was becoming harder for him and he felt the moment was right to step aside. He asked the coaching staff to drop him so the younger players who would eventually replace him could be given experience. They refused – he was too valuable to the side – but he could not accept seeing his standards fall, even if he was still an integral member of the team, and he gave it up to return home to New Zealand and concentrate on his young family at the end of the season.

When my body tells me it is time to give up and I am no longer moving forward as a player, I will go too. Martin Johnson showed how it should be done. Every professional sportsman would be envious of his farewell from Test rugby. It was a fairytale ending for him, to walk away from England after an unbeaten season, a Grand Slam and with the Webb Ellis Trophy under his arm.

There is no timescale on the rest of my career, only that I want to leave at the top, to step aside before my performances begin to deteriorate. That could be after the next World Cup when I will be twenty-eight or the one after when I will be thirty-two. The enforced lay-off may have added extra time on to the end of my career – who knows?

I can't say I will achieve all the goals I've set in whatever time is available, but what I can guarantee is I will give myself every chance. I have no excuse not to do the best I can because, as I've said before, I have it easy. Life has been put on a plate for me.

Off the field everything is taken care of. My parents have turned their own lives upside down by upping sticks and moving from Surrey to Northumberland to be on hand for me. Dad has given up his own career as a financial adviser to work full time managing and taking care of me to ensure that nothing ever interferes with my rugby. Alongside him, Tim Buttimore and Simon Cohen work to look after the commercial and legal side. A more trustworthy trio of people you could not wish to meet.

Blackie and Otis make sure I'm in top condition, Dave Alred is always there for me and my kicking, and all the coaches I work with at Newcastle and hopefully England again continually help me to move on as a player. All I have to do is turn up to train and play. If I didn't pay them back by giving my all, I don't know how I would live with myself.

I have recommitted to leaving no stone unturned in my quest to improve. I am having a gym installed at home. The design leaves a space for a patch of artificial grass on which to practise drop-kicks. You never know when one might come in handy again.

The work goes on. Even though the World Cup has gone, I have too much unfinished business in rugby. At twenty-six, I know I'm only part of the way to becoming the player I want to be. As far as I am concerned, the slate is clean. Chapter one is over; chapter two of my career starts now.